COLDER THAN
SIN

COLDER THAN **SIN**

Toni Anderson

Colder Than Sin

Cover design by Regina Wamba of ReginaWamba.com

Print ISBN-13: 9781988812120
Digital ISBN-13: 9781988812137

Contact email: info@toniandersonauthor.com

For more information on Toni Anderson's books, sign up for her Newsletter or check out her website (www.toniandersonauthor.com).

ALSO BY TONI ANDERSON

COLD JUSTICE – MOST WANTED

Cold Silence (Book #1)

COLD JUSTICE – THE NEGOTIATORS

Cold as Ice (Book #5)

Cold Cruel Kiss (Book #4)

Cold Wicked Lies (Book #3)

Colder Than Sin (Book #2)

Cold & Deadly (Book #1)

COLD JUSTICE SERIES

Cold Blooded (Book #10)

A Cold Dark Promise (Book #9~A Wedding Novella)

Cold Malice (Book #8)

Cold Secrets (Book #7)

Cold Hearted (Book #6)

Cold in the Shadows (Book #5)

Cold Fear (Book #4)

Cold Light of Day (Book #3)

Cold Pursuit (Book #2)

A Cold Dark Place (Book #1)

THE BARKLEY SOUND SERIES

Dark Waters (Book #2)

Dangerous Waters (Book #1)

STAND-ALONE TITLES

The Killing Game

Edge of Survival

Storm Warning

Sea of Suspicion

'HER' ROMANTIC SUSPENSE SERIES

Her Risk to Take (Novella ~ Book #3)

Her Last Chance (Book #2)

Her Sanctuary (Book #1)

For Dee.

Content Advisory: this book contains graphic violence (sexual assault, murder). For more information: https://www.tonian.dersonauthor.com/content-advisory

CHAPTER ONE

Saturday August 8th. Nabat Island in the Flores Sea, Indonesia.

CHIEF OF THE FBI's Crisis Negotiation Unit, Quentin Savage, leaned against the bar near the exit, wondering how long before he could reasonably escape. Unfortunately, not only was he meeting an old Army friend for a quick drink but, having delivered the keynote speech at the closing banquet of this symposium, he was duty-bound to stick around for a while in case people had questions.

People *always* had questions.

They always wanted to talk to negotiators. They assumed negotiators possessed some secret spiel that enabled them to get their own way and influence others.

It wasn't true—if it were, he wouldn't be here.

It did take some special qualities to be a good negotiator. Patience was definitely a virtue, as was the ability to think on your feet and not get emotionally invested. And, sure, there were specific techniques to influencing the actions of others, but the single biggest factor to being a great negotiator was the ability to listen. To *hear* what people said, verbally and non-verbally.

Being a negotiator was like being a therapist, except the other person was almost always in crisis by the time the Bureau arrived on the scene.

Quentin glanced at his watch impatiently. He wanted to check on the latest updates regarding a female volcanologist who'd been abducted off a remote volcanic island in the Banda Sea a few days ago. He was so close to the location where she'd last been seen, he itched to fly out to examine the area for clues. But if this was a straight kidnap for ransom and the kidnappers heard about the FBI's interest, they'd either jack up the price, or kill her to eliminate any larger potential problems.

He pushed her out of his mind. He had to retain some professional detachment, else he'd compromise his ability to rescue anyone. Burnout wasn't something he courted, even if he didn't have much of a life outside the Bureau. Not anymore.

He wasn't exactly roughing it here in Indonesia. The hotel, a large old Dutch colonial that had been tastefully modernized, was pure colonial splendor, complete with that indolent atmosphere that catered to the supremely wealthy. But even in the cooler evening, with the trade winds blowing, the air conditioning units and ceiling fans struggled to keep up with a room this large and this full of people. Delegates lounged on rattan furniture, drinking and eating complimentary finger food served on silver trays by uniformed staff.

Quentin made a face into the contents of his glass.

The setup reminded him of when he'd been a waiter at a country club many years ago. He'd grown up in SoCal, one of five brothers, and they'd all pulled their weight to support their mom after their dad left them for a younger woman. Quentin found it hard not to notice the people who were supposed to disappear into the background, probably as he identified with them more than he identified with the rich elite, or with the politicians or powerful CEOs.

He received a government paycheck and the sort of responsibility that would make most of them choke. He knew his own worth, and it wasn't measured in dollars or cents. It was measured in the lives of the people he saved and the prison terms of the criminals who failed to beat the system.

Quentin paid for two beers, adding a decent tip. He didn't like crowds. Didn't like taking time out of his busy schedule to give presentations, even though it might ultimately save lives. He really didn't like being the center of attention.

Unlike some people.

Holy cow.

An elegant blonde goddess came in from the gardens. The woman wore a gold dress with a plunging neckline and spiked heels that had her towering over the locals and most of the delegates. She made her way to a group near the bar, catching his gaze as she glanced around. He'd seen her a few times over the last two days, although he hadn't been introduced. Pity. He was pretty sure she was staying in the room next to his.

When she didn't look away, he raised his beer in salute, and she raised her champagne flute in response.

"That's Haley Cramer, in case you didn't know."

Quentin turned to the man who'd pushed into the space to his left. Quentin pointed to the pint on the bar. "You're late. That's for you."

"Cheers." Chris Baylor, a friend from boot camp days and three years of back-to-back deployments, raised the glass to his lips and took a big swallow. He put the glass down and followed Quentin's gaze across the room.

Haley Cramer had turned her back on them both.

So much for that. Not that anything would have happened between them, but he enjoyed looking at her. She was old-school Hollywood glamour in an age of Instagram selfies.

Hotter than sin, and probably twice as much trouble.

Chris handed Quentin a cigar. It was an old tradition for their now rare nights out. It was the only time Quentin ever smoked. Quentin put it in his pocket for later.

Another man who seemed to know Chris joined them.

"Quentin Savage, meet Grant Gunn. Grant was in the 10th Mountain Division in Shoh-I-Khot same time we were."

"Fun times," Gunn joked, ordering himself a beer.

The fierce battle in the eastern mountains of Afghanistan hadn't been fun for anyone, but that's how soldiers got through it. Humor. Brotherhood.

Unable to stop himself, Quentin glanced toward the blonde again.

"You never met Haley Cramer before?" Chris asked.

Quentin shook his head.

"Of 'Cramer, Parker & Gray'? Alex Parker works with you Feds in Quantico. Rumor has it he was a spook." Chris filled him in on the gossipy details.

Quentin sipped his beer. He didn't know Parker personally, but he knew him by reputation. Cramer, Parker & Gray was one of the top security firms in the US. Smaller than many of the others represented here, but with a stellar reputation. Top of the game in the cybersecurity and well regarded in close protection circles.

"And, according to Chris, she's as hot in the sack as she looks," Gunn added with a sly grin.

"I didn't ask," Quentin pointed out sharply.

"But you wanted to know." Gunn's grin was full of assholery. "What red-blooded man wouldn't?"

What Quentin wanted was nobody's business but his own. He turned to his friend. "You dated her?"

Chris was no longer the skinny, raw recruit Quentin had known back in his Army days. Years of training and grueling, physical work meant the guy had filled out across the shoulders and chest. His cheeks were a little fuller than they had been, a little more florid.

"I wouldn't call it dating…" Gunn guffawed into his beer.

Quentin frowned at the guy.

"We saw each other for about a month, but it was never gonna last." Chris wiped his mouth with the back of his hand.

"What happened?" Quentin asked, curious how the guy could have screwed up something so monumental.

He cut Quentin a grin that didn't quite reach his eyes. "You know me." He shrugged. "I can't resist a pretty face."

Which meant he'd cheated on her.

"You're even more of an idiot than I realized."

Chris drank his beer, not disagreeing. The military had turned an optimistic young man into a battled-hardened cynic, but boy scouts didn't last long in a war zone.

In those early Army days, they'd often exchanged bullshit stories about female conquests. Quentin wasn't a dumb eighteen-year-old anymore. He was not interested in games or chasing women who needed to be chased. He'd finally come through the dark shadow brought on by the death of his beloved wife and stillborn child five years ago, but he never wanted to endure that kind of heartbreak again. He was living life, even dating occasionally, but…like any good hostage negotiator, he didn't plan to get emotionally invested any time soon.

Quentin eyed Haley Cramer with a touch of regret. No doubt he would have enjoyed getting to know her better, but not in front of this crowd. Too many egos. Too much testosterone. Too much rabid speculation and potential blowback for both of them.

"She hates my guts, so I probably just ruined any chance you might have had with her. Sorry, buddy." Chris changed the subject. "I enjoyed the speech, by the way. Impressive for a man who can barely read."

Quentin ignored the jibe. His dyslexia had always been the source of much amusement to his buddies, but he was used to it and never let their ribbing get to him. "How's Nick?"

Nicholas Karlovac had been another grunt in their squad, and the three of them had been best friends back in the old days. Nick and Chris had gone on to become elite soldiers who'd formed their own private security firm upon getting out.

"He's back home running the office."

"You ever get tired of being in the field?" Quentin asked Chris.

Chris hunched his shoulders. "Someone's gotta do it. Nick's stuck with his wife and kids all needing a piece of him."

An attractive black woman with blue braids gave Quentin a grin across the room. Tricia Rooks. He'd sat beside her at breakfast yesterday. He smiled back.

Gunn glanced her way and then raised his eyebrows suggestively. "Looks like Haley Cramer isn't the only possibility in the room."

Quentin ignored the man.

An older gentleman entered the room, and the atmosphere ramped up as a hundred pairs of eyeballs latched on to him. Chris's hand tightened around his glass of beer. Haley Cramer's head turned.

Quentin hadn't seen the newcomer at the conference, but

he wasn't here to brown-nose or grease palms. The stranger might also be an innocent hotel guest, but from the way the other delegates were sniffing the air like wolves scenting blood, Quentin didn't think so.

The new arrival was a short, heavy guy. Balding. Blue silk shirt with sweat darkening his pits. White linen pants. Two burly men rode his shoulder like mismatched pilot fish. Bodyguards. To bring bodyguards to a security conference suggested a special kind of paranoia. Or a wealth of bad experiences…

The conference had been co-organized by the Indonesian government and was taking place on a small island in the Flores Sea. Most attendees had flown commercial to the small local airport and therefore weren't armed. Not an easy sell for most of these guys, but they were only here for three days, and the meeting had provided security. That security had wound down as soon as the foreign minister had left following the banquet earlier that evening.

Maybe that's why this newcomer hadn't appeared before now. Guns were banned, and his bodyguards were definitely packing.

The man worked his way through the crowd until he reached Haley Cramer. He grabbed her by both arms and leaned towards her, leading with puckered lips. The woman turned her face sideways at the last moment and got a sloppy kiss on the cheek.

Quentin glanced around the room and noticed the mood had soured. "Who's the guy?"

Chris scraped a tired hand over his square jaw. "Cecil Wenck. Tenth richest man in the world. Owns ARK Mining, the largest company in Southeast Asia and Oceania."

"Looks like Cramer is gonna screw us all, but only one guy in the room will get to fuck her tonight." Gunn tipped his glass up and finished his beer.

"You need to tone it down, pal," Quentin instructed quietly.

Gunn shot him a glare.

"Cramer, Parker and Gray don't have the personnel," Chris muttered, ignoring Quentin.

"You better hope they don't have the numbers," Gunn said cryptically.

Quentin's gaze was drawn back to the woman in the gold dress. Her blonde hair shone brighter than the gown, but it was her eyes that interested him. Intelligent and guarded, a keeper of secrets. She wasn't a fool. She knew the dangers of being a woman in a man's world but was here anyway.

Good for her. He hoped it didn't bite her in the ass. And now he needed to get that image out of his head with an ice-cold shower. Quentin slapped his old friend on the back. "I'm done."

"What?" Chris's eyes widened. "I had plans to drag you into town to a local bar."

"Town" was twenty miles away along a dirt road.

"I need a clear head in the morning." He needed to work on the Alexanders' case—a couple of seniors abducted off the South China Sea six months ago. And now this other young woman. He tried not to dwell on her fate. A lone female was prey to so many dangers. Had she been taken for ransom like the Alexanders? Or abducted for some deviant's pleasure? Or to be sold into the sex trade? Or kidnapped by an extremist group who didn't like strong, independent women?

"Come on, buddy. How often do we get the chance to

hang out?"

Quentin refused to feel bad. He wasn't that easily manipulated. "We'll catch up next time you're in D.C."

"I'll come into town with you," Gunn offered.

And now Quentin definitely wasn't going.

Chris ignored Gunn. "You're really skipping out on me?"

"I have an early flight." Kidnapped Americans were his priority. Trying to figure out how to get them released and how to stop them being taken in the first place.

Chris stared at him, clearly surprised at his refusal. In fairness it was probably the first time in years that he'd turned the guy down. After Abbie died Quentin had been all over too many drinks during downtime. Maybe that's why he no longer allowed himself too much time off.

Chris nodded. "Okay. Fine. Let's do that."

Quentin slapped his old friend on the shoulder and walked away, relief washing over him as he exited the crowded room. Half the people here wanted to make the world a better place—he counted himself in that group. The other half wanted ever-increasing amounts of power and money. They were the ones who viewed violence and unrest as opportunity. Those were the people he avoided whenever possible.

He was grateful to live in a democracy where federal agents did their best to protect the vulnerable and uphold the Constitution. That was what bound him and his fellow agents together, the rule of law, the strict adherence to the rules. But outside of the States, it was a different matter. It was his job to negotiate with people who used others as commodities and bargaining chips, not caring about the human toll. Quentin wished he could track all the kidnappers down and help put them away for life, but the most he allowed himself to hope for was getting hostages home. Making them safe again.

He'd definitely settle for that.

He went to the hotel registration desk to pay his bill so he wouldn't have to do it in the morning. When he looked back into the bar area, he saw the woman in gold, Haley Cramer, surrounded by powerful men all vying for her attention.

Some sixth sense had her looking up at him at that exact same moment. A silent message passed between them. One as old as time, and one neither intended to act upon.

Her expression grew almost sad.

He turned away, unwilling to explore the puzzle of a beautiful woman who, even surrounded by admirers, appeared lonely. Maybe he was projecting. And maybe he was sick of being on his own. He should be used to it now. And, if he were honest, he was scared to rock the status quo, no matter how beautiful the temptation.

CHAPTER TWO

HALEY WATCHED THE federal agent walk away, regret seeping through her that their paths hadn't crossed. She'd listened to his talk from the shadows of the auditorium, enjoying the content but also the deliveryman. Quentin Savage's dark eyes held a hypnotic quality, as did his sharp features and raven hair—hair worn slightly too long for a respectable federal agent. There was something compelling enough about him to keep pulling her gaze in his direction, but also strong enough to keep her feet firmly planted where she was.

She liked to be in charge of relationships and had a feeling a man like that wouldn't let her dictate terms.

Of course, they didn't need to have a *relationship*. But if she simply wanted a fuckbuddy there were a hundred guys here who could perform the act, men who didn't intrigue her with their soulful good looks and tragic eyes. Men she could control. Men she would never care about on a deep, personal level. Men like Chris Baylor whom she'd dated for an entire month last year before she realized he was a liar and a cheat. Luckily, she hadn't been hurt by that betrayal, but she'd been wrong to trust him and upset she'd been played.

And here was Cecil Wenck, billionaire mining conglomerate owner, playing games with her probably because she was the only female owner of any of the private security firms represented at this symposium.

She kept her smile in place even as Wenck's hand brushed the side of her breast. She twisted to pick up her wine off the bar, breaking the unwanted contact. She raised her glass, and someone handed the man a beer so they could chink glasses.

"A toast." The Australian smiled jovially, but his eyes were as cold as the red snapper's she'd eaten for lunch. "To the most beautiful security consultant in Indonesia, if not the whole bloody world."

She smiled, even though his words irritated her. Cramer, Parker & Gray might be a relatively small outfit, but they had an excellent reputation. The fact they were trying to expand into providing security for infrastructure, private firms, and government facilities was something she'd been pushing for years. Dermot and Alex had finally given in to her pressuring them, even though they were satisfied with their current niche.

"You look like a million dollars tonight, love."

Haley's smile barely concealed her annoyance. Men like Wenck were the reason Dermot and Alex hadn't wanted to pursue this line of business. Between the billionaires, sheiks, and crooked politicians, the super-rich thought they owned the world and everything in it, including women.

Especially women.

The fact she liked to wear pretty clothes and high heels and makeup had nothing to do with her business acumen and everything to do with the fact she liked pretty clothes, high heels and makeup.

The private military industry was an old boy's network full of people who'd served together. She didn't fit into this world, so she didn't even try. Many of their connections were forged either on active duty or in seedy bars in war-torn locations around the world. Alex Parker was the only one of the partners who'd been in the military. Dermot didn't know one end of a firearm from another. He was the world's biggest dork, and a brilliant software engineer. She wanted them both to be wrong about expanding the company into this arena.

Time to figure out what Wenck's play was. "And here's me thinking you didn't like me," she said sweetly, taking a sip of champagne. It was cold and tart on her tongue.

"Nonsense. Of course, I like you," Wenck assured her gruffly.

"Then why is my firm the only company not to get a one-on-one meeting with you today?" It hadn't taken long to figure it out. She wasn't dumb.

"I was saving the best 'til last, love." Wenck winked and sidled a little closer. The bodyguards weren't far behind, and the result was several men pressing too close to her side.

She shifted away along the bar, hating that she was forced to retreat but not surprised. She was used to men trying to take more than she offered, which was why she generally went on the offensive.

"I can meet you first thing in the morning to go over the quote we gave you," she said.

Wenck frowned, even as she smiled brightly at him. He was head of ARK Mining Corp., based in Darwin. Every private military company in existence wanted the contract that was coming up for renewal to provide security for his mines, industrial plants, and headquarters across Australia and Asia.

Keeping Cramer, Parker & Gray thriving was important to her. Important enough to ignore the misogynistic comments and slights she received whenever she attended meetings in this male-dominated world. She didn't care what they thought of her or what they said behind her back. She'd been fighting the patriarchy since she was a teen—fighting and winning. But she did care what they said about her firm.

"I'm leaving at six AM." Wenck pulled a "sorry" face.

"We can meet for breakfast at five."

He laughed, his voice raucous and grating. "I'm not a morning person, love." He checked his watch. "If you want to go over the contract now, I can accommodate you, but only because you're a beautiful woman."

Her smile hid what she was really feeling. Even though her company was one of the premier firms, she only got to play on a distinctly unleveled field because of her face and figure?

Somedays she thought she hated all men, and then she remembered Alex and Dermot and some of the operators who worked for them. She didn't hate them all, just an awful lot of them.

"Let's go somewhere quieter to discuss this matter," Haley suggested. The bar area was too noisy and crowded to talk the nitty gritty of a multi-million-dollar contract. Plus, she didn't want the opposition to overhear and lowball her offer.

Wenck nodded. "Sounds about right."

She followed Cecil out of the room, clutch bag under one arm, Wenck reaching back and grasping her other arm as if he were laying claim. Her high heels clicked, and she was aware of many narrowed eyes watching their progress. From the expressions on their faces, they seemed to have forgotten they'd all had meetings with Wenck today, the same way she was about to. Of course, they all thought she'd sleep with the guy to get him to sign a contract. The fact her company was every bit as good as theirs seemed lost on them. It was insulting, but she was used to that too.

Hatred gleamed in Grant Gunn's eyes as she passed him. Chris Baylor turned away with a sneer. What had she ever seen in the guy?

Wenck led her toward the elevator, but she put on the brakes.

"There's a quiet room over there." She pointed to a cozy space she'd discovered on her first day. Even though it was Indonesia, it had an open fireplace, though thankfully unlit. White walls and large leafy ferns created a calm, opulent space. Haley took out her phone to text Alex and Dermot that she was meeting with Wenck.

"I don't discuss business where someone might overhear, love. It's not worth the risk. We'll go up to my suite."

The man was probably paranoid. Considering his financial worth was the same as some third world countries, it wasn't surprising. He was also notoriously difficult to get face time with. This might be the only opportunity she ever had for a face-to-face meeting.

Haley debated for a moment about the sense of going alone to this man's hotel room, but she never let being a woman hold her back from doing what men would. Her heels clicked loudly on the black and white tiles. Yes, she'd rather do this in a public space, but she also knew that he'd been meeting everyone in his suite all day. Still, there was a vibe in the air that made her uneasy. She tapped on her phone's recording app and slid the device back in her clutch.

Dermot and Alex constantly warned her to be careful, and she wasn't stupid. Haley could handle herself and she doubted Wenck would physically attack her. Proposition her, sure. She could deal with being propositioned as long as he could deal with her saying "no."

And if he couldn't?

She balked but found herself shuffled into the elevator as the doors opened. She stood at the back, trying not to let her sudden unease show.

They got out on the fourth floor. Her floor, not that she'd tell Wenck that.

They entered his suite and one bodyguard swept the room for electronic listening devices, while the other one made sure nobody was hiding in the closet or under the bed.

She watched them work. Professional and well-trained. Would they help her if the situation presented itself? Presumably not, although Wenck was considered stingy, so she might be able to buy their cooperation if push literally came to shove.

It wouldn't come to that.

The room was all brocade-upholstered furniture against soft white walls. White net curtains billowed as the bodyguard opened the window onto the balcony.

Haley took a seat on the sofa.

"Drink?" Wenck walked to the old-fashioned drinks cabinet and picked up a bottle of single malt.

"Sure. Scotch on the rocks." She wasn't planning on drinking it, but it made the man relax a little when she accepted the offer.

He brought their drinks over and sat close enough that their knees brushed. The two bodyguards exited the room, which bothered her on several levels. They didn't know if she was some would-be assassin ready to stick her stiletto heel through Cecil's fat gullet. Also, why leave? They'd surely been present at all the afternoon meetings and knew private details of Cecil's business.

Her eyes narrowed.

Wenck was staring at her expectantly.

"Do you have a copy of my proposal on your laptop?" she asked, reminding him of the reason she was here. "Or should I email you one now, and we can go over it?" She put her drink down and went to pull out her cell phone.

He stopped her when he ran a stubby finger down her bare arm. "You don't really want to discuss business, do you?"

"That's why I'm here, Mr. Wenck." She meant his suite, but it applied to Indonesia in general. Sure, it was a good symposium, but Wenck's rumored attendance was the reason the event had sold out in record time.

His beady brown eyes took her in, his gaze catching on the low "V" of her dress. Her breasts were completely covered. It was the skin between her breasts that was on show. It held his attention, nevertheless.

She wasn't ashamed of her body, but his gaze was tactile and made her skin crawl.

"I don't know if you had the opportunity to read the bid our company submitted…" She again tried to draw his attention back to business. "We can provide the same standard physical security measures all the other firms offer with the added bonus of customized alarm systems and cyber intrusion prevention and detection measures at a competitive rate. You won't get our level of sophistication from any of the other firms."

"Huh?" His gaze sharpened and, for a brief moment, he looked more interested in her words than her bare skin.

"Our competitive edge is our cyber capabilities, which compared to any of the…" She snapped her fingers to get his gaze off her chest and said with exasperation, "Mr. Wenck, I'm here to talk business."

He groaned. "I think I've had about as much business as I can stand for one day. I was hoping for something else from you. Something none of the other firms can offer." He licked his lips and went to run a finger down her arm again, but she shifted away.

"Surely a man like you must have hundreds of women who want to have sex with them?"

His cheeks grew flushed. "Who said I wanted to have sex with you? Anyway, if you weren't up for it, why wear the revealing dress and heels that show off your tits and arse?"

His argument was all over the place.

"Trust me," she snorted. "I can tell when a person wants to have sex with me." She tried not to sound irate. "How I dress bears no relation to how good my firm is." She went to rise, but he grabbed her wrist.

"What would it take?" He suddenly sounded a lot less friendly.

"To what?" she asked.

"You know what." He shot a glance at her body.

Her mouth opened a little in shock. And, yet, she wasn't completely surprised. People had been trying to fuck her against her will since she was fourteen years old. She was now a smart, successful, independently wealthy woman and yet men struggled to deal with her as an equal.

"Mr. Wenck." She strove for patience, feeling like the only adult in the room. "I'm here to conduct a business meeting." She carefully removed his fingers from the vise-like grip around her arm and stood. He grabbed a handful of her dress and jerked her back down again, the smile on his face a clear indication she wasn't getting out of this that easily.

Shit.

"Everyone saw you flirting in the bar, love. Not one of them would believe I had to force you, and you know it."

The first hint of fear rippled over her nerves. *Force her*? The guy was seriously thinking about raping her?

She weighed her options. Scream? It was unlikely anyone would come to her aid. There were only a few suites in this wing of the hotel, and she and Cecil occupied two of them. His bodyguards and PA might be in the neighboring ones. Plus, if she screamed, his bodyguards might intervene on her behalf, or they might hold her down while Wenck raped her. She wasn't willing to take that chance.

Violence? She could hit Wenck, but then she'd still have to get past the bodyguards. And if Wenck called the authorities and said she assaulted him, she might end up in an Indonesian jail while he flew safely back to Australia.

No one would prosecute him.

Men like Wenck were untouchable.

No, she needed to use her guile to get out of this situation. Then she'd think about how to deal with the man later. She'd certainly never work for this disgusting piece of human garbage now that she'd met him.

She let him kiss her for a moment as if his wet lips would somehow convince her to change her mind. She mentally rolled her eyes at the sloppy attempt, although it wasn't his technique that was lacking. It was the fact he was attempting to stick his tongue down her throat when she'd told him she wasn't interested.

"Wait. Wait. Cecil." She laughed as if excited and short of breath, then slid from beneath him. She fanned herself and got up to pace behind the couch. "Give me a moment to think about this."

He followed her to his feet. "What's to think about? You're a beautiful woman, and I've got a hunger that needs to be appeased. Then, if you're any good, I'll give you one of the biggest security contracts the world has ever seen."

Any good? She raised her brows. Like he wouldn't blow like a rocket as soon as she touched his pathetic dick.

"It's not like you're ever gonna win their respect down there anyway." He pointed toward the bar.

That was true, but she'd like to retain her self-respect and compete in the business based on merit. Old fashioned, but what the hell. "What about the relative caliber of the different firms and their bids?"

"Oh, I know your firm's got a good rep, but there are three firms who can do what I need them to do, for less money." He leered. "Only one representative is wearing a dress I want to rip off her body before screwing her blind."

She gave a little laugh. *Ha, fucking, ha.* "Well, when you put it so romantically…"

He hitched his belt as if to draw attention to the bulge at the front of his trousers. "I don't do romance, love. I'm a former miner who got very lucky and was smart enough and ruthless enough to get what he wanted—which is more money than you can even imagine." He looked at her like he was in charge of her decisions and this was a done deal. "That means I can buy anything I damn well please, including you."

Haley liked to imagine she could see the evil in Wenck's smile, but he looked like any other man. That's what made predators so dangerous and difficult to spot.

"Right now…" Wenck began. "I want you to suck me off, and I'm willing to pay you millions of dollars to do it."

Haley already had millions of dollars and didn't need a penny more. Even if she'd been homeless, she wouldn't have touched this cockroach. Not for the first time, Haley wished she'd been born a man. Her life would have been so much simpler.

She stepped up to him, staring down at his mouth like he didn't turn her stomach. She ran her finger down his chest and stopped on his belt buckle, pressing hard enough to push him back a step. "Well, if you put it like that how can I resist? But I want that contract signed upfront as I'm not about to take your word for it."

His face transformed into arrogant conceit. "We'll see."

She ignored the comment. "While you're printing and signing the document, let's at least pretend this is more than a monetary transaction." She grabbed her clutch and headed to the bedroom, praying the suite had the same setup as hers. She looked inside. It did. She paused in the doorway and turned back to him. "Give me five minutes to make myself ready for you while you deal with that paperwork." She gave a pointed look at his tented pants. "Then we'll talk, big boy."

CHAPTER THREE

BIG BOY.

She gagged.

Nothing like being treated as a whore to drag your ego into the gutter. She closed the door to the bedroom and waited a second to calm her racing heart.

What a slime ball.

She strode to the balcony and slipped through the French doors, closing them quietly behind her and hoping Cecil didn't come out here via the living room. A warm breeze blew over her clammy skin, cooling the perspiration that had formed on her nape and her brow.

She stared out at the darkness. The sounds of the jungle were all around. How had it come to this?

Years ago, while teaching her self-defense, Alex had tried to instill in her that avoiding confrontation was far more important than winning a fight. It had taken her a long time to internalize the message, but she understood it now.

She pulled off her heels, tossed them and her clutch onto the stone balcony of the adjacent suite some four feet to her left.

No Jimmy Choo got left behind.

She hiked her skirt all the way up to her waist and grabbed onto the vine creeping up the side of the building to have an anchor as she stood. It wasn't that far of a jump, but it was high enough to make her stomach pitch. And she had to be quiet, because for all she knew, Wenck had rented this next-door suite for his staff. She heard movement in the bedroom behind her—that Wenck was premature was not a surprise.

She leaped the gap and grabbed the banister, her breath leaving her lungs in a *whoosh* as rough stone grazed her fingers. She gripped tight as she found her balance, then swung her leg over the railing as Cecil started calling her name. The balcony doors to this room were open, so she snatched up her belongings and ducked inside, remaining hidden behind the flimsy drapes. She froze when she heard Cecil come out onto his balcony looking for her.

"Where are you, you conniving, bloody bitch?"

She held her breath, sensing his presence even when he stopped cursing her out. His anger was palpable—a man not used to being thwarted. Her heart hammered in reaction to everything that had happened. As soon as he was gone, she'd jump to her balcony, one room over, and lock the doors until morning.

Strong arms wrapped around her, trapping her arms at her waist and covering her mouth, pinning her against an unyielding, male body.

Panic seized her heart. *Oh, god, no.* She knew what happened next. She wasn't sure she could stand it.

She began to struggle, but she didn't even begin to break free of the man's iron grip. She kicked out behind her, but her bare feet made little impact.

A voice whispered softly against her ear, "Quiet, or he'll realize you're in here."

She stiffened, then sagged in relief. She recognized the

voice of the tall, dark-haired federal agent who'd given the keynote lecture, the same guy she'd seen in the bar earlier. Quentin Savage.

Those strong arms of his released her, and she reached out for the wall to steady herself.

Savage was staring at her with those intense, dark eyes she'd noticed in the bar. His features were too sharp for him to be called pretty, but he was utterly compelling and fiercely attractive. He gave her a slight smile of calm reassurance before sauntering outside onto the balcony and casually lighting a cigar.

How had he figured out what was going on so quickly? Was he spying on the billionaire in the next room? Or was it the logical conclusion from the fact she'd obviously escaped Wenck's clutches via the freaking balcony?

Sweet aromatic smoke drifted toward where she remained immobile next to the wall, trembling. Adrenaline probably. Not fear—not anymore. Somehow being in the FBI agent's company made the fear evaporate.

"Is there a problem?" Savage asked Wenck in an unruffled voice. His tone held a different kind of arrogance to the scumbag Australian, one drawn from lawful authority rather than greed and power.

"Yeah right, mate," Wenck replied in irritation. "Just taking in the view. How ya going?"

Haley wondered if Savage could hear the underlying anger and suspicion in Wenck's words.

Duh, he was a hostage negotiator. Of course, he could hear it. Words were his bread and butter, his currency.

Haley looked around. A single bedside lamp lit Savage's room and showed her the massive four poster bed—similar to the one she'd been sleeping in—surrounded by mosquito netting. The furniture and layout were similar to that of her room, but Savage didn't have a sitting room. There was a gorgeous antique chaise and a giant sweeping fan that stirred the air like a lazy hand trailing through water.

His carryon luggage was open on a chair beside the bed. It looked like he was packing to leave, even though the conference wasn't officially over until tomorrow at noon.

She heard a door bang as someone entered her suite on the other side of the wall, and her bottom jaw dropped. *Son of a bitch*! Wenck must have bribed one of the hotel staff for a key or used a social pretext to get inside her room.

Fury washed over her. That they thought she was some sort of object to be taken and possessed. A thing to be used by men who figured they were powerful enough to do whatever they wanted without consequence.

It wasn't the first time. Old shame reared up inside her in a rush.

After a minute or so, the door to her room slammed shut. Haley tensed. Would they break in here too? She edged behind the velvet drapes in case the baboons were foolish enough to trespass on an FBI agent's domain—the way she had.

Savage spent a full ten minutes out there, unhurriedly smoking that expensive cigar and chatting to Cecil Wenck, never hinting he knew a woman had run away from the man only moments before.

Haley retrieved her cell from her clutch and turned off the recording app. Had it captured his threats? Would the words without the actions be enough to convince people she'd been in real danger? She wasn't sure. She needed to listen and think. To figure out how to handle the traumatic incident. She texted

Alex and Dermott that the meeting had been a bust. She didn't want them to worry.

Savage's tone never changed as he made small talk that drew information out of the rat bastard like toothpaste from a tube. Wenck was married with a young daughter. Savage said he didn't blame the man for not bringing them to this country, even though it was relatively safe at the moment. Religious extremists, small pockets of revolutionaries, corrupt officials, pirates were always active. The Fed made it sound like a hot bed of terrorist activity, which, considering they were staying in the height of colonial luxury, seemed a stretch.

"Want to join me for a nightcap?" Savage asked, finally stubbing out the cigar into a handy plant pot.

"Nah, mate. I appreciate the offer though." Wenck sounded genuinely regretful. Savage had charmed the beast. "Think I'm gonna turn in. Call the missus."

"Sounds like a great idea. Goodnight, Cecil."

"G'night, Quentin. Good talking to ya."

The Fed came inside and locked the balcony doors behind him.

His eyes glittered when she stepped out from behind the curtain. She opened her mouth to say something, but he stopped her by placing a finger on her lips. The move felt shockingly intimate. He smelled like tobacco and tropical paradise.

"Keep it to a low whisper, Ms. Cramer," he murmured. "The walls are thin, and my badge carries no legal authority here."

He stepped back.

She shivered and rubbed her hands up and down her bare arms, which were now covered in goosebumps. "Thanks for helping me," she whispered. "I'm so sorry this happened. If you give me a few minutes, I'll head back to my room." She pointed at the wall behind the enormous bed.

"That wouldn't be smart." He didn't try to stop her though. He headed to the bathroom, and she heard him wash his hands and brush his teeth.

He came back into the room and flicked on the TV, leaving the volume low enough to provide soft background noise. He poured two glasses of scotch and carried one over to where she stood like a mannequin against the wall. He held out the glass.

She took it, their fingers brushing but both pretending there hadn't been that little shock of electrical activity that woke up all the dormant nerves in her body.

"I really am sorry." She sipped the amber liquid, grateful for the warmth that flooded her mouth and spread down her throat as she swallowed.

"Did he hurt you? Do you want to press charges?" His dark eyes burned.

She heaved out a sigh and finally moved away from the window. She sat on the edge of Savage's chaise. "He invited me to his room to discuss business and then made it quite clear I wasn't leaving until I fulfilled a few sexual services, after which my company would win the contract up for tender, and we'd all be happy." She grimaced, and nausea burrowed deeper into her stomach.

"Did he touch you?" Savage's eyes were obsidian, gaze like a razor blade.

"When reason failed, I let him kiss me to give him the impression I agreed to his proposition." Did that mean it was her fault for leading him on? It had been a survival mechanism, pure and simple.

Wenck had scared her, more than she wanted to admit. She sucked in her bottom lip. She'd been a fool to trust the man. "I'm sure you think I had it coming to me for being so naive as to go to his room alone." It was hard to contain the resentment that spilled over, or the past that had shaped her.

Savage sat heavily beside her on the chaise. "Because you're a beautiful woman who wears heels and lipstick in a way that makes men fantasize about sex?" He gave a short huff of a laughter. "Pretty sure that isn't illegal." His voice firmed, even though he spoke barely above a whisper. "Attacking and trying to force someone to have sex with them is a crime. You are an American citizen, and I'm a federal agent. Do you want me to initiate a report and investigation?"

Lamp light struck that angular face of his, emphasizing the perfect bone structure. A heavy five o'clock shadow formed on his jaw, suggesting he probably needed to shave daily. The dark brows and sharp slice of a nose spoke of natural authority. Soft lips hinted at something more sensual.

She blinked, trying to concentrate on what he'd said. It was difficult. Her thoughts were jumbled. The fright Wenck had given her had her second guessing all her actions, which in turn made her angry.

Did she want to report Cecil Wenck to law enforcement? Sure she did. Did she want to go through hell and get her company blackballed? Hell, no. "Aside from some ugly threats and that disgusting kiss, nothing much happened."

"Enough to have you leaping across a balcony thirty feet up." Savage sipped his drink casually, although the energy he gave off was anything but relaxed.

"I'd rather not go through the wringer of making an official complaint." She had the audio recording to use as a safeguard should Wenck decide to try and smear her name. But what if he did this to someone else, and she didn't try to bring him to justice?

She bit her lip. She didn't know what to do.

"I understand. The process isn't easy—"

A bitter laugh escaped her lips.

Those eyes assessed her critically. "He wasn't pleased you got away from him and even though I de-escalated some of the anger, I suspect he's a man who doesn't like to be bested." Savage glanced down at his drink and then back up. "You can stay in here tonight with me. You have my word you'll be safe from any sexual advances. I highly recommend you leave with me on the first flight to Jakarta in the morning. How long will it take you to pack?"

Haley's head spun at the ramifications of what he was saying to her. She still wasn't safe…

She didn't want to stay here with Savage like a fugitive, but she wasn't dumb enough to head back to her room alone either—not if Savage thought it would be a foolish idea. The idea of running away pissed her off, but she wasn't on home ground and had no idea how much pressure Wenck could exert on local authorities. Accepting help and leaving with a federal agent seemed like a smart idea.

"I don't need long, just a few minutes to throw everything into my case." She looked down at her pretty dress. It was one of her favorites, but she'd never wear it again without thinking of Cecil Wenck and his repulsive proposition. She'd leave it behind and hope someone here got some use out of it. "I need to change."

Savage's brows pinched together as he stared her up and

down. “I can lend you some running shorts and a t-shirt to sleep in. In the morning, we can go quietly grab your belongings and come back here to get ready.”

“There are thousands of women who might enjoy what he had to offer,” she said. “Why chase one who isn’t interested?”

One side of Savage’s mouth twisted in a smile that held no humor. “We both know it wasn’t sex he was hungry for. It was power and domination. The thought of keeping you fearful and off-balance every time he saw you in a business meeting. Of repeatedly assaulting you. Of letting all the other guys in your sphere know that he was fucking you as if that would somehow make him more of a man.”

Haley’s stomach cramped, and she thought she might throw up. Cecil Wenck would have gotten her firm on the hook with a contract and then attacked her every chance he got. That’s what he’d imagined, anyway.

“We will not be taking that contract,” she said firmly.

Savage looked unconvinced.

“We don’t need it.”

“But you wouldn’t mind shoving it down the throats of all your competitors?”

The imagery conjured by those words had her shooting to her feet and dashing to the bathroom. Thankfully, she made it to the toilet before she threw up. Despite all the years of fighting for her place in this world, there were still people, lots of people, who thought she was nothing more than a walking sex toy designed for their pleasure. And that hurt. That really hurt.

She sat on the bathroom floor, holding her hair back with one hand, waiting for her stomach to settle.

Savage gave her privacy.

Thank god.

All these years, and she was back to this. It made her so mad, so angry. She spent a lot of time proving she was as capable and effective as any guy in this business. Proving she was an equal. Here she was running away and, worse, accepting help from the first man to cross her path. Fed—she corrected quickly. She was accepting Savage's help because of his position, not because he was a guy. It was his badge and his professionalism that were the draw, regardless of his gender. Feds were supposed to help. Supposed to protect.

She wiped her mouth and stood up to wash her hands. Her face was stark white except for her blood red lips. Her skin clammy. She used a tissue and some hotel soap to wash most of the makeup off her face, but she couldn't get it all. She eyed the gold dress and was suddenly overcome with hatred for the vibrant material, the plunging neckline, thigh high slit and everything it represented.

She needed to scrub away the feel of Cecil's eyes and hands along with the humiliation of what she'd gone through. She wished she could go smack Wenck on the nose, but that would be foolhardy under the circumstances.

She closed the bathroom door and eased down the zipper on her dress, stripping her underwear at the same time and tossing it in the corner of the room. She climbed into the shower, letting hot water wash away the shame and agitation of the ugly encounter.

Savage would understand. She knew that without asking.

Maybe she should be worried about the guy coming in here and helping himself, but she knew he wouldn't. Did that make her foolish to possess such blind faith in another stranger? Or did it mean she wasn't as jaded as she sometimes feared?

She found a bar of soap and lathered her skin, used the

hotel shampoo and conditioner on her hair until her scalp tingled. The words of that old song came back to her as she tried to remove even the memory of the man. "I'm gonna wash that man right outta my hair."

She sucked in several deep, calming breaths so she didn't laugh hysterically. She didn't dare make a noise in case Wenck heard her and broke into Savage's room. Then someone was going to get hurt and, no matter who it was, she didn't want to be responsible. And maybe she *would* report the asshole once she got safely back to the States, but the idea of facing those people downstairs again if she did… Of admitting she'd bitten off more than she could chew and that Wenck had attacked her rather than treat her as an equal… She didn't think she could handle that. Her pride wouldn't allow it—except, there were more important things than pride at stake.

Anger had her jaw clenching. She'd like to kick Cecil Wenck from one side of this island to the other. Reveal to his wife that her husband was a pig. But what she really craved was to forget what had happened or, better yet, take back control. Regain autonomy of her mind and body. Make her own choices. Follow her own desires.

Thoughts of the attractive federal agent in the next room made her skin flush and her pulse begin to throb. Her nipples hardened, and she cupped her own breast and imagined him doing the same.

It was an erotic fantasy, but one that could be a reality if she had the nerve to go after what she wanted. They were both leaving in the morning. She never had to see him again.

No one had ever said she lacked nerve, but if he wasn't interested…well, it would be an uncomfortable night for both of them, but it was a choice he'd get to make.

CHAPTER FOUR

QUENTIN WENT OVER to his luggage and dragged out his running gear and gave it the sniff test. He'd worn it briefly, but his workout had ended before he'd even broken sweat when he'd received news of Darby O'Roarke, the volcanologist's abduction. He hadn't planned on sharing his clothes, but he didn't have a lot of options. Haley Cramer had even less.

If she was too prissy to wear his workout gear when her personal safety was on the line, then he couldn't help her.

He heard Haley climb into the shower and sighed deeply, dropping his shoulders, wondering how he'd got himself into this situation. He didn't mind providing assistance, not at all, but he was pissed with not being able to do anything except apply a temporary Band-Aid.

He understood where she was coming from regarding pressing charges, especially as she seemed to have avoided the worst. That Wenck had been intent on pressuring her into sexual intercourse was appalling. The guy obviously got off on power. And it probably wasn't the first time he'd done something like this. Quentin would do some digging of his own when he got back to Quantico. Men like Wenck tended to exhibit a pattern of behavior that left a trail of victims in their wake.

He went over to the bathroom door, knocked, then opened the door an inch without looking inside. He hooked the clothes on the inner doorknob before closing it again.

It was possible Haley Cramer was playing him. She could have jumped the balcony and intentionally found him, a senior FBI agent, to act as a witness, crying sexual assault in order to blackmail the billionaire into either damages or signing what was presumably an extremely lucrative business deal.

However, false claims of sexual assault were exceedingly rare. And Quentin didn't think Haley had known who he was when he'd grabbed her to prevent her from crying out in fright. She'd seemed genuine when she said she was no longer interested in working for Wenck and didn't want to press any charges. Also, why had someone gone into her room searching for her? Unless she'd stolen something…

Her glittery purse sat on the table beside the unconsumed whiskey. Plain sight? *Ish*. He opened her purse and found a cell phone, a key card to her room, and a tube of scarlet lipstick. He examined the tube to make sure it was just a lipstick and not some fancy listening device or computer gizmo. As far as he could tell, it was just lipstick.

He felt like a bit of an ass for going through her stuff. He checked her wallet but found nothing out of the ordinary except a black American Express card that he'd assumed was a myth. It had *her* name on the front. Shit. He closed the purse and repositioned it back on the table.

It was better to be thorough than to look like a damned fool, so he emailed his secretary with a request for background information on Haley Cramer. Then he eyed the chaise-lounge. He wasn't looking forward to trying to contort himself on that thing all night, but he'd been raised with manners and would never allow a woman to take the couch. It wasn't even ten PM yet, but he had an early flight tomorrow morning, and if she had any sense of self-preservation, Haley Cramer would be joining him on it.

He quickly stripped to his boxers. Everything he'd brought with him, except his wash bag, was ready to zip up and head out the door. He set his alarm, grabbed a throw to nail home the point that he wasn't moving from the chaise, laid down with his eyes closed to at least attempt to get some sleep.

After five minutes or so, the bathroom door opened. Haley Cramer stood outlined by the light behind her, wearing a towel wrapped around her body, wet hair brushing bare shoulders.

"I hung shorts and a t-shirt on the doorknob for you to sleep in. You can take the bed. We have to be up early, so goodnight." He closed his eyes again, determined not to think about her naked under that towel. He wasn't going to get all worked up about sharing a room with a beautiful woman. She wasn't his type at all—except in appearance. He liked a simple life and uncomplicated women. Haley Cramer was not an uncomplicated woman. She was unstable dynamite left too close to a flame. She was the labyrinth beneath the pharaoh's tomb.

Soft footsteps came closer. If he was an asshole, he'd be hoping for sex, but he wasn't an asshole. Nope, he was a damn saint.

A light whisper floated on the quiet night air. "I don't mind sharing. The bed, that is."

He opened his eyes. He wasn't an asshole but apparently, he wasn't dead either.

"Although I generally sleep naked, which might bother

you." She undid the towel and let it fall to the floor. The light from the bathroom backlit her body, showcasing a silhouette of an hourglass figure. "And so there is no misunderstanding…this *is* an invitation for you to join me in bed. Naked. With sex on the menu if you're interested."

His mouth went dry. Every excuse he might have made evaporated on his tongue as blood seared through his veins, heading straight to his groin. He tossed aside the throw and sat up, swinging his legs around, finding her navel in line with his mouth. She stepped between his knees and he closed them tight, trapping her in place, taking a breath and struggling to think. There was probably a good reason not to do this, but for the life of him he couldn't remember what that might be. Her skin smelled like the hotel soap, but he could also scent her arousal, and it made him hard as steel.

He spread his fingers over the curve of each hip. Her skin was like velvet, but softer. Her curves tempted him, but he somehow managed to hold back. Not that he wanted to hold back, but… "You suffered an upsetting experience. You're not thinking straight."

She smiled and licked her bottom lip. "Oh, I know what I want. I've wanted you since the moment you stepped up on that podium today."

"Not the usual response I get from my audience." His voice cracked. *Way to play it cool, jackass.*

"How do you know? Are you a mind reader as well as a negotiator?" She tried to raise her leg to straddle him, but he didn't let her. If he did, all talking would end.

"No, ma'am. But I need you to be sure and not do something you might regret."

"I'm quite sure, Special Agent Savage."

He didn't correct her about his title. He wasn't *that* stupid. He cleared his throat. What if she was still upset? What if she mistakenly thought she owed him in some way for offering her shelter? "But—"

"Quentin." She sounded exasperated. "I'm positive. If you want to, that is. Otherwise, I'll sleep on the chaise. Alone." She sounded less certain now. "And never bother you again, I promise. No hard feelings."

No hard feelings? His erection *hurt*, he was so turned on.

She was so near, he couldn't think straight. He closed his eyes, needing to reason this through. But darkness heightened all his other senses, her scent fresh on the night air, her exquisite skin giving softly beneath the rough calluses on his fingers. His resistance crumbled.

He wanted to taste her. Needed to taste her. He leaned forward and dipped his tongue into the soft indent of her belly button. She gasped softly. He held her still as he traced his tongue over her skin, and then he moved lower, monitoring her reaction via the tension of her muscles as his tongue finally dragged through the naked folds of her sex.

This was new.

He liked her bare skin more than he'd anticipated, but then anything that made sex *different* was welcome. Anything that didn't elicit memories he'd rather forget when fucking another woman. He nuzzled her there, felt the hitch in her breathing as he used his tongue on her clit, keeping her trapped between his legs. She moaned, sifting her fingers through his hair as his fingers gripped her ass. He kept rubbing that small nub, feeling her react, stiffen and tremble.

She kept her cries down to a low whimper, her hips undulating against his mouth as he nibbled and tasted and drove.

There was nothing like the taste of a woman. Nothing like the feel of one coming against the flat of his tongue after only a few minutes of focused attention.

He pulled back, and she folded forward, her forehead resting on his shoulder. She was breathing heavily, giving him a perfect view of her breasts.

"I knew you were good with your mouth, but that wasn't what I was expecting."

He laughed and let her go from where he'd held her trapped between his legs. She pushed him back against the chaise. He captured her hand and brought her with him. Naked chest met naked chest, the satiny smoothness of her skin unlike anything he'd ever experienced before. His hands molded every contour, every perfect curve, searching out the heaviness of her breasts, teasing the rigid tips of her nipples. Pinching them with his thumb and forefinger before sucking them into his mouth.

Her hands spanned his shoulders, then his back. Grasping and exploring. Going lower. She moved front and center and found his erection, not difficult considering his dick was trying to climb out of his boxers to get her attention. Her fingers wrapped around him, and he leaned his head back and wondered how he'd gone from having a sensible early night to having sex with one of the most beautiful women he'd ever met.

His mind shied away from the thought and then shut down completely as she slid to her knees in front of him, eased him out of his boxers, and ran her tongue over his length. He was pretty sure steam sizzled off his skin.

She took him in her mouth, and he had to keep himself from thrusting forward.

His fingers sank into the upholstery in an effort to stop himself doing anything that might frighten her. She'd been through a terrifying experience earlier, but she hadn't seemed unsure or hesitant about this. No, she'd seemed keen to take control of the situation, and he was happy to help in any way he could.

Even so, he knew they shouldn't be doing this, but he couldn't seem to resist his attraction to her. Especially when he looked down and saw his length slipping between her lips and felt the wet heat of her mouth surrounding him. That vision must be wired to something primal, something handed down in his DNA as a way to short-circuit conscious thought and turn him into a mindless rutting creature.

The tight sensation in his balls told him he was going to come if she didn't stop soon, and, as desperately as he wanted that, he also wanted more.

He withdrew and almost groaned when she pouted. She had the sex kitten thing down pat.

How much of it was real? How much put on for his benefit?

Or maybe this was who she was, and she wasn't ashamed of any of it. Why should she be? There was nothing wrong with enjoying sex. They were both consenting adults, and he enjoyed the heck out of it.

And maybe he was thinking too damn much.

He took her hand and drew her to her feet. He headed for the bed but veered off to the bathroom along the way. He had condoms in his wash kit, because occasionally he wanted sex and sometimes, he was lucky enough to get it—like tonight. Whether it was a biological urge or simply a physiological reminder he wasn't dead yet, he wasn't sure, but he didn't fight it anymore. The sight of her gold dress lying in the corner had him pausing.

"This isn't about him." Haley tugged his hand. "It's about me wanting you. It's about me *choosing* you."

He grabbed a strip of condoms and dragged her to the bed.

HALEY HADN'T EXPECTED Quentin to be quite so assertive a lover. Although she should have guessed from the gleam in his eye and the confident way he handled himself in general.

Her clit still tingled from his tongue and, even though she'd come already, she felt as though they were only getting started.

He tossed the condoms on the bedside table and turned to face her. He sank his hand into the hair at her nape, pulled her forward, and kissed her on the mouth.

It caught her off guard, that simple kiss. He didn't try to force his way inside. Instead, he coaxed and teased, giving her the time she needed to adjust from sex to kissing. Kissing was an art form not everyone paid attention to. It was a getting-to-know-you move she didn't always allow. But she couldn't have broken that kiss if someone had put a gun to her head and threatened to pull the trigger.

It was an act of exploration and recognition, that was both familiar and at the same time unique. His tongue touched hers, tentatively seeking permission to come inside and play—somehow more intimate than him sucking her clit. His palm skimmed her side, barely touching but causing a rush of sensation in its wake.

She cupped his cheek though other parts of his body

tempted her. His muscles were well-defined and lean, a runner's build with no excess to slow him down. She absorbed his kiss and slid her fingers upward into the silky blackness of his hair.

Did he know how gorgeous he was? How spectacular?

She doubted it. He wasn't arrogant enough.

Suddenly the kiss felt too intimate, too revealing, and she pulled back, wrapping her fingers around his thick length.

"Hmm," she scraped her teeth along his bottom jaw up to the curve of his ear. "Let's see if you can talk your way out of this, shall we?"

"I must look way stupider than I realized if you think I'm even going to try." His voice was low and deep, only slightly above a whisper, reminding her Cecil Wenck could still be a problem that neither of them wanted to have to deal with. Quentin backed her up until her legs hit the mattress, and her knees buckled. He grinned, and she knew she was in big trouble.

He pulled her to the edge of the bed, sinking to his knees, his wide shoulders forcing her legs apart and opening her up to him.

"Tell me what you like, Haley. Tell me how to get you off as many times as you want before I get inside you."

She choked. *Holy crap*. No one had ever said anything like that to her before. She felt exposed and vulnerable and covered her insecurity with a light laugh. "Cocky much?"

One side of his mouth twisted into a grin. "Confident. But only with your help. Tell me what you like." He took her hand and sucked her finger into his mouth. "Show me."

She was shaking so hard, she wasn't sure she'd be able to. Then she decided why the hell not. This might be the best sex of her life and, after the awful things that had happened earlier tonight, she deserved it. They both did.

"I like to be teased for a while." She showed him, thrilled at how his eyes glinted at the information.

He copied her, painstakingly, slowly. "Okay."

Finally, he slid his tongue along her slit, and she almost shot up off the bed. But he didn't touch her how she really wanted, and she realized he was waiting for more instructions. Or teasing her into madness.

"I'd like your tongue inside me," she said carefully.

"Mmm." His tongue joined her finger, tasting and exploring her until she could barely breathe. He pulled her against his face, and her body shook with arousal. His hands pushed her thighs wider apart and, when he pulled away, his gaze was hot and intimate.

"What else?" His voice was rough now.

She swallowed, reminding herself not to scream because, dammit, *Cecil Wenck*. She slicked a finger over her clit. "I liked it when you sucked me here."

"Sucked you."

"It made me want to crawl all over you and fuck your face." She laughed.

He climbed onto the bed to lie beside her. "Your wish, lady."

She rose to her knees, a little intimidated even though she prided herself on knowing her way around the bedroom.

He drew her up his body until she straddled him. And then he sank his tongue inside her and made her gasp. The sensation was incredible, and she found her hips moving and pressing down without conscious thought. She froze, worried she was going to suffocate the guy. His eyes gleamed up at her, hands squeezing her thighs, driving her to move. His fingers found her nipples, and his tongue speared her clit, and she came apart into a million pieces of sparkling pleasure.

She tried to turn around to return the favor, but he shifted away from her.

"If you touch me with that mouth of yours again, I'm toast."

"Then you better get inside me quick."

He grabbed a condom, tension radiating from every taut muscle of his body. He covered himself. And the sight of him jutting out had her mouth watering. Her sex clenched at the thought of having him inside her.

He lay back, and she straddled his hips and bent over to lick each of his perfect brown nipples. His fingers bit into her thighs, the only sign of impatience he exhibited, but he didn't try to hurry her. He didn't try to rush this. His body was a marvel of tanned skin over solid muscle. His shoulders were broad, hips narrow. A smattering of dark hair covered his chest, narrowing into a thin line down his stomach and thickening around his groin. He was beautifully made.

There was a scar on his right side. She traced it. "Bullet wound?"

"Appendix." His eyes were amused at her exploration, but patient, so very patient. It might be the sexiest thing about him, and there was plenty to choose from.

Emotion made her throat close, and she didn't know why. To expel it, she raised herself up and eased down over him. He stretched and filled her, and she felt her muscles ripple and clench again. She was already over-sensitized and aroused to the point it was almost painful.

"You're so beautiful." He reached up and rubbed her bottom lip with his thumb, and the action shot something straight into her heart.

She didn't know what to do with the feelings though.

Usually sex was nothing more than a physical release. A little fun. A game. Exercise. Tonight, it felt as if the stakes had been raised.

Which was crazy.

It was probably some psychological response to Wenck's attack and her leap across the balcony.

To hide her reaction, she started moving on him, slowly at first, twisting her hips and deliberately squeezing her muscles around him every time he withdrew. Their pace increased, making them both gasp as sweat slicked their bodies. The friction was delicious and made her shake from the top of her head to her toes. Finally, as she was about to crash over the ledge one more time, he started thrusting into her deeper, hips pumping as he anchored her pelvis to him. Filling her hard and deep and so amazingly deliciously her breath came in hoarse pants. He growled softly as he came—spine bending, eyes closed, jaw clenched—pulsing inside her and setting off a chain reaction which blew the fuse on her orgasm so they both exploded together.

She collapsed, shaken to her core from the intensity of the encounter. He lay still for a few moments, holding on to her shoulders, his breath hot against her hair. Then, he carefully extracted himself and got out of bed and ditched the condom. She lay there in a sweaty heap. When Savage came back from the bathroom, he turned off the lamp, crawled in beside her and pulled her close.

He kissed her forehead. "Sleep well, Haley Cramer."

She huffed out an exhausted laugh. "Sleep well, Quentin Savage. See you on the other side."

She felt him smile against her hair, and she closed her eyes. Inexplicably happy, sated, and satisfied for the first time in what felt like forever.

CHAPTER FIVE

THE SOUND OF gunfire had Quentin rolling to his feet, reaching for his service weapon and finding nothing but empty space. *Shit.* The lack of a firearm was suddenly a major problem.

Haley Cramer sat up in bed then jumped to her feet, still gloriously naked. "What's going on?"

"Not sure yet."

He was impressed at how alert she was after coming out of a deep sleep, but gunfire did that to a person. His night vision was good, so he didn't turn on the lights—he could see plenty aided by the glow from the radio alarm—nor did he want to attract attention. They'd only been asleep for a short time.

This night was turning into one surprise after another. But give him sex with a beautiful woman over bullets any time of the day or night.

Quentin raked her figure with a glance, mentally tallying what they needed to do. He strode to the bathroom where his gym kit still hung on the door handle, then went to his luggage and tossed her a pair of socks and his sneakers. They were probably too big but better than going barefoot and certainly better than four-inch heels.

"Put those on."

She dressed without argument, then sat on the bed and

pulled on the socks and shoes he'd given her. Quentin grabbed his cell as he quickly tugged on a pair of boxers and black pants, followed by a dark t-shirt. Found a pair of socks and toed on his black leather shoes.

Automatic weapon fire sounded from the lobby.

This did not sound good.

He put in a quick call to the American ambassador's number, but the call didn't connect. No signal. Fuck.

"Could it be some sort of demonstration by one of the security firms?" Haley asked quickly, coming to stand beside him.

If it was, he was going to go downstairs and smash his fist through someone's face. But the screams told him this was no pantomime.

"Sounds like a terrorist attack. And I don't have a weapon." He didn't try to conceal his frustration. As much as he wanted to help people, he couldn't go head-to-head with an assault rifle and expect to last more than a few seconds before dying in a hail of bullets.

"Wenck's bodyguards have weapons," she added.

Give him a gun, and he stood a chance of saving some lives. Give him several trained people with weapons, and they could take these fuckers down.

"Stay here and only open the door for me, understand?" He eased it ajar and checked the corridor. Clear.

The sounds of gunshots, glass breaking, people screaming clawed at his conscience, but these weren't innocent tourists downstairs. They were some of the top operators in the world. The problem was, like him, none of them were armed and none of them were bulletproof.

Where was Chris? In the hotel? Or had he gone into town

for that drink? Quentin hoped the latter. He didn't even know where the guy's room was, but Chris was a survivor. He'd get out.

Quentin knocked on the thick wooden door of the suite next door. "Mr. Wenck? Cecil? It's Quentin Savage. Let me in."

Nothing.

Dammit. He couldn't risk standing here too long. If shooters got in the elevator or came up the stairs, he was a sitting duck. He went back to his room where Haley held the door. He closed it, locked it and added a chair beneath the knob for a little additional security.

More screams that tore through his conscience. Haley swallowed audibly. "We *have* to help them."

He gritted his teeth. Did she think he wasn't wracking his brain trying to figure out a strategy that might save lives? "We've got no chance unarmed against that sort of firepower."

"We can't just let people die." Her voice rose in anger.

He put his hands gently on her shoulders. "As Americans we are prime targets for death or hostage material. We have no weapons, and they're going to make your incident with Wenck seem like a spa day. We go out the window, and you hide in the jungle until the authorities arrive. Once you're safe, I'll see if I can pick off a terrorist with an automatic rifle and attempt to fight back. Anything else is suicide."

She jerked out of his hold, and her eyes went huge as another round of gunfire ended with a sharp scream not too far away.

"We can't help them, Haley. Not yet." But he could help her. She was his responsibility, and he didn't intend to let her be harmed if he could help it.

The sounds were coming closer. *Hell.* It sounded like attackers were shooting the locks off doors on the floor below and breaking into hotel rooms, probably killing people where they tried to hide.

They *had* to get out of here.

He grabbed his credentials and wallet and tucked them beneath the mattress. If captured, he did not want to be identified as a federal agent. They'd put a bullet straight through his brain, or worse...

"Follow me. We're going to jump to your balcony and use the creeper on the side of the hotel to descend to the ground level near the corner—it's not near any of the main function rooms. We'll check for tangos and if it's clear, we head into that patch of forest beside the hotel." He pointed southeast. "After that, we'll play it by ear, but we need to be quiet. No talking when we exit this room." He checked his watch. They had hours of darkness, which helped. Hopefully the authorities would be here soon to help stage a rescue.

She grabbed her cell from her clutch and stuffed it in the pocket of the shorts she wore.

He led the way, easing open the door onto the balcony and gazing out into the darkness. More screams from around the other side of the hotel and a slight whiff of smoke. They'd set fire to the building, either to destroy it entirely or flush people out of their rooms.

Quentin stared at Wenck's balcony. Dammit, he couldn't leave the man here to die when they stood a good chance of escaping this way.

"Wait here," he told Haley.

He jumped over to Wenck's suite and tapped on the glass of the door, hoping to hell the bodyguards weren't trigger happy. He tried the handle, and it opened. He poked his head inside. "Mr. Wenck? It's Quentin Savage. I think I know how we can get out of here."

He took a few steps inside then glanced into the living room. It was empty, and all the man's belongings were gone. It looked as if Wenck had checked out. Had he made it away before the terrorists attacked?

Quentin went back to the balcony and scanned the darkness below. Quiet for now. It wouldn't stay free of tangos forever, so they better get moving. He jumped back to his balcony where Haley crouched out of sight of anyone on the ground. He pulled her to her feet and climbed onto the railing and leapt across the short space to her balcony, feeling his heart wobble a little when some loose mortar rattled to the ground. He waited a second, then turned and held his arms out to Haley. She looked nervous but didn't hesitate.

He caught her, and pulled her against him. They both sucked in a breath of relief.

"Now to climb down to ground level," he whispered.

The sound of machine gun fire on the opposite corner of the hotel had them freezing in place. Someone screamed, and one of the conference delegates sprinted across the darkened lawn toward the pool that was lit up with tiki torches. It was a CEO of a big US security company. He was brought down with a blast of bullets to the back. Quentin pushed Haley's face against his chest to smother her sounds of distress.

The dead man had been a former Special Forces soldier, and he'd still known that, without the right equipment, the only reasonable option was to run and hide. If the terrorists spotted them up here on this balcony, they were next.

Someone started beating on the door to Haley's room. It

was only a matter of time until the militants broke in and found them.

"We have to go. Now. I'm going to go first to make sure it will hold our weight. I'll catch you if you fall."

"Who'll catch *you*?" Haley slowly released her grip on his shirt.

He smiled slightly. That wasn't how this worked. "Don't stop moving for anything. Not even if a terrorist starts firing. The aim of those AKs is for shit. Move fast. If we get separated head to the trees. Hide in the darkness and don't come out until you know it is safe."

Neither of them mentioned the dead contractor lying on the grass a hundred yards away.

Quentin grabbed on to the thick vine. It sagged a little unnervingly under his hundred-eighty-pound weight but held. If it supported him, it would hold Haley. He rapidly made his way down the vine, the scent of broken leaves mixing with gunpowder in the air.

He didn't have to tell Haley to follow. As soon as he hit the ground, her shadow attached itself to the vine with unnervingly pale limbs. The rustle of leaves as she quickly clambered down was unavoidable. More gunfire, and he hugged the building as shouts in the local language floated on the air.

The smoke was thicker now. Choking.

His heart beat in his chest like a war drum. He'd trained for this kind of mission, been involved in enough takedowns and arrests to know that adrenaline was the enemy as much as the guys with guns. Panic, and they were fucked. Keep a clear head, and they had a sliver of a chance.

Haley lowered herself far enough that he could reach her, and he lifted her into his arms before carefully placing her feet on solid ground. She was breathing heavily but not freaking out.

What he wouldn't give to be making love to her one more time rather than running for their lives through a jungle in the darkness. He took her hand and glanced around the corner of the building. Flames flickered orange near the entranceway. Most of the gunshots were coming from the bar area to the southwest that had probably been full of half-drunk delegates relaxing after a tiring few days.

Crouching low, he and Haley jogged across the short patch of grass and into the shrubs and bushes that marked the edge of the jungle. Rather than blindly crashing around, Quentin wound his way carefully and slowly through the trees, eyes and ears alert for tangos guarding the perimeter, on the lookout for escapees.

Haley's fingers gripped his. This was a terrifying situation, one he was woefully unprepared for, but she hadn't fought him on this course of action. If she was feeling half as remorseful as he was for leaving people behind, then she felt like crap.

A branch snapped about twenty feet ahead of him, and they both froze. He could feel her trembling.

They crouched low, not even breathing as a man detached himself from behind a tree and crushed a cigarette beneath his boot. Dammit. They'd almost walked straight into him.

With Haley behind him, they were almost invisible in the darkness. Quentin debated whether or not to grab the guy and steal his weapon, but he didn't think he could do it silently. His primary objective right now was to get Haley Cramer to safety, report the situation to FBI HQ, and then go see if he could save anyone else.

The terrorist moved away out of sight, and Quentin crept through the encompassing darkness, ignoring the buzz of insects seeking fresh blood. He hoped he didn't encounter any venomous snakes along the way. He hated snakes, but they were preferable to their human cousins right now. After ten minutes walking, the sounds of death and violent destruction were muted, but neither of them spoke until the soft lap of waves announced they'd reached the beach.

They stayed hidden in the trees. Being on the beach itself was too exposed, and they couldn't swim to safety. They had to hide.

North was a steep cliff with jungle so dense it was virtually impenetrable. South led to the hotel's private beach.

"Let's find a spot in the trees to regroup. I'm going to call Washington and see how fast they can send backup."

"Good idea," Haley whispered back.

They crept thirty feet into the jungle. Quentin cleared a patch of ground beside a huge tree using his shoes, hoping he was effective enough to scare away critters without being noisy enough to attract any unwanted attention from gun-wielding maniacs. He sat down on the ground, the relief of being safe for now mixing with distress at the knowledge others were suffering and in danger.

He checked his phone, grateful for the bars that indicated he had service thanks to the cell phone tower on the hillside above his head. He dialed a number for a friend at SIOC, the Strategic Information & Operations Center at headquarters. Indonesia was eleven hours ahead of everyone back home.

"McKenzie."

"Mac, listen up. It's Quentin Savage from CNU. I'm on Pulau Nabat, Indonesia, at a security symposium which has just been attacked by what I am assuming are heavily armed terrorists. Myself and a woman named Haley Cramer managed to get out of the hotel by climbing down the outside from the upper balconies. We're hiding in the jungle. I tried to get a call in to the US Ambassador in Jakarta but couldn't get a signal. I wanted to contact HQ directly with an update. You need to arrange for assistance from the Indonesian authorities." Quentin realized with a growing sense of despondency that there was very little he could actually tell the man. "I saw one guy shot in the back as he ran away. They've set fire to the hotel to flush people out of their rooms, or burn them to death, I—" He cleared his throat. "I don't have a weapon. I couldn't save anyone else..."

"Buddy, sounds like you did the only thing you logically could."

Logic didn't make Quentin feel any better.

A hand found his in the darkness and squeezed tight. Haley Cramer knew exactly how he felt. He pressed her hand back, hoping she got some comfort from him being here with her.

She'd had a rough night.

Where the hell had Cecil Wenck disappeared to? Had he decided to split in case Haley brought charges against him? Or had he decided on a firm and signed a deal and gone home to his long-suffering wife? Or had he been tipped off about the terrorists' arrival? All were distinct possibilities, the last was Quentin's most pressing question.

Haley called someone on her cell and murmured quietly in the darkness. He couldn't hear what she was saying, but he could feel her spine move against his back as she spoke. The human contact was reassuring.

"Can you tell me your exact location?" McKenzie asked.

"Near the beach beneath the hotel's cell tower."

"Are you safe?"

"For now," Quentin stated uneasily. "I'm going to creep back and see what I can observe from the woods. Maybe I can get a gun—"

"Negative. Stay concealed until the troops get there. Just heard from the Ambassador that Indonesian police are on their way. I am about to call SIOC's Section Chief and get him to talk to Defense. See if we have any ships in the area that can assist. Any idea how many US nationals are involved?"

"About a hundred? Many of the top private military contractors in the world are here." All unarmed unless they arrived by boat or private aircraft or arranged something to be delivered ahead of time. "I haven't heard anything that sounds like an exchange of fire. It sounds more like a massacre."

This was a massive coup for a group of militants. Had they read about the conference? Had someone told them about it?

"Keep out of sight. I have a US Navy vessel fifty miles offshore rerouting to the scene. Should be there before dawn. You need to hold on that long."

"Thanks. Talk to you later." Quentin hung up.

That's when he heard it.

The echo of laughter close by.

CHAPTER SIX

HALEY WAS SHAKING so badly as she dialed Alex's cell, she almost dropped the phone. He didn't answer. The guy had just had a baby, so she wasn't surprised, but this was more his field of expertise than Dermot's, and she needed a little advice.

She considered herself a competent professional, but nothing had prepared her for being attacked in a luxury hotel, knowing her fellow civilians were being slaughtered nearby and being unable to do anything about it. Nothing had prepared her for watching a man gunned down in cold blood while she stood by too terrified to even scream. Nothing had prepared her for the primal fear that had coursed through her veins, knowing people were actively trying to kill her, and the only viable option she had for survival was running for her life.

What the hell had happened to the security hired for the conference?

Alex's voice reached out of the darkness, and she wanted to sob in relief even though it was only his voice mail message. Damn, but she'd desperately needed to hear his voice.

Inhaling a calming breath, she cradled the phone with both hands and quietly told him her location, what had happened and who she was with. Then emotions bubbled up, emotions she normally kept battened down, because they didn't do any damn good.

"If anything happens to me, don't you dare try to take responsibility. You can't protect everyone, especially not someone as pigheaded as I am. Look after Mal. You've got a keeper there. Treat her like a queen. Kiss Georgina from me and find Dermot a wife for god's sake. He'll never get there on his own. I love you. Don't fuck anything up if I..." She swallowed hard. "Yeah."

She found herself back to back with Savage, leaning against him for support. She prided herself on the fact she didn't need anyone and yet, tonight, she wasn't sure she would have survived without him. He'd been a rock. But she shouldn't need a rock.

Her company helped prevent bad things from happening to others, and she was good at her job. But twice in one night her confidence in her own abilities had been shattered. Rather than proving she was an equal, she'd turned out to be the weak link.

Self-loathing rose up inside her. So much for her famous swagger. It was all just a front. She was furious with herself and yet didn't know what she could have done different and still be around to talk about it.

She straightened so she wasn't relying on Savage for support and instantly missed the connection. He turned and grabbed her thigh in a grip that was shockingly strong and full of warning. She hung up the call and pressed the screen against her chest to quench the light.

Voices.

Men's voices.

Oh, shit. Her skin went cold.

They weren't hiding but ambling casually through the

bush like tourists on a day hike.

"Conceal yourself under that bush and don't move. I'll hide under another one over here. If they catch me, stay hidden. Hold tight. Navy are on the way."

He seemed to drift away on the night air and disappeared into the ether, leaving her all alone. She moved carefully, easing under the thick branches and hoping to god there was nothing poisonous down here. The bottom line was, these men were way scarier than any other creature, no matter how many legs it had. Her pale skin and blonde hair stood out in the darkness. She made herself into the smallest possible ball and backed farther beneath the thick leaves. She moved slowly, so as not to rustle the bushes or draw attention, edging under the foliage into the void.

It was surreal.

How had she gone from cocktails in a gold dress and Jimmy Choos—shoes that had been abandoned with ease when life-threatening danger presented itself—to hiding in the jungle, crawling in the dirt, wearing a stranger's gym clothes, praying the bad guys didn't find either one of them?

She didn't want to die.

She hadn't realized how desperately she wanted to live until this very moment.

The chime of her cell phone made her heart stop beating. *No, no, no.* Terror spread over her skin like an electric shock. She uncurled enough to reject the call and turn the ringer to silent using shaking fingers on the button on the side. Then she wrapped her body around the stupid cell phone and closed her eyes, even though it was pitch black. If she couldn't see them, then maybe they couldn't see her, right?

The men had gone quiet. Haley heard nothing beyond the

drumming of blood in her ears. She forced herself to calm her breathing, which seemed as harsh as a siren in the night.

The systematic rustle of vegetation told her they'd heard the cell and were searching for her. She squeezed herself into an even smaller ball, holding her breath and trying to become invisible. Suddenly the branches were ripped away from over her head, and a strong hand manacled her wrist, dragging her to her feet. The man grabbed both her hands and pulled them behind her back, wrenching them so high she cried out in pain. She wanted to lash out, but the barrel of an AK was shoved into her chest, and she knew if she even blinked wrong, she was dead.

There were two of them, one tall and angular and the other, short and heavy. They jabbered with one another in a language she didn't understand. Moonlight glinted off belts of ammo wrapped over their shoulders. The smell of their sweat was rank and overwhelming, as if they'd been wearing the same clothes for days or didn't have access to a shower.

They were laughing at her. Mocking her. The man holding her wrapped something around her wrists and cinched it so tight pain shot up her arms. She doubted her blood could circulate. She was taller than both of them, but even with Alex's self-defense lessons, she was too scared to risk fighting them. The guns were too *there*. The slightest pressure of a finger on the trigger would mean a bullet, and a painful death.

She didn't look around for Savage. He couldn't do anything for her, and she didn't want to get him killed simply because she'd been too dumb to turn off her cell's ringer while hiding from hostiles.

She might not understand what the men were saying, but she recognized the change in tone, and understood their intent when they shoved her onto her back on the ground and dragged her shorts down her body, off one leg.

Oh, god.

She wanted to scream but didn't want to bring more attention to their little tableau. The furtive way these men were acting suggested they knew they shouldn't be doing this, and not because it was a moral outrage.

The position of her arms and hands beneath her back was agony. Despite knowing she should lie still and pretend it wasn't happening she drew back her leg and kicked the closest guy in the face.

They'd shoot her anyway after they raped her, so why the hell not? The heavier guy punched her, and a white flash of pain crashed through her brain. Her lip split, and she tasted blood. Her head fell back against the ground, and she lay there, dazed.

One of them turned on a flashlight and pointed it at her body. Rough hands parted her thighs and both men stared. Emotion choked her. Rage and humiliation wanted to consume her.

She squirmed and tried to squeeze her knees back together, but the taller man knelt down and forced them apart, planting himself there, fumbling with his zipper.

No.

This couldn't be happening.

Did she have some sort of victim symbol tattooed to her forehead? She lay frozen in horror and disgust. Shaking. Was this somehow her fault? Could she have behaved differently and none of this would ever have happened?

Yes, Haley, if you'd turned off the ringer of your goddamn phone this wouldn't be happening.

She stared up at the stars visible through the thick jungle canopy overhead. All these years, she'd been running away from this very act, taking control of her sex life while fighting to be taken seriously, to be treated as an equal. And yet these animals had taken one look at her in the dark forest and, once again, she'd been reduced to her most basic animal parts.

It was hard to see their expressions with the flashlight in front of them, but she could tell they were excited. *Duh.* The man between her thighs held her down with a heavy hand on her pelvis. Haley's mouth went dry, and her flesh went cold. She knew what was coming.

The second man stood behind the first, watching her nakedness with lust, waiting his turn with impatience. Suddenly, he seemed to sag, his neck bending in an unnatural fashion before he floated to the ground.

The man holding her reached out to touch her with his filthy hand, and she flinched. She hated him with every cell in her body. Despised him. Wanted to kill him but instead lay as inert as stone. Silent.

He noticed his friend had gone quiet and looked around, but it was too late. Big hands wrapped around his jaw and jerked his head violently to the right. Her attacker went limp and fell heavy across her thigh. Quentin dragged him off and tossed him aside.

She tried to close her legs, but her movements were stiff and awkward.

She wanted to hide herself, even though Quentin had seen every inch of her naked body. There was a distinct difference in being naked when she was having consensual sex versus any other time. Quentin seemed to understand she was struggling to cope and quickly pulled the shorts back up her legs and over her hips, treating her as if she were a helpless child. She lay there trembling so hard she didn't think she could sit up.

"Are you hurt?" he whispered desperately. "Was I too late?"

She shook her head, feeling the dirt and twigs beneath her scalp. She felt violated and dirty and full of every form of loathing and disgust.

Quentin used the attacker's flashlight but kept the beam of light close to the ground so it couldn't be seen from a distance. He searched the body of the dead man beside her, found a knife, rolled her unceremoniously onto her side and cut through the cord that bound her wrists.

Blood rushed painfully back into her hands and fingers and she felt lightheaded as she sat up. But she was free of her bindings and had never felt more grateful to another human being in her life. Not that they had time to celebrate.

Quentin turned away and began collecting weapons and ammo off the two dead men. Building a small arsenal. Then he undid the one man's shirt and then his pants and boots.

He thrust the clothes at her. "Put them on."

Her stomach heaved when the warm fabric touched her skin.

"I can't." She shoved them away.

"You have to." Quentin crouched beside her, tone resolute. "Your skin is too pale and too easily seen. As is your hair. The next time someone comes looking for us, we might not get so lucky."

Her inhaled breath sounded awfully like a sob.

He grasped her upper arm. "I know you can do this, Haley. I know how tough you are."

She thrust his hand away. All his words did was remind

her how weak she'd been over the last few hours. But he was right about her skin. It virtually glowed in the moonlight. She grabbed the shirt and quickly pulled it across her shoulders, immediately fading a little into the shadows. She wished she could disappear into the earth, let it swallow her whole. She undid Savage's too big sneakers and dragged the would-be rapist's pants up her legs over the gym shorts. She could smell her attacker's sour scent, and her stomach turned, but she held it together.

That asshole was dead. She wasn't. She wanted to remain that way.

She went to put Quentin's sneakers back on, but he stopped her and tossed her the man's boots instead.

"These are smaller. Wear them."

She toed them on. It was funny. She wasn't normally good at following orders. In fact, she was abysmal at it. Alex and Dermot would be open-mouthed at her interaction with this senior FBI agent. However, what Savage said made sense and arguing might cost them both of their lives, so she didn't bother. Despite her blunder with the cell phone, she wasn't an idiot.

Plus, he'd saved her from a brutal gang rape, not to mention helped her after Cecil Wenck had accosted her. She wouldn't repay that with some prima donna bullshit.

"Do either of them have a hat?" she asked.

Quentin glanced at her. He'd pulled on the other militant's shirt, even though it was tight cross his shoulders. He searched the guy's pants, and she thought to do the same with the trousers she was wearing.

"Found one." She jammed it over her bright hair. She would scour every inch of her body with bleach when she got home. Maybe shave off her hair and start from scratch. but first she needed to survive this ordeal. Quentin nodded with approval and dragged the two bodies a little deeper into the bushes.

She picked up an AK.

"You know how to use that?" he asked.

"Yes."

"Good." He crouched beside her on his knees in the dirt. The fact he didn't question her abilities made her heart melt a little. "I want you to make your way up the hill, find a dense bit of jungle and hide there until rescue arrives. When it does, when you know for sure they are the good guys, take off your hat and camo shirt and leave the weapon behind. The last thing we need is them mistaking you for a terrorist."

She clutched his arm. "Where are you going?"

He gave her a full smile that dazzled her. She'd been attracted to his looks earlier and wowed by his skill in the bedroom, but she hadn't realized exactly how devastatingly handsome he was until that moment. And she hadn't realized how little he smiled.

"Back to the hotel to check on the situation. See if there is anything I can do that might save some lives."

"I'm coming with you." Though she was terrified. She had a whole new respect for soldiers and law enforcement who kept civilians safe.

"No."

"Yes." She climbed to her feet. "I'm sick of people treating me like I'm nothing but a receptacle for their junk. Present company excepted."

Quentin broke into a surprised grin. "I appreciate the exception." He turned off the flashlight, and moonlight etched the side of his face. "One of the people I'm hoping to help is my friend Chris Baylor. I realize you two didn't part on good terms, but as a federal agent, I am looking to save anyone I can, and that includes men like Chris. If you have a problem with that..."

Haley couldn't stop the residual tremors that affected her limbs. "I have more of a problem hiding in the woods while other people die."

The look he gave her verged on pity, and she hated it.

"Your lack of training will probably hinder me rather than help me."

Like what had just happened with her cell phone? He didn't say it, but then he didn't have to.

Emotion squeezed her throat. Shame too. His honesty was refreshing and unwanted.

"I can point and shoot," she argued.

"We're going to need stealth and guile too."

Haley swallowed. Was it selfish of her to not want to be left alone? Some people thought she was nothing but a selfish bitch, but she could help. She knew she could and wanted to prove it.

"I'm a good shot and I know first aid," she told him. She needed to be useful. Not to be a liability. Not to be the victim.

Quentin cupped her cheek gently. "This is my job, Haley. And right now, I feel good that I've helped to keep one person alive tonight. If anything happens to you..."

She squeezed her hand over his, ashamed of her dependence. "I don't want you to get hurt either. And I'm scared," she admitted, though it almost choked her. "I'm begging you not to leave me behind."

CHAPTER SEVEN

QUENTIN KNEW HALEY was afraid. Who wouldn't be? He didn't want to leave her but didn't want to jeopardize her safety either, and he needed to see if he could help anyone else.

They stared at one another. Different people than they'd been a few hours ago, different even to the strangers who'd hooked up for a round of incredible sex.

He'd killed two men.

They'd have raped Haley and put a bullet in her head as soon as they were done. Quentin wasn't sorry, but he could still feel the moment their necks had snapped in his grip. It was a sensation he'd never forget.

"I want to help," she told him, holding the AK in a way that suggested she was competent with firearms.

He had to admit he was impressed despite himself. The woman in the gold dress and high heels had looked too glamorous to be handling an assault rifle with authority. The woman who'd lain in the dirt had looked too traumatized to try to persuade him to let her come on a high-risk mission. It was hard to believe all these different sides were part and parcel of the same woman, but he had no doubt she was sincere in her desire to help.

The sound of voices had them both tensing. A group of men headed in their direction, someone angrily barking out instructions.

Quentin took Haley's hand and drew her farther away from the beach, up the gully that ran along the bottom of this hillside. His night vision had adjusted so well he could easily make out the forest floor. Haley moved quietly beside him. No crying or panicking the way many civilians would have by now.

Was this the armed group making their escape before authorities arrived? Sure looked like it. Meanwhile, at the hotel, survivors or critically injured people would need first aid.

The appearance of those first two hostiles made more sense now. The group had probably left their boats on the beach, and the two guys had been the forward party to get everything ready for a rapid withdrawal. As soon as it was noted that those men weren't where they were supposed to be, the bad guys might instigate a search. If they found their comrades' bodies, the broken necks would tell them that not everyone on the island was dead.

Would they come after them or make their escape? Quentin didn't know, but he wasn't waiting around to find out.

He kept moving through the jungle, going as fast as he dared, choosing speed over stealth in order to put a little distance between him, Haley, and the tangos.

Up the hill, to the left of the cell tower, they pushed forward until his thighs screamed, and his breath grew harsh. Suddenly they burst out into a clearing. The road, he realized. He steered Haley back into the bush. The road was risky. Too exposed.

An orange glow lit the sky ahead, visible through the

branches and leaves. The smell of smoke was cloying and thick. The hotel was burning.

Haley's fingers tightened on his in silent apprehension. The roar of the flames grew louder the closer they got. The fire spit and crackled as sparks flew into the air. The heat made sweat bead on his brow even from a distance.

They reached the edge of the jungle where it met carefully manicured lawn. One side of the hotel, the side most people had been staying on, was engulfed in red-hot flames. The other half of the hotel seemed largely untouched for now.

He scanned the surroundings. No one seemed to be moving. No terrorists. No victims. No survivors. Surely not everyone was dead?

After watching for a full minute, he turned to Haley and leaned close to her ear, so his voice didn't carry. He thought he heard gunfire, but it was hard to tell for sure over the roar of the inferno. "I'm going to check out the ground floor area near the bar and see if there's anyone who can be rescued. Stay here—"

"No." She shook her head, took off the ugly cap and stuffed it in her shirt pocket, probably so she wasn't marked as a terrorist in the unlikely event the good guys turned up. He slipped out of the camp shirt for the same reason. He was pretty sure the hostiles had made their escape, but who knew for sure?

Haley was a grown woman. If she wanted to put herself in danger to save others, that was her choice, even if he didn't like it. She wasn't his subordinate or his responsibility. But after everything they'd been through, the idea of anything happening to her cut sharply through the armor he kept around his heart.

"Let's make our way around to the other side of the building via the woods and enter through the garden doors." That way they wouldn't have to make themselves more obvious targets than they already were and could look inside the building before they risked revealing themselves.

He felt her nod and realized he was still holding her hand, but as she didn't seem to mind and he liked knowing exactly where she was, he didn't let go.

It wasn't exactly date night.

They ran at a crouch. The going was easier here, still jungle, but jungle that was kept under control by groundskeepers. Quentin wondered if the terrorists had let the locals live. Presumably they'd targeted the foreigners at the security conference to make a mockery out of the proceedings and draw as much attention to themselves as possible. And what was the point of terrifying people if the world didn't hear about it? Killing locals would make it more likely that people would turn on them and reveal their identities...assuming anyone survived.

Once they reached the outside of the bar area, they scanned the scene from a distance through the glass. Orange flames licked the edges of the interior. By some miracle of electrical wiring, the fans still swirled lazily, fanning the flames, but the rest of the world had changed in a few short hours.

"You can still stay here out of danger," Quentin murmured close to her ear. "Keep lookout," he suggested.

She reared back to look him in the eye. "You'll need help bringing out survivors. I'm coming with you."

He dropped her hand to check his weapon and side-eyed her as she did the same. She appeared to know how to handle the AK, so hopefully he wouldn't get a bullet in the ass. But the night was young. Who knew what was going to happen next?

"Let's go." He ran across the lawn, half expecting the rat-tat-tat of automatic gunfire, but nothing happened. He got to the door that opened out onto the patio. He tried it, but it was locked. A look through the door showed him that someone had secured a cable tie around the handles so it couldn't be easily opened. The tangos hadn't wanted survivors to find a way out. Assuming there were survivors.

"Oh, hell," Haley said, staring into the room.

It was carnage, but Quentin didn't allow himself to acknowledge the blood or gore. He looked for signs of life. No one moved.

He smashed a glass pane in the door with the butt of his rifle. Reached through with the borrowed knife and sliced the plastic tie, shoving the doors wide open.

Smoke billowed out, and they both fell back, coughing. The fire intensified from the direction of the main building.

"Keep low," he told her.

Beams had already fallen in the lobby, blocking the main entrance to the hotel. Showers of sparks spat into the air.

He darted behind the bar, stepping over two dead bartenders—the terrorists had killed everyone—before dunking two towels into a sink full of water. He wrung them out and handed one to Haley and tied the other around his nose and mouth.

"We can't stay here for long." The heat was intense, and the roof might collapse. "Check for pulses. See if anyone's alive."

Haley immediately went from victim to victim, touching the necks of people who'd been having a quiet drink when hell had rained down on them. He did the same. Mostly they were guys, tough guys. Hardened men who'd spent years in combat zones, both looking for and avoiding trouble.

Quentin tried not to think about them as people he'd spoken with a few hours ago. He'd been so nervous about giving the keynote thanks to his dyslexia, but now it barely mattered. They'd never had the chance to talk themselves out of this onslaught.

The first five people he checked were dead. A lot of them had gunshot wounds to the torso but also shots to the head, as if someone had gone around execution style. Bullet casings were everywhere.

The sixth person he checked made him pause. It was Tricia Rooks. She was hidden beneath an overturned table and a dead guy. He rolled the dead guy off with a silent apology. Unlike the others, she didn't have a gunshot wound to the head but was bleeding from a chest wound.

He pressed his fingers more firmly against her warm skin. Was that his imagination? There it was again, the faint murmur of a pulse.

"Haley, this woman is alive. Help me drag her onto the lawn."

Haley ran to him, eyes reddened from the smoke in the air, hair streaked with soot. They weren't gentle, but they didn't have time to do anything except heave Tricia out by the arms and leave her lying on the grass in the fresh air a good distance from the burning building. He immediately returned to the bar. Flames were moving closer now, and the idea of someone surviving a massacre only to burn to death gave him chills.

"Hey!" Haley shouted above the noise of the flames. She

pointed at the hotel entryway. "Chris. It looks like he's trapped back there, but I think I saw him move his arm."

Quentin squinted at where she pointed. Sure enough, Chris was a little beyond the doorway. Flames licked the walls around him, the staircase was engulfed. Haley grabbed Quentin's arm as another beam fell. "You can't go back there. The roof is going to come down."

Chris was now trying to drag himself across the tile floor, but he was stuck or wounded, or both.

"I can't leave him to die." They'd been through too much together over the years. Quentin shoved away the fear of burning to death. Not how he wanted to go. "Stay here. See if anyone else is alive."

Quentin handed Haley his weapon and ran past the bodies of other victims, bypassing overturned tables and chairs and broken glass. He scrambled over a large beam that had come down, half blocking the double doors, while trying to avoid long nails and searing flames alike.

He reached Chris, knelt down and the other man met his gaze. There was a Glock near his hand as if he'd been trying to fight back. Quentin scooped up the gun and stuffed it in his pocket.

Chris grabbed Quentin's pant leg. "My foot's trapped."

Quentin worked his way down the guy's body to the large piece of what had previously been ceiling pinning Chris to the floor. Heat seared his skin and made the air too hot to breathe. God knew how Chris felt, but at least he was on the ground out of the toxic black smoke that was starting to crowd the room.

Coughing continuously, grateful for the wet towel over his face, Quentin lifted the obstruction, and Chris desperately clawed himself across the tiles until he was free. Blood soaked his neck and shirt. The only actual wounds Quentin could see were what looked like a gunshot to the top of the guy's left arm and a contusion that was bleeding profusely from his scalp.

He looped Chris's arm over his shoulders, and they staggered awkwardly over the beams and furniture, stumbling into the bar the way they'd drunkenly stumbled out of so many in the past. Haley had put the weapons down and was dragging one of the servers across the floor and down the steps, trying to keep the man's head from hitting the flagstones.

Chris staggered to his knees. "How did you get out?" he rasped.

"Luck," Quentin replied, attempting to get the man back on his feet again.

"Reminds me of Baghdad," said Chris.

Except they'd had Nick laying down covering fire and saving their asses in Baghdad.

Haley came back inside and helped support Chris. He wobbled, and Quentin gripped him tighter, wondering how much blood his friend had lost and how hard he'd been hit on the head.

They got him outside, but it wasn't easy, even with the two of them putting their backs into it. Chris was a big guy.

Quentin didn't have time to do anything else for him. He needed to get back inside to find more survivors.

Haley moved to come with him, but he stopped her. "Stay here and treat the injured."

He ran to the door, but she followed him in anyway. He almost smiled, but the last thing he wanted was for her to burn to death or get crushed by falling masonry. Shit.

She really was stubborn. It made him like her even more.

They found another man who was still alive despite terrible wounds. Quentin picked him up and put him over his shoulders in a fireman's carry. A terrible shudder ran through the whole building, and one of the ceiling fans crashed to the floor. Fire started to rain down from above as the smoke started to ignite.

Haley shouted and gestured at him. "Use this window. Quick." She opened it wide and jumped through. Quentin looked around at the bodies lying on the floor of the bar, wishing they had more time, but flames were everywhere now, the heat ferocious. He used a chair to access the window and, as he stepped through it, the entire roof collapsed behind him. He leaped, and Haley helped steady him on the other side. She caught his arm and pulled him away from the flames, and they stumbled onto the lawn. Quentin laid the injured man down on the grass and fell to the cool earth, exhausted.

He and Haley lay next to one another panting heavily, trying to catch their breath. Her hand found his and gripped him tight. "Is it over?"

Smoke filled his lungs and made his voice rasp. "I think so."

Then a shadow detached itself from the darkness and pointed a gun at them both.

Quentin swore.

The bastard yelled something at the top of his lungs. Quentin didn't understand what he was saying. What he did realize, deep in his bones, was that despite everything they'd endured and overcome, they were still going to die.

"GET UP."

The stranger's voice jabbed at Haley like a sharpened stick, but she laughed. Hysteria, probably. Despite her troubled teenage years, she'd never been this close to losing her mind.

Quentin stood, pulling Haley to her feet, shielding her with his body. She tried to stand beside him, but he wouldn't let her. She was too mentally exhausted to be annoyed. It had been a long time since she'd experienced anyone being chivalrous towards her, but when did she give anyone the chance? Alex and Dermot knew better than to try.

The man with the gun took something out of his pocket, a crumpled piece of paper. "FBI?"

Haley gasped softly against Quentin's back. His fingers squeezed hers. It was obvious this militant was looking for Savage specifically. Unfortunately, the gunman didn't look like a rescuer. He was dressed exactly like the men who'd tried to rape her in the woods.

This couldn't be good.

Quentin appeared to weigh his choices. "Yes. I'm FBI."

The man's face lit up. Then his gaze went to where she stood behind Quentin and hardened. "Away." He instructed, raising his weapon.

Quentin tensed, and his grip on her wrist tightened, silently telling her to stay put. "No. If I move aside, you'll shoot this woman."

The man seemed to understand exactly what Quentin was saying, even if his English wasn't perfect. "No hurt pretty lady, FBI. Away." The voice went from friendly to sharp. The gun barrel jerked rapidly, indicating he wanted them to separate.

Haley's gut churned, and a fresh wave of terror washed over her. "It's okay, Quentin. We better do as he says."

Savage shook his head firmly. "No." He grabbed her other wrist, pulled her so she was flush against his back, arms wrapped around his waist and unable to move. "Pretty lady is with me," Quentin told the gunman.

He inched them forward. Toward the militant with the deadly weapon pointed right at them. Quentin was going to attack the guy and probably die doing it.

"Quentin, let me go," she said frantically, trying to pull free. It was over.

His grip was relentless. He kept easing them forward. The terrorist's eyes widened, and he started shouting at them.

"Don't move!"

Or what? He'd shoot? Haley wanted to guffaw, but none of this was even remotely funny.

Suddenly more shadows spilled out of the darkness and whatever hope Haley might have harbored about getting out of this alive withered and died.

There was a rapid exchange in Indonesian. A burly man stepped forward. "What's your name?"

"Quentin Savage. This is my wife, Haley—"

The sounds of helicopters in the distance made everyone raise their heads and look north. The man in charge shouted at his men, and they rushed her and Quentin, dragging them apart, pulling a sack over her head that made it hard to breathe. Her heart hammered as she braced herself for a bullet. They wanted the FBI agent, and it was painfully clear from the death toll they didn't care about anyone else.

The sound of a bullet had Quentin screaming her name and then what sounded like a scuffle. "Son of a bitch!" Quentin managed to push past their captors and grab her arm.

"It's okay. I'm not dead. *Yet.*" She might have peed her

pants a little. Or someone else's pants. Crazy laughter echoed inside her head.

Then her mouth went dry as she realized they'd probably shot the injured man Quentin had risked his life dragging out of the burning building.

The bastards didn't want any witnesses.

She braced for the shot that would end her life. God, she hated them, their casual violence and total disregard for human life.

Her smoke-damaged lungs struggled to find oxygen through the thick, musty hood. It was hard to breathe, and even more difficult to think, to sort any of this into a compartment in her brain that made sense.

She was hurried along but tripped constantly, being almost completely blind. That alone was terrifying. Someone dragged her roughly to her feet, and their fingers bit into her upper arm. It hurt, but she did not complain. Were they going to shoot her, or weren't they? What were they waiting for? What was happening? Why did they want Quentin? It couldn't be good…

"Move, quickly now, or we put a bullet in your wife."

She realized they were using her as a threat to get Quentin to do as he was told.

Who knew how long that would last—until they reached the boat or other means of escape? Until they got to wherever they planned to take Quentin? Maybe they wanted to kill him on camera and probably her too. The idea made her want to puke, but the only option right now was to keep moving forward.

She wished she'd had more time with him—wished she'd gotten to know him better. Wished she'd maybe finally allowed herself to take a risk.

But she didn't have the time or mental energy for regrets right now. She was shoved forward again. Her entire existence compressed into the next few seconds. Tomorrow didn't matter. All the meetings she had planned for next week didn't matter. She tried not to think about how excited she'd been to see Alex and Mallory's baby. She had to take it one second, or minute, at a time. Everything else was wishful thinking.

She made herself keep up, in spite of her ankle twisting painfully on the uneven ground. She dared not slow the troop, even though slowing them down might give whoever was headed their way in the helicopter time to catch up and rescue them. Chances were the terrorists would either shoot her or use her as a human shield.

She did not want to die.

She stumbled down a small embankment and went down on her knees in the sand with a scream.

"Haley!" Quentin called out sharply. He was still worried that they were going to kill her. So was she.

"I'm here," she said softly, but the grunts and sounds of metal hitting flesh told her their captors were beating him. "Stop! Please, please don't hurt him. Quentin!" A fist hit her in the stomach, so hard bile rose up in her throat. Then they were rifling through her pockets, and one of them found her cell phone and took it away. She'd hoped to keep hold of it, knowing Alex would be able to track the signal.

She ignored the despair at its loss.

One step at a time.

Right now, she was still alive, and so many other people weren't. Arms hauled her up by her arm and threw her into a boat. She landed in a heap on top of another person lying on the bottom of the rigid hull.

Quentin?

It was Quentin. She could tell from the scent and shape of him. She pressed herself against his back, trying to soundlessly offer her support and thank him for saving her life.

He didn't move.

She slipped her arm around his chest in the darkness to check he was breathing and sagged in relief when she felt his lungs fill. He was alive but definitely hurt. Unconscious.

Men climbed in beside them, and she tried to protect Quentin from being stepped on, but they didn't care, and she held back a cry of pain when some asshole trod on her sore ankle. The boat was pushed into the water, and someone started an outboard motor. Another engine started up nearby.

Two boats. RIBs probably. She'd used them while scuba diving. Fast and nimble.

The hulls bounced wildly over the surf and then pounded against the surface of the water in a hard *thwack*, *thwack*, *thwack* as they traveled fast. Every bone-jarring motion sent pain running through her body. She tried to press Quentin down so he wasn't thrown about or injured even more. She slipped her arm beneath his head to provide a cushion, ignoring the painful bangs that she knew would leave bruises, if she lived long enough. Sea spray splashed them and collected on the floor of the boat, soaking through their clothes. The cold was a welcome relief after the heat of the fire, but it didn't take long for the seawater to start to itch.

She didn't know how long they traveled. It seemed to be forever. Hours and hours of being battered by the elements.

Eventually, the boat scraped along the sandy bottom of the seabed. Men began shouting as they jumped overboard.

Someone pulled her with them, and she fell into the water, taking in a mouthful of ocean before staggering to her feet.

Impatient hands pushed her along like she was oxen. She fell again, and a man muttered, "Stupid whore."

"I can't see where to put my feet," she snapped, bitterly. *You try it, asshole.*

The hood was whipped off her head. She blinked in surprise. A man—one of the terrorists—wore a bandana over his mouth and nose. Dark eyes glared at her. She glanced over his shoulder and saw a spectacular bay in the moonlight with a white crescent beach and dark blue water. A small yacht at anchor. Then she spotted two men dragging Quentin along by his arms.

"Please, let me help my husband." Words she'd never expected to utter, but the lie had already saved her life, she had no doubt. She was going to keep up the pretense for as long as possible, as long as necessary until they got out of this hellish situation.

"Move." The man shoved her along, not even bothering to threaten her with his gun. She was on an island somewhere in the middle of Indonesia, thick jungle rising up all around. She stumbled ahead, following a dirt track through the trees and up a long incline. Up and up until her legs wobbled with fatigue, and her lungs hurt, but she didn't complain. Finally, when she thought she couldn't go on any farther, they came upon a small group of huts. Haley was pushed through a low doorway, and relief filled her as Savage was dumped on the cot beside her.

But he was still unconscious, and she was terrified he might be dead.

CHAPTER EIGHT

EBAN WINTERS HAD his feet up on his boss's desk, sipping a fresh cup of java. He was holding down the Crisis Negotiation fort on a lazy Saturday afternoon. Dominic Sheridan was on leave after his girlfriend had been shot. Quentin Savage, his boss, was keynoting an important conference in Indonesia. Charlotte Blood had flown out last night to Washington State to see what the latest Freemen insurrection was all about. It wasn't a full-blown incident, but it wasn't something they wanted to ignore, either. The Bureau had a lot more success with long, drawn-out sieges nowadays than they'd had at Ruby Ridge or Waco, mainly by avoiding full-scale confrontation and watching and waiting for people to be reasonable.

Wasn't easy.

The ability to think critically and rationally appeared to be getting rarer every day.

Nor was their new approach newsworthy, which was both good and bad. Good, that the media didn't incite an escalation in hostilities—on either side. Bad, because failures of the past were never replaced by successes in the public eye.

He was familiar with the antigovernment mentality. He'd grown up in a remote town in Montana called Stone Creek. Many people he'd known growing up there liked to stay as far off the grid as possible. Some were preparing for the apocalypse; most were avoiding the IRS or warrants for their arrest.

As a kid, he'd liked horses and dogs way better than he'd ever liked people. But he'd been drawn to the FBI from a young age with stories of agents tracking down the Unabomber not that far from where he'd lived. The idea of danger had also been an attraction for him. Although, as everyone liked to point out, no negotiator had ever been killed over the telephone.

Eban took another sip of coffee and basked in the quiet of the office. This was the life. This was perfect. Relaxed. Peaceful. He looked out the window at the lush greens of the forest that surrounded the National Academy and Critical Incident Response Group compounds. He took a bite out of an apple and savored the sweetness. Maybe he'd go for a run or hit the firing range. Everything around here seemed to be running like clockwork.

The phone rang, and he snatched it out of the cradle, still leaning back in his boss's chair. "Winters."

"Eban. It's Steve McKenzie. I've got some bad news."

"What's up?" Eban had worked with McKenzie at SIOC in the spring when someone had attempted to bomb headquarters.

"I received a call from Savage not long ago. The hotel he was staying in was attacked by armed terrorists."

Eban dropped his feet off the table and stood. "Where is he now?"

"I don't know." McKenzie cleared his throat. "Local police arrived by helicopter, but the bad guys were gone, and they'd set fire to the hotel and, apparently, it's a bloodbath. They found a couple of survivors who were seriously injured. They are being transported to Jakarta for treatment. The legat will interview them as soon as they can talk. Neither of the survivors were Savage."

The piece of apple Eban had eaten soured in his stomach. Quentin had to be okay. "What's being done to work the scene and track the militants?" *To find Quentin*?

"The conference was attended by many different nationalities but primarily Americans. Wealthy and powerful Americans. We're sending a forensic team including a forensic anthropologist to identify the burned remains of as many people as we can as quickly as possible. Indonesian government is cooperating. People are searching for survivors..."

"I'm going out there."

"That's not up to me."

"I wasn't asking," Eban said. "I'll meet up with the negotiator we have in Jakarta. He's due to be relieved soon anyway. I'd like to do whatever I can to help."

"Can you contact the FBI office closest to Savage's next of kin? They need to hear about this from us before they see it on the news."

Eban dropped his chin to his chest. "You think he's dead, don't you?"

"Maybe Savage got away and is hiding for unknown reasons, or he's injured and lost in the jungle. We won't know for sure until we get forensic teams out there examining bodies and search teams scouring the area."

"The other option is he was taken hostage." Eban refused to believe Quentin had been murdered. He was a great guy. A brilliant guy. Eban wouldn't lose hope until he knew for certain Quentin was gone.

McKenzie huffed into the receiver. "It's definitely another

possibility. But these terrorists murdered close to a hundred delegates and about twenty locals. That's the rough estimate. Why would they take Savage and not some rich CEO?"

"You know why."

To embarrass the US government.

McKenzie was quiet for a few moments. "Interestingly, the Indonesian foreign minister and an Australian billionaire, Cecil Wenck, both left the hotel a few hours before the attack. Wenck had been scheduled to stay until morning."

Eban had heard of Wenck. Most people had. Head of the world's largest mining conglomerate. "You think they were tipped off?"

"I'd like to know why Wenck's plans suddenly changed that's for sure. We need people to interview him and see if we can get a warrant for information on his incoming calls or texts, but I doubt he'll want to talk to us."

"You think he was warned but didn't tell anyone else?" Rage stirred within Eban.

"I don't know. Talk to your unit chief—"

"Good idea," Eban snapped. "My unit chief is in Indonesia, so I'll go find him to ask."

McKenzie sighed tiredly. "Look, a flight leaves in three hours from Andrews Air Force Base with the rest of the team who have been assigned. I'll put your name on the list. Don't be late. Now I have to call Alex Parker to tell him that his business partner and one of his best friends is also feared dead."

Eban ground his teeth together.

Feared dead.

It sucked, but he didn't have time to dwell on emotions. He had a million things to do before he caught that flight, but the most important was calling Quentin's family in SoCal.

One thing was for sure. He had no intention of being left behind.

CHAPTER NINE

Pain stabbed Quentin's brain with needle-sharp spikes. Sunlight hurt his eyes. His mouth tasted like smoke and blood, and he was so parched, it felt as though someone had blowtorched his throat. Sweat poured off him in the unbearable heat, and his clothes stuck to his skin. A damp cloth pressed against his brow. The coolness was welcoming, and he groaned and strained toward it.

Memories from the night before flashed through his mind, and he opened his eyes and found himself lying on an uncomfortable cot in a primitive hut. Haley Cramer sat on her knees beside him on the dirt floor.

He caught her hand.

Thank god she was still alive.

"You're awake. I was beginning to think they'd fractured your skull, and you were in a coma, and I couldn't do anything to help you..." Her voice was a furtive whisper with smoky undertones. She blinked rapidly as if to staunch tears. She must have been scared out of her mind.

He sure as hell was.

The back of his head throbbed like a motherfucker where one of the attackers had smashed their rifle butt into his skull. Bastard could have killed him.

Why hadn't they?

"How long have I been out?" He kept his voice down. The last thing he wanted was anyone knowing he was awake or coming to check on them. Separating them. Hurting Haley. He needed time to gather whatever wits he had left.

"A long time. Hours." She checked her watch. A fancy one with a silver band. He was surprised she still had it. Plus, there were sparkles in her ears that were probably the real thing.

Although there wasn't any rush to steal their belongings. He doubted their captors thought they'd be going anywhere soon.

"We were in the boat for two, maybe three hours, traveling flat out. Then we were dumped in this rather luxurious accommodation around dawn. You've barely moved since. Half the time I couldn't tell if you were still breathing." Her blue eyes looked distraught, and she bit her lip. "I am so sorry they hurt you for trying to defend me."

That was a lot of guilt to carry. Not trying to protect her would have caused him more.

He brought the back of her hand to his lips. It was a different sort of intimacy to what they'd shared in bed last night. "I thought they were going to kill you on the beach and decided I'd rather die fighting than let them eliminate us one at a time like cattle in a slaughterhouse. I had Chris's Glock in my pocket, and I grabbed it and pulled the trigger."

Her eyes went wide. It was hard to remember they'd been strangers less than a day ago.

"Chamber was empty, but they weren't happy that no one had thought to search me, so I got a beating. The question is, why didn't they kill me?"

"They specifically targeted you. I found this…" Haley dug into the pocket of her stolen camo shirt and pulled out a crumpled piece of paper.

She handed him a printed picture of him from the conference handout. A generic FBI portrait in front of the flag that the public relations office had sent out. *Shit.*

Did these terrorists want to make an example of him? Sell him off to the highest terrorist bidder? Pump him for information or simply humiliate the shit out of him for entertainment and revenge value? Was he the reason all those other people had been murdered?

"Did they bring anyone else from the hotel?" he asked.

Haley shook her head, sending her soot-darkened, blonde hair into her eyes. She pushed it back behind her ears. "I didn't see anyone else get out of the boats."

Quentin levered himself up off the cot, ignoring the stabbing pain where his ribs had taken a hit, until he was sitting upright. His brain spun inside his skull, and he grabbed his head, trying to squeeze the tension away. He gave himself a moment of breathing deeply and evenly as Haley watched him with concern.

"Tell me everything you remember," he murmured to distract them both and also because he wanted information. What the hell was going on?

She did so, ending with a description of where they'd landed. "There was a yacht anchored in the harbor."

"A yacht?"

"About a thirty-eight to forty-footer. My dad had one about the same size when I was growing up." She nodded. "The gunmen forced me to walk up a dirt path through the jungle for about forty minutes. Someone carried you and put us in here. One guy brought a bowl of water to wash off the blood." She dipped the cloth and went to wipe his brow again, but he took the cloth from her and tentatively dabbed at the wound on the back of his skull where his hair was matted with blood.

She looked at the water longingly. "I didn't think I should drink it, even though I'm really thirsty. You must be too."

"At some point, we will need to drink, but let's see if we can find potable water that these guys also drink first. That source might make us sick, too, but it's the best we can hope for."

She swallowed and nodded. "I know. I guess I'm pretending to myself I'll have a choice."

Having your free will violently yanked away was a terrible thing. At least the Army had prepared him for some of it. "I'm sorry you got caught up in all this. Obviously, they were targeting me."

She sat back on her heels. "Are you kidding me? None of this is your fault. Without you, I'd have been repeatedly raped and then shot." She gave a laugh that sounded anything but happy.

"I wish I knew what they wanted with me. And why the fact I told them you were my wife meant they let you live too." He didn't get it. "Why the hell are they interested in me? For some sort of terrorist coup? Because bringing down the wrath of the US government isn't worth it." He tore the crumpled picture in half and handed it back to her. Vertigo hit him in a wave. "Can you get rid of this? Rip it into tiny pieces and push it out through the gaps in the rushes. We don't want them to know that we know."

He'd take any advantage he could get until they figured this out.

She stood and did as he asked. Tearing off tiny bits of

paper and pushing them through the sides of the hut and letting the wind catch them. The shack was built from branches interwoven with leaves. She moved around so there was no accumulation of the paper on the ground.

He watched her, thinking through their options. Didn't like any of them. Usually the best thing for a hostage to do was to wait for a ransom to be paid, even though it could take months, even years. The US government was unlikely to let this situation stand though and would come after these assholes with everything they possessed. Also, the chance of being beheaded on some jihadist online video was too high for him to trust the process he usually endorsed. Plus, there was Haley…

She sat beside him on the cot. A gray blanket was spread over the branches and dried grass that formed the mattress. At least the bed was raised up off the floor, so less chance of snakes and insects joining him and spreading disease, although who was he trying to kid?

The cot was narrow, and they'd have to share if they were lucky enough to remain together. He wasn't sure how she'd feel about that, considering what had happened to her over the last couple of days. Just because they'd had sex once didn't mean she'd want to be physically close again. No denying he was attracted to her, but there was also no chance in hell he'd behave inappropriately while in a terrorist camp. But she didn't know that. She didn't know him.

"No one has come to check on us yet?"

"No." She sighed deeply, dark circles around her eyes emphasizing her fear and fatigue. He doubted she'd slept. "I need to use the bathroom, and I'm insanely thirsty, but I'm too scared to ask them."

He could tell she wanted to cry. He wanted to tell her it would be all right, that he'd figure out a way to save them both but in reality, he didn't know what they were dealing with yet. And, as a negotiator, the only lies he told were to bad guys who'd exhausted the process of talking and were about to receive the sharp end of the CIRG playbook.

Honesty had always been his default.

"Haley, I've no idea what's going to happen next, but I doubt it'll be pleasant. No matter what, I want you to promise me something. Don't try to rescue me. If they take me for what is probably going to be regular beatings, make yourself as small and insignificant as possible. I won't think less of you. I'm not going to fight them, not until I'm able to win anyway. I will try to figure out a way for us both to escape, but I don't know when that will be."

She went to open her mouth, but he gently placed a finger on her lips, and she stopped.

"They think you're my wife, and they might use you to get to me. Do not tell them the truth about us not being married." He took her hand, spread her fingers and entangled them with his. "These are not nice guys. They are criminals and sociopaths looking for a way to justify their lifestyle choices. You're a beautiful woman and being blonde makes you stand out." He swallowed uneasily. "Sexual assault is a possibility, because that's how men like this often assert power. Pretending to be my wife should help protect you in the short term."

Her eyes were huge, and she swallowed repeatedly. He wasn't saying this to make her uncomfortable. He was saying this so she understood what was going on here. What might happen even though he'd do everything in his power to protect her. He couldn't guarantee he'd be able to save her.

He thought about Abbie and their child. He hadn't been able to save them either. He forced those memories away. "We need to avoid them splitting us up and getting you alone if at all possible."

She grabbed his other hand and squeezed. "You said I wasn't allowed to rescue you, but you're not allowed to rescue me either if they end up deciding to rape me." She was shaking, even though her voice was unwavering.

He wanted to argue, but she spoke over him.

"I can survive being raped if I have to. I've done it before." Her direct gaze held his unflinchingly, and his heart broke at the truth he saw there. "But I don't think I can survive this ordeal without you."

He was shaking too, and it wasn't just dehydration. The fact she'd been raped made him mad as hell, and yet now wasn't the time to indulge in his own rage or curiosity.

He nodded. "Okay. We'll both do whatever it takes to get out of here alive, hopefully untouched."

"No man left behind?" The smile that played on her face was watery.

"No *person* left behind. So." He moved on to the practical. That's what he was good at. "A few details in case they ask. We got married in secret a few weeks ago, which is why it isn't common knowledge. We met at a social event in the summer at—"

"A wedding. My business partner, Alex Parker, married FBI agent Mallory Rooney. Lots of other agents were there. It was in a vineyard in Virginia. I was in the wedding party."

"Okay, good. You looked amazing, and it was love at first sight. So where'd we get married?"

"Vegas," she suggested.

"I think those online records are available too easily."

"Bali?"

He shook his head again. "They might know someone they can ask for confirmation within Indonesia."

"What about the Caribbean? I own an island down there—"

"You *own* an island?"

"A small one."

Quentin tried to mask his surprise. Who owned an entire island? "Well, thank goodness it is just a small one."

She sensed his incredulity and tried to withdraw her hands, but he didn't let her.

He knew she was not usually shy or retiring—her confidence and vivaciousness in the bar last night while wearing that gold dress and then in his bed, naked, told him that—but being held captive changed everything and made you question what you thought you knew about yourself. He appreciated this academically. He figured he was about to endure a practical lesson.

"It's good, in fact it's great. You're rich. That's another reason for them to keep you alive." Unlike him. What the hell did they want with him? The only thing he had going for him was his FBI credentials, which he doubted they appreciated for his expertise.

"We can use the island thing. Private ceremony. A colleague of mine, Eban Winters, has a license to officiate, and that gives us an added bonus, because if they contact him for confirmation, he's a trained negotiator and can think on his feet."

Quentin thought back on a conversation he'd had with Dominic Sheridan last week, about how if he was ever in a tight spot, he'd want Dominic doing the talking before the bad guys chopped off anything vital.

Didn't seem so amusing now.

"I suspect these guys are hiding their evil beneath the shield of religious fundamentalism, so we need to get out of here before they figure out the truth about our relationship. As soon as the media find out we've been captured, they will dig through all the records and probably end up ruining our story."

Hopefully the FBI would keep a lid on his abduction for as long as possible, but with last night's massacre, it was only a matter of time before the story broke. His mom and brothers would be worried, as would his colleagues. While he was sorry about their pain, there was nothing he could do about it right now.

He looked at the filthy water in the wash bowl. "We also need to get out of here before we get so weak or sick we can't physically move more than a few yards without assistance. Feds will have people looking for us, but we can't assume they'll find us or that they will be successful in a rescue without accidentally killing us both."

That was the most dangerous time to be a hostage—during a rescue attempt. It was something he tried to avoid when he was running a K&R case, but he wasn't in charge of local police or military, and he generally didn't get much of a say about rescue attempts. He held Haley's steady blue gaze. "We need to work together. Whatever happens. Understand?"

Up close, those eyes of hers were like planets. Staring into them was like looking at the cosmos for the first time.

"Partners," she agreed.

He kissed her knuckles, which were knotted tightly with his. "Strength, Haley. We'll get through this but don't expect it to be easy."

They both tensed as footsteps approached the hut.

CHAPTER TEN

As an adult, Haley had never been scared to speak her mind. She knew how to stand up for herself and advocate for her position. Hell, Dermot said she was a steamroller when it came to getting what she wanted. She didn't quite see it that way, but maybe he had a point.

She'd run away from home at sixteen and managed to finish school, thanks to her determination and the love and care of her obscenely wealthy grandmother. Back then, she'd discovered that men in general wanted her to be seen and not heard, so she'd made a point of loudly voicing her opinions and objections as often and as frequently as required to prove a point.

Apparently, pointing the barrel of an automatic rifle at her was a much better way of shutting her up than her father's threats had ever been.

"Out," the guard ordered. He had greasy hair and grazed knuckles. A green, fringed scarf covered his nose and mouth, but the hostility in his dark eyes was easily identifiable.

For all Haley's usually ballsy bravado, she didn't even consider defying him. She'd never dealt with this type of humanity before. Her inexperience embarrassed her, revealing failings she hadn't been aware of.

She was aware of them now.

Savage released her hand, and she climbed stiffly to her feet. He held his ribs as he attempted to stand, and she tried to help him, but the armed guard grabbed her upper arm and dug his filthy fingernails into her skin.

Ouch.

"Outside. Now."

She ducked through the low door, and the man pushed her from behind, and she sprawled onto the dirt.

A large group of men stood around laughing. Her pulse skittered, and her heart beat so violently she worried it was going to burst. Quentin followed her out of the hut, shoulders hunched over, still favoring his side. She didn't know if he was pretending to be hurt or if they'd actually broken a rib or two when they beat him. She hoped it was the former. She staggered to her feet and another man shoved her next to Quentin, who put his arm around her shoulders to steady her.

His embrace provided such an intense feeling of comfort—it made no sense, and yet she yearned for it never to end. She knew he couldn't protect her if these rebels turned nasty. She hadn't been lying when she'd told him she didn't want him to intervene if they decided to attack her. He was one man against a heavily armed mob. Brute strength would not get them out of this nightmare. They couldn't fight their way to freedom, and she didn't think she could survive without him.

And survival was all that mattered right now.

Quentin Savage's presence was her most precious weapon of all. The thing that kept people alive even during the worst atrocities.

Quentin gave her *hope.*

It was tenuous at best.

Their captors were dressed like guerrillas in army fatigue

pants and shirts over droopy, sweat-stained t-shirts in every color from orange to what had probably once been white. Most wore headscarves over the bottom half of their faces and were draped in bullet belts. All of them carried automatic weapons.

Were they violent extremists or some sort of tin pot revolutionaries? Either way, they wouldn't like dealing with a woman as an equal, she didn't need anyone to explain that to her feminist heart. It was implicit. They ignored her and addressed Quentin. It might have been cowardly, but she was relieved.

One man stepped forward. He wore a clean-looking uniform with a buttoned-up shirt, black pistol holstered on his thigh. Extendible baton in his hand. He wore a hat and dark sunglasses and didn't sport a bandana. He was clearly the leader from the way he spoke and carried himself. "So you're the FBI agent."

The FBI agent?

The words gave Haley chills.

Quentin nodded. His skin was pale, and blood crusted in his hair from the scalp wound that wouldn't stop bleeding.

"You have me at a disadvantage." Quentin's words made her smile on the inside. "Who do I have the pleasure of addressing?" He held out his hand to shake, but the other man ignored it. So much for introductions.

"How did you escape from the hotel last night?" the man barked.

Quentin cocked his head. His expression was mildly quizzical. "We heard gunfire and hid in the jungle."

The leader slapped the baton into his open palm as if getting a measure of its weight. "You were not in your room?"

Quentin shook his head, and the man looked confused. "We took a stroll in the garden before we headed to bed. We were supposed to leave first thing in the morning and wanted to enjoy our last night on Nabat."

Haley didn't know why he lied. Maybe so these bandits would underestimate their badassedness? Climbing down the outside of a building? Hiding in the jungle at night? She hadn't even blinked.

"Can I ask why you attacked the hotel last night? What is it that you want?" Quentin was polite without being obsequious. Factual without being judgmental. It was his tone, Haley realized. Firm without being confrontational.

"You Americans," the man sneered. "Carrying out your proxy wars in other countries and raping lands of precious resources for your own gain."

Haley didn't know what direction the guy was going in. Was he an environmentalist, or did he simply hate Americans?

"You think you can come here and take whatever you want. *Kill* whoever you want without consequences?"

Oh, hell. Haley looked down at the camo pants she wore with trepidation and knew where the guy was going with this little show and tell. The terrorist leader caught her gaze when she glanced back up. She could not force herself to look away or lower her jaw, even though Quentin's words about fading into the background roared through her mind.

The man held out the baton and pointed to the pants. "Where did you get those?"

"I found them?" She tried to sound subservient, but definitely failed.

Quentin tensed beside her.

"You killed two of my men." He addressed Quentin this

time, because obviously a woman couldn't do that. Haley was angry that she hadn't been able to do that. She was mad at the assumption. Mad at the reality. She knew women who were badass as hell. She wasn't one of them.

"Two men attacked my wife. I did what I had to do to protect her."

The leader brought the baton down hard on Quentin's shoulder. Haley covered her mouth and tried to hold back a scream. Quentin didn't try to defend himself. He crashed to his knees.

This was all her fault. If she'd turned off her cell phone, not only would she not have attracted their attention, those men wouldn't be dead, and these bandits wouldn't have known anyone was still alive on the island, and Quentin wouldn't be getting the shit beaten out of him.

Two men grabbed Quentin by the arms and hauled him upright. The leader punched him in the stomach with the end of the baton, and two other men joined in with punches and kicks.

Quentin gagged and grunted, bent double.

Haley wanted to cry out or throw herself in front of him to protect him, then remembered what he'd told her about not trying to rescue him. He'd expected to be beaten. But it was one thing to agree in theory. It was another to watch him being hurt.

She wanted to beg and plead for them to stop but was terrified to make a noise. Her whole body shook. From fear, terror, dehydration, shock. From enduring what was happening to Quentin and being helpless to stop it. From fear she'd be next, and it would be worse because they wouldn't just hit her. They'd violate.

Everything she thought she knew about the world had been ripped away. This was who she really was. This scared, pathetic, silent wretch.

"Enough," the leader snapped. The men immediately stopped hitting Quentin. Then the leader pointed at her legs.

Haley froze again.

Oh, god.

"Those clothes do not belong to you. Take them off."

When she hesitated, the bastard went to strike Quentin again.

"Stop! Please stop. I'm doing it." She quickly began undoing the button and zipper of the pants, thankful beyond reason that she was wearing Quentin's gym shorts beneath. She was taller than everyone here except Quentin, and they all stared at her like she was an alien being. The men around her seemed disappointed she wasn't naked—but if they really wanted to see her bare, she wouldn't be able to stop them. The commander had complete control of hers and Quentin's life, and he knew it. Their complete destruction was one simple order away.

She hated all the eyes on her. It was one thing to be the center of attention when you felt confident in your world, another entirely when surrounded by heartless killers. The last thing she wanted was this warlord's interested gaze on her long legs or blonde hair.

She quickly tugged the trousers over her boots. "There. There are your pants."

"Pick them up and bring them here," the leader commanded quietly as his men watched with avid gleams in their eyes.

She didn't hesitate. She wasn't about to start a battle of

wills with a mini despot. She squatted down to pick up the dusty pants, well aware that the men's gazes took in every detail, especially the curve of her ass. She shook the pants out and folded them as best she could. She held them out to the man with her head bowed.

She was going to be smart and as strong as she was able. Rescue would come. It was just a matter of time. She was counting on Alex and Dermot, and the FBI who'd want their man back. And maybe a few Special Forces soldiers for good measure. They'd get them out of here. She just had to survive long enough to be rescued.

"Not to me." The commander sneered like she was dim-witted. She gritted her teeth. "You give them to Lyrita who lost a husband and the father of her children when your husband murdered him."

The crowd of men parted, and a young woman wearing a brightly colored dress and a head scarf walked forward. Her expression was angry as she snatched the pants out of Haley's hands. Then she spoke in some local dialect and spat at her. Haley jerked back, startled.

Had it been the tall skinny wannabe rapist or short burly one who'd been married to the woman? Big loss, Haley was sure. Forget that she and Quentin had been fighting for their lives—

She clamped down on all the things she wanted to say. This was not about reasoned debate. Starting an argument could get them both killed.

"It seems that you took us because we're American…" Quentin stated.

Deflecting attention away from her.

"Americans think they own the whole world!" the commander went off on another rant.

God, she could fall for a guy like Quentin Savage. The fact he was good in bed was an added bonus, but not even in the top ten reasons she wanted to kiss him on the lips.

Finally, the commander ran out of steam in his monologue, but he wasn't done. He circled around them both, and she felt him brush up behind her. Butterflies rose in her stomach, as large as the exotic birds that flew from branch to branch amongst the trees.

Oh, god.

"You are the big negotiator, correct? The man who helps get US captives free?" The crowd followed his lead and jeered, although Haley couldn't imagine they all spoke English or understood what their leader was saying.

The leader grabbed her hair and roughly forced her to her knees, sending shock ricocheting through her body. He drew a knife and held it against the bottom of her nose. The sting of the blade had her swallowing convulsively. She'd never imagined there could be something worse than rape.

Two men grabbed Quentin when he lunged for the commander.

"I'm going to cut off your pretty wife's nose. See how much you enjoy sleeping with an ugly monster at night."

Haley shook from fear. She'd never considered being disfigured. Didn't know if she'd be able to stand the physical pain or the mental anguish. Did that make her shallow, or human? She swallowed slowly, her throat painfully dry while her palms were slippery with sweat.

Quentin didn't meet her gaze. He was looking at the commander. "It seems like the only objective that serves is punishing me, which I realize you believe I deserve. But is that how you'd want your wife treated if our roles were reversed?" he asked. "Is your idea of justice for the oppressed to punish innocents?"

The commander moved the knife to her throat, and Haley's pulse took off like a freight train careening off the rails.

"Talk me out of slitting her throat, and maybe I'll just cut off her ears or fingers…"

The fear was so overwhelming it made reasoned argument impossible. She wanted to beg for her life but didn't dare move a single muscle.

"Unlike me, my wife comes from a wealthy family. You see the diamonds in her ears? Her watch? They're worth thousands of dollars. If you want to send a political message to the US, then do that with me, but she's a valuable asset. Her family won't pay if you disfigure her."

"They'll pay." The commander laughed. "They always pay."

So he'd done this before?

Quentin shook his head. "Not Haley's family. They're a bunch of snobs. Looks and appearance are everything to them. If she's mutilated, they won't want her back or in the news. They'd rather you just kill her."

She tensed as the commander moved the knife from her throat and came dangerously close to slicing her face as he pulled the diamond studs out of her ears one at a time, examining the hallmark. They were from Tiffany's.

"Give me your watch," the man demanded, holding out his hand.

Her hands visibly shook as she removed the timepiece. It was an antique her grandmother had bequeathed her and had sat in the old woman's safe for sixty years. The idea of giving it up wrenched, but it was better than losing her nose. "I-it's a rare *Cartier* model made in 1926. There are only four of them left in the world."

She had never been more grateful for the trappings of wealth than at this moment where she was bartering them for body parts. It was barbaric and sadistic, and the commander was clearly enjoying scaring the shit out of her.

"Maybe I'll let you keep your pretty face for now. My men might prefer it that way when the time comes..." The threat was implicit. This was how he intended to keep her in line. Pure fear of consequences. Cowed obedience.

She tried not to lose herself in Quentin's gaze, but she was so grateful he'd managed to think of something to say that had prevented the monster from maiming her, even temporarily.

The commander turned back to Quentin. "And you are also valuable, Mr. FBI."

Someone took a photograph of her, and she blinked against the glare of the flash. They did the same to Quentin, whose only reaction was the subtle tightening of his jaw.

He shook his head. "My family is not wealthy."

"Ah, but you underestimate yourself. What do you think it is worth for every freedom fighter in the world to see you at our mercy?" A smirk twisted thick lips.

"Is that what you want?" Quentin asked. "Credibility on the world stage?"

"You think I lack credibility?" The terrorist leader stared at Quentin for long, unnerving seconds. So long, in fact, that the flies that buzzed around Haley started to settle. She itched to swat them but dared not move. Dared not break the spell or draw attention back to herself. Too chicken. Too cowardly. She ground her teeth and hated this man, all of these men, except Quentin, and she hated herself most of all, for not being brave enough to stand up to them.

As the commander stood in front of Quentin, staring him down, Quentin returned the look but with no animosity. His gaze was measured and respectful. He wasn't going toe-to-toe with the guy. He was doing what Alex taught her was the most important thing about self-defense—defusing the situation. Avoiding a fight.

Considering how easily Quentin had taken control of their predicament last night, and killed two men with his bare hands, she wasn't fooled by his impassiveness, but this bandit seemed to be. He chuckled, turning and barking an order at his men in his own language. They all laughed and started to scatter. All Haley could see was the man's pistol on his hip so close she could reach out and snatch it…

Quentin clasped her hand in his and squeezed in warning, helping her to her feet to disguise the movement. She let out a long, shuddering breath. Her throat was so dry, she was beginning to sway from dehydration.

"Would it be possible to get some water, *Silahkan*?" asked Quentin with a slight bow. "And use the lavatory? It would be a great kindness, especially for my poor wife."

The subtext "weak woman" was in there but right now, she felt weak, and it suited their purpose.

The commander turned slowly back to face them. Then he nodded to the guy who'd brought them out of the hut earlier. "Ramon. Take them to the latrine." His smile turned a little evil. "But it is Lyrita who is in charge of your food and comfort. She will bring you water and food when she has time."

Haley pressed her lips together at the unfairness. Any

protest from her would make things worse. She needed to save her energy.

Ramon pushed her along, and she drew in a deep breath to stop herself snapping at him. She knew, without a doubt, they were goading her so she would break. Then they'd either punish her, or they'd punish the man they believed was her husband, the man who'd saved her so many times, she didn't know how she would ever be able to repay him. She wished they'd woken up in each other's arms without anyone being hurt or dying. But wishes would get her nowhere, and she had to concentrate on reality.

Quentin followed, and she noticed his shadow move directly behind her, protecting her again, the only way he could from the man with the shovey hands.

Children played in the dirt, chasing lizards with sticks. A dog walked alongside her for a few strides before heading off to join the children in their lizard hunt. She wanted to stroke that dog so badly...

She glanced around. Some of the structures were more substantial than others. One building was sturdy and wooden, men lounging around on hammocks and on the steps. An older, more ramshackle house built on stilts sat back from the main village—if you could call it a village. The house had a thatched roof and what had probably once been an actual lawn before being reclaimed by the jungle.

They arrived at some huts on the edge of the camp that were being used as a latrine. Quentin entered one side, and the guard pointed her towards the one a few feet away that was obviously for women.

Her stomach turned at the stench, and she gagged. Bile rose in her throat. Flies buzzed. There was a wooden board with a hole in it. She had to toughen up. She pulled her shorts down and sat, keeping herself covered as much as possible with Quentin's t-shirt, aware of the gimlet eye of the guard peering through a narrow gap in the rushes. She wanted to throw up but her whole life, she'd kept telling people how tough she was. She wasn't going to let the lack of toilet facilities or a voyeuristic pervert get her down.

A bowl of water sat nearby with a scoop that she used to rinse herself off as best she could. It meant her shorts got a little damp, but the heat was so overwhelming that was okay. They'd soon dry.

"Hurry." The mean voice barked into the small hut. He was mad she hadn't given him more of a show but thankfully, Quentin's shirt provided good coverage.

She rinsed her hands with the scoop and wondered how thirsty she'd have to be to drink the water out of that bowl. She wasn't there yet, but the headache was building, and dehydration in this climate would kill her sooner rather than later. It wouldn't take long.

Everything she ate and drank could potentially cause her to get sick here. She'd kept up to date with all her vaccines and boosters, but her body wasn't resilient to the bugs and bacteria that the locals had grown up with. Even a bad case of diarrhea could kill her. A mosquito buzzed in the dank air of the toilet—another insidious threat. Her malaria pills were back at the hotel, burned to a crisp.

An image of that man being shot in front of them on the lawn, of all the victims in the bar last night, flashed through her brain in vivid technicolor. She pushed aside the memory. Couldn't deal with it right now. They were people she'd known professionally, had competed with. People she'd both liked and disliked on a personal basis. She didn't know what this would mean for their industry as a whole. She couldn't even think about that right now. She would mourn for them as soon as she had the mental space to do so, but the industry would have to sort itself out without her in the meantime.

For her and Savage, their current existence was all about survival, doing and saying whatever it took to make it through the next encounter. She pressed her lips together as she exited the latrine and found Quentin waiting for her. His concerned gaze warmed her, and she swallowed at the dryness in her throat.

He had no idea how much he'd come to mean to her in such a short amount of time. With him by her side, she had no doubt she'd get through this, but without him?

Without him she didn't stand a chance.

CHAPTER ELEVEN

IT HAD BEEN an infinitely long trip but, finally, Eban had reached the paradise that, for so many, had morphed into a nightmare. He walked slowly toward the still smoldering ruins of what, according to the website, had been a beautiful, luxury hotel, a converted Dutch-colonial mansion that had survived WWII and the fierce fights for independence in its wake. But it hadn't survived a security symposium attacked by a group of armed terrorists.

Who was responsible?

And why?

Where was Quentin? Was he alive or dead?

These were the questions that filled his head and swirled along with the anger and grief that wanted to pummel him. But he wore his game face. He was a professional.

Paper booties covered his shoes, and nitrile gloves made his hands sweat. Under the circumstances, it was a miracle the crime scene had been even vaguely preserved.

It was afternoon, and the sun set early in this part of the world. The Indonesian military were setting up what looked like massive stadium lights so that the forensic teams could start recovering human remains as soon as it was deemed safe to go inside the main structure of the hotel. A blackened beam crashed to the ground, underscoring the weakness of the structure and the danger to those embarking on the search.

At the start of the week, Eban had glibly offered to take his boss's place at this conference. Looking around at the evidence of a massacre, he was glad Quentin hadn't accepted his request.

Several bodies lay strewn around the grounds, bloodstains marking their method of murder. Eban went from one corpse to another, each time bracing himself to find the body of a boss he liked and respected. A man he considered a friend.

An FBI photographer accompanied him, the flash on the camera blinding Eban every time the man took a snap, shocking his retinas the same way the brutal slaughter shocked his soul.

Images were being sent straight back to the States via satellite and run through facial recognition programs. Video was being streamed direct to SIOC where a team worked the leads.

The FBI's legal attaché to the region, Reid Armstrong, was watching the proceedings while talking to an official from the local police. Voices were raised, and Eban glanced over, hoping he wouldn't have to break up a fistfight.

Emotions were running high, and the US Government wanted swift and forceful action to be taken to bring the terrorists to justice. The US was happy and ready to help if the Indonesians couldn't carry that out on their own. The warship sitting in the bay emphasized the point.

Max Hawthorne, a negotiator and friend from CNU who'd been based in Jakarta for the past six weeks, was also walking the scene with another photographer, looking for Savage's body while trying to identify other victims.

Eban returned to his grim task.

Because there were so many dead Americans, the FBI was jointly running the investigation with Indonesian counterparts. Crime labs here were helping out and providing laboratory facilities where necessary. Only three survivors had been found so far, one local who was in critical condition with a bullet in the head, an American woman who'd been put in an induced medical coma to give her the best possible chance of survival, and another man with a nasty concussion and a gunshot wound that wasn't life threatening. He was under armed guard in the hospital, the only living and conscious witness to what had happened here last night.

Another man had stumbled back from a bar in the nearest town, so drunk he could barely walk straight. The sight of the raging fire and dead bodies had sobered him up fast, and he and his taxi driver had done an about-face and gone straight back to town.

Someone needed to question the guy ASAP.

The top ballistics expert in the FBI was measuring trajectories and marking the location of different rounds. Considering it looked like a war zone out here, the man had his work cut out. Shell casings and bullets were being systematically collected for ballistic and trace evidence analysis. It was doubtful the terrorists' fingerprints or DNA were on file, but when the bastards were found, and they *would* find them, it would help with their criminal conviction.

Indonesia believed in capital punishment.

The noxious smell of burnt meat and toxic smoke laced the air. Eban found himself wanting the assholes to pay the ultimate price, so long as they caught the right culprits.

He and the photographer kept walking. Skirting the manicured lawn until they reached the back of the property, which looked out over the ocean. The scenery was spectacular, except for another murdered man lying on the lawn—shot in the back as he'd tried to escape. Tall, lanky, dark-haired, lying face down in the short grass.

Eban clenched his fingers and braced himself as the photographer took pictures before they gently turned the guy over.

Flies buzzed, and a wave of nausea engulfed Eban at the stench. Decomp came on fast in the tropics, and he made himself examine the features carefully to be sure. But it wasn't Quentin. It wasn't his boss. Thank god.

He straightened.

That was it. They'd checked all the corpses so far found on the grounds. Searching the hotel ruins was going to take longer, and the chances of any of the victims being anything except blackened corpses was remote at best.

He called McKenzie at SIOC, even though he had no doubt it would be a bad time. He couldn't remember the time difference and didn't much care that the guy was probably in bed.

"Did you find him?" McKenzie answered immediately, his voice low with concern.

"Negative." Eban looked out over the sea that glistened in the sunshine. Not long ago, Quentin had probably stood here and admired this exact same view. "Tell me where he said he was when you spoke to him."

"I wrote it down. Hang on." There was a rustle and a knock as if McKenzie were putting something heavy on a table. "Okay, *on the beach, beneath the hotel cell tower.* Wait. Actually, he said *near* the beach."

Eban looked east. The cell tower stood proudly on top of a nearby hill, the highest point of this particular part of the island. He scanned the horizon and saw a multitude of small isles dotted in the distance.

Despite being the world's fourth most populous country, nine thousand of Indonesia's 17,000 islands were uninhabited. More than 255 million people lived in the place that was more a collection of diverse cultures than a unified country. As if to make things even more exciting, volcanoes marched across the region, any number of which could erupt at any moment.

That factoid reminded him of Darby O'Roarke, a graduate student volcanologist who'd been kidnapped a few days ago from an island in the Banda Sea.

Was that related?

Seemed unlikely, considering the attackers had mown down so many potential hostages indiscriminately, but Indonesia *was* a predominantly safe country. Exactly how many independent pockets of terrorists were there? He needed to know how many groups were active at this moment in time. The legat should know the answer to that question.

"I'll go check out the area he mentioned now," Eban told McKenzie, who remained silent on the line, both of them contemplating the long odds of Quentin being one of the few to survive this atrocity.

"He was with Haley Cramer," McKenzie reminded him. "Her business partners want in on any information that pertains to her."

"We can't share information on an open investigation," Eban argued.

"This time we can. Alex Parker is an FBI consultant and, if anyone can find them using electronic communications, it will be him or his team. Trust me, we need to work with this guy."

That was assuming Quentin and Haley Cramer were lost

and not in the blackened shell of the hotel. Eban scratched at his skull as a mosquito tried to suck out his brains.

"I'll let you know if I find anything." He hung up. It was easier to be coolly professional than to really think about what he was looking for. A corpse. The body of one of his best friends.

Chances were small Quentin was alive. If he was, he'd have come out of hiding the moment Eban and the other Feds arrived. Quentin was either dead, unconscious, or he'd been taken.

"I need to go search the forest down by the beach. You ready?" Eban asked the photographer.

The guy looked around. "Let's bring some others with us in case we run into a tiger."

Eban firmed his lips and hoped the guy was joking. "Tigers are the least of our worries."

He waved Hawthorne and his ERT tech over to join them, and the four agents headed down a narrow path in the general direction of the cell tower.

"Lot of tracks heading in this direction," Hawthorne noted. The federal agent was a former SAS soldier who had been a dual British/American citizen. He'd joined the Bureau after spending time in the States training FBI agents in close-quarter protection techniques. Hawthorne could read tracking sign better than anyone Eban knew.

Eban let him go ahead. They all had flashlights, which they flicked on to help combat the shadows beneath the thick canopy.

"Oh, yeah," the former Brit said. "*Lots* of people came this way. Do we know the direction from which the attack took place?"

"We know almost nothing," Eban stated bluntly, "except a lot of people died, and the wounds weren't self-inflicted."

Hawthorne nodded. "My guess is the attackers came from this direction. Probably landed boats on the beach. The alternative is a helicopter ride, but that would have lost them the element of surprise, and more people would have scattered into the woods to hide."

Eban carefully followed Hawthorne so they didn't trample all the potential evidence, even though he wasn't sure what it might tell them. After about five minutes, the trees thinned out, and he could see the beach. He paused.

"Savage was supposed to be hiding in the woods at the base of the hill." He swept the powerful flashlight over the underbrush in that direction. Something brassy glinted on the forest floor. He and Hawthorne moved cautiously through the foliage. The photographers shot film every step of the way.

It was a bullet belt. They needed to get that to the lab.

"Looks like some sort of confrontation happened over here. Look at all the flattened bushes and broken leaves," Hawthorne said with a frown.

Eban spotted a bare human foot sticking out from beneath a fern. He couldn't swallow the trepidation that crowded his throat and prevented him from breathing.

The photographers took pictures. Hawthorne found a stick and used it to push aside the branches.

Air rushed out of Eban's lungs when he saw it wasn't Quentin. Two male bodies, stripped of some clothing but not naked, lay there in the undergrowth. No visible bullet wounds. They wore sweat-stained vests and scarves tied around necks; necks that had clearly been broken. One man was missing his trousers and footwear.

Eban stood back to let the photographers in to take pictures to send back to HQ. "Two of the attackers, do you think?"

Hawthorne squatted beside the bodies. "They have some tattoos I want a better look at." The photographers got in closer, and Hawthorne rolled the body enough to provide a better shot.

"Someone broke their necks." Eban scouted the nearby area but didn't find anything else.

"Let's check out the beach," Hawthorne suggested.

Eban nodded and followed his colleagues.

Who'd killed the two men? Savage? This woman Haley Cramer? Someone else?

Where *were* they?

Eban blew out a frustrated breath. It would take days to search the brush properly. Maybe the Indonesian government would let the US Navy assist. Give the sailors something useful to do.

They hit the beach, and Hawthorne held out his arm to stop them going any farther.

"Drag marks over there. Two boats. Get some images," he told the photographers. The two men started down the beach, ranging out to the side before cautiously moving forward.

They got twenty feet before one called out. "I got a handgun and some blood here." His flash lit up the objects in the sand. "A couple of cell phones too."

Bingo.

Eban had to hold himself back from running as he and Hawthorne swiftly joined the other men. As soon as the photographer had enough snaps, Eban bent down and carefully picked up one cell phone by its outer edge and placed it in a clear evidence bag.

Hawthorne did the same with the other phone. Eban recognized Quentin's work cell. It was tempting to turn it on, but he didn't want to mess up anything for the tech guys.

"Let's collect the blood and pistol, and we'll get more evidence recovery people down here to see if they can salvage anything else." It was a miracle it hadn't rained in the last twenty-four hours, but the miracle wouldn't last much longer.

"Are you thinking what I'm thinking?" Hawthorne asked quietly.

Eban stared out at the seemingly endless ocean. "That they took Quentin and this Cramer woman with them?" Eban met the other man's worried gaze and nodded. "Yeah, I think I am. And now we have to find them."

CHAPTER TWELVE

QUENTIN DIDN'T SPEAK as they were paraded like prize cattle back through the makeshift village. He exaggerated the pain in his ribs and shuffled tiredly, wanting to appear weaker than he currently was. He could probably overpower the one guard, but he wasn't sure he could overpower him without the asshole crying out for assistance or getting a shot off from the AK he held so casually in his hands.

And if they attempted an escape and failed, their captors would beat the living shit out of him. Not that it'd been fun so far, but he was keenly aware from all the reports he'd read over the years that he and Haley had gotten off relatively easy. He still had his head, and she hadn't been violently assaulted.

Yet.

He had no doubt the threat to disfigure Haley was genuine, but it was also designed to keep them fearful and compliant. Follow the rules or bad things would happen. As if they needed a reminder after last night.

He did not want to be responsible for Haley being mutilated, but they needed to make an escape plan and not succumb to fear of the threats. Easy to say when you weren't the one who stood to lose a piece of your face, although he was pretty sure they'd want his whole head when the time came, and not just part of it.

He tried to scope out the place while keeping his head bent and only moving his eyes. Judging from the main house, and the small, sturdy, wooden barracks, this appeared to be a semi-permanent camp. Terrorist HQ.

Didn't mean these people owned this property. It was probably abandoned, or they'd killed the original owner and taken over the place.

The ramshackle huts that some of the people lived in looked as if a strong wind would blow them over. Presumably, they didn't want to invest time or energy building more permanent structures when they'd have to leave everything behind in a hurry should the authorities find them. But the presence of women and children suggested they were fairly confident the authorities *wouldn't* find them here…it was a conundrum.

Something about the leader, plus last night's highly orchestrated attack made Quentin think the guy had been in—or more worryingly, was *still* in—the military, which meant this group might be smarter than your average K&R opportunists.

They were Muslim, but most Indonesians were Muslims—peaceable ones.

Was this group affiliated with IS or Al Qaeda? Or did they have a local axe to grind?

Ironically, he didn't know much more about them standing in the heart of their camp than he would back in his office.

He tried to gauge the size of the island but couldn't. The dense jungle canopy meant he had no visual beyond ten or twenty feet in any direction. He caught a glimpse of the blue ocean to the south. Overhead, the leaves were impenetrable, except for the narrow line along the track.

Quentin glanced up at the thin slice of bright blue sky. A

satellite could pass right above them and he doubted it would spot the buildings or the people walking around on the ground below.

No cell tower in sight. The commander probably had a radio in his house or the barracks or both. Getting to that and sending a message might alert the authorities to their position, but he and Haley would be dead or moved to a new island before rescue had the chance to arrive.

Was this the same group who'd kidnapped the Alexanders and Darby O'Roarke? If so, where were they being held? Quentin hadn't seen any sign of them, but Haley had spotted a yacht which could be the Alexanders'—or some other poor traveler unlucky enough to pick the wrong spot for a secluded vacation.

The fact Darby O'Roarke was a single woman who'd been working alone meant the chances of her being assaulted or even forcibly married to one of the creeps who stole her was high. It was part of the reason Quentin had pretended Haley was his wife although, at the time, it had also been a desperate bid to keep her alive. The gambit had paid off and now meant they'd be less likely to be separated. Quentin needed that proximity if he wanted to try to keep her safe, and to take her with him when he made his bid for escape.

They arrived at "their" hut on the edge of the camp. Behind was thick forest and a steep drop off. The scenery was wildly beautiful and intimidatingly remote.

Escape? Escape where?

A woman shrieked behind them, and he slowly turned. Lyrita, the widow who couldn't have been more than eighteen, scurried toward them holding a covered bowl of something and a jug of water.

The guard said something to her, but she swung the food away from him and gave Haley a fierce show of teeth along with an audible snarl.

Lyrita held the bowl out toward him, and he took it and bowed slightly to appear less threatening. "*Terima kasih.*"

It meant "thank you" in Bahasa Indonesian. Although most of the islands had their own indigenous languages more than 220 million people spoke the official language. Hopefully, she was one of them. Unfortunately, Quentin only knew two phrases. *Please*, and *thank you* so that was the end of his conversational piece.

The woman glowered. Then she spat in the jug of water and thrust it at Haley who had to lunge to catch it before it smashed on the ground.

"*Terima kasih,*" Haley shouted after the furiously swaying hips of the retreating woman.

The woman threw her hands up and shrieked in outrage again.

Quentin hid a smile. The fact Haley had a sense of humor despite everything they were going through meant she might survive this nightmare.

Hopefully.

He remembered what she'd said about being raped before, and that old familiar rage stirred. But that was for another time. They needed to face these new dangers head-on, one minute at a time. Kidnappings often took months to resolve, but Quentin wasn't going to stick around that long if he could help it.

He'd been in the Army, and he'd undergone jungle survival training in Borneo, which wasn't dissimilar to this environment. He had enough survival skills to get himself out of here, assuming they didn't restrain or beat him half to death first. It was getting them both out that might prove difficult, but he was not leaving Haley behind.

The guard ducked his head into the hut as if looking for reinforcements—maybe a couple of handy dandy Navy SEALs, which would have been okay under the circumstances. As an Army guy, he would prefer Delta Force, but beggars couldn't be choosers. The guard turned back to them and jerked his rifle to urge them inside.

Quentin indicated Haley go first. "After you, my love."

She quirked a brow at him but went ahead anyway. He didn't want the guard to be alone with her if at all possible. Not even for a moment. He'd seen the way the man's eyes followed her and the way he couldn't keep his hands off her, even if it was in the guise of pushing her around.

He knew that mother-fucking type.

Quentin ducked through the opening, and the door was shut and padlocked behind them. Hardly Fort Knox, but a tiny gap in the rushes showed the guy slump down against a nearby tree, staring resentfully their way.

Getting away wouldn't be easy, but Quentin was confident he could pick the lock as long as the guard fell asleep.

He and Haley sat side-by-side on the cot, silently contemplating the jug of water and the covered bowl which he set on the ground in front of them. Thirst was making his tongue stick to the roof of his mouth, and his stomach grumbled.

He hadn't expected to be fed. Not yet. Although who knew what was under the lid. Could be anything from fried spiders to jungle rat. It could also be a cruel joke. He had killed Lyrita's husband after all.

It could be red ants or warm turds.

"Ready?" he asked.

Haley nodded and took a sip from the jug of water, spittle or no spittle. He felt ridiculously proud of her in that moment, and almost rolled his eyes at himself. *Jerk.*

She passed the jug to him, and he took a sip too. She seemed to know without him saying anything that they needed to ration the water, but not too slowly in case the damn guard came in and took it away from them again, or kicked it over in a rage.

Quentin cautiously removed the lid on the food dish. Haley held on tight to her stomach and then let out a breath of relief that sounded almost like a laugh.

Fried crickets.

Okay.

This wasn't so bad.

He picked one up and bit into the crunchy insect. It wasn't awful. Food was food, and it didn't taste bad. Kind of nutty.

Haley tentatively reached out and put one in her mouth too.

"Pound for pound insects have more protein than beef," she told him with a grimace.

He nodded, impressed. "Did you do a SERE school or something?"

Search, Evasion, Resistance, Escape was a staple of military training.

She shook her head and pulled a face as she chewed. "I'm not a personal fan of pain or deprivation." She picked up another insect. "I had a massive crush on Bear Grylls." She crunched the hindquarters. "Do you think she spat on these too?"

"I think you could take that bet to the bank."

She huffed out a horrified laugh. "I don't even care anymore. I know we can't afford to get weak from lack of food."

He had another drink of water and offered it back to Haley who took it.

They both looked at their bowl of crickets.

"I don't know whether to be grateful we're getting fed or suspicious and wonder if they are lulling us into a false sense of security," he told her honestly. "The guards seem pretty lax with security, almost to the point where it's like they know that, even if we try to escape, we'll fail. I'm guessing it has something to do with the fact the island is uninhabited except for this rebel group, and they presumably guard the boats. I mean, maybe there is a helipad or even a runway somewhere..."

"Can you fly a plane?"

"Unfortunately not." He laughed and then caught himself. It wasn't funny.

"What do you think they want with you?"

"I don't know." He cleared his throat, not wanting to tell her his worst fears, but that would be foolish. They couldn't keep secrets if they were going to trust one another. "It could be a routine ransom demand. There were a couple of American seniors who were kidnapped off their yacht in the South China Sea about six months ago. The yacht was never found—a thirty-eight-footer. A militant group have been asking for a ransom of ten million dollars. The family have been selling everything they own trying to raise the cash, but they have only been able to gather just over a million bucks. Another young woman was taken a day or so ago. A grad student volcanologist. No demand yet, but it usually takes a few days before they try to make contact with the relatives.

They probably think if they have me, the government will have to negotiate, but that's not how this works."

Haley touched his hand. She did that often, he'd noticed. Touched him. He liked it. He liked it a lot.

"I could raise enough money to buy all our ways out of here."

Quentin shook his head. "And then this organization is empowered to go out and kidnap more Westerners. And they'd keep asking for more money until they bleed you and the other families dry. The government will never allow a ransom to be paid for me—if they did, they'd open up every US official in the world to the K&R game."

Haley's mouth twisted, obviously unhappy with his reply. "Seems like they are already in the kidnap-and-ransom-US-officials game."

"True, but give them that kind of cash and imagine the weaponry they could purchase and how many people they could hurt with it."

She tucked her knees up to her chin, obviously disappointed it wasn't so simple. He was disappointed too.

They sat quietly, side by side. Finally, she spoke again. "You said it *could* be a ransom demand. What else could it be?"

He looked away. "A PR campaign. They might be planning to torture me," he cleared his throat, needing to be honest, "*us*, live on the internet to raise their cachet in the terrorist world and give the US the finger. Also, to give those other families more incentive to come up with the ransom. The fact that they now know you're wealthy means I think they'll keep you alive."

"With or without a nose?" She looked like she was going to

be sick. "Do you have a plan that will keep me from losing my mind?" She picked up another fried cricket and crunched down on it with determination.

He put his arm around her and leaned his head against hers. She was beautiful and smart and hadn't completely freaked out despite living a nightmare. First rule of survival—don't freak out.

"You'd have made a great agent, you know."

She laughed but didn't sound happy. "Because I'm so brave?"

"You *are* brave."

"I have done nothing except hide behind you since we met." She looked disgusted at the idea.

"We did do something else." He bumped her shoulder gently.

Her eyes flared at the reminder, and a zing of attraction passed between them as she laughed. "And I'm glad we did. It'll be something positive to remember if..."

He'd been going for a distraction but had obviously failed.

"Is it wrong that I'm happy I stumbled into your bedroom last night, and not someone else's?" she said quietly.

They stared at one another for a long moment, the air heated between them.

"Not wrong. I'm happy it was me too. I haven't felt like that since—" He cut himself off. Haley Cramer wasn't the sort of woman who'd appreciate being compared to his late wife, and Abbie deserved better. And maybe Haley would have slept with anyone who'd rescued her, simply to reassert her control over her body. He didn't know where to put that thought or the slight feeling of hurt that accompanied it. They had bigger issues to deal with.

He cleared his throat. "I thought we'd try to escape sooner rather than later, even though they'll be watching us closely to start with. I think we could probably pick the padlock and creep out while it's dark. Head down to the cove and steal the yacht or another boat."

"It's risky." Her eyes were huge.

"It is. They'll punish us if we get caught, and it will make today look like a kid's birthday party."

"They might be guarding the boats," she warned.

"I assume they will be. But if we can't get to the boats, we can hide out in the jungle until we figure out another way off this island. It's better than sitting here at these guys' mercy."

"I agree." She shivered and rubbed at the goosebumps that had formed on her arms. "The longer we stay, the worse it's going to get. I'd rather die trying to get out of here than wait for that asshole to cut off my goddamn nose."

He kissed her hair, the scent of smoke lingering there. She turned and smiled at him, and he found himself looking at her lips and then blinked, horrified at himself. What the hell was he thinking with all the touchy-feely shit? Just because they'd had sex, and he needed this human connection didn't mean she would welcome it. She was the victim of multiple assaults—

She leaned forward and kissed him on the lips, as if they were a real married couple and an affectionate peck was par for the course.

"In case they're watching," she murmured quickly, her cheeks heating a glorious red.

The little he could see of the guard suggested the man was sleeping.

A lump lodged in his throat. After years of being emotionally dead when it came to women, he'd finally met someone he could care about again. Haley Cramer. Who looked like a million bucks even without all the gilding, and who was sharp and honest and resilient.

Odds were they'd both be dead in a week.

The universe sure did have a twisted sense of humor.

Even if they got to the yacht, the bad guys had speedboats, and radios and AKs and knew their way around these parts. He had some old SERE's training, a lot of determination, and the help of a woman who apparently liked mad English survivalists.

He picked up another cricket, determined to keep up his strength. Then the ground shook beneath his feet, and Haley screamed.

CHAPTER THIRTEEN

"SO ON TOP of everything else, we're sitting on an active volcano?" Haley couldn't believe their luck. What the heck had she done to upset the universe? Whatever it was, she was ready to repent.

"Seems like it."

Their captors were chattering excitedly, but their attention seemed intent on the mountain, not them.

Quentin had a good poker face and was probably trying not to scare her, but she was done being courageous.

"How can you be so calm?" she hissed. They were both careful to keep their voices low enough that the guards couldn't overhear their conversation.

He gave her a lopsided smile. The fact that the man was gorgeous despite being dirty and disheveled and having a jaw darkened with scruff didn't make anything okay.

Nothing was okay.

Especially her being angry with him.

Tears filled her eyes, and she tried to stop them, but they rushed her defenses and started leaking out of her face. God, she hated tears. She found herself hauled against a strong male chest and then she started quietly sobbing. Not wanting to draw the guard's attention, she stuffed her hand into her mouth as Quentin rocked her back and forth, the way a parent might a child. Except it was a comfort she'd never received from her aloof father, and it made Quentin's actions even more poignant.

"It's okay, Haley. I've got you. For as long as it takes, I've got you. Let it all out."

Tears blinded her, and sobs wrenched out of her chest despite her attempts to keep quiet. He rubbed his hands up and down her spine, absorbing some of her pain, soothing some of her fear and hurt. He murmured nonsense sounds against her hair and she wept and wept, unable to get a hold of herself. After several minutes, she shuddered and stilled. She was done.

Quentin dipped a tiny corner of the blanket in the water and dabbed her face.

"I'm sorry." She felt better, more in control now. She didn't even know the last time she'd cried. Probably when Alex Parker had been incarcerated in that Moroccan jail on some bogus charge, and she thought she'd lost him forever. "I didn't mean to fall apart. We haven't even been here twenty-four hours, and I'm whining like a baby."

He squeezed the excess water from the blanket and dropped it back onto the cot.

"My turn tomorrow." He gave her a smile that was subtle in its humor, but she suddenly remembered he was the one who'd been beaten several times, and she hadn't even asked if he was okay.

"Are you injured?" She stopped squeezing him so tight. "I didn't even ask. Your ribs—"

"They hurt a little, but I was laying it on thick for our friends. The punches weren't fun, but they weren't that damaging. I'm not pissing blood which is a good sign."

She tried to forget the feel of that steel blade beneath her nose. "I don't want to think about how much worse it could get or think about how long we might be stuck here."

It was getting dark outside, and she knew that night would drop like a curtain, and they had no flashlight or candle. A mosquito buzzed, and she swatted it. "Ugh." She wiped the sticky carcass onto a piece of wood.

She had another drink of water, pacing herself because there was no way she was going to the creepy toilet with the creepy guard in the middle of the night. Not unless it was part of an escape plot.

"We should probably try to protect ourselves as much as possible from getting bitten. You take the blanket—"

"No."

"But—"

She shook her head. "Don't give me special treatment because I'm female. I need to pull my weight whenever I can. We're not in the nice, polite world anymore. We are partners fighting for survival."

Quentin's lips twisted. "I wasn't sure how you'd feel about sharing a bed given what's happened over the last couple of days and the fact you've been raped in the past. I don't want to trigger PTSD or some sort of flashback."

"Oh, my god, Quentin." Haley gave a short laugh, even though she'd never talked about what had happened to her. Not outside her family and regular therapy sessions. But more than twenty years had passed, and she was able to handle it better now. "I don't think I've ever met someone as considerate as you."

He pulled a face. "Pretty sure the people who work for me wouldn't say the same."

She didn't believe him. Not for a moment. "Sleeping with someone has never triggered PTSD in the past. I know it doesn't guarantee I won't have nightmares in the future, but I have never felt safer than when I'm with you."

He met her gaze with his dark chocolate eyes full of contrition and remorse for things that weren't even his fault. If other men were half as good as he was, the world wouldn't be the mess it was. He looked away, clearly uneasy with her faith in him. "I'm going to try to get a few hours' rest."

Haley moved the almost empty bowl of crickets to the end of the cot and offered him the water, which he took.

Then he eased down carefully, telling her that while he might be pretending the beating hadn't hurt, in reality he was sore. He edged over to one side, and she lay next to him. She draped the gray blanket over both their legs and drew it up to their chests. It smelled musty, but it was all they had, and she was grateful for it.

She lay on her back and tried to get comfortable without hogging the available space.

It was *impossible.*

"Lie on me," he said after five minutes of her fidgeting.

"I don't want to hurt you," she protested.

He raised his arm and she not-so-reluctantly adjusted herself so she lay against his chest, being as careful as possible of any injuries he might not have told her about. She slipped her knee over his, searching for a comfortable position.

He pulled the blanket over her, even covering her hair, making it hard for the mosquitoes to find exposed flesh. "Tell me if you start to panic. About anything."

"I'm beyond panic." But she knew what he meant. Her hand formed a fist on the center of his chest. She didn't know the last time she'd simply slept with a guy. Probably Chris Baylor when they'd been dating. That relationship was a record for her. She'd had others that had theoretically lasted longer but they'd been long distance, so she'd spent less time with them. Alex said she always picked the losers and users. The thought reminded her of the horrors of last night.

"I think they shot the man you saved before the roof collapsed yesterday. I knew him a little. He was a former Marine who was excellent at close protection work. He spent a lot of time in the Middle East, and I tried to tempt him to join our firm a couple of years ago." If he'd worked for them, he wouldn't have been at the conference, and he wouldn't be dead. "Do you think Chris survived?"

His arm tightened around her. "I don't know. He might have heard the terrorists come back and hidden himself."

She wondered about Tricia Rooks and the other person she'd rescued. Had they survived? Without Quentin's intervention, Haley knew she would most definitely be dead. Maybe that's why she felt such a strong pull to the man—except she'd felt it even before the terrorist attack, before they'd had sex.

It hadn't diminished.

The sounds of the villagers going about their daily business continued as the darkness thickened. Apparently, the rumble of a volcano wasn't that unusual. The sound and scent of cooking tainted the air with wood smoke. She didn't think she'd ever smell smoke again without thinking of the victims who'd been murdered last night. And now she and Quentin were surrounded by the people who'd done that to their fellow humans.

She couldn't afford to forget that. These sons of bitches

were rapists and killers. They'd have no mercy.

"How'd you and Chris get together?" Quentin asked, murmuring in the blackness. Maybe he could feel her heart racing.

"We met in D.C. He was very charming, until he wasn't."

"Sorry." The way he said it sounded like he thought it was his fault.

"Why are you sorry?"

"Because when we were in the Army together, I didn't beat him to a pulp every time he cheated on a girl."

A bittersweet huff of air burst out. "I only found out he was cheating after I discovered he was trying to break into my computer to steal company secrets."

"You have got to be kidding me."

She felt him try to meet her gaze, although it was too dark now to see his expression. "I wish."

"I can't believe it."

She stiffened.

"I don't mean that I doubt you, just… What did you do? Press charges?"

"No, my partners devised some misinformation about a contract we were both bidding on that meant his company lost a lot of money underbidding. Then Alex infected his computer system with a virus that shut down his company financial system for two weeks. We didn't want to compromise boots on the ground, but I was fine with Chris sweating a little. Ugh. I suspect that isn't strictly legal so forget I told you about it."

"It was an asshole move on his part."

It had been.

"You two met in the Army?" she asked. She wanted to know more. Not about Chris but about Quentin. If things didn't work out the way they wanted, she might have all the time in the world to explore his personal history, or she might have none at all. She didn't want to think about that.

"Bootcamp. I wanted to get my GI degree so I could apply for the FBI. It was the only way I could afford to go to college."

"You always wanted to be an agent?"

She felt him laugh and then wince.

"Yes. Seems like a stupid thing for a kid to aim for."

"It isn't stupid," she assured him. "It's pretty admirable."

"Right now, I'm wishing I'd gone for high school math teacher."

"I don't know," she said. "High school seems almost as dangerous as war zones these days."

"Don't remind me." He hugged her closer, and she didn't even know if he realized he was doing it. It didn't scare her, didn't even feel sexual. It felt good and safe and comforting.

Not that she didn't find Quentin attractive. He was hot on so many different levels, but here in this rickety hut with the disgustingly scary guard outside? She couldn't even begin to think about sex and was glad he didn't either.

"So you and Chris are BFFs? Must have been nice to catch up with him at the symposium."

"We were tight for a long time but drifted apart. There were three of us back then, another guy called Nick Karlovac."

"I know Karlovac."

"You don't sound impressed."

She shrugged, still keeping tucked close to Quentin's chest despite the humidity. He smelled good—not squeaky clean, but good—and the feel of his arm around her was even better. "We're competitors so we generally don't hang out for brunch."

But it was more than that. Karlovac and Baylor were both in-your-face alpha males who thought it was okay to try to intimidate her. Hadn't taken long for them to figure out she wasn't easily intimidated, especially with Alex Parker and Dermot Gray as her partners. "I have a hard time seeing you with them, if I'm honest."

"The Army is a melting pot of personalities. I was used to that sort of male-dominated situation—I have four brothers—and I made friends easily. To be honest, I needed that familiar shit-talking bonding when I first left home. We were young and stupid. I like to think I grew out of it but…" His voice grew serious. "I hope Chris made it out okay. Then I'll kick his ass for you."

"I hope he made it out alive too, but I don't need you to kick his ass. We dealt with it. It's over."

"Let's try to get a few hours' sleep," he murmured again, sounding tired.

She wasn't surprised.

One part of her was terrified to let go and surrender to the darkness, but the other part of her was barely hanging on to consciousness. She'd hardly slept in the last two days and needed to be rested and cognizant for whatever came next.

"Thank you," she said. "For having my back."

He didn't reply. She was pretty sure he was already asleep.

The mountain rumbled again, quietly, like a hibernating bear rolling over.

CHAPTER FOURTEEN

LATER THAT EVENING, Eban walked through the busy corridors of the hospital in Jakarta where the survivors were being treated. Getting here from the airport had been the usual mind-scrambling exercise of too many people, grid-locked traffic, and insane motorcycle riders and rickshaw drivers slipping through the interstitial space. Even inside the hospital waiting area, it was loud and chaotic and the last place he would want to find himself injured or sick.

The rest of the FBI team had stayed out on Nabat Island to help process the evidence, including the dead, but he needed to interview the survivors ASAP.

He asked directions to ICU and had to show ID to get past armed security. A good sign. The locals were taking the threat seriously as the FBI had been urging them to.

Eban had spoken briefly to Grant Gunn, the man who'd gone for a few beers and, by some miracle, missed the massacre. Gunn claimed he hadn't seen any of the attackers. Only the carnage left behind. The task force was investigating his background, and Eban had urged the man to head back to the States on the next available flight.

Chris Baylor was being treated on this floor for logistic reasons and not because he needed intensive care. The guy was lucky to be alive and, if the terrorists found out there were witnesses to the atrocity, who knew what they'd do. The attackers had been careful not to leave anyone alive. Not that Chris Baylor or Tricia Rooks might be able to tell them anything useful in identifying these bastards, but then again, they might get lucky. You never knew.

Eban was directed down a corridor with lots of side rooms with big glass viewing windows.

A tall, black guy stood staring into one of the rooms with a scowl on his face. Eban glanced through the window as he walked by and stopped. Turned back. The woman lying in the bed inside the room had bright blue hair, but apart from that she looked like the photograph he had for Tricia Rooks.

He stepped closer to the window, and the tall guy watched him in the reflection of the glass.

"You a relative of the patient?" Eban asked.

"Who's asking?" American accent. Operator eyes. The man maintained a bland expression that didn't fool Eban one bit. He was pissed.

Eban pulled his creds from his jeans pocket, held out his ID. "FBI Supervisory Special Agent Winters. I'm looking for two patients, one of whom is Tricia Rooks."

Eban wasn't dressed for business. He was dressed for travel and working a crime scene. The smell of smoke still clung to his clothes. He should probably have stopped to change, but he wanted to blend into the environment for this investigation, something wearing a suit and tie would make impossible. Plus, he couldn't stand the idea of wasting even a moment until he'd figured out exactly what had happened to his boss.

"That's Tricia Rooks." He pointed at the unconscious woman who was intubated. "Who're you?"

The man relaxed. "Sean Logan." The guy retrieved his passport out of his back pocket and showed it to Eban. "I work with Tricia at Raptor. You figured out what went down yet?"

"Still working on it." Eban would never discuss an ongoing investigation with someone outside the Bureau. "I was hoping to interview Ms. Rooks about the attack."

"Yeah. Me too." Sean slipped his passport back into his pocket. "The doctors induced a coma to help her heal. We're trying to get her on a medivac home tomorrow, if she's stable."

Eban pressed his lips together. "I really need to talk to her about what happened last night. See if she can give me any information about the attackers or the sequence of events."

Sean nodded. "I understand, but her health is our first priority."

Eban looked away. He totally got that. It was his concern that there might be live hostages that increased his sense of urgency, but he wasn't about to tell a stranger his suspicions about Quentin and Haley Cramer. For all he knew, they were two of the many corpses being pulled from the wreck of the hotel. Until he knew for sure, he wasn't going to stop looking for them.

"Any clue how she got out alive when so many others didn't?" Eban asked.

Sean shook his head. "But she's a hell of a smart and determined person. If anyone could survive, it would be Tricia."

Room had been full of smart, determined people.

"When she wakes up, call me." Eban handed the man his business card. "Any time, day or night. We need to catch these people before they attack anywhere else, and Tricia might know something useful."

Sean's brown eyes were determined when they met his.

"Personnel at Raptor are ready and eager to help."

Eban nodded stiffly. "Appreciate that. This is a top priority case for the FBI." He hesitated. "Is there any group you know of who might have gone after this particular conference?"

A mirthless smile sliced Sean's face. "No, sir, but I can guarantee they made a serious error in judgment when they did so."

"That they did." Eban went to turn away.

Sean's next words stopped him cold. "If the Feds don't catch these bastards, then one of the private military contractors who lost people will. I can guarantee every one of us has operatives working the data and leveraging our contacts in the region."

If Quentin was alive and some gung-ho private army went in, guns blazing, not realizing captives were being held in the camp, his boss wouldn't stand a chance. The same hazard existed if the US military or Indonesians went in hard and indiscriminately. Eban needed to figure out if Quentin was alive ASAP so they could strategize his rescue, not carpet bomb the militants.

"The US government appreciates any information anyone uncovers, but private organizations going vigilante will not be tolerated," Eban warned sharply. "American hostages are being held in this region and there's every chance they're being held by the same people who attacked the symposium." He could say that much without revealing he thought Quentin might be one of them.

"I guess we'll see what happens." Sean crossed his arms over his chest, clearly reserving judgment.

Eban stared past him to the woman who lay unmoving on the bed. She was lucky to be alive. He thought about his boss.

All the unanswered questions with zero leads…

"I'd appreciate you keeping me updated on Tricia's condition. We need to talk to her. It'll be faster if she allows that rather than us having to go through official channels or take her into protective custody…" He held the man's dark eyes, because that was a warning. The FBI did not fuck around. Speed in getting answers was vital. Cooperation was vital.

Sean seemed to remember they were on the same team and nodded. "I'll let you know when she's awake."

Eban said goodbye and walked farther down the corridor, shoes slapping the vinyl tiles, too loud for this space full of seriously ill people.

He turned the corner, saw a man in a room at the end of the hallway, sitting up in bed, furiously texting into a smartphone.

He recognized Chris Baylor, co-owner of Bay-Kar Inc., another major private security firm. These terrorists couldn't have picked a better target for their rage and revenge.

Had they planned it? Of course, they had. With help from someone on the inside? Is that why the Indonesian foreign minister left when he did? Eban needed to get other agencies involved, or perhaps the legat had connections they could leverage. Although, it wasn't exactly diplomatic to ask the host nation if they were complicit in a terrorist incident against Americans.

Indonesia was a complex country. Peaceful and amiable for the most part, with small pockets of violent hardliners. Same could be said for most places these days.

Chris Baylor glanced up as Eban got closer. At least sixty CEOs or high-level managers had been killed yesterday. Someone from almost every major private security company in the world. The grief and indignation were no less acute for them being in the security business. If anything, it was worse, asking how the hell this could have happened to such a savvy group of professionals.

"Mr. Baylor?" Eban asked, holding out his hand.

"Who's asking?" Chris Baylor looked suspicious as he shook hands.

"My name is Eban Winters. I'm an SSA with the FBI's Crisis Negotiation Unit. I need to interview you about what happened last night."

Chris's eyes widened a fraction. "Take a seat." He indicated the chair beside the bed.

"You have anyone here with you?" asked Eban.

"Nah. I told them not to bother coming. I have a gash on my leg, a concussion and a minor gunshot wound but apart from that, I got off easy. I feel like a fake being here." He pulled up the edge of his hospital gown sleeve and revealed a white bandage on his arm.

"You were shot?"

"Just a graze."

Eban spotted butterfly sutures running along a nasty scalp wound on the back of the man's head, and he was one of the lucky ones. "Did anyone take your statement?"

Chris shook his head. "Not really. A couple of the guys who first arrived on the scene asked what happened, and I told them. Another woman from the embassy checked on me when I arrived here. Nothing since then."

Everyone was at the scene. "Is it possible for you to talk me through what happened last night?"

Chris shrugged. "Bunch of armed terrorists burst into the hotel and started shooting." He rubbed the back of his head and winced. "That about covers it."

"How did you survive?" asked Eban.

"I didn't think I was going to."

"Can you tell me exactly what happened?"

"I can try, but it's all a bit hazy. I was in my room when I heard gunfire downstairs. I grabbed my pistol, but there was no way I was going to go up against bad guys with automatic rifles with nothing but a Glock and a couple of spare mags."

"How come you were the only one to have a firearm?" Getting hold of a weapon would have been too much hassle for most people attending a three-day symposium in a foreign country.

"I've been working between Papau and East Timor for the last six weeks and got a local pilot to fly me into Nabat at a cut price." Chris raised his brows. "I brought the Glock along as I don't like being anywhere unarmed."

"What about security for the conference? Was there any?" Eban had been trying to reach the organizers, but no one was answering their phones. They were possibly all dead.

"Meeting had security. Even had metal detectors to go through for the auditorium." Chris wiped a line of sweat from his brow. It was hot as hell inside the hospital, even with the A/C going full blast.

"Did they return fire when the terrorists arrived?"

Chris smiled grimly. "They left along with the politicians after Quentin's keynote speech."

"Quentin?" Eban asked sharply.

"Quentin Savage." The corners of Chris's mouth dragged down. "He was an old friend."

"You know Quentin Savage?" Eban asked in surprise.

Chris pressed his lips firmly together as if trying to get

ahold of the emotions surging through him. “We were in the 101st Airborne together. Screaming Eagles.”

Eban filed the information under interesting details he needed to follow up on. “Did you see Quentin during the shooting?”

“Yep.”

“What happened to him?” Eban said, trying to stem his impatience.

“I got hit on the head by a falling beam in the hotel foyer and knocked unconscious.” Chris gingerly touched his scalp again. “Quentin appeared out of nowhere and saved me from burning to death. Him and Haley Cramer. She helped drag me out of there too.”

That confirmed the link between the two.

“Did you see the attackers?” Eban asked.

Chris shook his head. “Not really. I wasn’t sure what to do when I heard the gunfire. I stayed in my room waiting for anyone to try and break in. I couldn’t exactly go John McLean and save everyone’s asses, but I could do some damage if anyone came for me.”

Eban nodded.

“It got to a point when I couldn’t stay in my room any longer because of the smoke. I put a wet cloth over my face and made my way downstairs. I couldn’t get near the front door, so I headed into the bar. Next thing I know, I’m trapped under burning rubble.”

“Go on.” Eban was using minimal encouragers to keep the guy talking. It was one of the cornerstones of active listening devices—keep people talking.

Chris reached over for a glass on the bedside table and took a long swallow of water.

"I woke up and tried to free myself. Then suddenly, Quentin is dragging me outside and dumped me on the lawn. Then he and Haley ran back inside to rescue others." Chris's voice broke. "The roof came down on top of their heads right before I passed out again." He swallowed noisily, but Eban was still trying to process his words.

Quentin was dead?

Eban's theory that Quentin and Cramer had been somehow seized by the attackers and that was why their bodies hadn't been found near the beach had just been blown out of the water.

Shit.

His throat closed, his skin suddenly drenched in sweat. Sorrow made him want to walk away and grieve, but he had a job to do. He could contemplate his loss later. First, he needed to find the people responsible.

"You engaged with one of the terrorists?" Eban pointed at the wound in Chris's arm.

"Yeah." Chris inspected his bicep. "There was one guy still in the lobby, waiting to ambush anyone who tried to escape, thankfully he was a lousy shot."

"You killed him?"

"I don't know. He might have been crushed when the roof fell in." Chris grimaced. "It was hard to see."

"Do you know a man called Cecil Wenck?"

Chris grunted. "Everyone knows Cecil Wenck. Is he dead too?"

Eban shook his head. "He left before the attack."

"Lucky bastard." Chris's lip curled. "Last time I saw him, he was heading to his room with Haley Cramer. She was all over him."

That was new and unexpected information. When and how had Cramer ended up with Quentin?

Eban was impatient for someone to interview Wenck, but the guy was an Australian citizen. The FBI couldn't force their way into interrogating the billionaire, and his high-priced lawyer was stalling.

Haley Cramer had been at the heart of everything that had happened. Maybe he'd have people dig deeper into her background too.

"Any idea when I can get out of here?" Chris asked. "I'm taking up a bed that someone who is genuinely sick could use."

"Right now, you are the only survivor of this massacre who's talking so we need to keep you safe." Eban wanted Chris protected at all times.

"I didn't see anything," Chris argued.

"They don't know that."

Chris frowned. "You think they'll send someone after me?"

"It's a possibility. I wouldn't go back to East Timor until we've rounded up the people responsible."

Chris swore. "I've got thirty well-trained and well-armed men to keep me company in East Timor."

Eban shrugged. "I can't tell you what to do in Indonesia, sir, but why would you risk bringing about an attack on yourself and your own personnel?"

Bloodshot eyes narrowed on him. "My guys can handle themselves."

"And who knows how many innocents might die in the crossfire?"

Chris grunted. "I guess the guys can manage operations without my help."

"Once I have a written statement from you, I suggest going somewhere these people won't find you for a while." Eban scratched his head. "Raptor is organizing a medivac for Tricia Rooks back to the States. Maybe you can catch a ride with them?"

"She woke up yet?" Chris asked.

Eban shook his head.

Chris gave a harsh laugh. "I doubt Raptor would want me onboard."

"I think they'd be willing to overlook old rivalries to help a fellow survivor."

Chris's face softened into a smile, and he gave a shrug that was almost boyish. "I guess they might." Then his face crumpled. "I wish Quentin was here…"

Eban didn't want to talk about his boss. The grief was like a hammer driving a nail slowly through his heart.

"Would you be willing to write a statement while I go talk to the Raptor operative guarding Ms. Rooks to ask about that ride home?"

Chris looked startled. "Yeah. Sure. Thanks. Grab me a pen and paper. It'll give me something to do."

Eban hesitated. "The FBI would also appreciate if you could refrain from talking to the media until we've processed the scene and know more about the attackers. We have to identify the dead and inform families."

Chris's jaw hardened. "I'll think about it but no promises. This is good publicity for my company, and I'm not going to waste it."

Eban raised his brows. He shouldn't be surprised these guys were so mercenary given their profession. He pulled a pen and paper from his laptop bag and found a clipboard from the end of the bed for the guy to lean on. "As much information as possible. The slightest detail might prove important. I'll be back in twenty minutes. Want me to grab you a coffee?"

Chris nodded. "Black with two sugars." He was already scribbling the date on the top of the sheet.

"You are a very lucky man," Eban said sincerely.

"Doesn't feel lucky to almost die in a terror attack and lose one of my best friends." Chris gave him a hard stare.

"I suppose not." Eban walked away. When he was in line for coffee in the hospital foyer his cell phone started vibrating. "Winters."

"SSA Winters. My name is Alex Parker. I'm a consultant for the FBI. We need to talk."

CHAPTER FIFTEEN

QUENTIN WOKE UP and lay staring into the thick blackness of the night. He took a few seconds to get his bearings and listen to the sounds of the camp in slumber. The woman pressed against his side was warm and soft, her legs tangled with his, her breath deep and peaceful.

He hated to wake her. Hated that she was in danger and might die if he messed up. The odds were not in their favor.

The noises of the Indonesian rainforest rang out like percussion. The terrorists had gone quiet, probably in bed after a hard night's work the previous day, killing and burning. Despite his training, he couldn't shake the feeling that now was the time to act, before they got weak, before their captors imagined they'd try to escape.

He eased away from Haley and shook out his shoes before putting them on. Then he took a big drink of water, leaving enough for Haley to slake her thirst.

Who knew the next time they'd have something to drink?

He knelt near the doorway of the hut and observed for long minutes. The slumped silhouette of the guard remained unmoving beneath the same tree as earlier. Quentin scanned the darkness, although it was hard to make out anything else in the shadows. The village appeared asleep, and the guard also.

Only one way to find out.

Quentin broke a short, thin stick from the branches of the hut and worked his hand through the twigs and branches until he could reach the padlock. It was a big, old-fashioned iron one and it only took a few seconds to pop the lock. The guard didn't stir.

Quentin went back to the cot and gently shook Haley awake.

She stiffened for a second, then found his hand and squeezed in recognition without saying a word. The fact she didn't scream in terror spoke of a survival instinct as strong as any soldier's on a mission. She groped around for her boots and shook them out before pulling them on.

He handed her the water jug. "Finish it." His words were a murmur on the warm air, but she heard them and raised the jug to her lips, draining it.

He put the pitcher and earthen bowl on the bed and draped the blanket over it, even though he was tempted to steal the blanket. Still, the time it might buy them when dawn arrived and the guard glanced casually inside might prove vital. He had no idea how many hours of darkness remained.

"Let me take care of the guard," he whispered into her hair. "Then we'll follow the path down the hill toward the beach. Our night vision should be good enough to see by. If we hear or see anyone on the trail, we fade into the bush, moving nice and slow and crouching close to the ground. Movement draws the eye faster than anything else." Quentin glanced down at her long, pale limbs. Damn, it was the same dilemma they'd faced in the woods near the hotel. Her skin was too pale even in the darkness. Nothing in the jungle glowed like alabaster.

He quietly scooped up the blanket. "You're going to need this if we're to have any hope of getting past them. Drape it around your shoulders like a cape."

He did it for her. Haley stood tense next to him as he tied the corners around her neck. She shook slightly, obviously terrified as anyone with a brain cell would be.

"If you don't want to do this we don't have to," he reassured her. But things would get progressively worse from now on. Having an agent of the Federal Bureau of Investigation of the United States of America would prove too tempting not to use and abuse. Wouldn't be long until the video cameras would be rolling and the machetes sharpened.

They hadn't mistreated them too badly yet, because they were lulling them into a false sense of security. These were not merciful individuals. If they'd simply wanted money, they'd have grabbed twenty Western hostages all worth a hell of a lot more than he was.

No, he was here for some sort of negative leverage campaign.

They might keep Haley alive, but it wouldn't go well for her either.

Many men in positions of power abused women when they had the opportunity. Quentin liked to pretend humans were civilized, but he'd seen abuse regularly as a street agent.

The US would come for them, guns blazing once videos surfaced on the internet. The US would annihilate this entire island if that's what it took, and Haley would still be dead. Contrary to the advice he usually gave captives, it was better for them to attempt an escape now rather than sit here like lemmings.

He went to the door of the hut and double-checked the

guard hadn't moved. He hardened his heart; he couldn't afford weakness. Haley couldn't afford for him to be weighing his humanity against their survival.

"Stay here," he whispered into her ear.

He unhooked the padlock and worked it back inside through the rushes. He slowly pushed open the rickety door, which creaked like a gong on the night air. Quentin tensed. The guard didn't move, instead a soft snore escaped.

Quentin crept forward, using combat training skills he'd thought he'd long forgotten. He didn't want to kill the man, but he had little choice. If the guard woke and checked on them during the night, their plans for escape would be sunk. Quentin steeled himself.

Breaking someone's neck was about as up-close and personal as two people got outside of sex. Quentin did not hesitate or give the guard a chance to call out a warning to his fellow terrorists. It was fast and brutally efficient. A small piece of Quentin shriveled up and died when the bone cracked. He'd take that slight loss of humanity over lying down and surrendering, especially if surrendering meant sacrificing Haley too.

He propped the man gently against the tree and went through his pockets. He left the AK. No way could he take on a hundred terrorists in a firefight and win. Rifles were heavy and noisy. He took a pistol and knife and slid them into his waistband and back pocket, found a water canteen that was almost full, which he slipped over his head and shoulder. No phone, which was surprising as social media was huge in this part of the world.

Was that intentional—the lack of phones? Had the paramilitaries figured out that the cell phone signals could be used to track them? Probably.

Quentin went back to the hut, and Haley stepped out, the blanket keeping her from being too visible in the moonlight. He quickly shut the door and replaced the padlock with a dull click. Then he took Haley's hand and found the path, moving silently down the hill and away from the people who wanted to chop off Haley's nose and his head. Praying that luck was for once on their side.

THEY MOVED GINGERLY, the path wide enough and her night vision sharp enough that Haley could see where to place her feet and avoid any roots that might trip her.

She'd watched Quentin Savage live up to his name as he killed another man, and yet she couldn't bring herself to be anything except grateful.

The jungle was raucous with sounds she didn't recognize. A few nights ago, the idea of walking through the forest at night would have made her wig out. Now her ears were focused solely on listening for human activity. Humans were the most terrifying predator of all.

Twenty minutes into their escape, the chink of metal against metal had Quentin stopping and leading her quickly off the main path to hide behind a tree. He adjusted the edge of the blanket and pulled the musty wool up over her hair. Then he wrapped his arms around her under the blanket and tucked his nose into the crook of her neck.

The mustiness tickled her nose, and she'd never been more afraid of something as simple as a sneeze in her entire life. Her heart hammered in fear. If they were caught, she knew they'd follow up on their evil threats, and she did not think she could survive being carved up for someone's amusement.

She could feel Quentin's exhale through the coarse fibers of the wool and quieted her own breathing to match his. The strength of his arms felt like a buttress of support for her to lean into as a small group of men trudged up the pathway toward camp, laughing and joking. Staying still and quiet was the hardest thing she'd ever done in her life. Way harder than running away from home. Way harder than competing for business in a competitive and male-dominated world. She owed Quentin her life and her sanity. Even if they never escaped. Even if they died in the next few hours, she owed him everything.

They waited a full minute after the men had passed.

She raised her head, and Quentin ran his hand over her jaw, his touch warm and comforting. He pulled her back onto the path, and they increased their pace until they were almost jogging, the increasing sense of urgency punching her ribcage with demanding thuds.

As soon as those men reached camp, they'd likely come upon the dead guard and raise the alarm. She and Quentin needed to be on a boat and out of here before that happened.

Less than five minutes later, they could hear the steady, constant beat of the ocean. They slowed and approached cautiously, hiding in the brush along the edge of the beach. The yacht bobbed temptingly in the moonlight. Even more enticing, two rigid inflatable boats were moored close to the rocks on the far side of the cove. In between lay what looked like a small makeshift camp.

"What do you think?" Quentin whispered in her ear.

"The yacht would be easier to swim out to and steal, but they can catch up to us easily in the inflatables, and we're back to square one."

"What bothers me is there are too many men on this island for those two inflatables. They must have access to a plane and runway or bigger boats for moving camp."

"But those boats are probably the only way they can catch us in the next hour, assuming we can get to the open ocean," said Haley.

"True. Okay. We need to work our way around to the other side of that encampment to those RIBs. I doubt they have more than the minimum number of guards on duty as they're on home ground, but let's not assume anything."

"Why were those men moving between camps at night do you think?"

"I don't know," Quentin answered softly. "We have to get moving though. They'll reach the other camp soon. Keep the blanket over your hair." He adjusted it slightly, and Haley felt her breath catch. Crazy under the circumstances, but who wouldn't fall for a man this handsome and considerate who was also trying to rescue her from ruthless killers?

She nodded. She wasn't going to be the dumb blonde who screwed up. Not this time. They were getting the hell out of here.

They crept through the bushes and skirted an area with tents that seemed to be where the men slept.

A small, dilapidated, wooden shack sat at the far edge of the camp with a hurricane lamp burning outside. A single guard stood on duty there. He seemed to be the only one awake in the whole place.

Was that where the camp commander slept? Seemed odd

when there was a better house up the hill. She and Quentin both froze when the door opened, and a man slipped outside with a broad grin on his face doing up his zipper. He slapped the other guard on the arm, and they changed places almost furtively.

That was weird.

Quentin's grip on her hand was her only safe anchor in the darkness. They carried on past the hut but both froze when a cry came from inside the structure. It was a woman's sob of anguish. "Please, no."

Haley sucked in a breath. Those men were abusing a woman in there. An American woman by the sounds of it. Quentin's grip on her tightened, and they moved farther away from the shed, into the bushes that skirted the beach.

"We can't leave her," she whispered. It could have been her back there. Abused. Hurting.

There was enough light for her to see Quentin's expression, and she could tell he felt the same way.

"This might cost us our chance to get out of here," he murmured softly.

No matter how desperate she was to get away and avoid the same fate, she couldn't abandon this woman.

"Can you handle starting the boat?" Quentin asked.

She nodded. She'd handled RIBs plenty of times while diving or playing around on the ocean.

"I didn't see any guards but check again before you leave cover. If no one is looking, sneak into one of the boats and make sure it is ready to go as soon as I get there with the woman. Tie the other boat to the back of the first so they can't use it to chase after us. And keep down, okay?"

She nodded.

"And if I'm not there in five minutes, leave without me."

She shook her head.

"Promise me, or I'm not going anywhere but with you."

Stubborn man.

"Fine." Like hell.

She edged down towards the rocks where the boats were moored. She looked around carefully but didn't see anyone guarding them—the sentries were apparently doing other things instead. A rush of anger hit her in the throat. That poor woman. That was her fate if they were caught.

She slipped into the water between the rocks and the boats and undid the knots mooring one of them. Fear was alive and swimming in her bloodstream as she released the rope from the metal loop on the wall and pushed the first craft farther into the surf. It was heavy but deep enough in the water that she could manage it alone. She tied the one boat to the side of the other, knowing that if they had to book it, they might have to dump the second boat. She hoisted herself over the edge of the inflatable that was still attached to the wall. She checked the oars, then crawled to the outboard motor. She did an internal happy dance when she realized whoever had driven it last had left the keys in the ignition. She flipped on the gas line, although she was unable to check the amount of fuel in the tank given the lack of light.

She unhitched the rope that kept it tethered to the rocks but kept the rope looped through the metal ring so it didn't float away.

Ready to go.

She hunched low in the boat, holding onto her nerves and subduing the rev of her heart. Where was Quentin? Had he been caught? Had he rescued the woman? Was he dead? The idea made her want to throw up.

She searched the darkness for some hint of him, but all she heard were monkeys in the trees and wild shrieks that scared the crap out of her. The jungle was alive with danger, but it wasn't half as terrifying as the monsters who'd taken them hostage.

QUENTIN WAITED FOR Haley to move away from the shed, then went back to crouch in the shadows. He couldn't afford to wait for long. He lobbed a rock into the bushes on the other side of the cabin. The guard stood up and went to stare into the darkness. Behind him, Quentin eased around the side of the building and up the steps. He jammed his hand over the bastard's mouth to stop him screaming and drew the knife across his throat.

It didn't take long for the guy to collapse, dead in his arms. Quentin pushed him off the step into the bushes at the edge of the jungle.

Swiftly, Quentin headed to the door and eased it open.

The scene inside broke his heart and enraged him in equal measure. He quietly closed the door behind him. A young woman lay on a thin, dirty mattress, curled on her side with her back to him. The man faced away from Quentin, fixing his clothing. Without looking up, the guy said something and chuckled, obviously thinking Quentin was one of his fellow asshole guerillas here to take a turn. Quentin grabbed hold of the guy, but his hands were bloody, and his grip slipped. He dropped the knife onto the bare wooden floor, and it clattered loudly.

Shit!

The man spun around and Quentin hit the guy hard in the face and followed up with a knee to the balls. Quentin fell on top of the bastard, arm pressed across his trachea, cutting off his air supply, not giving him an inch. If the guard caught a breath, he'd scream. If he screamed, Quentin, Haley, and this young woman, who he recognized as Darby O'Roarke, were as good as dead.

Out of the corner of his eyes, he watched the guard's fingers strain toward the knife, and Quentin gripped harder, unable to let go. Hatred spat at him from that spiteful gaze. The feeling was entirely mutual. Quentin pressed down harder, knowing he was too late. Haley would be leaving any second, and he'd failed to rescue this young woman from her kidnappers.

The guard's fingers brushed the knife, but the girl snatched it away. Quentin's grip tightened even more as the guard started to moan.

Quentin felt the thrust of the knife into the man's body beneath him and winced. Quentin held the man as life slowly drained from his body. Finally, the guard went limp. As soon as it appeared the man was dead, Quentin climbed to his feet.

Darby O'Roarke wore a filthy rag that might once have been a sack. She crouched away from him, brandishing the knife, her eyes wild.

"Darby. I'm a federal agent." He spoke in his most soothing voice. "You need to come with me, but we have to go now, and we need to be absolutely silent. We don't have much time. The woman I'm with is on the boats, and she is supposed to leave if I'm not there in five minutes."

Time was distorted in these life and death situations, so

maybe they could still make it. If they hurried. He held out his hand for the knife and prayed she understood he was there to help.

Darby licked her lips nervously, then hesitantly handed the knife over.

What courage had that taken? To give up her one chance of defense to a stranger?

He wiped the blade clean on the dead man's chest and stuck it in his belt. "Are you ready?"

Her eyes opened wide, and she nodded. He opened the door, and she hobbled in front of him. Limping down the steps.

He went around to her side and tried to help her though she flinched away. She staggered onwards, making more noise than was wise when she fell to the ground. His heart broke for her, but they didn't have time for anything except getting the hell out of here.

He bent beside her. "I'm going to carry you, Darby. I don't mean to rush you, but if we don't get to the boat in the next thirty seconds, we're right back where we started, and we will never get off this island."

She whimpered in the darkness, and he helped her to her feet and then put her over his shoulder. He jogged down to the beach. As he got closer to the water, he could make out Haley huddled in the stern of one of the boats, even though she should be long gone.

The water was a cool relief to his skin as he waded through the surf, trying to keep Darby dry.

"Start her up," Quentin whispered as he rolled Darby unceremoniously into the boat.

The engine roared to life just as a radio crackled on the

shore.

Haley was already driving the boat in reverse as he dragged himself up over the bulbous sides and into the hull.

"Get us out of here ASAP."

He didn't have to tell her twice. A rope whizzed past his ear as she poured on the gas. The other boat bumped along the side, but it was good cover, and no way did Quentin want the tangos to have a way to pursue them. They needed to put as much distance as possible between themselves and this island.

Bullets whizzed overhead, and he swore, but Haley kept going, hugging the edge of the bay and, as soon as they were able, turning the corner and getting them out of sight.

"They might shoot at us from the bluff." He pointed toward the headland in the darkness. "We should head straight out to sea until we're out of range, and then we'll figure out which way to travel."

He lay there panting for a few minutes, unable to believe they'd escaped and not quite trusting it yet. The terrorists might have more boats in another bay. They might have more gang members on the surrounding islands.

Remorse hit him as he realized the Alexanders, the older couple whose release he'd been negotiating for months, were probably back on that island too. That was definitely their yacht sitting in the harbor. They'd probably been kept in one of the huts in the makeshift village not a hundred yards from where he and Haley had been confined.

Dammit.

"Quentin." Haley raised her voice above the wind that was whipping past them. "Can you take over?"

He sat straight up. "Are you shot? Are you injured?"

"No. No, it's not that." He could just make out her features by the moonlight. God, she was beautiful. She nodded in the direction of Darby, who was huddled in the bottom of the boat. “I want to try to help the girl.”

“Her name is Darby,” he said softly. “She was kidnapped five days ago.”

The fact they’d got her out of there was a miracle. But now they had to find safety in a remote region where they didn’t know who was friend and who was foe.

He took the rudder and wished to hell he was back in Quantico negotiating with assholes who didn’t want to pay federal taxes, rather than being in the middle of some unknown sea with two vulnerable women as they all desperately tried to avoid armed terrorists.

CHAPTER SIXTEEN

FIVE DAYS... IN some ways, that was hardly any length of time at all, and yet, Haley knew the young woman had endured torture for every second of those five days in what must have felt like a never-ending nightmare.

Her own experience with rape had replayed a thousand times in her head over the years and had almost destroyed her at one point. But she'd eventually found her support system and taken her power back.

What would this brutal experience do to this woman?

Haley made her way unsteadily to the front of the boat as Quentin took over the helm.

"Are you okay, Darby?" she asked.

The woman curled tighter into a ball, and Haley's heart clenched at the pain telegraphed by that reflexive movement.

It *was* a stupid question.

She wedged herself next to the woman on the damp floor and used her woolen blanket to cover them both. The woman froze at the brief touch.

"I won't hurt you. I won't touch you unless you want me to, but I am here for you to hug if you need me." The breeze off the ocean made Haley shiver. "I wanted to share my blanket with you so you don't get cold."

Quentin had slowed the pace of the boat as it was dangerous to travel too fast when you couldn't spot obstacles in the water. The island where they'd been held captive was a monstrous shadow behind them, bigger than she'd imagined. Thankfully, there was no sign of pursuit but no sign of any other land mass either.

"I know you've been through a terrible experience, Darby, and I wish I could tell you you're safe now, but we don't know that for sure yet. We are trying though and will not leave you behind." She wanted to stroke the woman's hair, but that was up to Darby. She wouldn't cross that line without permission. "Quentin and I were taken from a hotel those men attacked late last night."

It felt like a lifetime ago.

She swallowed, and grief for the people who'd been murdered pushed to the surface. Her voice became gruff, obstructed by remnants of fear and a fresh welling of sadness. "We were the only ones taken alive. They killed everyone else."

Haley looked up at the endless sky. She felt small and insignificant on this seemingly gigantic body of water. "Quentin works for the FBI. You can trust him with your life, and he *will not* hurt you." It was crazy how much faith she had in the guy, but she felt like she knew him down to his DNA. He was a good man. "Can you tell me where they took you from?"

At first, she didn't think Darby would answer, but then the woman turned around and faced her. "I'm working on an uninhabited island in the Banda Sea. I was supposed to be there for a month setting up GPS arrays as part of my research." Her voice was croaky as if her throat was sore. "I study volcanoes. A few days ago, some men came to my tent in the night. T-they attacked me and, and, *took* me." She threw herself against Haley's chest, sobbing. "I was so scared."

Haley held onto Darby, knowing she'd give everything she possessed to change what had happened to this young woman, knowing it was impossible.

"They *hurt* me." Darby's sob caught the wind and echoed hauntingly.

Haley felt helpless and didn't know what to say.

"I didn't think it was ever going to end. I started praying for death, and then you two arrived." Darby went to pull away and then changed her mind and tightened her grip instead. "Maybe I am dead, and you two are angels."

Haley met Quentin's gaze across the boat. She wanted to cry along with Darby, but she also wanted to rip those bastards apart.

She kept a firm hold of the other woman, rocking Darby gently, knowing she would have suffered the same fate if they hadn't escaped.

"How hard would it be to figure out which island they are on?" Quentin asked, raising his voice to be heard over the motor.

"Not hard at all." Darby wiped her eyes. "We know roughly when the volcanic quakes occurred. USGS should be able to trace the origins."

"Good. At least we can tell the authorities where they are."

Darby looked up, eyes huge. "Do you have any water? I haven't had anything to drink today."

Oh, god.

Haley's stomach twisted. She and Quentin had been shown every hospitality compared to how Darby had been treated. Quentin unhooked the strap from over his head and swung the canteen across to her. Haley caught it and passed it to Darby.

"We need to either find a town where we can call for help, or hide somewhere safe once the sun rises."

"How do we know who to trust?" Darby clasped the flask so hard Haley could see her knuckles gleam in the moonlight. After a long swallow, she stopped drinking and capped the bottle, handed it back.

"Unfortunately, we don't," Quentin said pensively.

"Surely we can find a tourist resort or something? Or flag a passing ship?" Haley suggested.

The look Darby and Quentin shared suggested it wouldn't be so easy.

"How far did they move you, do you know?" Quentin asked contemplatively.

"Not that long. An hour by sea at most." She wiped her eyes again. "Why?"

"Did you travel from the north, south, east or west of the island we were on?"

Darby cleared her throat. "North."

"Think you could find the island where you were doing your research? Know anything about navigating using the stars?"

Darby snorted out a laugh that gave Haley hope that the girl might get through this, assuming they weren't recaptured.

Darby looked up at the sky. "I know we can't see the North Star, because we're below the equator, but the Southern Cross is over there." Darby pointed to a small cluster of five bright stars and then to two shiny stars to the right. "And those are the pointers. So south is that way." She made a general slice in the direction with her hand. "If we head north, Pulau Gunung Rebi, which is where I was working, should be pretty easy to spot. It has a lava flow that drops straight into the ocean on the north side."

Great, another active volcano. Haley refrained from doing a jig.

Quentin turned the boat in that direction. "I doubt they'll think you'd return there."

Darby's teeth started to chatter. It was fear, even though she didn't say anything.

"Did you have any methods of communication at your field site?" Quentin asked.

Haley began to see what he was driving at.

"I had a satellite phone, but they smashed it."

Darby responded well to questions, losing some of the traumatized quality that unsurprisingly surrounded her.

"Could we use the GPS sites you were setting up to somehow signal for help?" Haley asked.

"Like how?" Darby sounded doubtful.

"Move a bunch together to write an SOS?" Haley suggested.

"It would take days to move that many GPS units and set them up in that way. The data is collected twice a day and not necessarily analyzed in real time."

"Maybe we could move enough that the scientists on the other end would take a look at the satellite images, and we could write SOS in some other physical way that can be spotted from the air?" Haley didn't know if the scientists would be looking, but she knew Alex Parker and Dermot Gray would be.

"That is a *great* idea." Quentin's voice was warm with approval.

She felt like a goddamn rocket scientist.

"I don't like the thought of going back," Darby admitted.

"We can conceal the boats and hide ourselves from passersby. Wait for the cavalry to arrive."

"How will we know who the cavalry are?" Darby asked, clearly not onboard with the idea.

"We wait until we're sure," Quentin assured her.

Haley knew the US would be pulling out all the stops to find a federal agent who'd been kidnapped—assuming they knew he had been kidnapped. They might assume he was dead with all the other conference delegates. Her too. She didn't say that in front of Darby. Darby needed all the optimism Haley could muster.

"Is there a supply of fresh water on the island?" Quentin asked.

"Yes. There's a natural spring. I even left some MRE packs in a cooler that I doubt they would have found." She looked around anxiously. "I'm scared," she admitted.

"We're going to be real smart about this, Darby. We're going to make a plan and wait for the authorities to come get us. If you can think of a better idea, then let's hear it, otherwise, we head there so we can get off the water before daylight."

After a long moment, Darby nodded reluctantly. "I can't think of a better plan. And I do know the island. If we get there, we might just have a chance—"

The engine chose that moment to splutter and die.

QUENTIN SCANNED THE inky surface of the sea, searching for obstacles as he motored steadily north, northwest. They'd clambered into the second inflatable and ditched the first one to decrease drag and hopefully maximize fuel efficiency, taking anything with them that was even vaguely useful.

They'd found flares and a compass but no radio. The flares might prove handy but not until they knew exactly who was out here and who might respond to their cry for help.

Darby had fallen into an exhausted heap against Haley, both of them slumped in the bottom of the boat out of the wind. Haley's blonde hair caught in the breeze.

She was still the center of attention—his attention, anyway. He tried not to think about that. Despite everything she'd snuck under his guard.

Circumstances.

She wasn't for him. He was a government grunt who moved around at the FBI's whim. She was a wealthy CEO who'd survived a difficult past. He pressed his lips together, wondering why he was even thinking about their non-existent relationship—non-existent in the real world at least. Out here they were reliant on one another for support and survival. Back home she wouldn't even know he existed—and not just because all he ever did was work or sleep.

None of that mattered. All that mattered was getting these women to safety and then going back to attempt to rescue the Alexanders. The US wouldn't let these assholes get away with the wholesale slaughter of its citizens, and he had no doubt the terrorists would use their American captives as a shield. But he could help. It was his expertise—although negotiating with sociopaths was always a challenge.

He wasn't sure if returning to the location of Darby's abduction was a smart idea. He figured it was better than the wish and prayer and the wide-open seas that was their other choice. It was a known quantity. A risk, but a calculated one.

The sky was starting to lighten to the eastern horizon, which made him nervous. He wanted to be off the water by the time dawn came.

A sea bird swooped alongside him, startling him, and his heart gave a bang.

To the west, he caught sight of a vertical line of intense orange. Lava. He turned the rudder so they headed in that direction.

"Darby," he called even though he didn't really want to disturb her. But better that than to end up back on the island from which they'd recently escaped.

She came awake with a start, terror in her eyes for that split second before she realized where she was and who she was with.

Quentin nodded at the lava flow. "Is that your island?"

She craned her neck over the side of the boat to see. Then she nodded, expression pensive. "Pulau Gunung Rebi. Head around to the west from the north side. There's a small beach we can land on."

Quentin narrowed his gaze at the orange glow. "It isn't about to blow, is it?"

"Erupt, you mean?" Darby's eyes gleamed for the first time since they'd met. He was surprised she wasn't catatonic from the brutality of her experience, but he suspected she'd blocked a lot of it out. For now. Or maybe she was just as resilient as hell.

Survival had many forms.

"Not according to the measurements as of when I left." The glow in her eyes diminished. "But a lot can happen in five days, even for volcanoes."

Her words made his throat go tight, because now she was clearly thinking about her own experiences.

"I'm sorry you were hurt. I promise the US authorities will pursue these men—"

"Will everyone have to know?" she interrupted sharply.

Quentin stared at her, assessing. "I have to report what I saw."

"Why? It wasn't you who was raped."

The harshness of the words took them both aback, as did the bitterness in her tone. But what was worse than being violated?

The whole world knowing you'd been violated.

He wanted the kidnappers punished, but if that caused Darby more pain… He paused, trying to remember the things that had made him a good negotiator. Trying to remember the behavioral change stairway model that helped him influence people's actions—active listening, empathy, rapport, influence, behavioral change.

But maybe he had no right to try to influence this woman. Maybe he should let her make her own decisions.

"I can make my report such that it doesn't lay out any graphic details, but investigators will ask, and you shouldn't lie to them. Lie to them about one thing, and it will undermine anything else you say."

Her mouth tightened.

"You'll need medical treatment. You'll need counseling."

"I could be pregnant. Or have some terrible venereal disease." She glared at him. "I didn't get a contraceptive injection before I left and now, I might be pregnant." She looked away, her chin thrust out in anger.

The anguish of Darby's words hit Quentin unexpectedly.

He was used to dealing with people in crisis, but her vulnerability drew out his protective instincts. "I'll make sure you receive the medical treatment you need, Darby. Whatever that is. For however long you need it. I will make your care my priority and a priority for the team in the Crisis Negotiation Unit. There are others in the FBI who can help. We have victim advocates. We have medical practitioners. We can help you through this ordeal. I promise you."

Her lips wobbled as she looked at him. She finally nodded, accepting him at his word.

She switched to lecture mode. It was easier on both of them. "The lava has been flowing intermittently for about five years now, and the whole region has definitely been more active recently with Krakatoa and all the excitement over that. But this particular volcano has been fairly stable, and I doubt that's changed. I will check the readings on the tiltometer to make sure."

Quentin could live without the excitement of witnessing a volcanic eruption in person, especially from this sort of distance. He let her talk.

"The Japanese held prisoners here during the Second World War. Mainly Dutch ruling class." She roped her hair nervously between her fingers. "There's a graveyard where they buried the dead and the remnants of some of the old guard towers, but it wasn't used for long and they moved the prisoners to some of the main camps on Java after some seismic activity in early 1943."

The harm human beings did to one another never failed to depress him. That civilizations did not learn the lessons of history was equally disturbing.

The sun was creeping up the horizon, and Quentin wanted

to do a little reconnoiter of the place before they committed to this plan. Even as the thought entered his head, the outboard started to splutter as it ran out of fuel.

Dammit.

He squeezed as much juice out of it as he could, and then when it finally died, he came forward, grabbing the oars. Darby passed him the water bottle, and he took a sip before setting off.

The currents were strong, but the wind was working in his favor. After a while, the muscles in his shoulders burned, but he ignored the discomfort.

He rowed until he got a glimpse of the beach Darby had mentioned. They both scanned the area intently. Haley was still fast asleep. She must be exhausted.

"What do you think?" he asked the young woman.

"I don't see any signs of anyone else being here."

"Do we risk it? Or do we keep rowing until we find a boat to pick us up?"

He wanted to give her the choice, so she could start taking control of her life again. He didn't know what he'd do if she decided to stay at sea. They could easily die within a couple of days if they didn't find water or rescue.

Darby's green eyes widened. "A random boat?" It was light enough now to see her visibly shudder. She was a pretty woman with bright red hair and eyes that held a world of pain. "No, I don't want to risk that. I know every nook and cranny on this island. They won't catch me unaware again. They won't catch any of us unaware."

Good.

"And the sooner we start moving your GPS units, the sooner help will arrive." Quentin maneuvered the RIB awkwardly. It had been a long time since he'd rowed anything, let alone something this size. Darby eased beside him on the bench seat, taking one of the oars from him.

"I can help," she said.

Quentin didn't say anything. It was important for her to reclaim her independence and autonomy. It would aid her recovery. And he appreciated the help.

It didn't take the two of them long to row to shore, even though Darby was shaking with exertion by the time they got there. She was so skinny he doubted she'd eaten much since her capture. Not even a few fried crickets.

When they hit the sandy bottom, he jumped over the side and grabbed the rope, hauling the boat a little farther in.

The island rose up from the beach in a wide grassy plain. Forest flanked the lower edges of the island, which was maybe three miles across, green and lush.

"I'm surprised this place isn't inhabited. It has fresh water, and there looks like some fertile farmland."

"The locals think it's cursed." Darby grimaced. "They might be right."

Quentin didn't know what to say to that. He pointed to the margin between sea and sand. "Let's take the boat closer to those trees before we haul it out. Then we can drag it into the forest or cover it with leaves to hide it from view."

"Without leaving big drag marks up the beach and giving away the fact we're here." Darby gave him a look of approval, which made him smile considering their relative positions in life. She was obviously confident and intelligent, or she'd never have undertaken this sort of solo adventure.

He hoped she didn't lose that but possibly added a layer of security. But that was on the college and her supervisor, not her.

He glanced at Haley, whose eyes were starting to blink awake. Something inside his chest gave a little jolt when she smiled at him. He got that feeling whenever he looked at her.

Darby surprised him by jumping over the side of the boat and into the surf. When she disappeared beneath the surface, he froze and took a step forward. Then she reappeared, washing herself using seawater. He could only imagine how desperately she wanted to be clean.

Haley touched his hand. "Let's give her some space. I'll help you with the boat. She'll be okay."

Haley's lips were dry and cracked, eyes puffy and tired, dark circles beneath them, but she was still just as stunning as the woman who'd held his attention in the bar a few short days ago. A woman he'd made love to.

He wished things had gone differently after that. Wished they'd had the normal sort of interaction where he texted her and asked her out on a proper date. That would have been fun. As opposed to being on the run from people who would slice them to pieces if they caught them again.

He managed to drag his gaze away. Reminded himself they weren't home free yet. Not by a long way. He needed to concentrate. To protect them, to keep them both safe.

Don't get distracted, Savage. Stay in the *now*.

Together they dragged the heavy rubber dinghy over the pebbles and into the bushes. He used his stolen knife to cut branches from nearby bushes, covering the metal of the engine and gleam of the sides.

"I haven't thanked you properly," Haley said after they were done and stood admiring their handiwork. Her hands were on her hips, and she was wearing his gym kit, no longer whispering for fear of being overheard. For the first time in days, they could talk normally. "You've saved my life so often, I don't know what I'd have done without you." She forced a smile, but her eyes held a sheen they both pretended wasn't there.

Haley Cramer had already broken down once in front of him. He doubted she'd want to do it again. He took her hand in his and rubbed the cold skin of the back of her hand, bringing it to his lips without thinking. "I couldn't have done it without you."

"Yes, you could," she argued.

"We did it together, Haley. Every step." He didn't want to admit that he cared about her in a way he hadn't cared about anyone in years. Even knowing either of them could die at any moment, he'd allowed himself to get involved. He simply hadn't had a choice.

He went to let go of her hand, but she didn't let him.

"You're a good man, Quentin Savage." She looked at him, and what he saw in her eyes made him wish for so many things. "I'm glad it was your bedroom I wandered into."

That comment niggled just a little. Was that the only reason she'd had sex with him? Because he'd been there? Because he'd given her a safe space? Was he a pity fuck?

There'd been attraction in the bar, but so what? He frowned because he didn't know, and he was irritated it bothered him.

"Do you think Cecil Wenck was warned about the attack? Do you think he left for that reason?" she asked.

Quentin pushed thoughts about the whys of them hooking up aside. "Until we know whether he survived or not, there's no use speculating." His voice came out a little firmer than he intended. The fact was authorities might not even be looking for them yet. They might assume he and Haley were both dead. "Let's get moving."

Together, they waded through the surf back to Darby, who looked better. Her wet hair was darker now and plastered to her skull. The ragged material she wore clung to her body. He didn't even know what it had been. A sack? A stitched together blanket? He averted his gaze, not wanting her to be uncomfortable with a man seeing the outline of her body.

"Let's avoid walking in the sand and making tracks. We'll go up through the woods. That way, if anyone does a quick scan of the beach, they won't see fresh footprints."

"Definitely smart," Haley said.

Hell. Praise from her made him want to puff out his chest like a rooster. If his team could see him now, they'd be laughing their asses off. He rolled his eyes at himself.

"Can you take us to the stream to collect water, and then we'll see what supplies you have left?" Quentin asked.

He was starving, but Darby hadn't eaten in *days*. She needed to keep her strength up as part of her recovery.

"Then we'll get to work on the GPS stations." Darby nodded emphatically.

"Let's do this." Haley held up her hand to high-five them both. He slapped her hand, enjoying the fresh sparkle in her eyes after everything they'd endured.

Darby high-fived Haley and then turned to him. She hesitated briefly and then smacked his open palm.

He held her gaze, and some of the horror of what she'd been through leached into those mossy eyes. The raw anguish he saw there made his teeth clench. Even so, a small smile teased the corner of her lips.

"Don't let the bastards get you down," Haley murmured quietly.

Darby nodded, then stared at the waves breaking around her ankles for a long inhale. Then she looked up. "Let's go screw up the USGS data and see if anyone is paying attention. I, for one, want my life back."

CHAPTER SEVENTEEN

THE PHONE RANG on the bedside table, and Eban jerked awake. He'd fallen asleep fully clothed with the TV jabbering in the background. Jet lag, combined with long working hours, meant he'd passed out as soon as he'd got to his room at some point in the early hours of the morning.

Dammit.

Groggy, he grabbed his cell, cursing the charging cord that knocked his notebook off the table. He detached the cable. "Yeah?"

It was the legal attaché, Reid Armstrong. Eban had met the guy last time he was on rotation out here. "Evidence Response Team found what was left of Quentin Savage's creds in the ruins of the hotel."

The words were like individual punches to the face. A quick one-two followed by a giant uppercut. Eban closed his eyes, wanting to deny what the evidence and eye-witness accounts were telling him. But until he knew for sure, until they identified Quentin's body, he wasn't giving up hope.

Armstrong cleared his throat as if uncomfortable with his own emotion. "I managed to get a meeting with Foreign Minister Ini Kanawela's assistant first thing this morning."

What time was it? Eban glanced at the time on the hotel clock and tried to wrap his brain around what the numbers seven one five actually meant. He thought it was probably morning but wasn't one hundred percent certain.

"What did he say?" Eban sounded like he'd swallowed razorblades.

They'd all been working non-stop trying to figure out who these terrorists were, where they were. Bodies had been transported to a makeshift morgue at the outskirts of a military base on Java. Portable laboratories were being used to run DNA from each skeleton's molar. No one had taken responsibility.

"*She* says the foreign minister left immediately after Quentin's keynote, because he had an important meeting to attend the next day in Manila. A meeting that had been scheduled for weeks."

She? Eban wondered if Reid was sleeping with her because seven fifteen...AM, apparently...was a hell of an early time to have already finished a meeting.

"So you're telling me the minister didn't receive a last-minute tip off telling him the bad guys were on their way to kill everyone in their path and to clear out. Bummer." That would have been too easy, and Eban could have beat the shit out of the guy to find out exactly who had warned him and who the hell had massacred all those people.

And that was why Eban wasn't the Legal Attaché. Armstrong was a hell of a lot more diplomatic than this Montana homeboy.

"It raises an interesting point," Armstrong agreed. "Did the terrorists know that the minister had departed, which left the conference with zero security, or was it chance they arrived at exactly that moment?"

Eban didn't believe in that degree of chance. "My money is

on the terrorists knowing exactly what was going on inside that building. Maybe someone contacted them as soon as the coast was clear, or they had a solid read on the schedule. I have an FBI consultant called Alex Parker looking at cell tower information. Let me check my email. See if he came up with anything."

"You know he was a spook, right?"

"What? Who? Parker?" Eban hadn't known, but rumors flew around the Bureau the same way gossip spread in high school. "I don't care if he was a cold-blooded assassin as long as he delivers what he said he'd deliver." Eban opened his laptop and watched his email load. His eyes ran down the list of messages until it hit the first one from Parker.

It was a spreadsheet.

"He sent me all the cell phone numbers that pinged off that tower and matched them with the owners' details. Shit." He knuckled the sleep out of his eyes. "There are a lot of numbers here."

Armstrong was silent on the other end of the line.

Most of these people were dead.

Parker had highlighted Quentin's and Haley Cramer's cell numbers. They'd both made calls after midnight—Cramer to Alex Parker and Quentin to SIOC. Interestingly, no one else inside the hotel had called anyone.

Eban quickly scanned the rest of the message. "Parker says it looks like someone probably used a signal jammer inside the hotel so no one could call for help."

"That's a pretty sophisticated setup for a bunch of bum-fuck bandits," Armstrong muttered.

Damn straight it was. "What are the Indonesians doing to track these people down?" Eban didn't have a lot of confidence in the local authorities.

"They've made a bunch of arrests, but who knows if they're scooping up the right people."

"Not good enough." Eban's skin itched with impatience. He was so angry and frustrated. He knew that wasn't how people got results, but he couldn't negotiate with anyone unless someone made contact, and no one was going to make contact if Quentin Savage and Haley Cramer were dead.

He kept pushing the thought out of his head, because he didn't want to believe it, but what if it was true and he was being an intransigent fool?

"The government here is constantly trying to crack down on violent extremists that adversely affect tourism and destabilize the region. But there are some hardliners in parliament who welcome the disruption, as they want the country to adopt a stricter form of Sharia law."

Eban wondered if the assistant was Armstrong's main source of information.

"Interestingly, one of the hardliners is the interior minister who made searing statements after the attack, criticizing the foreign minister for helping organize the conference on Indonesian soil. He's is not particularly friendly to the West." Armstrong grunted. "But the Prime Minister has mobilized large swathes of the Army to beat the bushes." Armstrong paused. "I can't help wondering if it wasn't ex-military who carried it out. They were certainly well-armed, and it was a well-planned operation," Armstrong spoke quietly, as if worried someone might overhear. "They don't even need to be *Indonesian* military."

They just needed to know how to kill effectively and disappear into the dense vegetation of Southeast Asia.

"Hurek?"

"Maybe. People here don't want to talk about him."

Darmawan Hurek was a former major in the Indonesian army and a suspect in the Alexander kidnapping case. They had zero proof the guy was even alive, let alone running kidnap or terrorist missions. Just the word of a murderer who was executed before the FBI could question him.

Still, it was a potential lead to follow when nothing else was popping.

Eban's stomach growled, and he realized he was starving. He hadn't eaten much except a rice bowl they'd handed out to personnel yesterday afternoon at the ruins of the hotel. No one had felt much like eating.

"You heard any updates on Darby O'Roarke?" Eban asked. No group had admitted to taking Darby yet. If she had been kidnapped for ransom, the kidnappers usually waited a week or so before contacting the family. Try to gauge what she was worth from the media frenzy her disappearance provoked. It was part of the reason the FBI tried to keep kidnappings out of the headlines. Tried to deal with them quietly without fanfare. Fanfare raised the price, and the families were already being screwed for every penny they had.

"If someone else took the O'Roarke girl, they might not want to draw any attention to themselves when the whole country is riled up against terrorists," Armstrong suggested.

That was true. Which might be bad news for Darby. Easy enough to slice a throat and leave someone dead in the middle of the jungle where she'd never be found.

Another email message pinged in from Alex Parker.

"According to Parker," Eban told the legat, "thirty-eight of the two hundred and four cell phones that were pinging off the hotel's tower during the conference are still active today."

"So thirty-eight people managed to avoid being slaughtered by the terrorists?" asked Armstrong.

"A lot of them are staff who weren't on duty that night, or guests who'd already left the hotel. Parker is compiling a list of names and last known locations for those cell phones so we can arrange to have the users questioned."

"Maybe one of them will have seen or heard something or, better yet, *be* one of the asshole terrorists who failed to turn off his cell during the raid and the ride home."

"That would be great," Eban agreed. He checked another email, one from a forensic scientist in Java. He pumped his fist in excitement. "*Yes.* The blood on the beach belonged to Quentin Savage. They compared it to a profile of one of his brothers they had on file as an active duty soldier."

Eban paced the room, trying to see how the events could have played out from the evidence left behind. The information in the phone calls back to D.C. The two terrorists with their necks broken. The eyewitness accounts of the fire. The cell phones on the beach…

"You can't actually believe he's alive?" Armstrong's tone held disbelief.

"We didn't find their bodies on the beach, and what are the chances Savage and Cramer both accidentally lost their phones? The Glock too—no way would Quentin leave behind that weapon unless he was forced to." The blood confirmed that for Eban. Someone had used the pistol to hit Quentin. "If they're dead, why take their bodies?" Ballistics had shipped the pistol back to Quantico along with about a thousand bullet jackets and used ammo. "Somehow they got out of the hotel before the roof caved in, but the bad guys found them and took them hostage."

"*Why*? Why take them when they killed everyone else?"

"I don't know," Eban admitted. More bodies had been found in the woods but not Quentin or this Cramer woman.

"Why haven't we heard any online chatter from the bad guys bragging they have an FBI agent?"

"I don't know that either," Eban snapped. "Maybe they wanted to double-check their safeguards, make sure they didn't screw up on the raid before they risked bringing the wrath of the US down on their heads? If he's alive, we'll hear something soon."

"I'll pay the damn ransom myself if you're right," Armstrong muttered.

"Me, too," Eban agreed. "If they call with a monetary demand, we need to change tactics for this one. No haggling. We need proof of life, and then we agree to pay whatever they want and get information for a drop."

"You don't really think they'll ransom him, do you?"

Eban raked a hand over his scalp. "Probably not." He firmed his voice. He was a professional and needed to detach from the fact they were talking about a friend. "A lot depends on their motivation. Money? Cementing their reputation as badasses? Having leverage over the US? If it's the former or the latter, they should keep him alive, especially if we tell them we'll pay big bucks to get him back."

"And if it's anything else he's as good as dead," Armstrong finished for him.

"Unless we find him first," Eban said firmly. *Assuming Quentin is alive.* Big assumption, but one Eban was hoping for regardless. Another email hit his inbox with a ding. "Hold on." It was from Charlotte Blood, who was now holding the fort back in Quantico.

The FBI had received a ransom demand ten minutes ago, along with photographs which suggested Savage and Cramer had survived the terrorist attack.

"We just received a ransom demand." Eban raised his face to the ceiling. He'd known it. He'd damned well known it. After inhaling a calming breath, he read the rest of the email.

The bad news was, the terrorists wanted twenty million US dollars' worth of bitcoin *each* for Quentin Savage and Haley Cramer, and they wanted it by eight PM that day. If the FBI failed to deliver the money, they were going to start chopping them up and mailing them back to Quantico one piece at a time.

CHAPTER EIGHTEEN

TRUDGING UP THE path behind Quentin, Haley found herself admiring the shape of his backside and muscular thighs outlined by the black pants he wore. It shocked her a little, that after everything she'd recently experienced, she could still feel lust. But she'd decided a long time ago that she wouldn't let the monsters steal her sexuality. Her brain shied away from some of the things that *had* been stolen.

She believed in sex between consenting adults—good, healthy, mutually pleasurable sex. Sex for sex's sake. Sex for that kick of excitement. Sex for the fleeting ecstasy of orgasm as addictive as any other high known to man, or woman. From the way her eyes gobbled him up and her pulse quickened, her body had just remembered that Quentin was damned good at it too.

The power of basic pleasures should never be underrated. And her freedom to choose a partner—male, female, or someone in between—was something she'd guarded fiercely all these years.

She looked around as some sort of sea bird squawked high in the sky. The view was spectacular—almost as nice as her place in the Caribbean which, thankfully, lacked a volcano.

She felt refreshed. They'd washed in the sea, the astringent seawater good for the cuts and grazes they'd accumulated.

They'd washed again in the freshwater of the stream. Then they'd eaten some MREs, and drunk about a gallon of water each. Thankfully, the terrorists hadn't found Darby's main cache of supplies, which she'd placed in coolers in a small wooded glade.

They'd passed her tent, but Darby had avoided going inside. Haley knew why. It was no longer a refuge. She'd felt the same way about her bedroom as a teen, although for a time, she'd had to sleep there anyway, until she'd finally worked up the courage to run away.

She bent down to adjust the wet socks that rubbed on the heel of her stolen boots. Irritating but relatively minor. She'd dry them out later. She still wore Quentin's gym clothes and these damn boots. Darby's clothes were too small for her, the girl was petite and fine-boned. They'd all slathered on sunscreen Darby had packed in her supplies so at least their skin wouldn't roast in the midday sun.

Who knew how long it would take to build their signal, but Haley was almost looking forward to it. Freedom was a heady feeling, and she wasn't afraid of hard work.

Darby walked twenty paces ahead of them, seemingly indomitable, striding up the hill wearing hiking boots, a clean pair of khaki shorts and a green canvas shirt with a floppy hat stuffed on top of her curls. She was beautiful and so much tougher than Haley would have been had their situations been reversed.

Determination had the girl's shoulders pulled back, her jaw tilted to the angle of a survivor. Bruises of all different colors covered her exposed skin, suggesting the bastards had beaten her at regular intervals during her captivity. The idea of this defenseless young woman being abused sickened Haley and made her own experience at the hands of her father's younger brother pale into insignificance.

Her feet stopped moving, and she found herself swallowing repeatedly, suddenly fighting emotion. That experience had shaped her whole life, but Darby hadn't even known if she would live or die—or how long she'd have to endure the nightmare…

Pathetic. Haley was completely pathetic. She'd spent years running from her past. Years bitterly using it as an excuse never to get close to a man, because she wouldn't allow anyone to control her that way again.

She clawed for her self-control. God, she couldn't lose it again.

Quentin turned back, as if somehow sensing her distress. Darby carried on hiking up the hill away from them, out of earshot.

He came back and put a hand on her shoulder. The contact felt good—warm and familiar, but brand-new and exciting all at the same time. "You okay?"

Of course, is what she'd normally say with some sort of forced sexy laugh.

Aside from her family, Haley hadn't told anyone except her therapist about being raped. Not even Alex or Dermot. Certainly not any of her former lovers. She hadn't wanted to expose that fault line. It was her secret, her pain. But Quentin already knew, because she'd blurted it out when she'd thought they were going to die.

Her throat hurt from trying to keep the shame buried deep inside. "I was thinking about my experience with sexual assault and how it pales compared to what Darby has endured," she admitted, not knowing how to explain all the emotions whirling inside her.

He shocked her by hauling her against his chest and squeezing her so hard her ribs hurt.

God, it felt good.

He rested his chin on the top of her head, an action that pierced her heart. "Trauma is trauma, Haley, no matter the degree." He leaned back and held her gaze. "I am sorry you went through that."

"It was a long time ago. I'm over it, really, and I don't want to even think about my past experiences when Darby's are so fresh."

Those dark, sober eyes of his held hers, and she couldn't look away.

"One day, if you need to talk about it, I'm here for you. I'm a very good listener." He smiled, and her knees wobbled for one feeble moment. "But Darby might welcome you talking about what happened to you—knowing that she isn't alone even if both experiences are unique. Don't ask her for specifics about what happened to her, but perhaps tell her what happened to you—if you can bear to talk about it. I can make myself scarce."

Words choked in her throat. The problem was, she didn't know how to talk about it. It was too difficult. Too humiliating.

Whatever he saw in her expression had his gaze turning somber. "It's okay if you don't want to, Haley. Whatever you choose to do is perfectly fine."

And with that, he took her hand and kissed it the way he had several times since they'd been taken captive, and her heart gave another little quiver.

"Come on. Let's catch up before she decides to come back

and herd us along."

Haley laughed, and they started up the path together still holding hands. She hated that she loved it. Loved the comfort and reassurance of his touch. She hated that she wanted more of it. A lot more. That was not who she was under normal circumstances.

When they were rescued, if they were rescued, she could pursue her usual independence and equilibrium. She and Quentin might even enjoy a short celebratory fling and then go back to being who they really were. The idea made her fingers clench anxiously around his hand.

They crested the ridge, careful to keep low on the horizon in case someone somewhere had eyes on the skyline. They'd be tiny, but no one wanted to risk it.

Something had brought the terrorists here when they'd grabbed Darby the first time.

Haley was sweating after another ten minutes of hiking steadily uphill over ever steeper ground then up barren volcanic rock.

Darby didn't slow. She was like a dynamo of energy. You'd never guess she'd been assaulted unless you looked at the marks or caught the trauma in her gaze.

Victims did that.

They blocked it out and carried on as normal, and then people said they never noticed a change in their behavior. Found it hard to believe the truth when it finally emerged.

Survival mechanisms didn't always make sense unless you'd been through that kind of ordeal yourself.

Quentin kept hold of Haley's hand, helping her along when the air grew thinner, and her body started to shake with fatigue. Darby eyed the connection between her and Quentin with an assessing glance. Haley suspected that the idea of any relationship, even friendship, might be hard for her for a while.

Not that Haley and Quentin were in a relationship, at least not a conventional one. Maybe one based on mutual survival, which was a little too close to need in Haley's estimation. She let go of his hand and took a drink of water. He took a drink too, and they both scanned the view.

Small islands dotted the sea in the distance. Not close, but close enough to make their kidnappers still present a threat. No boats were in sight. She didn't know if that was a good thing or not.

After a short rest, they trudged over the next rise. Darby reached a bright yellow tripod held in place with some large rocks. A white disk sat on top.

When Haley and Quentin caught up, Darby explained it to them. "We call it a benchmark." She gestured at the concrete cylinder planted in the ground beneath the white disk. "Geophysicists intermittently come back and take measurements at fixed reference points marked by concrete blocks, so we can assess changes over time. We also have permanent, fixed GPS stations, but this will be easier to move, along with the portable solar panel."

"What's that over there?" Quentin pointed to some sort of concrete structure.

"It measures the angle of tilt. As a volcano grows, we see an increase in the tilt, and that change in tilt speeds up the closer we get to an eruption." She walked over to it and grinned. "Don't worry, there hasn't been a dramatic shift since..." Her voice faltered. "Since I was taken."

Haley changed the subject, trying to skate over memories

Darby would never outrun. "What exactly are you studying?"

Darby blinked. "My dissertation was supposed to assess any deformation in the geology of this volcano in the wake of Krakatoa's recent increased activity. Deformation is usually caused by magma building beneath the surface. We measure it by doing a campaign GPS network on the volcano's surface using these benchmarks."

Darby looked off into the distance. Her hands started shaking as she began spooling the wire that led from the solar panel to the battery. "I have no idea if I'll be able to finish the work here or if I even want to, after…"

She couldn't finish her sentence.

"You don't have to make any decisions right now, Darby," Quentin said softly.

The woman drew in a stuttering breath. "My supervisor is one of those professors who doesn't believe in excuses—"

"What happened to you is not an *excuse.*" Quentin's tone was firm. "It wasn't a failure on *your* part that led to the attack. If anything, it was a failure on the university's part not to provide adequate protection for one of its students, and I will be talking to them about it, trust me."

"But what if I don't want them to know?" Darby's voice rose, and her expression grew stricken. "How can I look my supervisor or fellow students in the eye if they know what happened—"

"It doesn't change who you are," Quentin said quietly.

But he didn't understand. It did change you. It assaulted every truth you thought you knew about yourself.

Even so, Haley was shocked Darby would consider hiding what had happened to her. It was such a violent attack. Except…wasn't that what she'd done? When her father had refused to believe her over his brother, hadn't she buried it so deep no one would ever find it unless she allowed them to?

"You don't need to make any decisions yet," Haley assured her. "All we need to do right now is figure out how to be rescued by the good guys."

Darby's eyes went huge, and she nodded, the fear of their captors returning ten-fold. Haley wanted to say something to ease her anxiety, but nothing came. What if the bad guys did track them down? What if the terrorists found them? They were not out of danger yet. They were trapped on this island until they were rescued—and figuring out who the good guys were could be a problem.

Darby folded the legs of the tripod so it formed one long unit, but before she could shoulder it, Quentin took it from her.

"Is there another one of these not too far from here?" he asked.

"Yes." She tipped her chin to the west. "Over the ridge. Not far."

"Do you think two GPS units will be enough to get someone's attention?" he asked.

Darby shrugged. "I don't know. They might all be watching more active volcanoes, like the one on the island where we were kept." Her voice tripped.

"Why aren't there volcanologists there?" Quentin asked, moving off in the direction Darby had indicated.

Haley brought up the rear.

"It only recently became active. I'm sure teams will be arriving there soon to set up monitoring stations."

"Where from?" asked Quentin.

"The States usually deploys a team."

"Which means presumably the bad guys will need to find somewhere else to set up camp," Haley said.

"Which is probably why they came here in the first place," Quentin added. "Looking for somewhere to relocate."

"Oh, god." Darby gripped her throat. "They'll come back."

Haley exchanged a look with Quentin. *Shit.*

"They might," Quentin agreed cautiously. "Or they might head to one of the thousands of other uninhabited islands around here that isn't a volcano. So, the sooner we get these signals transmitting with our cry for help the better, because I don't know about you guys, but I want to catch those bastards and make them pay for everything they've done."

Darby started hurrying to the next station, and Haley's heart broke for her again. Along with it came fear for herself and Quentin. If the terrorists did catch them again, she'd suffer the same fate Darby had endured, and Quentin would be killed.

The realization that they still weren't safe had her stomach cramping with dread, so she hurried to catch up with the others so they could figure out a way off this goddamned volcano.

QUENTIN WOULD BE lying if he said he wasn't worried about the terrorists tracking them down to this island before he could secure their safety. He worked for the FBI. He was responsible for protecting American citizens. He had one pistol with a single magazine of ammo and a knife he wasn't afraid to use, but that wouldn't be enough against a small army of murderous thugs.

Having these two strong but vulnerable women in his company made his apprehension worse. The thought of anyone hurting them made him furious. They'd both been hurt too much already.

The three of them needed to use guile and brains to get to safety, not rely on violence or brute force.

He thought about Abbie and what she would have thought of him hiding out on an active volcano after escaping a terrorist camp. Of him having killed five men with his bare hands. She would have hated that. She'd been a soft and gentle soul who couldn't even swat a wasp.

The memories and loneliness of missing his late wife didn't cut quite as deep as they usually did. It was both a guilty relief and a terrifying prospect, because he knew why. Maybe it was the "almost dying" part that had gotten him to finally shake loose some of his emotional paralysis. Maybe it was the inexorable passage of time. Maybe it was the amazing sex with a stunning beauty. Or maybe it was simply allowing himself to care about another person as both a lover and a friend. They were usually one or the other. Although there was nothing usual about Haley.

Currently she was taking it in turns with Darby to carry the second tripod and flexible solar panel downhill to a location above the tree line that Darby thought would be a suitable place to build their SOS signal. It was hidden from view on land and from the water. If the terrorists flew directly over it, they were screwed, but they had to take that risk.

The heavy tripod was cutting into his shoulder, so he adjusted it slightly. Almost there.

"You move these things around on your own normally?" He didn't want to be sexist, but Darby was five-two tops and slight with it. He was over six-foot and fit, and he was feeling the burn in his muscles.

Darby slicked sweat from the side of her face onto the shoulder of her t-shirt. "The helicopter dropped the crates close to where each benchmark needed to be set up. I only had to move them twenty or thirty yards."

He flashed his brows in acknowledgement. She was tough. She'd need to be.

Finally, Darby stopped walking and helped Haley carefully lower the heavy unit to the ground and set it up on its feet. He surveyed the patch of ground and walked thirty paces away so the tripods would mark the two ends of the three letters.

"We have to make the SOS as large as possible so that it can be seen from space, and heavy enough it doesn't blow away if the breeze gets up." He put his hands on his hips. "How about Haley and I look for rocks while you set up the GPS?"

"Okay." Darby glanced around nervously.

They needed to instigate a watch system, but this came first. It was their only chance of rescue.

"We won't go far," he assured the girl.

She nodded sheepishly. "Sorry. I'm not normally such a scaredy-cat."

Haley opened her arms, and the two women embraced. "You don't have to apologize to us, Darby. Quentin and I know what you endured, and we are both so impressed with your strength and spirit." Haley laughed, but it was a half-sob. "Feel free to fall apart any time. I know I do."

Funny that he was the one who was supposed to be good with words, but she knew exactly what to say.

Haley gave Darby one last squeeze.

"Right." Haley sniffed. "Come on, Savage. We get to haul rocks."

One side of his lips lifted in a smirk. He liked the bossy side of her. The fact she was regaining her rather magnificent self-confidence after their shitty ordeal bolstered his own spirits.

They started building a pile of stones and scouring the adjacent area for anything they could find. Pity they didn't have some white paint.

As soon as Darby was done setting up the two GPS stations, she set to work on marking out the letters. First, she loosely created the outline so they knew how many gaps they'd need to fill. Having exhausted the rocks in the immediate vicinity, he and Haley headed over a small rise into what was probably a stream bed when it rained. Right now, it was dry.

Haley bent over to pick up a rock, and her legs looked a million times better in his gym shorts than his did. The phantom weight of them around his hips had blood diverting to his groin.

"Like what you see?" She'd caught him staring at her ass.

Rather than looking away, he told her the truth. "I'm thinking about what happened back at the hotel. Hoping it happens again some time when we're not running for our lives."

Her eyes widened, pupils dilating. "Oh."

He laughed. "Oh? That's all a guy gets for being honest?"

She blinked, and her sudden loss of composure had him panicking because, shit, maybe she wasn't ready for any mention of sex after living under the threat of violence. And maybe the two of them had been a never-to-be-repeated one-night stand. Perhaps he was the only one who thought the sex had been stupendous.

She laughed. "I thought I was going to have to work a lot harder to persuade you to do that again."

"Persuade me?" He mirrored her words, angling for more insight though he was mentally fist pumping.

"Persuade you to have sex with me. You don't think I could do it?"

She only had to breathe, and he was volunteering for duty. He let her come closer, her walk turning seductive, her eyes sparkling and her smile… like she knew every dirty fantasy he'd ever imagined and probably a few he'd never dreamed of.

When she got within touching distance, he cupped her face while she was still trying to turn this into a competition, because that's how she made it less personal, less about them making love and more about the power play of an explosive hookup.

That's how she usually operated. He knew it without her telling him. And he knew why.

She stood toe-to-toe with him, and he stared into those eyes of hers, blue planets in unknown solar systems. The lust was sparking for sure, but so was something else. Something timid and unsure that he didn't want to think about too deeply, because he knew it was reflected in his own. It was something she wouldn't want or know how to deal with. He didn't want to deal with it either, but he recognized it. He kissed her so neither of them had to think about anything except how the other tasted.

Her lips were soft and parted for him immediately. His arm went around her waist, and he pulled her to him so that she knew the effect she had on him even if they couldn't do anything about it any time soon.

He bent her back over his arm and swept his tongue into her mouth, tasting her, exploring her. Not in the same feral rush of a few nights ago, but savoring, coaxing. Nipping, soothing, murmuring as he drew her further and further into him, into this.

And she responded like magnesium to a flame, sizzling in his arms. She slid her tongue into his mouth, tangling it with his as she savored him. He purposefully kept her off balance. His free hand smoothed over the curve of her waist, over the rounded hips until he spanned his fingers across one globe of her ass, wishing he could do more than rough out the territory. They couldn't risk leaving Darby alone for long and needed to get this SOS signal constructed as soon as possible so the civilians could be rescued, and he could get back to helping bring these bastards to justice.

Slowly he raised his head and looked down at her slick, reddened lips.

"Somehow, I don't think I'd need much persuading," he said, grinning at her. "And when I get the chance, I'm going to get you naked for two days straight and make you come every chance I get."

Haley went to open her mouth to reply, but a piercing scream rent the air, and Quentin almost dropped her. Quickly he pulled her upright and then sprinted for the top of the rise.

When he got there, he saw Darby dancing around on the spot.

"What? What is it?" He was so fucking happy there wasn't an army of hostiles surrounding her, but his heart was pounding.

Dammit they needed to set a watch.

Darby looked up sheepishly. Sweeping her hands repeatedly over her arms and legs. “Spider.”

Haley raised her hand to her mouth and failed to hide a laugh. A grin tugged at his own lips.

Darby finally stopped hopping around and started to laugh, but after a few moments of hilarity, her face crumpled in sadness once more. Haley went and put her arms around the young woman, and Quentin went over and loosely hugged them both.

“We’re getting out of here,” he promised them both. One way or another, he was bringing these women home.

He looked up at the sky, wondering if the satellite that tracked these GPS signals had passed overhead yet. Wondered if, right now, someone somewhere was looking for him and Haley. Given the sheer scale of victims at the hotel and the raging inferno of flames that had engulfed it, they probably assumed they were dead like all the others.

But he wasn’t dead.

Ironically, he felt more alive than he had in years.

CHAPTER NINETEEN

"WHERE DID THE image originate?" Eban was in the legat's office in the US embassy in Jakarta. Legat Reid Armstrong sat next to him. Max Hawthorne, the other negotiator from CNU, paced behind them, wired after pulling another all-nighter at the scene of the hotel massacre. The scent of smoke lingered, despite the fact Hawthorne had showered down the hall a few minutes ago.

The photograph they'd received of Quentin had shown him looking tired and beaten, but essentially whole. The one of Haley Cramer revealed a beautiful woman who'd looked subdued and terrified—and no wonder.

Alex Parker was on a video-link cradling a sleeping newborn. "There's no identifying information in the metadata. Someone wiped it clean before sending it."

Which suggested a degree of sophistication that made Eban uneasy. These guys were pros.

"The email came from an anonymous account set up in Indonesia a few days ago," Alex continued. "No other messages to or from the account. IPS address of the computer where it was created was a busy internet cafe in Jakarta—no surveillance cameras. I checked. I think the most interesting thing is the fact they sent it to the same local detective who's been negotiating the release of the two Westerners abducted from the South China Sea. It kind of tips their hand despite their efforts to conceal their identities."

The FBI rarely dealt with the kidnappers directly in these kind of cases. The language barrier was one issue. Time was another. In this instance, they'd worked through a local police detective Hawthorne had been coaching. The detective had been doing a damn fine job, even though they hadn't made much forward progress.

"Any update on the other woman, Darby O'Roarke?" Alex asked.

The guy sure had gotten up to speed fast. Darby's abduction hadn't even hit the media channels yet.

Eban shook his head. "Nothing." He was more and more convinced she was dead.

Alex rocked the baby as it—*she,* if the pink sleep suit was any indication—started to stir. "What do we know about the Alexanders' kidnappers?"

Eban let Hawthorne take over as he'd been working the case most recently.

"Our main suspect is a guy named Darmawan Hurek." Hawthorne spelled it for the cyber security guy on the other side of the world. "A major in the Indonesian Army who went AWOL five years ago after getting caught stealing military equipment and selling it on the black market. A bunch of his men deserted with him."

Alex nodded, tapping keys with one hand. "Why do you think he's involved?"

"We didn't until about three weeks ago when a man was arrested for murder in northern Sumatra. He claimed he knew where the Alexanders were being held and that Hurek was behind the kidnappings."

"Did he give you proof when you questioned him?" asked Alex.

"Never got the opportunity. He was sentenced to death and executed immediately. By the time I arrived, he'd already been cremated." Hawthorne looked pissed.

They'd all been furious.

"Send me his name," Parker instructed. "Let's see if we can find out where he'd traveled or who he'd been communicating with in the months before he died. I'll get some of my team tracking other soldiers who deserted. Maybe we can triangulate some communication data."

It wasn't that long since the Indonesian government had been fighting against separatist groups in Aceh. Eban scratched his jaw, needing a shave but not caring. "Could the attack on the hotel have anything to do with the Muslim extremists who want the country to enforce stricter religious laws?"

Hawthorne paused in his pacing. "Finding tattoos on those dead terrorists in the woods would be unusual if that was the case. Many Muslims believe tattoos to be *haram*." Forbidden.

"The foreign minister who attended the conference is a known moderate." The legat got up and poured himself fresh coffee. "I would have thought that extremists would have attacked when he was there, rather than after he left if they were trying to promote a political agenda."

Eban had no clue.

"Well, whoever carried out the attack on the hotel definitely had some sort of military or militia training," Alex said. "They waited until virtually no security was on site. They shut down communications from the hotel so no one could call for help, then eliminated almost everyone there."

"Why take Quentin and Cramer and no one else?" Armstrong asked.

"It's often about money with these guys—even IS regularly released captives in exchange for cash. I suspect they took Quentin when they discovered he was FBI. Even if they couldn't ransom him, there are other groups who'd pay a lot of money to get their hands on someone from the Bureau. Haley was probably taken because she's beautiful and extremely wealthy." Alex's expression firmed, and he looked like he was struggling to swallow. The thought of his friend being taken captive had hit the guy hard. Eban knew exactly how he was feeling.

The FBI had run background checks on the woman and the company she and Alex Parker and another man owned. Everything came back shiny. But Eban was thinking the man on the other end of the video-link could alter any damn online thing he wanted if he was as good as his reputation suggested. Still, Haley Cramer was a multimillionaire who owned her own private island. She didn't need money, and their company didn't need this sort of attention.

Even though Quentin had requested a background check on the woman, it was possible that had been for personal reasons. FBI agents couldn't be too careful about who they hung out with.

Maybe they'd hooked up, or Quentin had wanted to. Which would have been good news as the guy had been hurting since he'd lost his wife five years ago.

Although—talk about bad timing or bad luck or both.

"Did you talk to the survivors?" Alex asked. The baby stirred again, and he adjusted her position against his chest.

"Tricia Rooks is in a coma. I spoke to Chris Baylor last night who apparently was in the 101st with Savage. They're friends. He says he saw the ceiling collapse on top of Quentin and Haley after they rescued him from the burning building, and is convinced they're dead. He was pretty cut up about it. Grant Gunn left Indonesia without me speaking to him. We'll track him down Stateside for an official statement. I had planned to go back to the hospital this morning, but then we received the ransom demand." He checked his watch. "Chris Baylor and Tricia Rooks were supposed to be on a private medivac chartered by Tricia's company, Raptor, heading back to the US right about now. We'll need agents on the ground to talk to them again as soon as they arrive. I want to know where they are at all times until we figure this out."

"What about Cecil Wenck?" Alex Parker's tone was mild, but Eban wasn't fooled.

"I've put in a request to the Australian authorities to interview him but no word yet as to whether or not he'll comply."

"There was a call from his room at around eleven PM," Alex told him. "He was at the airstrip and on his private jet by 11:30 PM."

"What about his cell phone activity?" Eban asked.

Alex rubbed his palm soothingly over the baby's back. "You'll need a warrant to access those records."

Eban held the man's gaze through the camera. There was no way Alex Parker would wait on a warrant, but equally no way he could admit that to a room of FBI agents.

"I'm sure if there's any suspicious activity we'll find out about it," Eban said with as much diplomacy as he could muster.

Alex tipped his chin. "I'm sure we will."

"Can we raise enough bitcoin for the ransom?" the legat asked the room in general.

"We can," Alex stated as if it were no problem. *Welcome to the private sector*. "We can even trace it."

Eban's brows went high. He'd heard it was possible but hadn't had that verified before now. Crooks thought they were invisible and untraceable. The fact they weren't made Eban bare his teeth in a grin.

"The US will not officially allow a ransom to be paid for one of its agents," the legat reminded them.

"They might if they believe it's fake money," Alex argued. "Also, maybe that's what the kidnappers are hoping for as an excuse to kill Quentin Savage. US policy. Then they can blame the Americans when they torture and kill him on YouTube."

Eban flinched. "Is it fake money?"

Alex Parker stared into the screen and avoided the question. "Before we pay, we need the kidnappers to prove Haley and Quentin are still alive. We need some sort of communication I can trace, which can be as simple as them opening an email."

"I'll craft a reply to try and draw them out in an exchange and buy some time." It wasn't unusual for kidnappers to start off behaving with violent aggression to frighten the family of their victims into action. It wasn't even unheard of for captors to kill hostages on deadline. But it was unusual for groups who actually wanted to claim their money.

The baby started fussing. Alex rocked backward and forward, but the crying grew louder. "Looks like I need to get this little one to her momma. Let me know immediately if the kidnappers get in touch. And send me the name of the guy they executed in Sumatra. I'll also see if I can track any of the calls the kidnappers made to your hostage negotiator in Jakarta in the past. Maybe they weren't as careful as they thought they were." He stood. "I'll be here if you need anything else…and, if you hear anything at all about Haley, *please* let me know, day or night. Even if it's bad news. I'd rather know."

Eban pressed his lips together and nodded. He felt the same way about Quentin. The sense of urgency, the need to do something, was escalating. They had mere hours until the first deadline.

Quentin was smart. He'd behave and make himself the perfect captive knowing these negotiations often took time. Eban grabbed himself a coffee while everyone got to work.

CHAPTER TWENTY

HALEY HANDED OUT food pouches for supper. Hers was pasta with a carbonara sauce with a side of M&Ms as a treat. She was starving after lugging all those rocks around. Their SOS looked pretty impressive by the time they'd finished and she knew Alex would be desperately searching for some sign she was alive. She would deal with the guilt of interfering with his new role as a father later, as soon as they were all home safe.

Please find us, Alex. She sent the wish into the air as close to a prayer as she got these days.

They'd decided to make camp in a small clump of trees farther up the mountain from Darby's original base. It gave them an excellent vantage point to watch the waters surrounding the island, except if someone approached from the north side, which was unlikely as it was composed of barren rock and steep-sided cliffs. The trees kept them concealed and protected them from the scorching tropical sun. They'd left Darby's tent in place in case her kidnappers came looking, but they'd retrieved her bedroll and sleeping bag, and the one small camp chair Darby had brought along to sit on. Haley still had the blanket she'd taken from the hut and had washed it in the sea and then rinsed it in the stream and left it to dry in the hot sun. It would come in useful tonight when the temperature dropped. Thankfully the bugs weren't so bad here due to the brisk sea breeze.

They'd also filled and ferried enough water containers up the hillside to see them through several days of needing to lay low should the terrorists appear.

Darby had packed a sudoku book for entertainment, and Haley spotted a sketchbook in one of the coolers they'd lugged up the hill earlier. All in all, they'd made the journey five times, but now their camp was well supplied, and they just needed to construct some sort of basic shelter in case it rained.

"I've only got one fork and one spoon," the young woman apologized, before handing Haley and Quentin the utensils.

They exchanged a look. Darby was holding it together, but it was only a matter of time until something snapped.

"You weren't exactly expecting visitors," Quentin said with a smile and then winced as if worried he'd said the wrong thing.

Darby forgave him with a smile.

"You have the fork first. I'll wait." Quentin handed it back to Darby who shook her head.

As a negotiator, he paid attention to the words spoken, Haley noticed, but he also seemed hyper vigilant about body language and tone of voice. She liked the fact he paid attention. It made the guy even sexier than he looked, and he was already in the hot zone.

She needed to remind herself not to go and fall for the guy. What they had could never be more than a fling. Anything more serious always threw her after a week or two. She couldn't stand being bossed around by anyone or having her decisions or movements questioned.

FBI agents seemed to be particularly assertive, which

might be fine while running for your life, but not so great while living it. Still, she liked him. Really liked him.

"Hang on a minute," Darby exclaimed, digging through the cooler with all the food. "Aha. I have a multitool with a fork thingy on it. I'll use that."

"Thingy" was so unscientific they all smiled. Finally, they could start eating.

"This is *so* delicious." Haley savored the linguini, which tasted way better than she'd expected from a packet—as good as any five-star restaurant back home.

"Mine too." Quentin was eating curry. Darby some sort of bacon and egg dish.

"I eat these packs when I'm hiking so I know they're good," Darby mumbled between bites.

It didn't take long for Haley to finish hers. She'd be embarrassed if the others weren't just as ravenous.

"Where are you from originally?" Quentin asked Darby.

"Alaska." Darby smiled. "I did my undergrad there and started a Ph.D. program last September. I always wanted to travel." She grimaced and looked away.

"Don't let what happened prevent you from pursuing your dreams, Darby," Haley said vehemently. The idea that being assaulted might stop this bright young woman from moving forward with her ambitions horrified Haley. "I'm not saying take crazy risks but with the right safeguards…" She trailed off because sometimes safeguards weren't enough. Sometimes the bad guys got to you anyway—which was why firms like hers existed.

She swallowed. "Look, I was raped when I was fourteen." A wave of ice rolled over her skin. "It was my father's younger brother, who happened to be living with us at the time after his wife kicked him out. He came to my room one night and said if I told anyone what he was doing, he'd tell them that I'd come on to him. He alternated that threat with threats against my life and my grandmother's, saying how easy it would be for her to trip and fall down the stairs. He kept telling me my father would never believe a filthy slut like me over the brother he adored. Turned out he was right."

Haley wasn't seeing the lush tropical island anymore, she was seeing the door of her bedroom ease open and a shadow loom over her in the darkness. He'd been drunk, or pretended to be that first time, as if that would somehow reduce his crimes.

She inhaled sharply, not knowing if this would help Darby or make things worse for everyone. Haley desperately wanted to help her. She didn't look at Quentin but knew he was watching intently. She didn't need anyone's pity, but she wanted Darby to know some people did get over being assaulted even though it wasn't easy and it wasn't simple. It was a process that could take years. "The assaults went on for over a year until one day I thought I was pregnant and finally worked up the courage to tell my mother what was happening." She snorted. "You can imagine how well that went."

"What happened?" asked Darby in a tiny voice.

"She didn't believe me. She told my father, and he confronted my uncle…who denied it. Said I must have been sleeping with some boy and wanted to cause him as much trouble as possible."

Resentment swept over Haley. The sense of hurt and injustice poured acid over badly healed wounds. She'd thought she was over this bullshit, but she'd never truly be over it until her uncle admitted his crimes. The problem with that was he'd been dead for over a decade after driving head-on into a garbage truck while three times over the legal alcohol limit.

She'd wanted to send the truck driver flowers but had decided that would reveal too much of her inner rage.

"I realized pretty quickly that my parents didn't believe me. I was scared what my father's brother would do to me if he caught me alone. I packed a bag one night and ran away to my grandmother's—my mother's mother. We hadn't been close until then, but I had no one else to turn to." Haley blinked at the rush of emotion that hit when she thought about that determined, old woman. "She took me in and believed me immediately. Made me an appointment at the clinic, but it turns out I hadn't been pregnant after all. The bastard had given me an STD. It went untreated for so long it spread to my fallopian tubes and I ended up…" she inhaled rapidly three times before she could finish. "I ended up infertile."

She met Quentin's gaze but couldn't read what he was thinking. Darby reached for Haley's hand.

"I'm so sorry that happened to you." Darby swallowed noisily.

How much fresher was the hell this woman had gone through? Haley covered Darby's hand with her other one as if she could cradle and protect Darby from all bad things.

"I'm terrified I might be pregnant. My father is pretty strict and if he found out, he'd make me keep it." Darby shook her head vigorously. "I don't want any reminders of what they did to me."

"I wouldn't want that either. You need to talk to a doctor and a therapist as soon as we get back," Haley told her. "Your father doesn't get to have a say in this. It is your decision."

Darby glanced at Quentin. "I know. But I'm scared to do it

on my own."

"I will make sure you get the help you need, Darby," Quentin said softly.

Haley leaned in closer to the other woman. "He's an FBI agent. He keeps his promises."

Darby cleared her throat. "What happened with your family, if you don't mind me asking?"

Haley raised up her face to the sky and laughed. "Actually, in the end there was some divine sort of justice. I mean, I didn't get to cut my uncle's dick off and feed it to him before he died, but he did come to a nasty end." The dreams of vengeance had been graphic and wonderful. "My grandmother let me live with her while I finished high school, and we bonded over chocolate cake and episodes of *Friends*." They couldn't have been closer if they'd been best friends. "She died when I was twenty-one, left me every cent of her fortune, which my father had assumed my mother would inherit. It left him a few million down from where he'd expected to be in retirement and he tried to sue me for it." Her smile felt sharp as a blade. "My grandmother had been explicit in her instructions and absolutely sound of mind. After Dad lost the court case, he divorced my mother." Haley watched clouds boiling on the horizon. They were overdue a storm given the time of year. "Mom and I reconciled our differences eventually, but I guess I've never really forgiven her for not supporting me."

"I would have believed you," Quentin stated.

She held his dark gaze and knew he was telling the truth. "Thank you."

"I'd have believed you too," Darby said quietly.

"Thank you." Haley shifted to look into the girl's green

eyes, seeing the shadows flickering there. "Don't let what happened destroy your dreams. Adapt them if need be. But don't let them beat you down. You are smart and beautiful and pure of heart."

"Ha." Darby wiped her eyes, and Haley realized there were tears on her cheeks too. Then the other woman raised her eyes to the skyline. "We're going to get rain within the hour."

Quentin got to his feet. "I'll build a shelter."

Haley grinned. "Very Bear Grylls."

"I have a machete in the cooler." Darby raised the blade from the plastic tub.

"I love a girl who's prepared. Hand it over. I want to impress Haley with my survival skills."

Haley took a sip of water. "It'll be more impressive if you take your shirt off while you're doing it." She wiggled her brows at Darby and leaned back on her elbows, enjoying the view as Quentin whipped off his shirt and flung it straight at her face. She caught it with a laugh, and her breath stopped at the same time.

Wowzers.

Her face went hot. It was the first time she'd seen him shirtless in the sunlight. He was hard and lean with well-defined muscles she wanted to lick. His dark hair flopped into his eyes as he grinned at her. The guy was smoking.

She let out a long slow whistle to prove she wasn't unnerved by his raw masculinity. Darby thankfully laughed at their horseplay.

"I always thought FBI agents were stuffed suits full of nothing but hot air, especially *negotiators.*"

"Exactly how many *negotiators* do you know?" Quentin held the machete in one hand and struck a pose, grinning like a pirate.

Her lips curved. "One."

Then he glanced at the sky and grew serious. "I think we're about to get soaked. If anyone wants to help before the clouds burst, that might be a good thing. I'm a little rusty in the shelter building arena."

Haley checked the horizon again and realized the gathering clouds were growing darker, the storm boiling toward them at a rapid pace.

"I have some string in the tent we could use." Darby glanced anxiously in the general direction of where she'd set up her first camp.

Quentin nodded. "As much as I'd like to prove myself better than some jumped up Englishman, it might not be a bad thing to cheat a little. Can you fetch it?"

Haley could tell from the way Darby gnawed her lip that she didn't want to go down to the tent on her own.

"How about I go?" Haley offered even though her thighs were burning from going up and down the hillside all day.

Darby nodded with relief.

Quentin looked up at the sky. "Be quick."

Haley hurried off down the mountain. A wall of gray obscured the horizon, and she suspected she was going to get drenched on the return journey. She went inside the tent and started grabbing what was left of Darby's belongings, including a notepad. A weird vibration started, and the sides of the tent buffeted hard in the wind. And it took a few seconds for Haley to realize that the rhythmic noise wasn't the wind, it was a helicopter. Did she make a run for the trees? It sounded close, but she had no idea where the machine was.

She edged to the front of the tent and eased the zipper

down enough to hide her from view.

Was this the rescue team or the terrorists tracking them down? She had no idea. She froze, curling herself into a small, rigid ball, the terror of her abduction, the knowledge that if the kidnappers reclaimed their lost prizes…she and Darby would have to endure daily horror. Quentin would be tortured, probably to death.

"Please, please, please." She begged whatever deity watched over desperate women in these parts. Not that they'd helped Darby much. "I'll do anything. I'll be a better person. I'll stop cursing so much, give up drinking and one-night stands, and go volunteer in a pet shelter."

The beat of the rotors became louder and louder until the drumming hurt her ears and punched her chest. She squeezed her eyes shut like a kid hiding in a closet playing hide-and-go-seek. Then she made a decision.

QUENTIN HAD JUST finished chopping the main support branches for their makeshift shelter when he heard the beat of rotors.

"Shit."

Darby looked up from where she was collecting leaves to spread over the roof of the structure.

"Help me get everything out of sight. Fast."

He grabbed the cooler and threw in everything they'd used for dinner, slammed the lid closed and dragged it into the depths of the trees. Darby grabbed the camp chair and bedroll. Stumbled after him with huge, desperate eyes.

"Is it them?" Her voice was high and thin.

"I don't know, but we can't risk them finding us. Get over by those bushes and cover yourself with this blanket. Don't. Move. No matter what happens." He thrust Haley's gray blanket at the young woman and she took it, fingers shaking so badly she almost dropped it.

That was what real terror looked like.

And he was feeling it too.

Where was Haley? Where was the chopper? Had they spotted her? Had she heard the noise and hidden before they got to her?

What if it was a rescue team?

What if it *wasn't*?

Fuck.

He piled leaves and branches and dirt over the coolers hidden in the brush then lay next to Darby, covering them both with the heavy gray wool. He drew the handgun out of his waistband and put a bullet in the chamber, ready to shoot anyone who tried to take them back to that island.

He drew the knife and handed it to Darby. She gripped it tight, eyes round with fear but jaw determined as hell. She'd already killed one of her attackers. She might not get another chance, but at least she wouldn't feel so completely defenseless.

"Do you think Haley is okay?" Her eyes frantically searched through the thin slit at the bottom of the blanket.

"I hope so," he said fervently. He wanted to run down the side of the mountain after her, but what if he led the hostiles straight to them? And how could he leave Darby to face this danger alone? Even for Haley?

"You like her."

He snorted. "Of course, I like her."

"No," she laughed, then swallowed nervously. "You *really*

like her. I've seen you watching her."

He gave her a look but didn't reply. What was not to like? Haley was a smart, beautiful woman, although so was Darby. So were thousands of other women in the world, but he hadn't looked at any of them twice since he'd met Abbie over a decade ago.

Suddenly the noise of the helicopter grew louder just as the rain began to fall in a deluge that soaked them to the skin in two seconds flat. At least it was warm rain and cooled his skin to a bearable temperature.

"Keep your head down and don't move," he ordered Darby as they anchored the blanket around them.

He watched through a narrow gap as a dark green helicopter rose up and into view, clearly searching the wide-open plain in sweeping movements.

Had someone noticed the signal? It seemed too fast for a response but what if… He scanned the aircraft for some sort of insignia, but there was nothing useful except a number he couldn't make out at this distance. He tried to get a look at the pilot and crew, but the rain was too thick, a wall of gray leaching color and detail.

He wished like hell he could run out there waving his hands like a twenty-first-century Robinson Crusoe spotting a rescue ship, but if he got it wrong it wasn't just him who'd suffer. It was Haley, and Darby. And he had no desire for his family's last memory of him to be that of a prisoner kneeling obediently as his head was sawn from his shoulders.

Fuckers.

After what seemed like forever, the bird wheeled around and streaked across the island towards the beach. Thank god they'd pulled the boat way under the trees. He doubted they'd spot it in this rain.

He put a hand on Darby's shoulder when she started to move. She flinched and then held still. The helicopter spent another thirty seconds working the coastline but not near where they'd set up their SOS signal.

Surely, if they'd come because of the SOS signal they would have headed there first?

Yeah, they would have.

These people had not come in response to their cry for help, which meant the chances of them being tangos just went up.

Rain ran in rivulets down his back, over his face, dripping off the ends of his hair. His beard itched like it housed fire ants.

To think, a few days ago, he'd been worried about presenting the keynote lecture. Now he was building shelters out of palm trees on a tropical island, hiding from armed militants and ready to defend himself and these women to the death.

His mouth went dry, concern for Haley eating at him. Finally, the chopper peeled away from the island and began heading south, back into the rain clouds.

He gave it thirty seconds before he threw the blanket off his head. "I need to go check on Haley. Stay here and stay out of sight."

What if they'd found her and taken her?

Darby grabbed his sleeve. "What if they dropped someone off on the island? Please don't leave me."

His heart felt like it was being wrenched in two. He counted to ten. Centered himself. "I don't think they landed, and there was no reason not to if they wanted to drop off a search party, but you're right, we need to be careful. I'll head down to the tent but scan every rise. I won't be long, but it could take an hour or more to get there and back. You stay here, hidden. You know how to fire a gun?" he asked.

"I'm from Alaska."

Right.

He offered her the pistol. "Swap you."

She took it and handed him the knife.

"Please don't shoot us when we come back. I'll make sure I call out, or better yet, I'll do an owl call and you do one back, okay?" Mimicry was the oldest bonding tool in the book, and this was a good shortcut. "But if I miss Haley somehow, don't forget she won't know about our signal so ease off on the trigger pulling until you see a face and know what's going on, 'kay?"

An unhappy smile wobbled Darby's bottom lip. "Okay."

"Okay," he said firmly. "Stay under the blanket. If it gets dark before I get back, do not use any lights. You are completely hidden from view here. We will find you. We will get through this."

Darby nodded vigorously. "Go, find Haley. I'll be fine."

He squeezed her shoulder. "I know you will be."

He headed to the side of the trees into a gully that ran down the mountain. It was running with water now but didn't make him any more wet. He jogged downhill, mindful of his footing for the sake of his ankles, but desperate to check Haley was safe and the bastards hadn't picked her up and taken her back to that island camp.

His foot slipped in the fine mud, but he kept going, his heart beating a little too hard from worry.

Close to where he believed the tent was, he scrambled up the side of the stream bank and peered over the edge, checking what he could see of the area.

Rain beat down on him, nothing else moving except for a colorful bird flying through the trees. The tent flap was zipped up tight. Was Haley hiding inside?

He watched for another minute before stealing over the top of the gully and running in a low crouch to the tent.

"Haley," he said, raising the volume to be heard over the rain. "It's me."

He raised the zipper and looked inside, feeling a punch in the gut when he realized she wasn't there.

He heard footsteps pounding the ground a split second before something hit him from behind.

CHAPTER TWENTY-ONE

HALEY HAD ONLY meant to hug Quentin in relief, but she slipped and crashed into the man, only to find herself flat on her back with a knife to her throat.

"Hi," she squeaked.

The knife disappeared. "Shit. Sorry."

"It wasn't your fault. It was my fault—"

"I should have known it was you, but I was so worried someone in that helicopter had taken you—"

"They hovered all around the tent, but they didn't get out and check inside. And I ran like a scared rabbit when they moved off. Was it the terrorists? Or the good guys?"

"I have no idea, but I suspect it was the terrorists. I am so glad you're okay." A wry grin curved his soft-looking lips, the beard almost full now after just a few days.

"I'm glad you're okay, too," she said huskily.

She ran her hand over his jaw and then stilled as the air charged around them. Energy spun like a billion electrons colliding off one another.

"You're wet." He glanced up at the rain, but she squeezed her legs together because she was wet. *Everywhere.* And hot. And starved. This was a terrible idea, but god she wanted him inside her as fast and as deep as he could get.

He saw it in her eyes. She could tell he did.

And he must have felt it in the way her nipples poked through the thin material of his borrowed shirt and gave him a very pointed "hello."

His lips pressed together, and his nostrils flared as he stared down at her lying in the mud.

Haley had never been shy. She wriggled until the t-shirt came up and pulled her arms out, then dragged it over her head until she was bare and there was no mistaking what she wanted.

His pupils dilated, but he glanced around.

She thought he was going to reject her, but instead he groaned. "We have to be quick."

She nodded, and he was already undoing his button and zipper. She shoved his hands away and dove in, stroking him. Wanting the press of that searing hot velvet that was rapidly morphing into steel.

He dragged her shorts down her legs and tested her with his fingers. She bucked against him, muscles clenching, already halfway to climax.

"Fuck. I don't have a condom." His mouth formed a frustrated line as he unerringly found that spot that drove her crazy, his palm touching her clit and making her bow against his touch.

"I'm clean, and I can't get pregnant. I get regular checkups and haven't been with anyone except you in a while."

"I'm clean too but…"

They held each other's gaze. It was a risk. Of course, it was a risk. But they'd been so close to dying and that visit from an unknown chopper had brought the danger they faced crashing back down over them. They weren't safe yet. They weren't free. This might be their last chance to be together.

She let out a sigh of relief when he wedged himself between her legs. She opened wider, lifting her hips, silently begging for him to take her hard and fast despite the rain, despite the mud.

Then he kissed her, and she took his tongue in her mouth as he guided himself inside. One thrust, and he was lodged deep, filling her so perfectly. She wrapped one leg around him, anchoring him to her pelvis as they began to move. Finding a rhythm that was wild and reckless and glorious. There was no finesse. They were rutting in the mud, grinding against one another in a rush to come. His hands pinching her nipples, his mouth devouring hers. Her hips rose higher and higher off the ground, and he turned them so she was on top looking down at him, riding the thick length of his arousal, using him to get off in an orgasm that detonated waves upon waves of pleasure throughout her body.

Then he rolled them again, and she didn't have time to catch her breath as he slammed into her, relentlessly pounding until he came with a roar that twisted his beautiful face into a parody of pain.

Her heartbeat boomed in her ears.

She'd never done anything like that before. Never felt anything like that before.

He closed his eyes and rested his forehead on her shoulder. She could feel his heart pounding against her breast as if he'd run a marathon. Was it the danger they faced? The adrenaline rush? Or was it them?

He withdrew and tucked himself away, pulled up his zipper, buttoned his pants while she lay there winded.

His expression was pensive. Dark eyes worried. He turned away.

"Are you all right? Did I do the wrong thing?" she asked, suddenly insecure.

He turned back, brows rising, and he snorted. "I think you've ruined me for any other woman when it comes to sex." But he looked uncomfortable, as if regretting what they'd done. "We have to get back before Darby comes looking for us and gets an eyeful she might not be able to deal with right now."

Oh, god. Of course. She didn't know how she could have been so selfish, except she'd needed it. Needed the release. Needed to screw Quentin's brains out one more time.

Just sex, she told herself as she forced her damp boots back through the leg holes of her shorts and pulled her t-shirt over her filthy body.

It wasn't true, but she knew how to fake detachment. She knew how to fake it until it became truth. "If you want to let off steam again, you know where to find me." She smiled as if she wasn't a bedraggled rat on a volcanic island, but rather the sophisticated femme fatale she spent most of her life perfecting.

Rather than replying, he watched her with an unreadable expression on his face.

"Let's go."

QUENTIN DIDN'T TAKE Haley's hand as they trudged up the gully. He knew that, for all Haley's ballsy, confident front, his post-sex withdrawal had confused her.

It had confused him too.

What had happened down there, when for the first time

outside wedlock he'd fucked a woman bare, had rocked him to his core. It had been the best sex of his entire life, and that felt like a betrayal of his dead wife and their short but incredibly happy marriage.

His sex life with Abbie had been loving and fun, and they'd certainly never stopped enjoying what happened in the bedroom. But rolling around in the open air, the rain beating down, mud covering every inch of exposed skin…he'd been incinerated by want and lust. It had ripped out his brain and replaced it with ravenous, uncontrollable need. He'd felt like an animal pounding into Haley's perfect body. A madman in the throes of psychosis.

He stopped, and she almost bumped into him.

"Did I hurt you?" he asked, turning back to face her.

She raised a brow. "Do you mean with the size of your cock or your unbridled passion?" There was an edge to her tone that hadn't been there before. Not since that first night at the hotel.

It masked her insecurities, he realized.

Shit.

He *had* hurt her, though not physically.

He used one of his negotiator Jedi-mind tricks to try to get her to say more. "Unbridled passion?"

If she started talking about his cock, he was going to want her again, and he wasn't sure why his desire for this woman seemed to take over his brain so easily. And didn't know why the fact it did bothered him so damn much.

"You know, where you fucked me like a mason drill."

His mouth went dry. He should have known she wouldn't be so easily manipulated. Which word to mirror now? Fuck? Drill? All of which he wanted to do again and again on repeat.

She must have seen the hunger in his eyes.

He turned away, but rather than hurrying up the slope, he twisted back just as she took a step forward. He grabbed her so she didn't fall backwards when their bodies collided. Held her close enough she could feel his erection. Her eyes widened.

They needed to have this conversation somewhere Darby wouldn't overhear them.

"I don't know how to deal with a woman like you, Haley," he told her honestly.

"What do you mean? A woman like me?" Her eyes were wary. Her mouth pretending it wasn't sad.

Everything about her reminded him of a wounded creature, and he thought of the rapist uncle and how she'd reclaimed her sexuality like a weapon to be wielded. But it hadn't been like that a few minutes earlier, *that* had been passion and honesty. He went with truth rather than guarding his own heart, because she'd been hurt too much, and he couldn't stand the idea that he might also cause her pain.

"A woman who burns so brightly I feel like I'm being blinded by a star whenever I look at her."

She blinked rapidly.

"A woman who will walk away from me without a backward glance as soon as this is over."

Her mouth opened in shock. She stared at his throat, avoiding his gaze. "I've never not wanted to walk away in the past..." She raised her eyes to his then, not in apology, but with fear. "I have no idea how I'm going to feel about you when this is over. I've never..." She swallowed her words then tried again. "I'm not a woman men want to get involved with for anything besides sex, Quentin, and the sex has been fantastic."

She stroked her hand down his chest, but he didn't let himself get distracted.

"Are you actually trying to tell me men walk away from you first?"

She gave him a look. Then laughed. "No."

"No?" He opened the negotiator's toolbox again.

The anger went out of her. "I always leave before I get emotionally involved. I don't want those clingy, awkward emotions. I don't need the distraction from my work."

"So, to be clear, you're saying, when this is over, when we are rescued," because they were going to be rescued, "you'll walk away rather than pursue a relationship with me?"

"Relationship?" she asked.

"You know. People who talk and date and have sex as often as possible."

She opened her mouth again, but no words came out. She stared at him in silence.

He went to turn away, but she grabbed onto his arm.

"I don't want a relationship," she whispered.

He blew out a long breath and twisted out of her grip. He should have been relieved. He knew exactly where he stood, and if they did have sex again, he could enjoy it without worrying about how that reflected on his marriage or the depth of feeling he'd had for his late wife. It would be a purely physical act with an incredibly attractive woman.

But for the first time since Abbie died, he had to wonder whether or not that would be enough.

CHAPTER TWENTY-TWO

THE SCREAMING FROM the video that had been uploaded online came to an abrupt end, cut off just as violently as the man's ear. The video was in black and white, but the blood was obvious. The video was twelve seconds long and hideous.

Eban's stomach churned. "Play it again."

The victim was held down by a knee pressing his head into the dirt. The only thing visible was the side of the man's head, thick black hair and a dark t-shirt.

Heavy panting filled the audio feed as if there'd been a scuffle. Next, another man's hands came into view, holding a large hunting knife. He grabbed hold of the top of the captive's ear and sliced through the cartilage and all the way down to the lobe, leaving the remaining flesh ragged and torn. The wound welled with blood as the victim screamed.

Eban closed his eyes. The message on the video stated they had twelve hours until they cut off Quentin's other ear. After that, they'd snip off his fingers and toes before removing his balls.

Eban grabbed his head between his hands. "Fuuuuck!"

Charlotte Blood was on one video-link, her complexion ashen. Alex Parker was on another *sans* baby, thank god.

"How soon can we get that money together?" Eban asked. The new head of the task force was on his way from CIRG, and

Eban didn't want the guy screwing this up with by-the-book procedures that would get his boss killed.

"It's ready to go," Alex said. "But I want proof of life for Haley before I send it."

"Guys," said Charlotte.

"Are you serious?" Eban asked Alex incredulously.

"Deadly." Alex's tone was implacable.

"Guys," said Charlotte.

"They just cut off his fucking ear," Eban snarled.

"Guys!" Charlotte snapped with impatience. "I don't think that was Quentin," She was doing something on her end. "Look at this photograph." She emailed Eban and Parker a picture of Quentin from the side taken at some wedding. The guy had shorter hair in the image—it was from before Abbie had died and he'd gone all Keanu Reeves on them.

"Compare the still of the person who just lost their ear with this picture of the boss."

Eban stared hard at the two images. Then sat up straight. Ears were as individual as fingerprints.

"She's right." Alex produced an overlay of the two images, and the ears were not even remotely the same shape.

Eban inhaled slowly. It wasn't Quentin who'd just had his ear shorn off, it was some other poor bastard. "Why pretend to cut off his ear?"

"And why the big hurry to get the cash? They know this usually takes months." Charlotte looked worried.

Eban blinked as facts collided. "Shit. They don't have him anymore." His elation rolled straight into despondency. He rubbed his hands over his face, all the stress and strain of the past few days hitting him like a tank. "He's probably dead." He stared up at the ceiling of the legat's office at the US embassy, choked by despair. Working kidnap and ransoms was always rough, but nothing had prepared him for what happened when the hostage was one of their own.

"He might have escaped," Alex argued.

Eban shook his head. "Quentin knows the best thing for a hostage to do is to wait for a ransom to be paid."

"Ask them for proof of life for Haley and Quentin, but tell them we have some money ready to be sent immediately as testament of our good intentions. Beg them not to hurt them any further." Alex narrowed his eyes at his monitor. "I'm not ready to give up on either of them until we have irrefutable information that says otherwise. Give me some time to track the video upload, and my data analysts are still working on all the cell data, but it's a lot of information. It'll take some time."

Eban straightened his spine and nodded, ashamed of his loss of hope. "I'll email them right now." Regardless of whether Quentin was alive or dead, Eban was going to hunt these bastards down. No one got away with attacking US citizens without experiencing the full brunt of US resources. No one got away with killing his friends.

"Do you have a hostage rescue team in place and ready to move if we locate these guys?" Alex asked. "Because I have a private group based in Colombia on a flight to Jakarta as we speak."

Eban nodded slowly. "HRT are on their way. Will be based onboard the Navy frigate near the site of the attack." Ready to kick some terrorist ass just as soon as they figured out where the bastards were.

CHAPTER TWENTY-THREE

"ARE YOU OKAY?" Darby asked anxiously when they arrived back at camp. He'd made the owl call as arranged, and she'd replied in kind, the signal that they were safe for now.

Dusk had crept in with the storm. The rain had finally stopped, and steam rose from his clothes in misty waves.

Quentin nodded, but decided to let Haley do the talking while he got to work finishing the shelter. He hoped they wouldn't be here long enough to need it.

He picked up the machete and started hacking at a few more saplings to shore up the roof. Then he layered large fronds over the structure, holding them down with more branches and repeating the process until he had what he hoped would be a waterproof covering beneath which they could sit out any future tropical downpours.

He slapped at a mosquito.

"Here." Haley held out a bottle of bug spray, and he took it from her, not meeting her eyes.

"Thanks." He sprayed himself, DEET hitting the back of his throat in a noxious wave.

Darby was out of earshot, digging noisily through the cooler looking for something to eat as a snack. They'd agreed to ration her supplies in case rescue took longer than they hoped, but she needed food. Tomorrow he'd see if he could catch any fish. Give Bear Grylls a run for his money.

He grunted to himself.

Haley leaned closer, and he was suddenly aware of every cell in his body.

"When I said I didn't want a relationship, what I really meant was that I don't *want* to want a relationship. The idea of being under anyone's control scares me..." she whispered.

"That is not what a relationship is about," Quentin said, trying to keep the edge out of his tone. Where was his late-night DJ voice? Or his good buddy voice that had helped talk down bank robbers and whacked out meth-heads? "One person doesn't control the other."

"I know that on one level, in the rational part of my brain." Her hands curled into fists. "But the fourteen-year-old girl buried not that deep below the surface is aware that without a wealthy grandmother, I would have been dependent on my parents, who didn't believe I was being abused in my own home—or I'd have been on the streets doing whatever it took to survive."

He wove another leaf through the branches. "You equate intimate relationships with subjugation and abuse?"

"Yes. No." She shook her head. "I don't know. Quentin, I just know that I...that I..." She started gulping air.

Ah shit.

He turned back to her. God, he was a jackass. "It's okay, Haley. Just breathe. I should never have brought it up. I don't want a relationship either." What the hell had he been thinking? "We are in a survival situation, it wasn't fair to do that to you and put you under pressure that way. I'm sorry."

She clutched at his forearms. "No. You were thinking like

a normal person. I'm trying to explain that I'm not normal. I don't think I've ever been normal."

He hauled her to him and then saw Darby staring at them with haunted eyes, looking lonely and lost. He opened his other arm wide, and Darby flung herself into the group embrace.

He stood there holding two scared women in his arms and staring up at the pristine navy sky as the silver moon started to rise. He grieved for what these women had lost. Grieved for the pain and suffering they had endured at the hands of men. He murmured soft words and rocked them both. He would do anything he could to protect them, even if it ended up leaving him open to hurt.

The wind dropped, and the clouds had disappeared as if they'd dumped everything they had onto this remote and vast wilderness.

"You know what I want to see?" he said, realizing it was true, even though he'd simply been searching for something to distract them all from their situation.

Haley straightened away from him, wiping her eyes and looking embarrassed. Darby followed suit. "What?" they asked in unison.

"A lava flow at night."

Haley snorted out a laugh, and Darby's eyes gleamed.

"We'll have to wait for the moon to rise fully so we can see the path," Darby told him, putting her hands on her hips and doing what she did best, organizing things.

"You two try and get a few hours rest until then." Even though it was early, they were all exhausted. "I'll take first watch."

Darby handed him the pistol, and he nodded to her and

grabbed the camp chair, then went off to find the best vantage point. They had to keep one step ahead of the enemy.

THE PATH WAS narrow and dangerous, but the moon was so bright and the night so clear it was almost as if it were daylight. Sweat beaded on his brow. His muscles ached from the steep climb. They'd been at this for nearly an hour, going steady, because breaking a limb might be a death sentence.

The rock underfoot was coarse. The air held the odor of sulfur and was so dry and hot he could feel the heat in his lungs.

They'd brought a canteen of water and a granola bar each.

"Did you ever get lonely out here all alone?" Haley asked Darby.

"Not really. I'm used to wide open spaces and like my own company." The young woman led the way, and Quentin noticed a sway in her gait that hadn't been there before. It gave him hope she could get through this, even though he knew it wouldn't be quick or easy.

"I spend a lot of time on a remote island in the Caribbean. After two days of solitude I'm clawing the walls." Haley huffed, clearly feeling the altitude. "I always think I want it, but when I get it, I don't want it anymore." She laughed.

"I'm the same." Quentin put his hands on her hips to steady her as she clambered up a small rockface. The look she gave him over her shoulder was full of so much passion, his fingers clenched reflexively on her hips.

She ran her hand across his cheek, almost tenderly, then hoisted herself up and over the ledge.

"The same as who?" Darby asked and laughed, oblivious to the sexual tension strumming between him and Haley.

Damn. He could barely remember how to breathe, let alone think.

"Do you like your own company or not?" Darby prompted.

He grinned as he hauled himself up the rock. Darby was still a shrewd and focused cookie, in spite of everything she'd endured.

"Well, I always *think* I enjoy solitude, but I'm not sure it's true, as I never take a day off work."

"Never?" Haley asked, incredulous.

Quentin shook his head. "Not anymore."

Haley frowned at him quizzically.

"How far is it to go?" He changed the subject, because he didn't want either of them catching on that something had changed, and that change had been the tragic loss of his wife and their stillborn child. Even though he knew every corner of their trauma, he wasn't ready to share his. Or perhaps he didn't want to burden them with more sadness. They were already suffering enough.

Darby moved to the top of a nearby ridge and planted her fists on her hips. "We're here!"

After making his way to join her, Quentin stopped short at the dramatic scene. Below them was a jagged slope dark with shadow. Midnight black except for a glowing line of fervent orange—molten lava moving inexorably toward a cliff before abruptly plunging into the sea. The stench was like brimstone.

"Welcome to Mordor," he said under his breath.

Darby grinned at him, obviously thrilled to find a fellow Tolkien fan.

"This isn't considered an active volcano?" Trepidation

seeped into Haley's tone. The red glow of the lava gilded the edge of her face, and he found it hard to keep his eyes off her. She was beautiful. Stunning.

"It's an active volcano, but a stable one for the last seventy years or so. USGS monitor it—hence me being here—but we don't have a full-time team assigned as it isn't showing any signs of imminent eruption, and the island isn't populated."

Quentin looked away from the spectacular scenery. "Any way to make it appear an eruption might be imminent?"

And grab someone's attention?

Darby pressed her lips together. "Well, moving the benchmark GPS stations might do it. Except, as they are portable, they might not be monitored automatically, the way the permanent, fixed, GPS stations are." She frowned harder. "If we unscrewed the casings and jiggled a few of the tiltometers *that* might set off an automatic alarm, but my boss and the USGS would be pissed we interfered with baseline data."

Her boss could go fuck himself. Quentin curved his lips, hoping he didn't look as pissed at the guy as he felt. "They can take it up with me after we're rescued. Come on, let's go stage a little seismic activity of our own."

THEY PILED BACK to camp with the tired, happy feeling of scouts returning from a long hike. It was crazy to feel that sense of deep satisfaction, but Haley was practically euphoric.

"I'll take first watch," Quentin offered.

"I think you already did." Haley rolled her eyes. He'd kept watch while she and Darby had slept earlier. If she had to guess, she'd say it was about three AM.

"I don't mind doing an extra shift," he insisted.

"That's not how this equality thing works." Haley shook her head. "I'll do it."

"No." Darby held her hand out for the weapon Quentin carried in his waistband. "I'll do it. I slept well earlier, and I've had enough nightmares for one night."

The euphoria died. Haley's mouth went dry. It was easy to forget Darby had recently gone through such a brutal ordeal. She was so collected and competent. But when she closed her eyes, she probably relived every detail. Haley ran her hand over Darby's shoulder, and the girl smiled at her ruefully.

"Four hours, and then it's Haley's turn," Quentin said sternly.

As soon as Darby trudged out of sight, Haley looked around for the blanket she'd been using. Quentin picked it up, shook it out and offered it to her, already knowing what she was looking for. It was scary how well he knew her already.

He unzipped Darby's sleeping bag and laid it on the sleeping pad then glanced at her standing there uncertainly. "It's big enough for two if you want to share."

That was all the invitation she needed. She hurried in beside him and once again found herself snuggled against a strong male body, resting her cheek on his chest. She adjusted the blanket over them both, the breeze off the ocean keeping the temperature tolerable.

She rubbed her hand gently over his chest. He grabbed her fingers and held her still.

"Keep touching me like that, and I'll never get to sleep."

Haley felt a shiver of desire whip over her skin. But it wasn't fair to Darby to initiate anything sexual when she might walk in on them. Not when her wounds were so fresh.

"Maybe we can go looking for more rocks again tomorrow," Haley suggested. "Get a little lost on the way back."

His hands tightened around her waist, and his voice got husky. "I like how you think."

The scent of him comforted her. The warmth of his solid muscles provided a reassuring sense of safety.

"I wish I could figure out why I was the only person they planned to take alive," he said quietly after a few moments of silence.

It was obviously eating at him. "Perhaps you were the target all along."

"Jesus, I hope not."

Haley lifted her head to look into his face. "It doesn't make what happened your fault, Quentin. You know that."

His dark eyes glittered. "I know it academically, but it's not the same as believing it in your soul."

"Do you think anyone else survived?" she whispered, laying her head back down.

"I hope so." He kissed the top of her head, and it felt like the most natural and elemental gesture in the world. It wasn't only sex he was good at. It was everything.

Sleep was dragging at her consciousness, pulling her into its depths. "I can't believe some lucky woman hasn't snapped you up," she murmured. She drifted off to the sound of his heart beating beneath her cheek and the wash of the ocean, a soft cadence against a distant shore. As far as being marooned on a tropical island went, this wasn't so bad.

THE PHONE RANG next to Eban's ear, and he bolted upright, heart pounding, blood thundering through his veins. It took him a moment to figure out where he was. Hotel room. Jakarta. He'd returned to get a couple of hours' sleep.

The phone rang again. He snatched it up.

"Winters." His voice sounded like someone had cleaned out his throat with bleach.

"I think we've got something." It was Alex Parker.

Eban tried to get his eyes to stay open, but it was like his lids were glued shut. It was six AM, and his alarm started to beep even as he threw his legs over the side of the bed. "What?"

"FBI identified one of the dead terrorists as one Kenga Kaswali. He was one of the men who deserted with Darmawan Hurek. Kaswali was married to a woman from Sulawesi."

"Tell me she phones home twice a week like a good daughter."

"Not quite. But every few months there's a call from Bandaneira in the Banda Islands. We found a similar pattern in some of the other phone data of relatives of deserters suspected of accompanying Hurek."

"Can you narrow it down further?"

"Ten minutes ago, I'd have said no, but then I intercepted some messages between US Geological Services personnel and the embassy in Jakarta. USGS were asking about getting a team back on the island Darby O'Roarke was abducted from as there'd been some unusual eruptive events recorded there. They wanted to know how stable the region was for foreigners. Embassy advised against travel to that part of the world following the hotel massacre until security improved."

Eban didn't know where the guy was going with this.

"I decided to take a look at the data they were talking about and then checked out some satellite images." Excitement vibrated through his voice. “Check out the screenshot I sent you.”

Eban looked at the image that appeared on his laptop. “Holy *shit*.”

“I don’t know where the terrorists are, but I think we might have maybe found Quentin and Haley. Or Darby.” The man sounded like he was trying to physically calm himself down. “Even if it is not them, it’s someone who needs help.”

Someone who’d gone to a lot of effort to build a giant SOS visible from space.

“Have you informed FBI HQ?” Eban went into the bathroom and turned on the shower. He stank.

“They’re sending the warship to the area. The thing is…the company I hired out of Colombia arrived in Jakarta last night, and they have a helicopter full of equipment fueled up and ready to go. Turns out they are acquainted with Max Hawthorne from having served together in the SAS. They also said they could squeeze the two of you on board if you wanted to go along for the ride. If it doesn’t pan out, they’ll refuel in Bandaneira, so maybe you can use the trip to ask questions of the locals about Hurek and his band of murderous thugs. Can’t hurt.”

“Give me directions—”

“I can do better than that. A car will pick you up in fifteen minutes. By the way, I get the impression that your big bosses don’t want us to do this little reconnaissance, so if you want to come along you, might want to not answer their calls until you’re airborne.”

And by then it would be too late.

“I’ll be ready. Get some sleep, Alex. I’ll call you when we get there.”

CHAPTER TWENTY-FOUR

QUENTIN TOOK SEVERAL quick, deep breaths in succession, then dove beneath the aquamarine surface of the crystal-clear water. It could have been the perfect getaway if he wasn't fishing so they had something to eat while Darby kept watch for their enemies from camp.

He duck-dived down to the bottom, searching for a fish to lunge at with his makeshift spear. He waited on the sea floor, slowing his pulse, calming his mind. The sun dappled the surface of the water above him, blinding when the solar rays caught it just so. Creatures darted around him. Too small and nimble for him to catch.

The pressure in the walls of his chest built. That need to draw in fresh oxygen. A flash of silver to the left drew his peripheral gaze even though he didn't move. Slowly, a large fish swam closer. Quentin waited for it to swim past before lunging with his multi-headed spear.

Yes!

Elation filled him as he successfully caught the creature. He swept it upwards and kicked hard, breaking the surface and drawing in a massive breath.

"Woot!"

He turned while treading water and almost dropped his catch.

Haley sat naked on a rock, her clothes wet and laid out to dry as if she'd just done laundry. She looked confident and provocative and was the sexiest woman he'd ever seen.

He climbed out on the rocks—they'd decided to avoid leaving any tracks in the sand—and dispatched the poor fish who would feed all three of them for several days.

Then he placed the spear on the rock while taking in the view.

She hiked a brow and smiled, drawing one knee up. She was going to kill him. Blood flow to his brain was going to be permanently cut off and diverted to his dick and that would be the end of him.

"Your skin is going to burn." His voice came out as gravelly as the bottom of the seabed.

"I washed my clothes." Haley ignored his comment and pointed to the t-shirt and shorts that had once belonged to him.

"I can see that." He stared down at the rivulets of water draining from the boxers he wore. "I washed mine too."

"Now you've caught dinner, you should dry your clothes on the rocks with mine."

"Then we'd both be naked."

Haley bit her lip in a gesture that shot straight to his groin.

Sold.

He stepped out of his boxers and slapped them down on the hot rock.

It was Haley's turn to stare lustfully.

He thought better of leaving the clothes exposed on the rock and gathered them up. He held out a hand, and she reached up to take it, and he jerked her to her feet, enjoying her surprise as she fell against him. She laughed and scooped up their footwear. He led her to the soft sandy earth beneath the trees where they'd stored the boat, out of the searing sun. He spread their clothes on top of branches to dry, then pressed her against a smooth tree trunk and kissed her, craving her mouth like she was that gasp of fresh air after holding his breath for too long.

It delighted him, the way she opened for him immediately. No hesitation. She tasted of salt and warm sunshine, and he could spend hours exploring her mouth. She drew her knee up the side of his leg and rested it against his hip. He lowered his head to suck on her pretty nipples, her skin already slightly reddened from the sun.

His hand slipped lower, through the folds of her vulva, before sinking deep into her wet heat.

She moaned as she rose onto the tiptoes of one foot, the other foot still hooking his hip. He loved the fact she wasn't afraid to show him what she enjoyed. He loved it so much his cock was on fire.

She went to slip a hand around him, but he wasn't done yet. Men were simple when it came to orgasms. Women were not. It wasn't just a case of mechanical stroking for women. They needed teasing and coaxing, and the clitoris needed worshipping with just the right amount of pressure. He sank to his knees, placing her foot on his shoulder so she was exposed to him. Then he started negotiating his way to her climax, using his tongue.

She resisted for half a second before sinking one hand into his hair and grabbing hold. She rested her head back against the tree trunk. He reached up to tease her nipples, one at a time, making them pebble against his touch. Then he found the exact tactics that worked for her, the rhythm that had her writhing against his mouth, seeking more pressure, seeking release. He worked her until she was gripping his hair tight enough to hurt and spreading her thighs wider in an effort to get even closer. When she came on his tongue, he absorbed her shudders and treasured her flavors. He grinned as he rose to his feet, right up until the moment she sank to her own knees and licked him from root to tip.

Oh, shit.

He held on to the tree as his knees almost buckled. It was a battle for him to hold on to his control as she did to him what he'd just done to her. But he wanted to be inside her again. Wanted to be looking her in the eye when they both came.

After a blissful minute, he eased away and drew her to her feet. He kissed her, closing his eyes so he could imagine them somewhere where they were safe, maybe her island or in his bed…

Her fingers found his painfully hard dick, and she guided him to her opening, teasing them both along the way. He lifted her up and thrust inside, cushioning her back against the hard trunk with an arm wrapped around her waist, the other beneath her ass as he worked himself in and out, wishing he had one more hand.

"Touch yourself. Make yourself come."

Her eyes held his as she slipped one hand lower, the other grasping him around the nape, holding on for dear life as he pumped inside her like a madman.

It took only seconds before he felt her muscles clench and quiver around him. She gasped out a quiet cry of ecstasy. His balls tightened, and pleasure shot along his length, white light crashing through his senses and leaving him blind, drained and sated, sweat sticking them together wherever their skin met.

He came back to the real world slowly, as if he were waking from a deep sleep. A buzzing noise sounded in his ear. He looked around for a bee or mosquito.

But it wasn't an insect.

Shit. He quickly withdrew from Haley who still hadn't caught on.

"That was—"

He put a hand over her mouth, startling her. Then she blinked, and the buzzing noise became louder. A boat engine.

They grabbed their clothes.

"Hide behind that large tree over there and don't move. I'm going to try and retrieve the fish I caught before whoever is in that boat reaches the cove. If we're lucky, it might be the good guys."

He ran, keeping low. No time to lose. He crouched at the edge of the woods, but the fish on the spear was out of range without him revealing himself.

He ducked as he spotted the boat approaching the beach at high speed, squatted behind the rock, quickly pulling on his clothes, which were still wet and lightly dusted with sand. Then he ran in a low crouch back into the woods, breathed a sigh of relief when he got to the tree he'd told Haley to hide behind. But the relief was short-lived. She was gone.

HALEY RAN UP the mountain path to camp. She was barefoot and felt hideously exposed but kept between the trees for as long as possible before scrambling on her hands and knees up the gully on the other side of where Darby's tent was pitched to avoid being seen from the beach.

Were these the same people who'd been in the helicopter last night? Had they spotted her running into the woods and decided to come back to scoop them up at their leisure?

Or was it a rescue team?

Haley hadn't stuck around to find out. She had to warn Darby, even if it meant abandoning Quentin. She swallowed painfully at having left him in possible danger, but he'd be more able to avoid being seen if he was alone.

Darby needed her. Haley couldn't leave the girl to face this new predicament unaware. She couldn't risk the young woman having somehow missed the arrival of the boat, strolling down to meet them, and walking straight into a deadly situation. She would not allow that to happen. She'd warn Darby, grab the pistol, and head back to find Quentin.

She didn't regret seducing Quentin. Their "relationship," for want of a better word, was the only thing that had been good about this entire nightmare episode. But she did regret letting her guard down at the worst possible moment.

She paused in her mad dash, as she needed to cross a few feet of ground where she could be seen from below. If she crawled, she should be hidden by the long grass. She peeked through the blades, and her mouth went dry.

Men with guns had beached their boat and were spreading out along the cove. They didn't look like good guys. It wouldn't be long until they found the RIB and knew that someone had landed here.

Assuming it was the same militants and not some new enemy.

She crawled through the grass, past a rocky bluff that stuck out and hid her from view from below. Then she ran, ignoring the sting of rock cutting into her feet.

Once in camp, she stood in the center of the small glade of trees and tentatively called out, "Darby?"

No reply, so she headed along another path to where they'd set up their watch position. There was a small overhang where you could sit in the shadows and look out across the ocean.

Haley arrived, calling out again. "Darby? Where are you?"

"Haley?" Darby hurried from around the corner with a worried frown. "What is it? What happened?"

Haley wished she didn't have to shatter this young woman's fragile calm. "A boat came."

Darby froze.

"I think it's the bad guys," Haley didn't try to cushion the blow. "Quentin's still down there. Give me the pistol. I'll sneak back down and be ready to rescue him if they find him. You hide. Okay?"

"I fell asleep. Oh, my god, I fell asleep and then I needed to pee, and they found us." Darby was hyperventilating and shaking so hard, Haley tried to calm her down.

"This is not your fault. It is not your fault. We are all doing the best we can, so please don't beat yourself up."

Darby nodded, swallowing noisily. She dipped into the pocket of her jacket and drew out the gun.

"I need to hide, but where?" The young woman bit her lip as she handed over the weapon.

Haley clasped her shoulder and peered down into Darby's big green eyes. "Don't tell me in case…" It was Haley's turn to swallow loudly. In case they caught her and tried to torture Darby's location out of her. "Just hide and don't come out until you know it's safe." She gave her another squeeze. "I have to go." Quentin was in danger, and she couldn't bear the thought of him being hurt.

"Wait," Darby ordered sharply. She ran over to a little bag of supplies she'd brought with her. She held out a green floppy hat. "It's not much, but it might help hide your hair and face."

Haley took the hat gratefully and placed it on her head, drawing the string tight. It was a long way from gold dresses and Jimmy Choos, but she was so very grateful for the gift if it might help save her life.

Darby's skin was ashen. "I wish I was brave enough to come with you."

"You are brave, Darby." Haley touched her arm, remembering what Quentin had said to her when the hotel was being attacked. "It would be nice if one of us survived this thing. It would make everything we do worthwhile. Go," Haley ordered. "Hide. We'll call for you when it's safe."

Haley headed back along the path towards where she'd left Quentin, using the gully to work her way down the mountain, never having felt so damn scared in her life. She hoped to make the woods at the bottom of the hill before any of the newcomers left the beach area. She reached the shade of the trees and blew out a huge breath of relief. A parrot flapped and squawked above her head, and she looked up, her right hand going to her throat in fear.

Her pulse raced, and she told herself to relax. "It's just a bird, dummy."

But as a strange man stepped out of the shadows, a malicious grin stretching his lips, she realized she should have been paying attention not to the bird, but to *why* the bird spooked.

The man was dressed in grubby fatigues and sweat-stained tee, and she recognized him from the village where they'd been held captive. He tried to grab her arm, but she was done being anyone's plaything or making it easy for them. She jerked away and raised her left hand and aimed, pulling the trigger of the pistol before he could bring his rifle around to shoot her.

He fell to the ground, still alive, still struggling to aim his weapon. So, Haley shot him again. Point blank range.

QUENTIN WAS SECRETED beneath an undercut bank with the roots of a large palm tree hiding him from view. A crab did its weird sideways walk before disappearing down a burrow. The waves lapped about three feet away from where he crouched. The soothing sound of the water made it hard for him to reconcile the fact that armed men were once again hunting them.

Where was Haley?

Had she gone to warn Darby or did he need to worry about them both being captured and hurt?

Haley was smart. Both women were. He was pretty sure she'd have gone up to the camp. From there the two women had supplies and could hide out long enough for some USGS grunt to pay attention to the fucking data and send a rescue mission.

The new arrivals were not friendlies, nor were they Indonesian military. They'd quickly discovered the boat hidden under the foliage, and he'd heard the excited chatter between the men even if he didn't understand the language. He didn't think they'd radioed their find back yet, because the radio was back on the inflatable they'd left unguarded on the beach.

If he could get hold of that radio, he could call directly for help.

If.

His options were limited. He could hide, which was only an advantage until these assholes reported back to base, and the island swarmed with terrorists who'd already proven their bloodthirstiness. Or he could attack, which would probably get him killed. But what the hell, he was trained. And protecting Haley and Darby was all that mattered.

The men had spread out, presumably to search for clues as to their whereabouts.

Quentin eased out of his hiding place and made his way back toward the rocks, keeping low and moving slowly to avoid drawing their eyes. From there he scanned the area. The two men he could see had their backs to him. He grabbed the spear he'd fashioned earlier and removed the fish from the end with a silent apology. The weapon wasn't much against an assault rifle, but it was better than nothing.

He made his way cautiously from tree to tree, searching for a target. If he could quietly pick off a couple of these guys, then odds became much more favorable.

He froze as one of the men came into view and headed over to the tree Quentin had originally told Haley to hide behind. The man must have spotted footprints in the dirt. Quentin didn't stare at him, didn't want to raise that innate survival instinct that told someone when they were being watched.

The man bent over and picked up Haley's boot.

Quentin didn't hesitate. The other bad guys were out of sight. He ran forward, choosing surprise blitz attack over stealth. At the last moment, the man turned. Quentin thrust the multi-pronged spear hard into the guy's throat before ripping it back out. His stomach heaved at the gruesome results.

The victim dropped his rifle and fell to his knees, desperately clutching the wound, trying to stem the blood pouring from his jugular.

Quentin snatched up the rifle and tossed the primitive spear aside. Pity made him want to assist the guy, try to stop the bleeding. Dammit, he didn't have time for mercy—these were ruthless killers. He slung the rifle strap over his head and the weapon across his back and took the man's hands in his. He wrapped them around the wound.

"Press hard to stop the bleeding." Quentin spoke quietly, pity for the man in direct competition with his need for survival. The dying man's eyes bulged, and then a calm seemed to settle over his features. A few seconds later he went lax, his chest no longer moving, clearly dead.

Quentin swallowed the fist-sized lump that had wedged in his mouth. He closed his eyes for a moment. He was good with words, but he couldn't negotiate with madmen, and he couldn't negotiate with people who refused to communicate like normal human beings. He didn't have time for self-pity or reflection. He needed to do whatever it took to get the women to safety and bring this group to justice.

A gun shot rang out, and Quentin's stomach seized. Then a second round was fired.

Had they found Haley or were they shooting at a feral pig?

Even as fear for the others clamored inside his head, he forced himself not to run, but to mark the location of each threat. Two of the men were in front of him heading up the path that led toward Darby's old camp—heading towards the gunfire. He didn't know where the other two were.

He paused. Should he double-back and get on the radio? But the idea of leaving Haley or Darby vulnerable made it impossible to turn away.

Dense underbrush on this part of the island meant it was difficult to see too far ahead. He jogged, rifle up, finger along the top of the trigger.

He used trees for cover. Then he heard the unmistakable sound of small arms fire and a man grunting in pain.

Someone was shooting at the terrorists, and he had to assume it was one of the women.

A burst from a fully automatic assault rifle shattered the peaceful tranquility of the island.

Men with AKs were going up against a woman with a handgun and limited ammunition. It was no contest.

Keep them safe. Keep them safe. Keep them safe.

Quentin headed right, to a place where he had both a view of the shooters and cover of his own. Whoever they were firing at was hidden behind a large fig tree. One man started to move around, flanking the target's position.

It was only a matter of seconds before the rest of the bastards turned up. Quentin took aim, catching the first man in the chest and dropping him to the ground, then sighting left and nailing the next guy before he even realized someone had the drop on him.

The silence that followed echoed with the knowledge there were more hostiles out there.

"It's me, Quentin. Are you hurt?" he called out softly. He didn't want Haley or Darby to shoot him accidentally.

Haley poked her head out, looking scared but not injured. He ran to the first man he'd shot and took his rifle. Tossed it to Haley who caught it. He wasn't sure if the man was dead or not, but he quickly searched him for comms. Nothing except a hunting knife that he tossed beneath the fig tree.

The other guy had caught a bullet in the skull and was definitely dead. Quentin grabbed his weapon, putting it over his other shoulder. Again, no comms.

"There are two more men on the island," Quentin told Haley.

"I killed one." Her skin was chalk white. "I took his gun, but it jammed when I tried to use it."

She must have been terrified.

"I killed another which leaves only one." But one guy could kill them all, or radio for help. "I don't think they have any communications except for the radio in the boat."

They needed to get that radio.

"No way he missed the ruckus. Let's head back to the beach, but we need to be careful." Quentin didn't want Haley in the line of fire, but they didn't have much choice. "Keep low and let's stay in the woods where we have some cover. And follow me but leave some space between us." As much as he wanted her close, they were tactically better off with some distance separating them so they couldn't be wiped out in a single swipe of gunfire.

He ran in a crouch, continually scanning the area for the last terrorist. He could be anywhere, but Quentin was betting he'd hightailed it back to the beach. And when his buddies didn't return, he'd flee.

Quentin hadn't seen anything resembling courage from these assholes. From attacking a conference of unarmed civilians, to kidnapping seniors and young women.

Through the trees, Quentin spotted movement. The man was desperately dragging the inflatable into the surf. Dammit.

No way could Quentin let him call for backup.

Shit

Quentin started running.

The boats were heavy and unwieldy to handle alone, and the guy was struggling. The surf had gotten up, with waves cresting on the small outer reef before crashing into the bay.

Quentin was sprinting flat-out now, sweat dripping into his eyes, but he didn't let it distract his focus. He leapt on top of the rocky outcrop as the terrorist rolled himself into the boat and quickly started the engine.

Quentin aimed.

As the man picked up the radio, Quentin started firing. The bullets ripped into the side of the RIB, and the man suddenly slumped over, obviously hit, hopefully dead. The boat didn't stop though. It headed full-pelt out to sea, and they had no hope of catching up with it.

Quentin swore.

They were still marooned, but it wouldn't be long until the kidnappers started wondering what happened to the search party they'd sent to Pulau Gunung Rebi. And they'd send another group to find out.

He stared at the fast disappearing inflatable. He should have gone after the radio earlier. He might have been able to call for help and end this nightmare. Dammit.

They needed to be smart. Get rid of the evidence. Play a game of psychological warfare.

"I'm going to dump all the bodies off a cliff into the sea," he said as Haley came up beside him. "Can you drag branches of leaves over the sand to hide the marks and footprints?"

He glanced down at the pink nail polish on her toes. She was wearing a floppy green hat, barefoot, and holding a rifle. It was surreal. Their world had done a complete one-eighty, and he had to wonder if they'd get out of this mess alive.

She worried her dry lips. "I should go tell Darby it's safe."

He shook his head. "Later. Let's do this first in case more bad guys come looking. I want them unsure as to whether their men ever arrived here or not."

They needed to either hide their inflatable or let it drift out to sea. But the idea of them being truly stranded was scary. Except, floating adrift on the ocean wasn't exactly a survival strategy either.

Surely someone would notice their signal soon?

"What happens if they come back?" Haley's blue eyes were wide with the horror of what they'd been forced to do.

"Then we hide." Grimly, Quentin patted the assault rifle. "At least this time we can fight back."

CHAPTER TWENTY-FIVE

EBAN WAS THRILLED his laptop had functional Wi-Fi, even though flying flat-out in the back of some bare-bones military transport helicopter wasn't the most comfortable space he'd ever worked in.

The others were catching up and shooting the breeze. The whole bunch were former British Special Forces who now worked for a private company called Penny Fan. Eban wasn't fooled. These guys were not private security the way Haley Cramer and Alex Parker were private security—otherwise one of them would have been attending the symposium that was attacked.

They were Black Ops working under the guise of security contractors. Apparently, Hawthorne knew most of the crew except the pilot who was a local they trusted and had worked with before. The guys spent most of their time telling embarrassing stories about things that had gone wrong and almost killed them at one time or another. They never seemed to run out of material.

He was online with the legat. Eban had managed to spin himself and Hawthorne getting a ride out to see the site of Darby O'Roarke's abduction as the next reasonable step in the case. Thankfully, McKenzie back at SIOC backed him up. McKenzie had the ear of the director after helping thwart an attack on HQ earlier in the year. Alex Parker had also helped stop that attack, which added weight to him finding this SOS, which he believed was a signal from Haley Cramer. The Bureau was happy to help him chase a lead even if it turned out to be nothing. The task force leader, a real hard ass, was not so happy. He had "repercussions" written all over his short, terse responses.

But this move did make sense.

The kidnappers had set up another demonstration of online ear removal—it was hard to watch, even knowing it likely wasn't Quentin on the receiving end of the mutilation. They'd also sent another photograph of Haley with a faceless man holding a knife beneath her nose, clearly threatening to cut it off. It appeared as if it was taken the same day as the first photograph. It had made his stomach lurch.

The communications had done nothing to dispel their working theory that the attackers no longer had Quentin or Haley in their possession, but it did nothing to dispel the theory that they'd already killed them either.

Alex Parker's grim determination that this SOS came from them was the only reason Eban had any hope left.

Alex had arranged to send a down payment of one-hundred thousand dollars on the condition the kidnappers stopped hurting the hostages and allowed them time to gather the full ransom. Twenty million was hard to liquidate at such short notice, but a hundred grand was a hell of a deposit.

Alex was following the money. A team of these former SAS dudes sat in a hotel in Jakarta, ready to move if they traced anyone picking up communications there.

Sending the bitcoin also created a false sense of security for the kidnappers. Why would the victims' families pay that amount of money if Eban and company were winging their way to liberate the hostages?

A team of analysts at HQ and at Cramer, Parker and Gray had been picking over satellite images of Pulau Gunung Rebi, and there was no indication of a terrorist camp—although nothing was one hundred percent certain as trees and possibly cave systems could hide them from view.

Those same analysts were checking neighboring islands with as much care as possible, but there were a lot of islands, and terrorists could be hiding in plain sight in a regular town or village.

"Ten minutes out."

Eban nodded and put away his computer and pulled on his ballistics vest. One of the operators, a big guy named Logan Masters who seemed to be in charge of the outfit, tossed him an earpiece for communication and then slid an MK5 across the floor of the bird. Eban nodded his appreciation. He hoped this was a rescue mission, but if they walked into terrorist central, he wanted to be ready for a firefight.

The sea beneath them was a deep dark blue with small islands dotted around and volcanic ranges jutting up out of the ocean like sharks' teeth. A paradise, but one full of potential dangers.

Max Hawthorne pointed out the window. Pulau Gunung Rebi. The island where Darby O'Roarke had been taken and where someone had written an SOS in a desperate bid for rescue—or to lure the unsuspecting…

They circled the island, first looking for movement or signs of life. A small, desolate-looking tent sat exposed on flat ground just above some trees on the leeward side of the island. A dramatic stream of bright orange lava flowed into the sea to the north. The helicopter circled until they were directly above the stones that spelled SOS, but no one ran out waving and rejoicing that rescue had come. Two large yellow tripods sat at either end of the letters. Eban didn't know their purpose, but they seemed to be properly assembled rather than randomly situated.

"Let's take it down," Masters told the pilot who nodded and started circling.

A weird noise of something pinging off metal made Eban frown. The pilot banked hard as Masters yelled, "Taking fire!"

Eban held on tight. Someone was certainly down there, shooting at them. The big question was whether or not they were hostages who needed rescue or terrorists hiding from the law. One way or another, they were about to find out.

The pilot circled around and put the bird down near the small tent whose canvas flapped in the downwash. The operators and two agents piled out, heading straight for the cover of the trees. The pilot took off back out to sea to wait until they'd secured the island or until he needed to refuel. Either way he was out of range of any bullets.

Eban looked across at Hawthorne who was grinning at him. The man was an excellent negotiator but obviously enjoyed being back in the field.

They huddled around in a circle, ten men in all with a lot of ground to cover.

Masters drew out a map folder and balanced it on one knee. "We split up into two four-man units plus one FBI agent each. One group takes the beach area, the other heads to where the shots came from."

The operators were dressed in full jungle camo with helmets and headsets. They looked like professional military rather than ill-equipped bandits. Eban and Hawthorne were in black tactical gear with FBI written clearly in yellow on their flak jackets.

If it was terrorists who'd shot at them, they'd be easily marked. But on the outside chance Quentin or Haley or Darby O'Roarke or even the Alexanders were out here, hopefully it would make them realize that he and this team were the good guys. And they were safe.

HALEY WINCED AS Darby started shooting at the helicopter that had flown over their SOS signal.

"Hold fire," Quentin ordered, pushing the rifle barrel to the floor.

Darby glared at him.

"It might be the rescue team. You see how they came straight to the SOS? That's someone who already knew the signal was there."

Darby stuck her lip out mutinously. "Bad guys could have access to satellite images too."

"Fair point," Haley murmured. They were all on edge, waiting for the next attack.

The helicopter flew out of sight, and Haley was guessing people were disembarking. The question was, who were these guys?

"We have to be really careful not to shoot innocent people who are coming to rescue us." Quentin looked concerned about Darby's mental state. Haley was worried about her too. Since warning her about the unexpected visitors first thing that morning, Darby had been jumpy and her eyes a little wild.

Haley understood, but the last thing they needed was to scare away or injure their rescuers.

"We want to get out of here, right?" Haley infused joviality into her tone.

The odds of them getting out of this mess alive had plummeted that morning, and it was quite possible this was a search party looking for their missing comrades who were now all dead.

"How will we know if they're good guys or bad guys?" Haley asked. They all clutched assault rifles and were in a dense thicket of trees, north of the signal.

Quentin pulled a face. "I was hoping it would be obvious, but it might not be if the Indonesians have their military looking for us also. Last thing I want to do is end up in a local prison for killing the wrong people. Or shot because they think we're the terrorists."

Quentin's dark eyes looked haunted. Haley knew that the death toll was weighing heavily on him. She was heartsick about having been forced to kill a man, but she would do it a thousand times over to survive. But how many times could Quentin's training and the surprise factor outcompete locals who knew the area and were well-armed, desperate criminals?

"What's the plan, Q?" she asked.

He glanced at Darby indecisively.

"It's okay to leave me alone." Darby sounded bitter. "I'll be all right."

His eyes flicked to Haley's, silently asking her opinion.

Haley nodded and turned to Darby. "Hide the same way you did last time, and we'll yell if it is safe to come out."

Darby nodded. She looked drawn today. Red hair escaping the band she'd used to try and tame it. None of them had eaten or drunk enough water today, and stress was beginning to reveal itself on their faces and health. All of them were waiting for the terrorists to show up again. For Darby it had to be the most terrifying prospect of all.

Haley reached out and touched her shoulder. "We'll be back. Hopefully with a rescue team."

Darby's gaze softened, and she nodded, dropping the nose of the rifle toward the ground.

Quentin eased to his feet. "Remember not to shoot first and ask questions later. Staying put and staying quiet is the best way to stay hidden."

"Yes, Dad," Darby muttered irritably. But she sounded rational again. Sane.

Quentin rolled his eyes and held out his hand to help haul Haley to her feet. His fingers were calloused but warm and strong. She trusted this man with her life, maybe even more than that.

They struck right, through a barely discernible goat path down the mountain toward the beach, keeping to the trees and trying not to make any noise. She wore her blanket as a sarong over the gym shorts Quentin had given her. Her stolen boots still rubbed her heel, but her skin was toughening up. Her pedicure looked surprisingly good under the circumstances.

When they got out of earshot of Darby she asked, "Do you really think this is a rescue bid?"

He turned and shot her a grin. God, the man was gorgeous, even all scruffy and bearded. "I figure it's fifty-fifty at this point." He kept the volume down. Sound traveled this close to the water.

She was getting fed up of the need to be quiet. She was going to spend an hour screaming her head off as soon as they got out of this mess. Hopefully Quentin Savage would be inside her the whole time.

They moved quietly and cautiously down the path. Birds flitted from branch to branch. Lizards basked in the sun before dashing away. The thick green coils of a snake had Quentin taking an abrupt detour.

He didn't like snakes. It was kind of endearing for a man who'd gone up against so many black-hearted thugs and won.

A minute later, he held up his hand, and she froze. They both sank to the ground beneath the height of the bushes. Through the gaps in the leaves, they could just make out the beach below and two figures were moving around near where they'd previously hidden the boat.

Men in combat uniforms. Heavily armed. Haley's breath seemed to lodge in her lungs, and she couldn't exhale. Quentin put a hand on the back of her nape and massaged the rock-hard tension trapped there. Slowly, her chest unlocked, and she began to breathe normally.

They watched silently. Then a black man in tactical gear stepped out from the shadows and walked across the beach toward the other men. He had F-B-I stenciled on his back in bright yellow letters.

She felt Quentin tense. "You know him?"

Quentin climbed to his feet. "I sure do. His name is Max Hawthorne. I'm his boss." He held his hands over his head and yelled down to the men on the beach. "Up here!" The men swung around to face him, and the guy called Hawthorne *whooped* loudly.

"Come on, let's go down to meet them, and then we'll go fetch Darby." Quentin took her hand, and they hurried through the brush, Quentin swatting the overhanging branches out of the way.

His fingers felt good around hers. She had the horrible feeling that once they were rescued, they'd go their separate ways, and she'd never see him again, and the idea terrified her. "I'd like to try that thing you mentioned, once we get back to civilization."

"What thing?" Quentin was barely listening. Her timing was terrible.

"The date thing."

He stopped so abruptly, she crashed into him. He caught her in his arms. "Seriously?"

She stared into those dark chocolate eyes. "I probably won't be very good at it, but hopefully I'll get a few meals that aren't fried crickets before we crash and burn."

He closed his eyes and rested his forehead against hers. "And, if we're lucky, some great sex. Let's not forget the great sex."

She chuckled. He slid his fingers into the hair at her nape and raised her chin to kiss her chapped lips. She looked a wreck, but he didn't seem to care. His beard was soft against her skin, and the emotion he put into that kiss was so profound, she felt bereft when he pulled away.

"Come on." He was eager and she was dragging her feet a little. What they'd been through had been horrible, but it had changed her. Made her stronger in ways she hadn't expected. Made her softer in other ways. Made her want to hold on to some of the good things she'd discovered—like Quentin, even if she didn't have the first clue how to make a relationship work.

They burst into the open, striding across the sandy beach, for the first time uncaring if they left footprints.

Quentin dropped her hand and embraced his coworker

who grabbed him around the waist and lifted him off his feet in a bear hug.

"We thought you were dead, for fuck's sake." The man's accent surprised her. A Brit.

"Ma'am." A dark-haired man in fatigues held out his hand to shake hers. "Do you need any medical attention?"

Another Brit.

"I'm okay. Nothing worse than a sunburn and some shattered nerves." She smiled, and everyone looked relieved and quickly introduced themselves.

"Are there any hostiles in the area that you know about?"

She shook her head. "We had some unfriendly visitors this morning, which is where we got these." She touched the butt of the assault rifle she carried. She'd gotten quite attached to the reassuring weight of it on her shoulder.

"Was it you who fired at us?" the man asked, not with censure but not exactly happy either.

Quentin answered, "No. Sorry. It was Darby O'Roarke. She's still a little jumpy after her ordeal."

"She's alive?" Hawthorne asked.

"Yes," Haley said, "but she was badly…treated." How the hell were they ever going to keep that secret? "We need to go back and tell her it's safe—"

"We have a team headed to the SOS site," the man assured her.

"Radio them and tell them to wait for us to get up there. She's not likely to trust a stranger," Quentin instructed quickly.

The men seemed to understand all the things they weren't saying, and the rise of their anger was palpable. One of the men radioed the other team, but a few seconds later the sound of gunfire lit up the quiet of the afternoon.

CHAPTER TWENTY-SIX

EBAN AND THE military contractors fanned out as they approached the area where the massive SOS had been spelled out with rocks. Whoever had shot at them was hiding or long gone.

"What are these things?" one of the ex-soldiers asked, pointing to the yellow tripods attached to solar panels.

Eban shook his head and then remembered Alex had mentioned the USGS talking about picking up some unusual readings from the equipment on the island. "I think they might be instruments that measure volcanic activity."

"You think that girl is still alive? The volcanologist?" One guy easily made the connection.

Eban didn't know. He was ashamed at the feeling of disappointment that wanted to creep in at the thought it was Darby O'Roarke and not Quentin Savage signaling for help. He walked to the edge of the clearing and stared into the thick green brush. He'd swear he could feel someone watching him, but he couldn't see anyone. Perhaps it was the unfamiliar environment getting to him. Tropical jungle and active volcanoes were not his usual turf.

But someone had shot at them. Someone had constructed this brilliant cry for help. Darby or Quentin?

Sweat had his t-shirt sticking to his skin under his body

armor, and there was an itch under his shoulder blade he didn't have a cat's chance in hell of reaching to scratch. His mouth was parched, and he could only imagine what a hostage must have to deal with on a daily basis. Never knowing if rescue was coming or if they were going to die a slow, anonymous death, or worse, a quick one, televised for all the sick haters.

He walked right up to where the dense forest started. Was he deluding himself with the idea that Quentin might still be alive? What state would he be in if he was? Would he understand they were here to help him?

"Quentin? You out there? It's me, Eban." He wanted whoever was out there to know he was an American. If it was Quentin, he'd have come out by now if he were able. Hope at finding the man alive once again plummeted. Eban felt sick to his stomach.

The operators surveyed their surroundings, assault rifles held in deceptively relaxed grips. One member of the group stayed out of sight.

Eban turned and headed back to the group.

"You're FBI?" A thin, quavering voice called out behind him. An American female. He scanned the area but wherever she was, she was well concealed.

"That's right. My name is Eban Winters. Who am I talking to?" Eban stared towards where he thought the voice originated. He kept his hands off his rifle but felt more than saw the rest of the team edge toward the margins of the clearing.

"Doesn't matter who I am. Prove to me you're who you say you are." The words were harsh and no nonsense.

"I have ID." He pulled his creds from his pocket and held them up. "I'm a negotiator for the FBI."

"Tell them to stop moving or I'm going to shoot!" The woman's voice was high-pitched and panicky. He held up his hands in warning, although no one wanted to stand in the crosshairs of an unknown entity.

"We aren't going to hurt you, but if you shoot, we will return fire. I don't know who you are, but I suspect you're one of three American women missing in this area. Women I'm here, along with these men, trying to rescue. Alice Alexander, Haley Cramer or Darby O'Roarke."

"Anyone could know those names—especially the kidnappers."

Whoever this was still had their wits, but had clearly been traumatized. They needed to go easy.

"It seems like you're going to need time to trust us. It seems like we make you nervous and scared which is understandable, but none of us are here to hurt you. Let me know what we can do to prove that to you."

"How do I know you aren't working with the men who kidnapped me?"

She sounded too young for Alice Alexander.

He held up his hands, palms up. "It's hard to prove a negative, but we have no intention of hurting you. We came in response to the SOS signal that a man named Alex Parker spotted on satellite imagery."

There was no reaction to Alex's name. Eban was ninety-nine percent sure he was dealing with Darby O'Roarke. He tried not to be disappointed. He wanted them all safe, but especially his boss.

Shots rang out, shattering the tranquility of this fake paradise. Bullets spat into the grass to his right. Sonofabitch. The woman yelled, "I told them not to move!"

One of the men shouted, "Darby O'Roarke! Quentin Savage is on the radio. He said he is on his way to get you. Please put the weapon down before someone gets hurt."

Eban swung to face the guy. "Quentin's alive?"

The man grinned and nodded. "Him and a blonde female."

Eban's knees sagged, and he held his head in his hands as relief crashed over him. Thank god. He drew in a deep breath. "Darby, I can appreciate why you're so scared, but I swear we are the good guys. I work with Quentin back in Quantico. Alex Parker, the guy who spotted the SOS, hired these men to find Haley Cramer. He's her business partner and friend. We have been going crazy thinking they were dead while waiting for your kidnappers to make contact. I've been talking to your father, and he's worried sick about you."

A shrill scream tore through the air and then the sound of a scuffle, then fists hitting flesh before something large crashed through the bush towards them. Eban had known one of the men would be working his way around to her position. He appeared suddenly, carrying an unarmed redhead at arm's length in front of him. The young woman's arms and legs were swinging and punching, but she was too small to do any real damage, and it was obvious the former soldier was trying not to hurt her.

But no one wanted a loaded weapon pointed in their direction, especially by someone who was emotionally fragile.

Eban handed his weapon off to the man next to him and went over to where the big man was trying to contain a furious hellcat without hurting her. There was something feral in her actions. Something so desperate, he knew without being told she'd been attacked and probably raped.

"Darby," he spoke calmly. "We are not going to hurt you. In fact, we would all lay down our lives to protect you."

The operator placed her on her feet and quickly backed away. She lunged at him and then pulled back.

She stood there, fists up, trembling, fear and rage battling in her eyes.

She was beautiful. Which took him by surprise. Bright red hair. The greenest eyes he'd ever seen. Freckles and pale skin.

The harm that had been inflicted on her raced across her features. Her expression was so fierce it broke his damn heart.

"We're not going to hurt you. I promise," he said softly.

She looked frantically around at all the men who were watching her with their guns pointed at the ground and their expressions understanding and sympathetic. She blinked and swallowed.

"You're really here to rescue us?"

"We're trying." Eban nodded and stood there, wanting to be there for her if she needed him.

"You really spoke to my dad?" Her voice cracked, and she looked over her shoulder as if ready to run.

He nodded. Jesus, what had they done to her?

"Dad's okay?" She turned back, waiting for reassurance.

"He's pretty upset, but we can call him shortly and let him know you're all right. You can talk to him if you want, but you don't have to, not yet," he added quickly when her eyes widened anxiously. "Whatever you decide is perfectly normal." Sometimes people who'd been held captive needed a little time to figure out their world again.

"*Normal.*" She huffed out a bitter sound, then rubbed her hands over her bare arms.

He registered marks there, and on her legs, but didn't let

his eyes waver from her face. “We’re here to rescue you, Darby. You’re safe now.” He opened his arms wide, feeling like a fool, but what the hell. If she wanted a hug, she could take one. If she didn’t, then he could deal with looking like an idiot.

She glanced around at them all and bit her lip. “I shot at your helicopter.”

“Yeah, better blame that on Quentin as I don’t think the pilot was too thrilled.”

“I’m sorry.” She swallowed repeatedly, blinking at the tears that shimmered in her eyes, tears she refused to let fall. Then she launched herself into his arms and held on so tight he thought she might strangle him, but he didn’t care. He closed his arms until he held her very gently, trying not to scare her.

Darby O’Roarke was safe in his arms and, though she was thin and bedraggled, she was more or less whole. She started sobbing, and he held the gazes of each of the operators one at a time, and they all wore identical expressions of misery and anger.

“It’s okay, Darby. We’ve got you. You’re safe now. We will keep you safe.”

CHAPTER TWENTY-SEVEN

QUENTIN MADE HIS way to a hospital room onboard the warship anchored north of Darby's island. It was full dark now, so they had a magnificent view of the lava flowing straight into the sea, but he'd never forget standing beside Darby and Haley in the moonlight looking down at that living fire.

Darby had insisted they put her yellow tripods back in the correct position before leaving the island. It had given them all something to do while waiting for the Navy to catch up.

He'd just got off the phone defending his right to be involved in the case at all, and also defending Haley. The head of the task force investigating the attack was suspicious of her, which pissed Quentin off. He'd explained that he'd requested the background check on Haley because of the incident with that slimy bastard Wenck who, it turned out, had survived the terrorist attack. The guy had left not long after the conversation they'd shared on the balcony.

Quentin hadn't confessed to the red-hot sex with Haley—the Bureau already knew too damn much about him. He had told them that he was now in a personal relationship with her and they, combined with Darby, were the best chance of finding and getting convictions against the terrorists. Against the task force commander's wishes, the director had let them continue with what they were doing, just so long as Haley wasn't allowed to access any confidential case material. Quentin had almost snorted. Like she hadn't lived every moment of that frickin' ordeal with him.

He knocked on the door and stuck his head inside. Rather than being in bed, Haley was sitting on the side of the mattress, talking on the ship's telephone. She looked up and waved him inside.

He'd hated being separated from her, but they'd all needed to be debriefed. A process that would probably continue once they got back to the States. A necessary evil, but irritating nonetheless.

She'd cleaned up. Wore a plain white t-shirt and some black leggings someone had found for her. Her feet were bare except for the pink nail polish. Her hair gleamed like honey, sun streaks and a tan making her look like she'd spent the week on a beach vacation rather than fighting for her life. She'd pulled her hair into a ponytail that emphasized the honed cheekbones and stubborn jaw.

Her eyes sparkled, and she laughed at whatever the person on the other end of the line was saying. "I love you, Alex Parker. Don't you ever forget that." She hung up the phone and looked at Quentin.

He crossed his arms and leaned back against the door. "You should have told him I love him too." Alex Parker was the man who'd spotted their SOS signal even though the dummies at USGS had missed it. He liked to think they'd have caught on eventually.

"You can tell him yourself when we get back to the States. He has a house in Quantico and a condo in D.C." She grasped her hands tightly together as if suddenly uncertain. "I'd like you to meet both Alex and Dermot, my business partners, who also happen to be my best friends."

So she'd been serious about giving this thing between them a try. This was difficult for her. It was difficult for him too.

He sat next to her on the bed, took her hand in his, rubbing his thumb over the base of hers. "I'd like that."

She met his gaze then, and her beauty stunned him, every single time. The fact a woman like her was looking at him this way, like she wanted to kiss the hell out of him and, even more inexplicably, that she wanted to sit here holding his hand was a miracle.

Was this his second chance? Even the thought scared the hell out of him. Losing Abbie had been catastrophic. Could he risk that sort of anguish again?

Haley leaned her head against his shoulder, and his throat closed. Damn if he didn't want to give it a try.

It was early days. He didn't need to leap fully into the void. They could take it slow. See how their feelings for one another stood up to real world challenges like him leaving the toilet seat up or her being messy and disrupting his orderly bachelor existence.

"Did you see Darby?" she asked. "How is she?"

"Doctors were happy with how well she's physically healing. We're trying to make sure someone from CNU is with her whenever she's awake. Eban Winters is there right now. She seems comfortable with him." He turned her hand over in his and then traced her lifeline down to the tendon beneath the delicate skin of her wrist. "She asked the doctors to sedate her for the exam." They'd run a rape kit, which had taken a lot longer than he'd hoped for. "She's on a course of intravenous antibiotics and prophylaxis." There would be no unwanted pregnancy.

Haley looked sad, and he remembered what she'd said about being infertile. "Does it bother you, not being able to have kids?"

"It's been a fact of life for me for a lot of years. I don't let myself think about it much." She looked pensive. "I've always been fine without children in my life. I get to play aunty to Alex's new baby. What about you? You ever want to be a dad? *Are* you a dad?"

The words were like bullets that raked his soul. He shook his head, unable to say the words even though he owed Haley an explanation about Abbie. He'd do it later when they were back in the States, and he could maybe explain exactly how much he'd loved his wife without making Haley feel like she had to compete with her memory.

That wasn't fair and wasn't necessarily accurate, because his feelings for Haley were intense. But he wasn't sure how much he could trust these emotions as they'd been borne by circumstances outside the norm.

He'd be lying if he'd said he wasn't relieved at the idea of Haley not being able to conceive. Losing his partner and their baby in one stroke was not something he ever wanted to risk again. So what if thousands of women went through childbirth every day? He was pretty sure he was jinxed, and even the thought of pregnancy made him sick to his stomach. And he was getting *way* ahead of himself. They hadn't even gone on a date yet.

"I heard Cecil Wenck and his bodyguards left before the attack." Her voice was calm but threaded with anger.

He nodded. He was furious but needed to let go of the

emotion if he hoped to stay anywhere near this investigation. "His lawyer is stalling when it comes to letting him be questioned by FBI officials." Wealth was apparently an effective shield when it came to law enforcement. The question was, why was he stalling?

"Did Chris survive?"

Quentin smiled. "Yeah, he did. As did Tricia Rooks and Grant Gunn who was busy getting drunk in town."

Haley smiled at him and bumped his shoulder. "I'm glad."

"Me too." Although it was a pitifully small number.

He checked the time and realized he was already late for a meeting. "I have to go see how plans are progressing."

"Can I come?" Haley asked.

He stared at her and frowned. Strictly speaking, it was government personnel only, but this wasn't classified information per se. She might remember something he didn't...

Quentin took her hand, kissed her fingertips and then let her go. "You can attend, but they might toss you out if things get sensitive, and you can't get pissy with them if they do. You and I are both here on sufferance."

She wiggled her brows and smiled. "Story of my life."

Wow, those words were a punch in the gut.

"Where are we going?" She slipped her feet into the same stolen boots she'd been wearing since the hotel attack.

"Hostage Rescue Team along with a few Navy SEALs and a few Indonesian Special Forces are going to conduct a dawn raid on the island. We're sending a drone for a look-see first."

Haley nodded and pulled her shoulders back like she was getting ready for battle. Revisiting that island wouldn't be easy, and they'd been relatively well looked after, just threatened and roughened up a bit.

Unlike Darby.

The only explanation Quentin could come up with was the terrorists had simply been too tired after the nighttime attack on the hotel, and he and Haley would have been beaten and tortured more if they'd not slipped away when they did.

It made the risk they'd taken worthwhile, especially as they'd found Darby. But what about the Alexanders? Their fate tormented him.

Haley followed him out of the room and along the narrow metal corridors. Quentin wasn't blind to the stir she caused amongst the mostly male crew. The white t-shirt she wore was thin and, if you looked hard enough, you could tell she wasn't wearing a bra.

Quentin narrowed his gaze at one guy who leered a little too obviously. It was one thing to admire beauty, it was something else entirely to ogle until he made someone uncomfortable.

"Relax." She ran her hand over his shoulder and down his arm in a possessive move meant to soothe him, which made him feel like a fool. "You're going to break your own jaw from clenching it so tight."

He forced himself to release the tension and let her go ahead of him up the metal stairway. The fact he couldn't look away from her ass meant he was just as base as these other men.

Dammit.

She was special. It wasn't simply her face or her figure. She was brave and smart and had a sense of humor even when things got seriously tough. But she was probably the hottest woman he'd ever been with, and that brought a pang of guilt right along with it. Abbie had been pretty and undeniably sweet but in a cute girl-next-door kind of way, whereas Haley was more international glamor.

He shook his head. It was like trying to compare rare jewels. Both were precious and unique and beautiful. Both had value that didn't diminish that of the other. He needed to tell Haley about Abbie, but the guilt still flayed him. He needed a little time to figure it out, to try to find not just the right words, but the right headspace.

He led Haley up another level and down a corridor. He knocked on the wooden door. A sailor opened it.

At the ensign's frown, Quentin stated, "Ms. Cramer is with me."

He indicated Haley go ahead and nodded to the people inside. Held out a chair for her to sit in while he stood. Kurt Montana, the HRT tactical commander, sat beside the ship's captain and all the HRT and Navy SEALs were lined up around the walls facing two large monitors. Even the head of the group of private military contractors who'd rescued them earlier had a seat at the table.

If Haley was intimidated by the amount of testosterone flooding the air, she didn't show it.

Eban Winters and Max Hawthorne arrived late—Quentin assumed that meant Darby was still out cold as he had been explicit in his instructions. The presence of the negotiators would hopefully remind people that the Alexanders were still believed to be captives, and a rescue attempt needed to be staged if possible. Unfortunately, the time for talking was definitely over. The US government no longer had the patience to bargain with these ruthless killers.

Now that everyone was here, the captain gave the signal.

The drone was hovering high above the island where they had almost certainly been held captive. There were so many islands in the region though, they needed to be sure.

The room became silent as the drone operator—somewhere onboard the vessel—took the aircraft lower. It had Tactical Nighttime Wide Area Surveillance and could detect moving targets.

Everyone in the room stared intently at the monitors as the feeds went live. The drone was whisper-quiet, so it was doubtful it would be heard over the nightly noise of the rainforest. The operator zoomed in on the small bay where the yacht had been moored. The boat wasn't there now.

Quentin made out the small shed were Darby had been held.

"That's definitely the right place," he confirmed. He would personally torch that shed as soon as forensics were finished there.

Quentin narrowed his gaze. He'd described to the drone pilot the route they'd taken up to the village, but it had been indistinguishable on the satellite images. He leaned closer as the thermal camera started to pick up the yellowish glow of human beings, but there was something odd about them. They were frozen in place. "Is there something wrong with the camera?"

Kurt Montana shook his head. "I don't believe so."

"Why isn't anyone moving?" Haley voiced the question everyone was thinking.

"They're either sleeping, or dead," Montana said grimly.

No one spoke as the drone pilot flew to the main camp. Again, people were visible on the heat profile of the camera, cooler looking than expected, lying haphazardly, all perfectly still.

Quentin clenched his fists.

The pilot moved the drone lower. A couple of dogs trotted out of wherever they'd been sleeping and looked up at the sky. None of the people reacted.

"What's the plan?" he asked Montana. The FBI was officially in charge of this operation, and Montana was in charge of the tactical side. The Navy might not like it, but they knew how to respect the chain of command.

Montana did not look happy, but that was an almost permanent state of being for the man.

"We need to assess the scene for biohazards before we go in, figure out if these people are asleep or dead. If they're dead, what killed them. We'll send in a small team fitted with biohazard suits and see what they find. Continue to monitor the area with the drone as they approach from the north."

As he'd suspected, there'd been another small harbor on the island with more boats and a helicopter landing pad. Most of those boats were still moored to the floating dock.

Quentin nodded. No one wanted to expose the team to potential hazards, but they needed to know what they were dealing with.

"I don't understand." Haley's eyes were huge.

"Neither do I. Let's go get some food from the mess hall and wait for these guys to report back."

Haley pushed back her chair, and he took her elbow, wishing he could shield her from what was likely to be a very ugly truth. Someone had murdered every man, woman and child on that island. The question was, who?

Eban and Hawthorne followed them out. "What do you want us to do, Boss?" Eban asked.

"Make sure Darby's okay. I want as much information as she can bear to give us on her captors. Hawthorne," Quentin narrowed his eyes at the former Brit, "find out whatever those guys discover as soon as they discover it." He pointed into the room they'd just exited. "I don't want to be left out of the loop."

Both men nodded and headed off in different directions.

Quentin led Haley down to the ship's galley where they both ate in silence. Haley yawned and suddenly looked incredibly tired. He felt the same way. He'd spent most of last night on watch.

"Let's catch a few hours' sleep. It'll take the team time to gear up and get to the island anyway."

At the door to Haley's room, he said goodnight and went to turn away, even though it felt weird not to be with her.

"Please don't leave me alone," she said quietly.

Quentin met her gaze. "Are you sure?"

Her soft smile was all the answer he needed.

CHAPTER TWENTY-EIGHT

HALEY STARED AT the moon through the room's porthole. Quentin had slipped quietly away half an hour ago, assuming she was dozing. But she was pretending. Before they'd gone to sleep, he'd made her promise not to mention, even to Alex, the fact that all the terrorists who'd attacked them appeared to be dead or drugged. The promise bothered her.

Hadn't Quentin figured out by now that Alex was one of the good guys? Without him, they'd still be on the island fighting off bandits. Didn't Quentin trust her judgment?

It was already starting—that awkward compromise between the "man in her life" and her friends/business partners who meant everything to her. And she wanted to watch the raid, but Quentin had said he wasn't sure she'd be allowed into the operations room for that, and that he'd call if she was.

She wasn't used to seeking permission or following orders.

Irritated, she reached for the tablet one of the nurses had loaned her and video-called Alex anyway. "Hey," she said brightly when he answered. "Am I bugging you?"

Alex's lips curved in a patient smile. He was sitting on the balcony of his swank D.C. apartment cradling baby Georgina. "Nope. We're out here giving Mallory some time to sleep. Seems like someone takes after her father and is a bit of a night owl."

"She's adorable."

Alex grinned. "I know. We're going to head down to Quantico to settle into the house with this bundle of joy in the next couple of days. Come stay with us when you get home."

"I'll be in the way."

"You're family. You're supposed to be in the way."

Her laugh came out all wobbly. "Okay. I'd like that."

"You still holding up?"

Haley felt her smile slip. "You know." She shrugged one shoulder.

His gaze narrowed. "So, you and the Fed, huh?"

She stared at him, astonished. "How did you know that?"

"I'd like to say it was my innate intuition or some funky bugging device you knew nothing about but actually, Mallory heard it from Lincoln Frazer. He heard it from Steve McKenzie who heard it from the Unit Chief of SIOC. Head of the task force investigating the hotel attack wanted Savage removed from anything to do with the case and flown home immediately, to get him away from *you* because *you* might have had something to do with the terrorist attack."

"What the hell? *Me*?" Her voice was a quiet shriek of outrage.

"It was a working theory after the task force discovered Savage had run a background check on you a couple of hours prior to the hotel attack."

"What?"

"I'd have done the same if I wanted to hook up with a stranger at a conference."

Haley knew her mouth was gaping wide open.

"McKenzie used his influence with the director, and they

managed to infuse a little common sense into the situation. You had no motive to kill hundreds of innocent people then get yourself abducted."

Their "relationship" had already caused trouble for Quentin, but he hadn't mentioned it to her. Hadn't blamed her in any way. "When Quentin told me not to contact you and divulge certain pieces of information…"

"He's trying to keep his job and follow the rules. Feds are big on rules. Ask me how I know?" He pulled a face. "Quentin staked his reputation on your integrity. Don't tell me anything you're not supposed to—unless you want him fired."

"Why would I *want* him fired?"

"So he'd be pissed off, and you two would have a fight, and then you'd have an excuse to dump him."

"Alex! What the hell?"

"Haley," Alex said with exasperation even as he kissed the baby's head, "I've known you for a long time. That's what you do, especially when you actually like someone. You put up with worthless dickheads twice as long as you'll date a decent man."

"Decent men are often excruciatingly boring or pompous assholes."

"Is Quentin?"

She stared at Alex through the screen for a long time, and neither of them spoke.

She'd already been putting up barriers she realized, so she could justify a retreat when a disagreement came up. That's why she was calling Alex. Because Quentin had asked her not to, and she didn't like being told what to do. It smacked of control the way her father had liked to control her.

But Quentin was simply doing his job, and she was acting

like a brat.

Dammit. She hated being predictable, hated perpetuating this cycle she was stuck in. No wonder she never had worthwhile relationships.

"Well," rather than admit Alex was right, she changed the subject, "I actually called to tell you more about the run-in I had with Cecil Wenck the night of the attack."

He was quiet after she'd relayed every detail of the story. Too quiet.

"I recorded it on my phone, but the FBI has my cell in evidence." Alex looked like he wanted to hit something. "You're not allowed to hurt him—not physically anyway. You're not even allowed to infect his computer systems with a virus as we would be the first people they'd suspect of such a move."

"No one would ever be able to trace it to me," Alex assured her.

"But the Feds would suspect, and maybe they'd stop working with us. Maybe they'd stop letting you work with Mallory."

He narrowed his eyes at the camera. "I can't believe you're so calm about this. I want to rip the guy apart."

And she wasn't the passive type, except when passive meant survival. "Trust me, I want him to get what he deserves, but I have bigger things to deal with first. Did you figure out why Wenck left early? Did someone warn him?" She might not be privy to investigative details, but Alex was *her* partner.

"He received a call on his cell around eleven. Headed straight to the airport and his private jet."

"He had to have been warned. Whoever attacked us didn't want him dead."

"I've had someone looking into the man's finances, and he

donates a lot of money to many different political candidates at municipal and national levels wherever he owns a mine, which is pretty much everywhere. He has a built-in protection network."

"I hate how corrupt this world is."

"We're never doing business with that douche or his company," Alex told her.

"I agree. Will you start digging around for me? See if there are any rumors of sexual assaults, or hints of affairs in his background? Some of the women might have been paid off or intimidated into silence."

"I can do that." Alex nodded, but the light in his eyes was icy cold.

"The FBI isn't having much luck getting an interview with him. I bet I could get in to see him."

"I don't want you near that..." He looked down at a sleeping Georgina before mouthing a vile curse into the camera.

She smiled grimly. "I'm not letting Wenck scare me, Alex. He's going to be knocked off his game regardless. And I think he'll want to see me to find out what happened during and after the attack. Or to see if we think he's involved."

Alex's jaw flexed. "Take the Fed with you, otherwise I will have to hurt the guy."

"Noted." Haley remembered something else. "One thing I forgot to mention earlier is the kidnappers took my grandmother's watch and some Tiffany diamond earrings."

"You loved that watch."

"They were threatening to cut off my nose at the time, and I'm more attached to that." Alex flinched, and she wished she hadn't said anything. "I was just thinking that it's almost bound to show up at auction at some point. I made a point of saying how valuable it was. The insurance info with photographs and more detailed information is in my safe." Which Alex could access in her Georgetown home. "It's the sort of thing you might track faster than the Feds, especially when they have other things on their minds."

Alex nodded. "I'll set up some web crawlers and trigger searches." Georgina started to fuss. "Feeding time."

Alex looked down with such adoration in his gaze, Haley felt another pang for what she couldn't have. "Talk to you tomorrow. Give Mallory my love."

She cut off the feed and sat there for a few minutes thinking about what Alex had said. Was he right? The idea she'd been running away all these years under the guise of fierce independence made her wonder what else she'd been lying to herself about.

She decided to go see Darby. It was early, but she couldn't sleep and wouldn't be surprised if Darby couldn't either.

Haley eased her feet over the side of the bed and back into her dead man's shoes. Truth was, she'd grown fond of the sturdy black military boots. She planned to keep them as a reminder of everything she'd been through, along with her gray woolen blanket.

She closed the door quietly behind her. Despite the hundreds of people onboard the ship, the area was deserted and quiet. She headed down the corridor to Darby's room and knocked on the door.

The door was opened by one of Quentin's colleagues, Eban Winters, who had similar coloring to his boss but was shorter and broader. And almost as handsome.

"She's sleeping." He didn't look particularly pleased to see her.

"Who is it?" Darby's groggy voice cut through the quiet.

Eban rolled his eyes and opened the door wider.

Haley slipped inside. "Just me. I couldn't sleep and thought I'd come check on you. If you want to rest, I'll leave."

"No. Please stay." Darby looked tiny amid the white sheets and pillows of the hospital bed. Her face was pale, her wild hair tamed into a tight, no nonsense braid, green eyes still worried. She held out her hand, and Haley walked over, took it, and sat beside her on the bed.

How long would it take before Darby stopped feeling that terror?

How long before Haley stopped feeling it?

"Where's Quentin?" asked Darby.

A notepad sat on the nearby chair, and Haley could see that Darby had been writing about her ordeal.

Haley eyed Eban. No wonder he looked strained and overprotective. She understood him better than he understood himself. The desire to guard this vulnerable woman had seeped into each of their souls.

"He's at some meeting that I suspect Eban should probably be attending too."

"I don't want Darby left alone..."

Interesting that he'd already claimed her.

"I'll stay." Haley toed off her boots and lay next to the other woman. Darby simply shifted over a few inches without a word. The time they'd spent together had bonded them more firmly than siblings.

Eban hesitated before picking up that notebook from the bedside table. Then he reached into his pocket and placed a phone in its place. "That's my personal cell. My work number is in the contacts." He reeled off the pin. "Call me if Haley needs to leave or if you get hungry or if you remember anything else you think is relevant."

That reminded Haley. "Did you find my cell on Nabat Island?"

Eban nodded.

"Any chance of me getting it back?"

"It's in Evidence back in Quantico now. You can put in a request."

Haley pulled a face. She needed that phone as it contained the recording of Wenck's attack on her. "I'll do that." She'd ask Alex to handle the request and a new phone in the meantime. She doubted they'd stay on the ship much longer. But she wanted to remain near Quentin which was unnerving. She didn't usually do clingy.

Eban went to leave.

"Will you come tell us…" Haley asked. "When you know anything?"

He pressed his lips into a thin line and nodded. Then he left.

Haley turned off the bedside light, and she and Darby lay there with their shoulders touching, each to the other a reassuring presence in an unfamiliar place. Darby's breathing finally eased into a steady rhythm, and Haley lay there, watching the water reflect off the ceiling and knowing that Special Forces soldiers were right now approaching the island, and that Quentin was in that briefing room watching the drama unfold. Still trying to protect her from unseen danger. Still trying to keep them both safe.

The armor around her heart was cracking, being pierced over and over again by the rapier that was Quentin Savage. She knew she wasn't good enough for him and wasn't sure how she was going to deal with the consequences when he finally figured it out.

BY THE TIME dawn came, Quentin was standing at the edge of the village where he and Haley had been held hostage a few short days ago. He wore full protective clothing with a military-grade air filter covering his nose and mouth. Not because the people here had died due to some unknown pathogen—death had been caused by the very obvious bullet wounds in each of their bodies. Unfortunately, those same victims now posed a danger to human health due to the spread of disease from their rapidly decomposing corpses.

US and Indonesian forensics teams were en route from Jakarta. Ballistics experts were being flown in from both the US and the Philippines so that there was no doubt as to the veracity of the results obtained. The US needed full transparency as it would be easy for someone to point the finger at them carrying out this massacre in revenge for the hotel attack.

It could have been one of the private military companies who'd lost people during the terrorist attack. While Quentin understood the motivation, one slaughter did not justify another. Whoever the culprit, the FBI would do their utmost to bring them to justice.

"You're sure these people were alive when you left?" Kurt Montana asked.

Ex-military with a knack for tactical operations, Montana considered negotiation a necessary evil derived from the launch of too many lawsuits when things had gone wrong in the past.

"Most of them were alive when I left." Quentin had already made out his reports about the men he'd killed during their escape. "I would never have committed this wholesale slaughter after the fact." Quentin's voice shook. Figuring out who was behind the hotel attack and his own abduction was now a lot more difficult. Most of the participants were dead.

He struggled to view the carnage unemotionally. These people had understood the kind of life they'd chosen. He glanced around, knowing from the thermal images he'd viewed that what was up ahead was going to be much worse than the scattered paramilitary soldiers he'd passed in the camp below.

"That's the hut where we were kept." He pointed it out to the videographer and ducked his head inside. Empty, except for the narrow cot he'd briefly shared with Haley. The dead guard had been removed and presumably buried.

Quentin continued into the village past the other huts. They ducked inside each one, making it a drawn out and depressing trek. All the dead were being catalogued. Photographed, fingerprinted and DNA samples collected for analysis, but Quentin didn't wait for the techs to process the bodies. He was looking for three people. The leader of this murderous troop—a man called Darmawan Hurek whom Quentin had identified from old photographs—and the Alexanders.

Someone had taken the yacht.

It could have been whoever attacked this village, but why would they give themselves away so obviously by being in possession of a stolen yacht that linked them to the crime?

Quentin was holding on to hope that the Alexanders had

somehow managed to flee when the village had been attacked.

He paused near the well. A large group of people had been rounded up here and gunned down. He spotted a brightly colored dress and recognized the young widow, Lyrita, clutching one of her children to her chest. She was barely out of her teens.

Bile churned in his stomach as he looked at the children. Innocents. Whoever had done this deserved everything the Indonesian and US governments threw at them. Sweat ran down his forehead and into his eyes even though the sun was barely up.

"You okay?" Montana asked him.

"Fine." Quentin carried on.

The men who'd found them on Darby's volcano yesterday morning had been part of this terror group. Had they left before the death squad attacked? Or were they the killers? The fact the villagers hadn't fled into the jungle suggested the shooters had been trusted enough to be walking amongst them.

Quentin had no idea. Maybe some people had gotten away and hidden in the jungle, but the drone hadn't picked up any human heat sources on the island.

He ascended the steps into the old plantation house. The place was dilapidated, water stains on the ceilings suggesting the roof leaked, moth eaten furniture that looked as if it had been around since the glory days of the spice trade. But it wasn't a total dump.

Several corpses littered the premises. One woman was naked in the bedroom, but it didn't appear as if she'd been sexually assaulted. Gunned down but not raped—the killers had been fast and systematic. A half-filled suitcase sat near the closet. A man's clothes filled some of the drawers and hung on hangers. Quentin was almost certain Hurek lived here. Was that his wife or lover lying there?

"Remind the forensic teams to get DNA profiles from the bedding."

Montana keyed in his radio and relayed the message.

No sign of the commander's body or his extendable baton which Quentin had wanted to shove in Hurek's face.

Quentin exited and went down the steps off the front porch. He walked farther along the path. Flies buzzed. Brass bullet casings were strewn in the dirt and in the brush. To the right was a hut with a large metal padlock securing the door.

"Bolt cutters," Quentin snapped.

An agent from HRT withdrew some from a heavy tool bag he'd lugged with him. Quentin let him snip the thick iron and gather the lock into an evidence bag before dragging the door wide. The stench hit as Quentin stepped inside, blood, sweat, and excrement. The overpowering sharpness took his breath and made his eyes water—that, along with the scene before him.

A tall, blond man lay stretched over the much tinier form of an older woman. Both of them were emaciated, hair long, frazzled and gray.

There were seven bullet holes in Erik Alexander's back. He'd died trying to protect his wife.

Quentin closed his eyes. He'd failed these people multiple times over. First, he'd failed to negotiate their freedom, and then he'd failed by not rescuing them when he and Haley had escaped. He stepped outside and let the other members of the team do their job. Unlike him, they were good at it.

"Hey!" Kurt Montana yelled. "Someone call for a medical

team."

Quentin ducked back inside. They'd rolled Erik Alexander carefully off Alice, and laid the guy on the floor. She was covered in blood, but his sacrifice had paid off. Even though it took a moment, Quentin made out the shallow rise and fall of the woman's chest.

"Sonofabitch. She's alive."

CHAPTER TWENTY-NINE

EBAN STARED OUT the porthole in Darby O'Roarke's room. He itched to get to work and help figure out what the hell was going on but didn't want to leave Darby alone. Haley Cramer was being taken on a tour of the ship by the captain. Eban had the feeling his boss wasn't going to like that.

Or maybe he wouldn't care.

Maybe theirs was one of those relationships that had sprung out of emotional intensity and proximity of the moment and would fizzle out just as fast. Eban didn't blame the guy. The woman was a walking wet dream. Eban didn't feel that way but, unfortunately for him, his weakness had always been redheads.

The door was open to make Darby feel more relaxed and to get some air moving around the small cabin. But they were in a metal boat near the equator and, despite some attempts at A/C, it was damn hot.

"What is it you aren't telling me?" Darby asked suddenly with a frown.

"What do you mean?"

She rolled her eyes. According to her files, she was twenty-four years old and had started her doctorate work at the Geophysical Institute, University of Alaska Fairbanks, last September. That she was smart was a given but what a paper record couldn't tell you was the spark of defiance that lit her clear green eyes when she managed to forget, however briefly, what had happened to her. Or how those shadows reached out and ripped his heart out whenever she didn't.

"Where are we going then?" she asked.

The ship's engines had started up thirty minutes ago.

"I don't know." *But he had a good idea.*

Darby gave a huff and kicked off the sheet that covered her bare legs.

He glanced over and caught sight of some of the mottled bruises and cuts on her thighs. One bruise looked like a handprint on her pale skin.

"Stop it," Darby snapped. "I don't need your pity."

What he was feeling wasn't pity. It was burn-the-house-down fury, but he doubted his manly rage would make her feel better. "I'm sorry about what happened to you, Darby."

She looked away and changed the subject. Sometimes, he noticed, she faced what had happened to her head-on. Other times she couldn't seem to face it at all. "I need something to wear."

He crossed his arms over his chest. "Where do you intend to go?"

She gave him a perplexed look. "For a walk?"

"The doctors want you to rest."

"I'm done resting."

"I—"

She held up her hand. "If you aren't helping me then you can leave."

Little Miss Pissy. He went to an overhead locker, opened it and pulled out a canvas bag of her gear. He tossed it on the bed, and she grinned at him and damn if he didn't feel like a goddamn hero. Apparently, his ego really was that fragile.

He stepped outside the room while she dressed. When she came out, she was wearing green canvas shorts and a yellow t-shirt with some sort of geology conference logo on it. She'd strapped river sandals to her feet and pulled a University of Alaska ball cap over that vivid hair which was now constrained in a ponytail. Looking at her, aside from the bruises that dotted her body, you'd never know she'd been brutally assaulted a few days ago.

Her eyes shied away from his, and she seemed to know what he was thinking. He pushed himself off the wall.

"Where do you want to go?" He sounded surly.

"The deck. I want some fresh air." She looked about uncertainly. "I don't remember which way it is."

"This way. Come on." Eban led her through winding corridors up several staircases and then up onto the main deck. They passed seamen along the way, and he felt Darby shrink every time she drew their attention.

Up on deck, she went straight to the railing and wrapped her fingers around the metal bars. She closed her eyes and raised her face to the sky, clearly enjoying the cool breeze if her flushed cheeks were any indication.

He couldn't look away from those slightly parted lips and the delicate line of her throat, until he hit the first bruise and turned away, disgusted with himself. She'd been hurt, and he was thinking how pretty she was? What sort of asshole acted that way?

A group of sailors came on deck, joking around, laughing. Darby's eyes startled open, and she angled herself so he was between her and them.

As soon as they spotted Darby, the sailors sobered, and

their expressions morphed to pity, and they shuffled away.

Darby turned her back on them and stared out at the sun low in the east. "Is this how it's always going to be, do you think?" she asked quietly. "Me acting like a scared rabbit and men looking at me with pity."

"Of course not." He hoped.

Her green eyes narrowed at him. "Will every man I sleep with treat me differently because of what they did to me?"

This wasn't exactly what he wanted to be discussing with her. He didn't have a psych degree. But pushing her to talk, to get every piece of bitterness out so she could start to heal…

"Most reasonable men would want to be careful they don't upset or scare you if they were lucky enough to find themselves in that position." He didn't even want to think about all the buffoons out there who might mess it up for her. "The best thing might be to let yourself fully heal before you become intimate with anyone. If they are in any way worthy, they'll wait."

"I was a virgin."

Her words struck him so hard he reached out and held onto the railing, his knees threatening to buckle.

"Pathetic, right? I was dating a guy before I started my Ph.D. He dumped me because I wouldn't sleep with him. It feels like such irony, like such a waste of time. I was a fool to guard something so fiercely when it could be so easily taken by force."

The words felt like a serrated knife being dragged backwards and forwards over his heart. He already knew the world could be a vicious place. He saw it regularly. But rarely was it this raw or personal.

"You weren't foolish, Darby. You made a personal choice.

One day you'll find a guy worthy of all that." He frowned. "And I don't believe that rape takes someone's 'virginity.' Rape isn't sex or making love. You've never had sex, never experienced genuine intimacy." He tried to keep his voice even. "You can still make the choice of who you want to cross that threshold with."

She pulled a face. "Would you have sex with someone who'd been degraded the way I have? Who jumps at the slightest noise and lashes out even at people who are kind?"

If he told her the truth, she'd run a mile, so he kept his mouth shut.

She huffed out a breath and turned away. "Thought so."

He shifted so they couldn't be overheard. She held herself stiffly.

"Ask me again when you're ready to start thinking about that part of your life. In the meantime, don't be in any rush to have sex with men who probably don't deserve to be in the same room as you, let alone in your bed." His voice was a little firm, but he meant every word. "Give yourself time to heal. Be kind to yourself because you deserve it."

She gave him a look he couldn't interpret, and then her gaze shifted onto the southern horizon behind him. "Where are we going?"

The dark silhouette of an island started to grow on the horizon. Her green eyes latched onto it and widened, then her gaze shot to his. "We're going back to the island."

Her nostrils flared, and she started to shake her head and back away. "I'm not going back there. I can't…"

"They can't hurt you anymore." He took her hand. "I swear I won't let anyone hurt you again, Darby. I *swear* it. And neither will the US Navy."

She stopped fighting him and simply crumpled against his chest as if someone had snapped the strings that held her up. She was sobbing so hard, Eban couldn't bear it. He picked her up, and she buried her nose against his shoulder as he carried her back to the sickbay, passing curious and pitying stares she would have hated if she'd spotted them.

Inside her room, he closed the door and went to put her down, but she clung to him. Instead he turned and sat, still holding her in his arms.

He rocked her until her tears ran dry, and the shudders stopped racking her body. Slowly she recovered her composure, but he held her in his lap, feeling the beat of her heart slowly settle and the soft heat of her body relax.

Her hand rose and cupped his chin, and he looked down at the reddened eyes and tearstained cheeks.

"Will you kiss me so I have one good memory to think about when all the bad ones crowd in?" Her eyes started to panic as soon as she asked. "Oh, my god. Of course, you don't want to kiss me, you're here to babysit me not be my personal sex therapist."

She tried to sit up, but she was off balance, and he decided that wasn't a bad thing.

"I'm so sorry. That was such a stupid thing to suggest—"

He leaned down and very, very softly touched his lips to hers. Just a brush of sensation. Just a stroke of tenderness. Then he pulled away and smiled into her shocked eyes.

"Try to remember that in the darkest times, Darby." Then he set her beside him on the bed and left the room, because the last thing he wanted to do was scare her.

HALEY SPOTTED QUENTIN arriving back on the ship now anchored off the island where they'd been held hostage. Even from a distance, he looked grim. She wanted to go to him but was aware he had a very important job to do whereas she was doing nothing of significance. She'd spoken to her assistant, Jane Sanders. Jane, who was the girlfriend of one of Haley's favorite operatives, had taken over running logistics for the firm. Jane had assured her she had everything under control and urged Haley to take some time to recover from her ordeal, but she was already bored.

Haley made her way down to her room, wondering if Darby wanted some female company and maybe Eban, some respite. She found him on sentry duty outside Darby's door.

"Is everything okay?" Haley asked.

He nodded, but his eyes looked worried. "She fell apart a little when she realized we were back at the island where you were all held captive."

Haley reached for the door handle but paused when a commotion started at the other end of the corridor. Someone was being stretchered into a room and a whole squad of men, including Quentin, crowded into the hallway. She and Eban went to see what was going on.

"Is that Alice Alexander?" Eban asked.

Haley recognized the name.

Quentin nodded, but he didn't look happy. "She's alive. Barely. Her husband was shot dead as he shielded her with his body."

Quentin's dark eyes held hers. They were black with emotion. His now cleanly-shaved jaw clenched.

"They were held captive in the same place we were?" Haley asked.

He nodded. "A hut between the plantation house and the latrines. In the jungle off to the east." He looked torn up over the admission.

"You can't save everyone, Savage." This from the shorter bullish man, Montana, who was as always dressed in black tactical gear.

Quentin shot the guy a death glare. "I didn't even try."

"You had your hands full getting two female hostages off the island, one of whom was in clear distress." Montana's low voice boomed. "You couldn't have known for sure the Alexanders were there. You did what you could, just like you did at the hotel when you and Miss Cramer pulled the few survivors out of the burning building. Without you they'd all be dead." He slapped Quentin on the back and went back to talk to his men.

Quentin's eyes returned to hers before turning to Eban and the third negotiator who'd appeared out of nowhere.

"Darmawan Hurek was not found amongst the dead. I suspect he escaped on the yacht." Quentin was clearly angry about what he had seen. "Justice won't be fully served until Hurek is captured. Darby will never feel safe until all those bastards are dead or behind bars."

"What's the next move?" Eban asked.

Quentin glanced at Haley, and she was reminded she wasn't an agent. He surprised her by saying quietly, "Everyone on that island was slaughtered, including all the women and children. Why?"

"Retaliation? For the hotel attack," Eban suggested. "Maybe Hurek ordered everyone killed to take the pressure off. After all, most of the terrorists who attacked the hotel are now dead," Eban suggested. "Maybe he thought that would appease the US and Indonesian authorities?"

"Well, it won't appease me," Quentin said through gritted teeth.

"And it won't appease me," Haley agreed.

"Or just to shut them up?" The other hostage negotiator, Max something-or-other put in. "No witnesses."

"Or perhaps you were kidnapped to order and whoever wanted you alive didn't believe Hurek when he told them you'd escaped?" said Eban.

"Seems a bit extreme," Max put in.

"Everything about this is extreme," Quentin bit out. "Someone took advantage of the fact they knew where I was going to be at a certain time and everyone else was collateral damage?" The idea clearly horrified him. He shook his head. "Why? And who?"

"Someone with connections. Most people can't pick up a telephone and dial the local terrorist to help with a kidnapping," said Eban.

"Did Cecil Wenck talk to investigators yet?" Haley asked.

Quentin shook his head. "They rescheduled for later today. Wenck was still too 'shaken' to be able to meet with them." His words dripped condescension.

"Or he was waiting to hear back about whether or not any of the terrorists survived this attack?" Haley mused.

Quentin frowned. "He showed no signs of recognition that night on the balcony. And I can't see a clear motive for him attacking the conference or him wanting me taken alive."

"Maybe he contacted them after he bonded with you on the balcony. Decided to keep you alive. His leaving when he did is highly suspicious." Haley crossed her arms over her chest. "I want to talk to him."

"No."

"I wasn't asking permission." She smiled at the idea. Federal agent or not, lover or not, he didn't get to tell her what to do. And if he wanted to, then better to find out now and end this thing before either of them got too emotionally involved.

Quentin stared at her long and hard. She wondered what exactly he was looking for. A crack in her resolve? Not likely.

"What do you want us to do, Boss?" Max was clearly amused by her defiance.

"We could detain Ms. Cramer for questioning," Eban suggested with a glint in his eye.

"Don't even think it," the two of them said together.

"They want the three of us back at Quantico ASAP. Crisis Negotiation Unit is short-staffed," Quentin added, clearly contemplating his options.

"We've been kind of busy," Eban argued.

"No kidding." Quentin smiled. "Thanks for coming to find me."

"Nothing was stopping me from being here." Eban clasped a hand on the back of his neck and looked away as if embarrassed by the depth of his emotions. "I'm just glad we found you alive."

Quentin appeared to come to a decision. "Eban, I want you to accompany Darby and Alice Alexander until they are safely back in the States. When Alice is able to talk, I want you to get a statement. Hopefully we can arrange a transport back to the States for all of you today. Max, you head back to Quantico on the first available flight."

"I don't mind staying." The tall, black man tugged on his ear.

"You're way overdue leave, and now all the hostages are

accounted for. The legat can handle anything that arises in Jakarta should Alex Parker dig up anything there. Go home. Take a short break then get back to the grind."

"What are you going to do?" Eban asked.

One side of Quentin's mouth curved up in a smile. "I'm heading back to Quantico."

Haley shuffled her feet and tried to hide her disappointment.

He shot her a look that told her he knew exactly what she was thinking. "Via Darwin."

She closed her eyes as relief shot through her. Wenck's attack had been a major trauma at the time but had paled after what had happened next. But she'd have been lying if she'd claimed she wasn't nervous about confronting the man alone.

"Between the two of us, I think we can get Wenck to reveal what he knows," said Quentin.

"Even if he's responsible for mass murder?" Eban said dubiously.

"Yes," Quentin countered. "He thinks he's untouchable. We just need to give him enough rope so he can hang himself."

CHAPTER THIRTY

CECIL WENCK'S MANSION was in the Fannie Bay area of Darwin in Australia's Northern Territory, a classically beautiful home largely hidden behind tall garden walls and massive security gates.

Quentin pulled up in the rented Mercedes and pressed the intercom. "Quentin Savage to see Mr. Wenck."

"Do you have an appointment?"

"No, but I'm pretty sure Cecil will want to talk to me. Tell him we met last Saturday night." If nothing else, Quentin was betting on basic human curiosity getting him through the door.

Thirty seconds later, the gates opened, and Quentin drove in before anyone could change their mind.

The gardens were green and lush, the landscaping elegant with a large stone fountain the centerpiece of the lawn area, gurgling away despite a recent drought. Quentin parked in front of the five-car garage.

Wenck came to the massive double door of the mansion, trailed by the bodyguards Quentin had seen in the bar the night of the attack. Quentin got out of the car but left the front windows rolled down. Haley had agreed to wait in the backseat so Quentin could try to establish a rapport with Wenck. The rear windows were tinted, and she was hidden from view. If they needed to shake the mining billionaire out of his comfort zone, she could confront him later. Right now, Quentin was happy she was safely out of sight.

She'd told him about the recording of the attack before they'd left the ship. He'd asked if the FBI could get a copy to add to the file they were building on Wenck. Even though it had to be deeply personal and upsetting, she'd agreed, as long as the recording was copied with Alex Parker present, and shared only with her express permission, excepting judicial proceedings. She'd had her lawyer draw up the agreement, and the DOJ had signed for expediency's sake—especially as no one had been able to access her phone data in the meantime.

Alex Parker strikes again.

Wenck's face lit up when he saw him. "Mate! Good to see you. I thought you were a goner."

They shook hands. Quentin searched for some artifice or deception in the man's ugly, round face but he was either an exceptional actor or genuinely pleased to see him alive.

"They told me everyone from the hotel died." The man gave a visible shudder. "What a bloody nightmare."

Authorities had told the media that there were no survivors in order to safeguard them until the perpetrators of the violence had been captured. The fact Wenck also seemed to believe it was interesting, assuming the reaction was genuine.

"I managed to escape the hotel, but the gunmen captured me. Took me to a remote island where I eventually managed to get away."

Wenck's eyes were huge, and he looked entranced. "You should get a movie deal out of that. I know people in Hollywood. I'll set you up."

The fact Wenck wanted to commercialize an event where

so many people had died sickened Quentin, but he could see why some people might like the guy if they took him at face value. It was one of the things that made serial predators so dangerous.

"Maybe when I retire." Quentin raised the sunglasses he'd bought that afternoon when he and Haley had resupplied themselves at a mall in the city. They'd caught a ride here on a private jet with the men Alex Parker had hired to help bring them home.

Quentin's laptop had been his biggest practical loss from the hotel attack, but mainly in terms of the amount of paperwork it would generate from the admin back at headquarters. Not to mention his creds and wallet and all the other things he didn't even want to start thinking about. He didn't even have keys to his condo.

"Is now a bad time to talk?" Quentin was actively fishing for a "no" response. "No" made people feel safe and secure. It gave them the confidence to hear someone out.

Wenck regarded him for a long moment and then seemed to relax. "No, mate. Come on in."

He led them through the white marble entrance, straight through an entryway and out into an area with a patio and a large pool.

"I'm assuming they sent you to get a statement about last Saturday night?" Wenck settled into an outdoor sofa and indicated for Quentin to join him. The bodyguards faded into the shadows.

"I'm not here in an official capacity, although obviously I am an officer of the law."

That surprised the guy.

Quentin only lied to people who were about to get the

sharp end of a tactical assault.

"I was curious because when I was escaping my room via the balcony, I first jumped over to your room to urge you to come with me, but there was no one there. FBI officials informed me you flew home before midnight."

A male staff member brought out two glasses of ice-cold sparkling water. Quentin wondered if the wife knew Wenck had grabby hands when it came to the female gender and kept temptation to a minimum.

When the server left, Wenck said, "The timing looks pretty suss, huh?"

"The timing?" Quentin mirrored.

"You know, me packing my bags, and then the hotel getting attacked."

Quentin held the man's gaze. "A little."

"It's not what you think. I didn't have anything to do with those bastards attacking the conference. They've caused me a major headache."

"Headache?"

"Yeah." Wenck took a long gulp of water and immediately signaled for more. It was hot outside, even though it was officially winter here. A fine mist began to appear around the bushes, the sprinkler system adding to the overall humidity and causing Cecil to wipe sweat from his brow. Quentin was goddamn roasting, but it was cooler here than in Indonesia, and he had deodorant now so that was a win.

"I went there to get more competitive bids on a security contract that's up for renewal at the end of October. But with all those execs dying last week and the heightened threat to Westerners in general most of the bids have been withdrawn as the companies regroup. I'm gonna stick with the firm I already use, for now. Less hassle."

The selfishness of the man was mind-blowing, but Quentin had to ignore that and instead make the man feel understood. Quentin paraphrased and repeated Wenck's words back to him to show him he was being heard. He summarized Wenck's position and ended with, "So the fact that so many security contractors died actually had a negative impact on your business dealings?"

"That's right." Wenck nodded eagerly.

Bingo.

"It all seems so unfair that you had to go back to the drawing board on something you thought was almost completed, and I'm sure something you want to make sure is taken care of properly. Security is obviously very important to you and your company. I can see why this would be frustrating for you and cost you a lot of time and money." Labeling and tactical empathy.

"Yeah, exactly. My costs have skyrocketed because of the increased threat. Those security guys take home a lot more than most miners for a lot less graft, that's for damn sure." Wenck spoke as if he wasn't the person paying the wages.

The man drained his second glass of water, and Quentin also accepted a refill this time. "How was it you came to leave so suddenly that night, or had you always planned it that way?" *Rape and run*?

Wenck scratched his face and huffed out a deep breath. "I'm not gonna lie." That usually meant someone *was* going to lie, but Quentin heard him out anyway.

Wenck looked around nervously as if someone might overhear and leaned closer. All the better for Quentin's cell phone to pick up his words. "I don't usually go in for all that divine intervention bullshit, but now I've got to wonder if someone up there isn't looking out for me."

"Looking out for you?"

"Yeah. After I finished talking to you, I went back to the room to call my missus like I said I was going to, remember?"

"Uh huh." Minimal encouragers. Non-judgmental tone. It wasn't easy when he knew what Cecil had done to Haley before their conversation.

"She beat me to it. Glenda. Bawling. So I knew something was crook. Said she'd been involved in a car accident. Some guy had driven straight into her when she drove home from the yacht club. Wrecked the fucking Mercedes—excuse my language."

"Was she hurt?" Quentin frowned.

"You'd have thought she'd lost a limb from the way she was carrying on, but thankfully she only had a few cuts and bruises. Those cars are built like tanks so he came off worse, but I rushed back to make sure she was okay."

"Huh." Quentin gave a soft laugh. "Her car accident saved your life? What are the chances of that happening?"

Slim to none.

Was Wenck telling the truth? If he was, could the accident have been orchestrated to get Wenck on a plane out of there?

"I'm still curious as to why you didn't want to talk to FBI? I mean, obviously you didn't have anything to do with the shooting, but why not tell them everything you knew? Nothing makes them suspicious like someone avoiding their questions."

Wenck grunted. "I don't owe the FBI any answers." He looked irritated. He rubbed a hand over his mouth. "Is this off the record?"

Quentin nodded. He wasn't a reporter, though. He was a federal agent. Nothing was ever off the record during a federal investigation. "The wife had had a few drinks and shouldn't have been driving. I mean, I pay a chauffeur to be on staff, but she likes to drive herself." His mouth tightened. "Police got involved, but I called the commissioner on the way to the airstrip and managed to get it squared away. I paid for all the damage," he assured Quentin as if that made it okay.

His wife had been driving under the influence and crashed into another car, and he'd used his connections to ensure she wasn't arrested?

"I know what you're thinking," Wenck said.

Quentin highly doubted it.

"Should've made her learn her lesson and take her punishment, but as it saved my life, I couldn't bring myself to be too hard on her. She won't do it again—I'll make sure of that." Wenck leaned back in his chair as if he got to make all the laws around here. Perhaps he did.

Quentin definitely needed to find out more details about that crash. He also intended to forward a copy of this conversation to a pal in the Australian Federal Police.

The sound of female laughter drifted through the hallways.

"That's the missus now. Don't tell her I told you. She'd be embarrassed."

What she should be was arrested, but he doubted the States was any less corrupt. All it took was a rich donor, a call to a politician, an angry governor coming down hard on a police chief. Yeah. As much as he wanted to believe they were better than this, he didn't. But he did believe in accountability.

A pretty brunette, five-four, a hundred-thirty pounds, around forty years old wearing a flowery sundress walked in with her arm hooked through Haley's.

Quentin thought Wenck was going to have a coronary. The man opened his mouth but didn't seem able to draw in a breath. His face went puce, and the vein in his temple started to throb.

Quentin stood. "This must be Mrs. Wenck."

"I can't believe you left this poor girl in the car on a hot day without the air con on," the woman scolded.

"She said she wanted to take a nap." Quentin smiled, meeting Haley's keen gaze.

"Passed out more like." The lady of the house waved at the male staff member. "Grab us some water and a nice bottle of white would you, love?"

Haley towered over the other woman and patted her arm like they were old friends. Haley wore skintight jeans that showed off every inch of her long legs and a hot-pink, strappy top that cupped her breasts in a way that made Quentin's mouth water. He had to smile at her footwear. She'd bought a pair of stiletto sandals but was still wearing those black combat boots. Her hair was shiny and bounced around her shoulders like some shampoo commercial, and she'd applied eye shadow and lipstick, giving anyone a run for their money in the kissability department.

"I didn't want to interfere with all the business talk." Haley's smirk was directed at Wenck, and he shifted his feet beneath his chair as if he was about to flee.

Wenck's wife held out her hand to Quentin and shook enthusiastically. "Glenda, Cecil's wife. Haley was telling me all about your recent escapades. I can't believe what the two of you went through." Her free hand clutched her throat.

Wenck swallowed repeatedly and kept looking nervously

between Quentin and Haley, obviously expecting them to reveal his abhorrent behavior. His expression started to turn belligerent.

"I'd never have gotten out of there in one piece without Quentin," Haley said. "He saved me numerous times. I don't know how I'll ever repay him." Her blue eyes shone with sincerity, and she gripped his wrist as she sat beside him.

"I don't need 'repaying'." The words came out sharp. But the last thing he wanted was her thinking she owed him anything. That's not how relationships worked, not even fledgling ones. "Haley is one of the brightest, toughest, and most determined people I've ever met. We worked together and got out alive."

"Aw," Glenda reached for Cecil's hand and squeezed. The man turned and looked at her with so much love and pain in his eyes it was hard to watch. He clearly expected them to tell Glenda about how he'd tried to force himself on Haley. And the man no longer wanted to pay the price of that attempted rape—he'd never expected to pay the price. He was a coward and a bastard, hiding behind his wealth and privilege.

Quentin turned to Haley. It was up to her how they approached this.

"It's your decision," he murmured so only she could hear. He wanted to keep the guy on side because he wanted to see what Wenck did after they left. Alex was monitoring Wenck's phone and computer lines, and the FBI had an agent ready to tail the billionaire in an unofficial capacity. Quentin was determined Wenck wouldn't get away with his crimes, but it could take time and patience to build a case. If Haley wanted to strike back at the man today, face-to-face, Quentin had no right, nor desire, to stop her.

She blinked rapidly a few times, clearly surprised that he was letting her be the one to choose. She took a glass of water and drank the whole thing down in one go.

Glenda laughed. "See, I told you she was thirsty."

Quentin smiled. Glenda seemed nice enough. But the fact she'd had too much to drink and then driven home was reckless, thoughtless, and criminal. He would be delving further into the "accident" that had brought Wenck home at exactly the right moment, and Quentin was sure the recording of this conversation would have consequences for local cops and politicians. Not to mention Glenda and Cecil.

The bigger questions were whether Wenck had something to do with that terrorist attack on the hotel, or the massacre on the island afterward? If he had, the FBI and Alex Parker would figure it out.

A squeal was followed by giggles, and then a girl erupted out of the entry way and cannonballed into the pool.

The splash washed over him and Wenck. Quentin welcomed the coolness, and the others laughed.

"That's our pride and joy, Katie. Everything I do is for her," Wenck said, clearly trying to build empathy.

"I doubt that very much," Haley said quietly.

Cecil's jaw hardened.

"You don't play golf for your daughter. You don't drink beer for her." Haley was staring at the little girl who was splashing in the pool.

Glenda laughed. "She's got you there, love. I keep telling Cecil he needs to start taking it easy. Hand over the reins to a manager or sell the company. It's not like there's anything we need. You could be like Bill Gates and give away half your fortune."

Cecil's eyes widened. "She's trying to kill me." He laughed, but he looked terrified by the idea.

Because his wealth and success defined him, Quentin grasped. Was that what drove Haley? Was she defined by wealth and success? He realized he had no idea what she liked to do outside work—then again, he did nothing except work. Maybe they could figure out this stuff together if they lasted long enough.

Haley swallowed repeatedly, and Quentin could see she was distressed. He pushed to his feet. "It was nice to meet you, Glenda." He gave Cecil's hand a firm shake, searching his eyes for any inkling of deceit, but still finding nothing. "I know you have connections in the region, Cecil. Perhaps if you hear anything about who might have been involved in the attack on the hotel, you'd do me the courtesy of letting me know?"

Cecil smirked, seeming to realize Quentin and Haley were not going to reveal his despicable actions in front of his wife and child—although the wife deserved to know the truth about the sort of animal she was married to. Wenck probably thought he'd gotten away with it and, to some degree, he had. It would be almost impossible for the Department of Justice to press charges without more evidence. But Quentin had no doubt there'd be other women and other incidents. He wasn't giving the guy a free pass. He was being patient and building a case.

Wenck stood and nodded, visibly relieved. "Always happy to help the FBI. I had my site managers put out a few feelers when this happened so if I hear anything back, I'll let you know."

Asshole.

Haley gripped Quentin's hand as if she sensed how close

he was to letting go of pretense and smacking the guy. She entwined his fingers with hers, reminding him this wasn't about him.

"Time to go home."

He nodded. He was looking forward to getting his life back.

CHAPTER THIRTY-ONE

THIRTY HOURS LATER, Quentin parked his SUV and jogged up the stairs to Chris Baylor's apartment near Dupont Circle, Washington, D.C. It was an expensive bachelor pad the guy rarely spent any time in. He was usually traveling abroad with work.

Quentin and Haley had flown home first-class at her insistence. Figuring out how to deal with their wealth disparity was something they'd have to confront eventually. But whatever issues might lie between them, he couldn't wait to see her again. Despite their exhaustion, they were going on their first date tonight in Quantico.

He'd visited Georgetown University Hospital where Tricia Rooks was being treated. She was intubated and fighting an infection. The doctors were worried she might struggle to breathe on her own. They'd also told him that even if she woke up, it was possible she'd never remember the attack itself. Those memories might have been wiped by the trauma before they'd had time to form.

Aside from Tricia, himself and Haley—who the world still didn't know had survived the attack—Chris was the only other Westerner who'd lived through the nightmare at the hotel.

Grant Gunn supposedly hadn't been at the hotel when the terrorists arrived and couldn't ID any of the attackers. That's what he'd claimed in his statement anyway and had been backed by the local taxi driver ferrying him around. Gunn lived in Arizona and had already been questioned by FBI agents on several occasions. The guy was not being particularly cooperative and had appeared on various news shows, plugging his survival instincts—which were basically to go get drunk—and using the event as a media stunt to promote his firm.

It was only a matter of time before the world discovered the link between the hotel attack and the massacre of a small community on what was supposed to be an uninhabited island in Indonesia. Then would come the news of the rescue of two female hostages, the death of Erik Alexander, and Quentin and Haley's ordeal. After that the media storm would swirl into a full-blown hurricane. He wanted as many answers as possible before the stories broke.

His priority was supporting the victims, protecting their privacy, keeping them safe. That included Chris although the guy wouldn't appreciate the suggestion he couldn't look after himself.

Quentin also wanted to see if he remembered anything that wasn't in the statement he'd given to Eban in Jakarta last Sunday. Quentin couldn't discuss what he'd found on the island, or the ongoing investigation, but there were things Chris might say to him that he wouldn't want in an official report.

Raised voices inside Chris's apartment made Quentin hesitate, but he knocked on the door, not wanting to eavesdrop. The door was flung open and there stood Nick Karlovac, obviously on his way out. The man's face was red, his chest heaving.

Nick's mouth dropped open in shock. "You *bastard.*" He grabbed Quentin in a bear hug. "I just bought a new suit for your fucking funeral." The man spoke into his neck, clinging so hard Quentin could barely breathe.

He felt his friend's distress and was sorry he hadn't set the record straight as soon as he'd been rescued. He'd had his reasons. He'd called his family from the ship in Indonesia but told them to act as though they still thought he was missing and presumed dead.

"I can't believe it." Chris came to the door and when Nick stepped back, he grabbed Quentin for a hug of his own. "I thought you were dead, buddy. I thought you were dead for sure." He pulled back, wiped his eyes. "What happened? How the hell did you survive?"

"Me and Haley Cramer jumped through a window a split second before the ceiling crashed. Then the terrorists found us and abducted us both."

"You and Haley Cramer *both* survived?" Chris shook his head. "Unbelievable."

"That is unbelievable," Nick told him. "Shit, I need to call Michelle. She's been devastated since we heard the news."

"I would have contacted you sooner, but I was incapacitated by a few dozen hostage takers."

"How the hell did you escape?" Chris asked.

"Long story. How did *you* escape?" Quentin asked.

Chris frowned. "You dumped me in the grass, otherwise I'd have been a crispy critter along with all the others. Don't you remember?"

They closed the door and headed inside Chris's apartment. Chris handed out beers, and they all chinked bottles. Quentin swallowed, appreciating the cool flavor that flooded his dry throat.

"I'm surprised the gunmen didn't find you on the lawn." And shoot him like all the others.

Chris scratched his brow. "Honestly? I have no idea what happened. I woke up in the bushes, and the hotel was still a raging inferno. Maybe I crawled there? Instinct telling me to find shelter. I do know you saved my life, you crazy bastard." His eyes shone with emotion. "Without you, I'd have burned to death in that godforsaken hotel."

Quentin sobered. So many people *had* perished. They were still in the process of identifying the dead and notifying the relatives. He hoped his survival didn't bring false hope to those who'd lost loved ones. The idea of causing more pain didn't sit well.

"We should have gone to that bar with that asshole Gunn like I suggested," Chris joked.

And Haley would likely have died in the raid. That reality smashed into Quentin like a sledgehammer. As despicable as Wenck's actions were, without them, Quentin doubted Haley would have come to his room or made a pass at him. She'd be dead. The realization that he'd probably have lost her without even knowing her made his stomach twist in knots.

"Want to go out and grab that beer now? Celebrate our survival?" Chris was already lifting his wallet from the kitchen counter.

Quentin shook his head and held up his hands, palms facing out. "I can't. I just got off the red-eye."

"Never stopped you before." Chris narrowed his gaze and swore. "I recognize that glint in your eyes. You're hoping to get lucky tonight."

Quentin kept his mouth shut.

"Anyone we know?" Nick asked curiously.

"You didn't mention you were seeing anyone when we were in Indonesia." The silence stretched between them until realization struck. "It's Haley Cramer, isn't it?"

Quentin said nothing.

"The competition." Nick rolled his eyes at them both. "She must be something in the sack."

Rage filled Quentin, and he clenched his fists. He held onto his temper, barely. Needling each other had always been part of their dynamic, but his late wife and new relationship were off-limits.

"I never thought you'd get over Abbie," Chris said with a shake of his head. "And I'd have thought Haley was too much of a ball-buster for you."

Quentin reminded himself he was a negotiator, but all he wanted to do was lash out. The sort of connection he shared with Haley wasn't the sum of moving parts, but he wasn't about to share his feelings with anyone until he understood them better himself. Exhaustion swept over him, and he reined in the anger. He was an FBI Unit Chief now, not a hot-headed squaddie.

"I have to go. Let me know if you hear or remember anything else about the attack. I also wanted to warn you that you might want to stay in a hotel or at your Virginia compound for a few days." The compound was about thirty minutes north of Quantico. "The media is about to be informed of the fact there were actually survivors from the attack, and you probably don't want your face all over the news." He turned to Nick. "Give my love to Michelle."

"You're really leaving already?" Chris asked, incredulous. "Oh, my god, you're serious about her." He started laughing.

"I give it two weeks before she gets tired of you and kicks you to the curb. When she does, come over and we can drown our sorrows and compare blowjobs."

Quentin decked Chris with an uppercut, then stood there shaking out his fist.

Nick laughed and hoisted Chris to his feet. "You're such a fucking idiot, Chris. You've obviously forgotten how possessive and overprotective he gets."

Chris mumbled something incoherent and tipped his head back to stop his nose bleed.

"I'll see myself out. Glad you got home safe."

"You, too, asshole," Chris grumbled.

Nick walked him to the door. "Ignore him. She was way out of his league." Nick shook his head. "Come see us for dinner when you feel up to it. Michelle would love to see you, and so would the kids."

"I'll be there." Quentin squeezed his buddy's arm and then jogged down to his SUV.

He was eager to see Haley again and already missed her face and her smile. And so what if he was out of his league, too? After losing Abbie, he wasn't in any rush. Hell, this was the first time he'd even considered seriously dating anyone in five years. One step at a time.

He didn't know if what they'd felt for one another would stand up to real life. And after everything he'd been through with Abbie, he needed to hold onto what was left of his heart if he was to keep functioning as a human being. Then he realized what he was doing—loss aversion. Where people were so scared about a potential loss they gave up on the chance of riches.

He closed his eyes and rested his forehead on the steering

wheel. Who was he trying to kid? He was already in too deep emotionally. Punching his old friend should have clued him in on the spot but he'd been in denial.

Now he had to figure out what the hell to do about it.

CHAPTER THIRTY-TWO

SINCE CONFRONTING WENCK in Darwin and then arriving home that morning, Haley had been mentally and physically exhausted. She'd spent most of the day asleep at Mallory and Alex's newly renovated Quantico home. When she'd woken, she'd rocked the baby, changed her first diaper, and doted on the tiny bundle. Then little Georgina had started screaming to be fed, and Haley had passed her back to her parents with a sigh of relief. It had been the perfect way to decompress after her adventures.

Before heading to Quantico, they'd dropped into the office in Woodley Park, and she'd been overwhelmed by the outpouring of love and support, impressed all over again by the hard work and ingenuity they'd employed to help get her home.

She had an idea for expanding their business, but she didn't know if Alex and Dermot would go for it. There probably wasn't a lot of money in it, but helping to find missing people might fit their ethos better than guarding mines or palaces. She was going to do some research and put a proposal together. Maybe they could create a non-profit arm of their company.

Haley had showered and changed into clothes Mallory had collected from her house in Georgetown. The other woman had even packed sneakers and workout gear. She and Alex obviously thought Haley was staying for a while. But now she was here, she wanted to be with Quentin. It was pathetic, and she was trying to resist the persistent urge. They weren't teenagers, and he'd probably resent her being too needy or eager or whatever the hell people called it.

It was less than a week since her entire world had shifted, so maybe she needed to slow everything down, but she missed him, and now he was here to take her out to dinner, like a normal person on a normal date. She stood impatiently waiting for Alex to open the wrought-iron gate of his house. Rather than letting Quentin drive inside, she ran out to meet him. Thankfully, he had the window rolled down, and she leaned in, grabbed his head and kissed him until neither of them could breathe.

"I thought it might be different back here," he admitted when they finally broke apart, staring into each other's eyes.

She kissed him again with zero finesse until he groaned and broke away again.

"Get in the car before I embarrass myself." The heat in his gaze made her want to find the nearest bed or secluded spot where they could park and try out the back seat of the SUV.

She ran around the hood and jumped in.

"What are you hungry for?" he asked.

She sent him a suggestive smile.

"I want to feed you something more enticing than deep fried crickets before I get you naked again in a real bed."

Those crickets had been disgusting, but they'd helped them stay alive. "I don't care what we have as long as there are French fries on the menu."

He reversed out of the drive. "A woman after my own

heart."

His words hit her in the solar plexus. Was she after his heart? Was this love? This horrible mix of excitement and anxiety fighting for dominance in her bloodstream?

"Think I have any chance of getting it?"

Oh, for god's sake.

What possessed her to ask that? She wanted to squirm and hide. She was putting herself on the line here, and what if he wasn't interested?

He stopped the car, put a hand around her nape and pulled her closer. "What do you think?"

That wasn't the answer she was looking for. She took a deep breath and plowed on. "I think whatever is going on between us feels unlike anything I've ever experienced before, and I don't know what it means."

A shadow flitted across his eyes, and he let her go. Put the car in gear. "Let's go eat."

She sat back in her seat and had the terrible feeling she'd said the wrong thing. She'd come on too strong. Been too demanding. But she didn't know how to do this, not when everything she did and said felt so consequential. She knew how to seduce and how to flirt. She knew how to fuck strangers she met in bars. She didn't know how to have a normal relationship with the expected slow progression of feelings and expectations.

She hadn't been *normal* since she was fourteen. Since before her uncle had moved in. She clenched her hands in her lap. Maybe this whole thing was one giant mistake. Perhaps she wasn't meant to be involved with anyone in a committed, monogamous relationship. Sure, they'd needed each other for survival in Indonesia but here? They didn't need each other here. They could part ways and both go on living. The question came down to what did they both actually want?

And why, after everything they'd been through together, had Quentin suddenly stopped meeting her gaze? What exactly was he afraid to tell her?

DINNER WAS AWKWARD. It wasn't the food or the atmosphere. It was him.

Quentin tried to shake the feeling that he was betraying his dead wife. Every time he looked at Haley, every time he thought about her mouth on him or how incredible it was to be inside her, it felt as if someone had stuck a spade in his chest and started digging.

In Indonesia it had been easy to separate himself from who he was back in the US. Now, on his own turf, his axis had shifted again, and his world felt off kilter. He wasn't sure of anything except the fact the tension was growing between him and Haley, and the widening chasm made his chest ache.

He didn't want to lose her.

The emotions churning inside him were unlike anything he'd experienced before. He'd been in love. Thoroughly and completely in love. And it hadn't felt like this. That's why Haley's words earlier had rocked him.

Did she have a chance of claiming his heart? He didn't know.

What he felt for Haley was volcanic and molten and hastily constructed on unstable foundations. Nothing like the rock-steady devotion he and Abbie had shared as soon as they'd met.

What if all he was feeling was simply lust? Haley was extraordinarily beautiful—with or without the makeup she liked to wear.

Were the cosmetics armor? It didn't matter. If she liked it, he was all for it. If she didn't, he was all for that too. He did know she'd been hurt before and had trusted him with deeply personal confidences.

But he still hadn't told her about Abbie.

He hadn't shared the single most important part of himself, not even when he'd thought they were both going to die.

And he wasn't sure how Haley was going to react to that.

How did he explain that if he'd still been married, he would never have looked at Haley twice? And yet, now, he could barely keep his hands to himself even though they were eating in a public restaurant.

Haley had said she was ready to try for a real relationship with him, but how could they move forward until he'd told her the truth about his past?

And what about everything else that separated them? He wasn't a rich man. His FBI position was his only income, and he wasn't ready to switch to the private sector to earn more.

"What is it?" Haley's eyes pinched with worry.

He was distracted as hell, and he could see her start to withdraw, to protect herself from the potential for hurt. Loss aversion was a very real thing. Emotional risk for those who'd already suffered could be paralyzing.

The difference in wealth was something they could figure out over time. The truth about his dead wife and child was something he needed to deal with right now. He reached out and put his hand over hers. "I need to show you something."

"That sounds ominous."

He shook his head, unable to speak. He couldn't joke about this. Abbie had meant everything to him, and her death still hurt. It would always hurt.

He paid the bill, and they left the restaurant and climbed into the SUV without saying anything. Haley bit her fingernail in a way that told him she was nervous. Shit. He was screwing this up. The most important negotiation of his life, and he was turning it into a goddamn fiasco.

It wasn't a long drive, but it took about a thousand years to get there.

He pulled into a parking space outside a cemetery and got out, walking around to open Haley's door. It was full dark although there were some lamps lit inside the grounds giving the place a ghostly feel.

"If this is where you reveal some weird graveyard kink, I think I'm going to have to disappoint you before we even start." She laughed nervously. She knew this was important. She often made a joke when things got serious.

He took her hand and led her through the large stone-flanked gates, shutting them with a painful grind of iron against iron. They walked along a gravel path, the smell of the Atlantic on the breeze.

Haley shivered, and he took off his jacket and draped it over her shoulders with a symbolism that wasn't lost on him.

Gravel crunched under their feet. Finally, he wound them between white marble markers until he came to the spot he'd chosen for Abbie and their stillborn child.

This area of the cemetery was lit brightly enough to read the inscription chiseled into the stone in an unalterable, permanent truth. The grass around the grave was neatly trimmed—he'd come out to tend the plot before he'd left for

Indonesia. Hell, he spent more time here than going on dates. Rather than flowers, he'd placed a couple of Abbie's favorite plants in ornate containers she'd purchased for their home—a lavender bush in one pot, a camellia bush in another.

Haley stared at the grave, clearly trying to make sense of why he'd brought her here, even though it was right there etched in stone.

Abbie Savage. Beloved wife.

He cleared his throat. "My wife, Abbie, died five years ago while giving birth to our son, Thomas. He died too."

Haley was quiet for a long time.

What was she thinking? "She'd quit her job as a sales associate and was ready to devote her life to raising our kids, but, hmm," he swallowed the old grief and pain, "it wasn't to be."

"This is why you went all quiet when I said I'd never experienced a feeling like this before." She took a step back, crossed her arms over her chest. "Because you have."

The band around his own chest constricted. "Abbie was sweet and beautiful and the kindest person I ever knew. She meant more to me than anyone I've ever met. I loved her to the center of my being."

Tears began running down Haley's cheeks. "I'm so sorry you lost her, Quentin."

She reached out and took his hand. Her empathy unlocking the pressure in his ribcage, because he should have known Haley wouldn't be jealous. She was better than that.

She shook her head slowly from side to side. "But I don't understand why you didn't mention her before."

Gravel shifted in his throat. "There never seemed to be a good time, then when we had Darby with us, I didn't want to say anything that might exacerbate her sadness."

"What about when we were alone? Or after we were rescued?"

He wanted to explain. He wanted Haley to know everything but couldn't minimize what Abbie had meant to him. He wasn't sure how to start. "I didn't know how to tell you that I'd been married. Happily married. Blissfully married. And when she died a piece of me died too." He dragged his hand through his hair. "But what I felt for Abbie isn't anything like the way I feel about you."

Haley flinched.

He opened his mouth to tell her that he was crazy about her, but the cell phone work had given him that day began to ring stridently, destroying the peacefulness of the setting. He fumbled to turn it off, but the next thing he knew, Haley was sprinting for the gates.

"Haley! Wait. Please wait." He called out, but she kept on running. Goddammit, the woman had legs.

Considering words were his business, he couldn't believe how badly he'd messed up that conversation.

Okay. He drew in a long deep breath. She'd wait for him by the SUV, and he'd explain exactly what she meant to him. That he was falling for her. That it terrified him as much as it did her.

Halfway to the car, he found his jacket in a heap on the ground. He picked it up and heard a car engine start and the car drive away.

When he got to the entrance, he looked around, but Haley wasn't there. He circled the vehicle. She wasn't anywhere. "Haley?"

Dammit. She must have caught a ride with whoever had

just left.

Quentin's temper spiked. He was terrified she was going to get killed by some psychopath only hours after arriving back in the States following their nightmare ordeal and all because she didn't have the patience to let him take a breath or turn off his cell? To gather his thoughts? To figure things out?

Who *did* that?

He drove slowly to the Parkers' home, working on calming his temper. When he arrived, he pressed the intercom button. "Is she here? Is she safe?"

"She's safe, but she doesn't want to talk to you." Alex Parker. Gatekeeper.

Quentin narrowed his eyes at the camera. "She hitched a ride alone at night with a stranger rather than have a conversation?" He pulled in another deep breath. He wanted to wind up his window and turn his car around and go home to get some sleep.

Except, without all the facts, Haley wouldn't make a balanced decision. She'd just keep on trying to outrun the potential for hurt. So, he put his heart on a platter because he already knew life was short and opportunities like this did not happen every day. Pride was a cold and lonely companion.

"Can you pass on a message for me?" The intercom remained silent, but he knew she was inside. Listening. "I needed to tell her about Abbie and the past I shared with my late wife so that perhaps Haley and I could start a relationship like we discussed back in Indonesia. When I said I didn't feel the same way about Haley as I did about Abbie, I didn't mean that I didn't…" *Shit*, was he really going to do this with a frickin' intercom?

"Tell her we need to talk." He strove for patience. Losing

his temper wouldn't do anyone any good, especially when they were all tired and overwrought. "And tell her she needs to work on her listening skills." And he needed to work on his delivery.

He reversed out of the drive and drove away. Being angry would get them nowhere. And maybe they both needed a little space. Space to figure out if what they'd found in that Indonesian hellhole was worth fighting for back on home ground.

CHAPTER THIRTY-THREE

DARBY WALKED QUICKLY from the bar back to her dorm at the FBI Academy, clutching a small box of pizza. The whole time she was aware of eyes watching her, trying to figure out who she was in her civilian clothes and visitor badge. They probably thought she was a visiting lecturer or police officer.

She liked that idea.

Worst was when someone recognized her. Some of the agents who'd been on the ship were around campus and when they smiled at her, there was pity in their gazes. She'd put her head down and run.

Footsteps rang out behind her. Fear spiked every nerve in her body, and she sped up. The pursuer did too. She was a half-second from sprinting in blind terror to the small room they'd given her when someone called out.

"Darby. Wait up."

Her heart gave a little flutter of relief. Eban. Eban Winters. They'd spent a lot of time together over the last few days but rarely alone since the victims advocate had arrived.

Darby had relived that soft, gentle kiss a million times since that day on the ship. Thinking about it had kept her sane when she'd woken screaming.

"Eban." She whirled and smiled. "How are you feeling?"

His brown eyes twinkled. "I thought that was my line?" He

rubbed the back of his neck. "I wanted to check on you before I headed home for the night."

It jolted her a little that he lived nearby. That he was back in his normal world while she was still in this weird limbo where she didn't really know what was going to happen in the future and wasn't ready to think about it. She had to tell her father what had happened. Her advisor too. The idea made her want to huddle into a tight ball and rock.

They kept walking.

"I was hungry so I popped out for something to eat. The only place open was the bar, but they let me take some pizza away." She held up the box like an idiot. She shook her head at herself and kept walking. At her door, she juggled food and a can of soda while she found her keys.

Eban waited patiently and then picked up the keys when she dropped them. She flinched when he reached past her to unlock the door, and he pretended not to notice.

She hated herself for being so jumpy. It wasn't like anyone could hurt her more than she'd already been hurt. Physically, she was almost healed. Mentally, she was up and down like a rollercoaster.

Once in the small dorm, she put everything on the desk and took off her shoes and set them by the door. "Come on in."

She forced a big smile so he wouldn't think she was worried about being alone with him.

He took a step into the room and let the door swing shut behind him.

"You live nearby?" She opened the soda and took a sip. There was no way she could eat right now, even though she'd been starving just a few minutes ago.

He ran his hands through his hair. It was slightly curly she'd noted. And although he'd shaved just before they'd arrived back in the States on the plane that morning, there was already a dark shadow of stubble on his jaw.

"I share a condo with another negotiator from CNU a few miles south of here. We're both gone so much it's rare we're actually there at the same time. It's more or less like living alone." He shrugged. "It works for now."

"What made you become an FBI agent?" She was desperate for him to stay, which was stupid. But hadn't he just told her by default that he wasn't married or involved with anyone?

Okay, the second was a reach for a good-looking guy like him, but she'd been turning something over in her mind…as a scientist she'd realized that it was impossible to replace a bad memory with a good one if she didn't have any good ones to insert.

She sat on the bed with her back against the wall. "Have a seat." She patted the bed next to her.

He gave her a measured look to make sure she was okay with his proximity, but he'd spent so much time with her since her rescue that she was starting to resent those looks. Yes, strange men made her nervous, but she wasn't scared of everything or everyone.

She wanted to be more than just a victim.

"I have something to tell you about your attackers."

Darby froze. Even the thought of them made her gag. She'd stabbed one, killed him with her own hand as Quentin had fought with him the night of her rescue. She would do it again a thousand times over.

"They're all dead."

"What? How?" A bolt of relief hit her. Had US forces

killed them? Before or after Alice Alexander had been rescued? They'd refused to tell her anything on the ship—even Quentin and Haley had seemed to be holding something back.

"We're not sure who killed them. They were found dead on the island when we went to arrest them."

Obviously, they'd all known for a while then, but no one had told her. Because she was *fragile*. She hated that word. "*Everyone* is dead?"

"Everyone found on the island is dead. Except Alice."

She frowned. "But it's possible some of them escaped. There was a group of men on the boat that came to Pulau Gunung Rebi. There could be others."

"It's possible but not likely."

Darby rubbed her brow. "I want to see photos."

"They were gunned down and brutally murdered."

Darby didn't care. "I want to see photographs of their faces to confirm they're all dead."

Eban shook his head. "I can't do that. You might not even recognize them if you saw them."

"I'd recognize them."

"With a bullet in the face?"

He'd wanted his words to shock, but if he'd gone through what she'd experienced, he'd realize that wasn't possible.

"I'd recognize them," she reaffirmed. She saw their grinning faces and disgusting leers every time she closed her eyes. Smelled their sweat and their breath and heard the sound of their labored breathing mingled with her cries of anguish. Maybe she looked fragile on the outside, but inside, she felt like she was constructed out of tungsten steel.

Eban looked like he wanted to ask her more questions but changed his mind.

He finally sat down beside her. "You managed to find your way around the academy okay today?" Changing the subject. Moving on.

She let it go. She'd talk to Quentin.

After they'd arrived that morning, Eban had left her with the victims advocate and gone into his office somewhere close by. He hadn't told her exactly where. He stretched his legs out across her bed and slouched back against the wall next to her.

On the island when Quentin had been on watch, Haley had shared that she'd reclaimed her autonomy by taking charge of her sex life. Darby wasn't sure how to do that, but she liked Eban, and the kiss thing had worked.

Perhaps if they had sex…

But how to get him to agree?

She felt awkward and obvious, as if her intentions were scrawled across her features in black marker. She needed to find something to talk about that didn't remind him of what she'd been through. Men liked to talk about themselves generally. "This room is like a college dorm. Is this where you stayed when you did your training?"

He smiled, which made his dark eyes crinkle. "My dorm was down another hall, but yeah, it was similar to this one except mine was two to a room. I shared with a guy called Mike Tanner who is a communications expert here at the National Laboratory. Great guy. Helped me study all the federal laws we needed to memorize."

"You enjoy being a negotiator?"

He smiled at her. "I do. I was on the SWAT team in LA, but I got a real kick out of watching negotiators talk the instigators out of a situation. I thought it was pretty cool to be able to do that, so I applied to negotiator school, and they said no. So, I volunteered on a suicide hotline and then asked to shadow the negotiators in LA. They refused at first, as apparently everyone wants to be a negotiator, but eventually, after I made myself as annoying as possible, my supervisor let me work with them, and I was accepted into the training school second time around."

"You learned the value of persistence?"

"Where I come from, we call it being a pain in the ass."

"Montana, right?"

"That's right."

She had one of those memories that stored information. It was useful for her studies. Not so much for other things.

"What's it like there?"

He smiled. "I come from a remote town in the high Rockies. It's probably the most beautiful scenery in the world, but the people are suspicious by nature and don't like strangers."

"Suspicion is probably useful to an FBI agent, huh?"

He laughed, and his gaze definitely dropped to her lips before shifting away. Had he been thinking about that kiss? She couldn't stop thinking about it, except when she was thinking about other terrible things. She forced those thoughts away. Licked her bottom lip and saw his gaze flicker again.

Aha. He might be a little attracted to her.

She wasn't sure how to get him to act upon it. And she really wanted him to. Desperately.

He started telling her about what was going to happen tomorrow, but she wasn't listening anymore. She shifted so she was touching his shoulder with hers, and then she slid her hand along her thigh just brushing his leg.

There was a slight hitch in his monologue before he continued.

"Eban," she interrupted and leaned closer. When he turned his head, they were only an inch apart. "I can't stop thinking about that kiss." He blinked. "I was thinking that maybe if we had sex it would have the same effect and help block out what they did to me."

His pupils dilated and mouth dropped open when she slowly slid her hand over this thigh. She leaned forward, and he opened his lips, probably to argue, but she kissed him. She kept kissing him even though she didn't really know what she was doing.

He sat there, balling his fists and breathing hard. He finally kissed her back.

"Stop. Stop. Stop." He pulled away and grabbed her hand, even though his chest was bellowing. "We can't do this. Not after what you went through."

She froze. "You mean if I hadn't been raped, you'd have sex with me?"

"Yes. No! *Dammit.* It would cost me my job, Darby. But more importantly, you *were* raped." He held onto her wrist now, facing her, so close she could see lines of gold striate the brown of his irises. "You were violated and traumatized, and I'm not going to be the man you use, thinking you're regaining control of your body, but actually you are systematically destroying your self-esteem."

She blinked at him. "I wasn't using you." She tried to pull away, but he wouldn't let go. For a few seconds it was fine, but the grip on her wrist tightened. Her heart exploded, and she fought him to get free. When she succeeded, he sat there, one dark brow raised in an *I-told-you-so* stare.

She leapt to her feet and paced. Rubbing the feel of his grip away from her flesh, bombarded by images and sounds and the scents. Sweat. Semen. Blood.

She started to hyperventilate, and Eban was right beside her. He sat her on the edge of the bed, helped her cup her hands over her nose and mouth.

"Breathe, Darby. Slowly. Deeply."

She dragged oxygen into her lungs like a fifty-a-day smoker. Her throat felt hoarse, and that triggered another wave of panic.

"In and out." He rubbed her back and spoke gently, soothingly and eventually, after what seemed like an hour, her body sagged and gave in. Exhausted and drained. Once again, he was rocking her against his chest. Once again, she was crying.

Finally, she drifted off to sleep. When she woke up, he was gone.

CHAPTER THIRTY-FOUR

HALEY SHOWED HER ID to the guard post, and the stone-faced Marine spoke to someone via his earpiece before waving her through to the next barrier. She was meeting with Darby who'd been given private quarters at the FBI's National Academy until she felt well enough to go home. That was Quentin's doing, Haley was sure. Protecting her. Keeping her safe.

It was noon, and she'd slept for ten hours straight last night. Alex had hugged her while she'd bemoaned her own cowardice. By the time she'd run outside to tell Quentin she was sorry for bolting, he'd driven away. Alex had taken her by the hand and told her to sleep rather than chase after the man right then. For once she'd actually listened.

Now she felt so stupid and couldn't imagine facing him again. Why would he want to be involved with someone as flighty or unstable as she was? Her palms were sweaty, and she wiped them on her favorite pair of Levi's.

She'd run because she'd been convinced Quentin had been about to tell her that he didn't love her and would never love her the way he'd loved his late wife, and her heart hadn't been able to cope. It had hurt too damn much.

How could she stand a chance against the memory of a perfect stay-at-home wife, one who'd been about to give him a child—something Haley could never do?

The real problem was she'd lost her nerve. Her self-confidence had been shattered by her experience at the hands of her captors, and she was trying to protect the most vulnerable part of herself—her heart. But that was not how Quentin deserved to be treated. After everything they'd been through together, she owed him an explanation for her behavior, and she needed to hear him out. To respect him. She'd messed up. Sabotaged their relationship the way Alex had warned her she might.

Adulting was hard.

She took a deep breath, trying to rein in her angst.

After she met with Darby, she'd find Quentin. Apologize, even though she doubted it would make a difference. She was so obviously not the kind of woman he usually got involved with.

She received a visitor's badge, which she pinned to the yellow blouse she wore. On her feet were the combat boots she'd gotten used to. They were comfortable. They also reminded her of what she'd been through. That she'd killed a man in order to survive.

She wasn't yet ready to submerge herself back into her old life as if the abduction had never happened. She needed to process it properly. Her devotion to Jimmy Choo wasn't dead, but at the moment she was enjoying the freedom and power of jackboots.

She drove up to the parking lot and left Alex's borrowed Audi in a visitor slot—he'd picked her up from the airport yesterday and insisted on driving her everywhere so she could rest. That meant her car was in D.C.

She checked her appearance in the mirror. Her lipstick

was her favorite shade of red and her makeup light. She got out and headed over to the main entrance, spotting Darby standing inside the shadowy foyer. The woman's red hair was loose around her shoulders, her skin pale despite the light tan she'd gotten in the tropics. She was one of the few people not to be wearing beige pants and a polo shirt. Instead she wore a beige t-shirt with khaki shorts and the ugliest looking river sandals Haley had ever seen.

She looked like a field geologist.

Haley loved every inch of the young woman and intended to take her out for a fun day of shopping and spoil her rotten with anything she wanted. She got the impression Darby worked hard for everything she had, and didn't have a lot.

They embraced, and Haley was aware of a lot of eyes watching the two of them. It was clear they weren't FBI agents.

"Did you have a good trip back?" Haley asked.

Darby smiled and rubbed her hands up and down her bare arms. "It was a good reminder why not to join the Army." Darby and Eban had flown home on some sort of military transport. "There were a lot of coffins on the same flight—from the hotel."

Haley winced.

"I'm so glad you and Quentin escaped that attack and not just because you rescued me."

Haley rubbed Darby's hand in both of hers. "Me too."

"How's Quentin?"

Haley closed her eyes for a brief moment and swallowed loudly. "I did something stupid."

Darby's eyes widened even more. "So did I."

"Let's go get a coffee and talk."

Darby led the way down the corridor, waving to a woman

with long blonde hair who was talking to a receptionist. Haley recognized her from Alex and Mallory's wedding.

"That's Erin Donovan, the victims advocate," Darby told her. "She's helping me figure out how to cope. I'm meeting her later today to talk about how I might handle my father and my supervisor. She also has some other rape survivors she wants to introduce me to. She thinks our shared experience might help me understand I'm not alone and give me someone to talk to about what happened, but I'm not sure." Darby sounded overwhelmed. "Right now, she's helping Alice organize Erik's funeral. I went to visit Alice earlier. They were held captive for six months." Darby's expression mirrored her distress. "I barely survived a week, and that poor woman was there for six months."

Haley stopped her with a hand on her arm. They hadn't done to Alice what they'd done to Darby. "You're one of the bravest people I have ever met. I had Quentin with me the whole time, and he protected me. You were alone and outnumbered, and you survived *and they didn't*," Haley whispered fiercely.

"But..." Darby trailed off.

"It's hard not to doubt yourself," Haley said knowingly.

And maybe that was the real reason she'd run from Quentin last night. How could she possibly compete with his perfect previously unknown, dead wife?

And *that* thought wasn't fair to him, and it wasn't fair to her, and it wasn't fair to poor deceased Abbie Savage.

"Sexual assault means you doubt yourself a lot, even though none of it is your fault."

They bought coffee and found a table.

Haley sipped the scalding brew and decided to go first.

"Quentin showed me his late wife's grave last night. I hadn't even known he was married, but I should have guessed. He's so damn perfect. I freaked out when he told me what he felt for me wasn't anything like what he felt for her, and I literally ran away."

Darby's green eyes were huge and dark. "He cares about you, Haley. How could you doubt that?"

Haley ran her fingers over the ridges in her paper cup. "It's easy when you've never let yourself fall for anyone before." She looked up and caught Darby's sympathetic gaze. The girl understood. "The reality of him having already lost the love of his life hit me hard." She pushed her hair away from her face and swallowed the knot that twisted in her throat. "I guess I can't imagine being the sort of woman he actually wants in his life." She clenched her fist in her lap. She didn't want to lose him, but could they really make this thing between them work? It seemed so impossible today when yesterday it had seemed unstoppable.

"I tried to seduce Eban Winters," Darby whispered.

Haley's eyes popped wide.

"That's pretty much how he looked when I kissed him." Darby's lips twitched with unexpected humor.

Haley rarely found herself speechless.

"It was what you said about not letting anyone rob you of your enjoyment of sex. I decided if I could have a good experience to think about rather than the…the rapes," she stumbled on the words, "I stood a better chance of getting past this."

Haley's brain screeched to a halt. At the time she'd been trying to give Darby something to hold on to. She hadn't known how long they'd be stuck on that island or if they'd ever be rescued. She'd wanted to give her hope. She wasn't a damn therapist and look how her love life was turning out. "What did Eban say?"

"He kissed me back for about a nanosecond, and then he remembered who I was. He also ran away."

"I'm so sorry." Haley wanted so badly to help Darby heal. "But if anyone found out, he'd probably lose his job."

Darby sighed. "He mentioned that, but I wasn't going to tell anyone except you and you *cannot* tell Quentin."

Because Quentin was his boss.

Haley reached over the table and grabbed Darby's hand. "I know you're trying to figure this out logically, but I think Eban made the right choice. It's too soon."

Darby looked mutinous.

Haley leaned closer. "I'm going to get you in to see my therapist. She's amazing and deals with survivors on a regular basis."

Darby's lips dragged down at the corners. "I live in Alaska."

"Take some time off. Come stay with me in D.C. And if you don't want to do that, you can set up video appointments with her."

Darby eyed her sideways. "You really think a therapist can help after what I went through?"

Haley nodded. "And if she doesn't, we'll find another one closer to you who can."

Darby played with a sachet of sugar that had been left on the table. "It's almost worth the price, you know."

"What is?"

"Meeting you and Quentin." Darby's eyes were shiny bright with tears she didn't let fall.

"Don't say that." Haley gripped her hand. "Don't equate the two things. I don't want to be associated with those monsters."

Darby leaned closer and whispered, "They're all dead. That's what Eban told me."

Haley nodded. "I know. I wanted to tell you."

"I asked if I could look at the faces, but he didn't think that would be wise. He probably thought I was a fruitcake at that point. No wonder he wouldn't have sex with me."

"Take some time…" Haley shook her head at herself. "You know, Darby, you do what you feel you have to do, but don't be surprised if it doesn't turn out how you expect it to. And talk to the therapist before you go picking up any strange guys in bars."

A bunch of men in black tactical gear walked into the cafeteria joking loudly and sweating hard.

Part of the Hostage Rescue Team, but not the group who'd been on the ship with them.

One guy looked at Darby, and Haley saw his eyes widen. In recognition or with attraction she wasn't sure.

Darby shrank away and hid her face with her hair. "I just want the crippling fear to go away," she mumbled to Haley. "I'm not scared of Quentin or Eban or even Max, but everyone else makes me want to run screaming down the hall."

"Time will help," Haley assured her and then blew out a long breath. Time did help, but who wanted to spend years being screwed up?

Darby nodded, clearly done talking about it for now. She checked her wristwatch. "Quentin told me he was going to the range at noon. Offered to let me shoot with him. Want to come?"

"Yes." Even though Haley both dreaded and longed to see him again.

She fought the urge to check her appearance in her compact. Quentin had seen her at her worst, and she wasn't that insecure—at least, she never used to be. But it wasn't her looks that were the problem, it was who she was—her lifestyle, her dedication to her work. And, having had time to think about all the things that stood between them, she suspected they didn't really have a hope of making this thing between them work. But she still needed to face him and tell him she was sorry for running out on him last night. She needed to stop being an emotional coward.

QUENTIN CAUGHT A flash of canary yellow in the corner of his eye and knew it was Haley.

When she'd run out on him last night, he'd felt like he'd lost something vital to his happiness and wellbeing. He'd also known that, more than anything, Haley feared losing control of her choices. With that thought in mind, after what they'd both recently been through, he decided to give her some space. He'd let her make the decision to come find him, rather than chase her and trigger her flight reflex. But now he was terrified he'd chosen the wrong option, and that she'd come to say goodbye.

Exhaustion and jet lag had knocked him out last night, but he'd woken early, immediately missing Haley pressed up beside him in bed. At the sight of her now, something reconnected inside his chest. To say he had it bad was an epic understatement. He had it so bad he wanted to invite her to his home, regardless of the fact he was supposed to be at work, and make love to her until she went blind with pleasure—or at least gave them a chance. Not what he should be thinking about when he had a loaded gun in his hand.

He emptied the Glock at the target, nailing the center repeatedly, but decided to quit while he was ahead. He placed the ear protectors on the bench. Then turned around.

Darby was clapping and grinning at him. He shook his head as he walked over to them. Haley looked incredible in that fitted yellow top and tight jeans and lipstick that made him want…

Okay. Time to reel in the sexual fantasies at work.

He hugged Darby and stood looking at Haley, awkwardly trying to read her expression. Her mouth was smiling, but her eyes were apprehensive. She looked rested though. The shadows that had been beneath her eyes for days were gone.

He should have known better than to lay a deeply emotional scene on her when they were both so exhausted and raw, but he'd been feeling impatient and guilty.

He should have known better, but he was human. He made mistakes. He took a step forward, cupped the back of her head and slowly pulled her in for a kiss. He gave her plenty of time to back out before he brushed those petal-soft lips with his. Then he let her go. This was the FBI National Academy, and he was at work. But he needed her to know he was sorry for messing things up last night and that he forgave her for running out on him. The kiss spoke without having to say all the words in front of an audience.

"You guys want a go at shooting?" He'd already checked with the firearms instructor. NATs—New Agents in Training—would be out here later this afternoon, but for the next hour, there were a couple of lanes free if they wanted.

"I do." Darby bounced excitedly on her toes.

She was bored and looking for a distraction that didn't involve thinking about how she was going to move forward in her life. There was plenty of time to figure it out. He'd spent an hour that morning on the phone with her Ph.D. supervisor. Quentin told the guy what he thought of him for leaving students out in the middle of nowhere alone with zero support. The professor had sounded genuinely upset and contrite, but Quentin would be keeping an eye on him from now on.

"I'm fine just watching." Haley took a step back. Her voice was scratchy and sexy as hell.

Shit. She turned him inside out just standing there.

"The instructor offered to let me try out one of the HRT sniper rifles." Dimples cut into Darby's cheeks as she grinned.

He glanced at Haley, but she avoided his gaze.

"You guys go talk." Darby waved them off. She looked happy, he realized. Maybe because she felt safe here.

He'd do everything in his power to keep her feeling that way but, unfortunately, she couldn't stay forever. He'd gained her a month's grace, which was a minor miracle of bureaucratic cooperation and good timing between courses. Hopefully the media zoo would have calmed down by the time she left.

His new work cell buzzed in his pocket. It was Alex Parker. "Excuse me," he said to them both. "I need to take this."

"Apparently the guy who caused the car wreck with Mrs. Wenck used a false identity to rent the vehicle," Alex said without preamble. "I can't get any clear shots of him on the security footage."

"Whoever it was had to be working in conjunction with

the terrorists at the hotel to make sure the billionaire left before the attack." Quentin swore.

Wenck hadn't done anything suspicious after meeting with them in Darwin except call his lawyer. The attorney hadn't sounded happy or surprised when Wenck had mentioned Haley and what she might accuse him of. Alex had also hired a private investigator to see if he could track down any other women who might have been attacked by the billionaire.

"Two more things," Alex said. "Haley's grandmother's Cartier watch just surfaced on a dealer's site in Australia."

Nice. "What's the other thing?"

"Someone used a mixer to move the bitcoin I paid in ransom to another account."

"Can you still track it?" Quentin asked.

"Yeah, I can track it." Alex sounded insulted. "If they use it to pay for something in the real world, I can nail the bastards. But if they put it through a second mixer, then tracking the money becomes exponentially more difficult."

Quentin swore under his breath. "I'll contact the cops in Australia about the timepiece."

"She really loves that watch," Alex said quietly.

Quentin grunted. His pal in the Australian Federal Police owed him one after the tipoff about corrupt officials up in Darwin. He hung up and walked over to where Haley was watching Darby put a specially modified Remington 700 sniper rifle through its paces. Holy shit the girl could shoot. He had no problem imagining what Darby was shooting at. He hoped the men who'd attacked her burned in the fiery depths of hell.

Haley's mind though, he realized as she turned toward

him, was an entirely different matter. He had no clue what she was thinking, and that couldn't be good.

They walked a small distance away so they had some privacy. She held up her hand almost in defeat. "I'm sorry about last night."

"I should have told you about Abbie earlier."

Haley pressed her pretty red lips together, dipped her chin. "There was never a good time to discuss things that weren't directly relevant to getting through our ordeal alive."

The sun glinted off her bright blonde hair. He could see other agents looking at her. She was the sort of woman everyone noticed. But her appeal went deeper than the surface for him. For all her tough façade, she was easily hurt.

He didn't want to be the person who hurt her.

"How about we take things slow for a while. See if we can figure out how we fit into each other's lives now we're not *running* for our lives?" he suggested. "Just enjoy ourselves."

She smiled, but a shadow of uncertainty seemed to cast itself over her features and dim the light at the edges.

His cell buzzed again. "Dammit." He checked the screen. "I need to take this too."

"You're working. I didn't mean to disturb you."

"Haley." He touched her arm so she looked at him, really looked at him. "You can disturb me any time. Working or not working. I—" His cell cut him off again, and he wanted to smash the thing to pieces. He turned it off.

She started to back away.

He made a desperate bid by going after the most important issue. "Please don't feel like you have to compete with Abbie's memory—"

"How can I not?" Haley stopped retreating, but her expression did not give him hope. "The woman you were blissfully married to was about to give birth to a child you craved when they both tragically died. It's heartbreaking, Quentin, and I am so sorry that happened." Her sad eyes broke his heart all over again. "But I'm not like her. I'm selfish. I'm not about to give up my job or turn into some little homebody."

"I never asked Abbie to give up her job." People were looking at them, but Quentin didn't care. "That was the choice she made."

"For you. Because of you, your schedule. The fact that your entire life revolves around work. You said it yourself—you never take a day off." She held her hair out of her face as the breeze took it.

He ground his teeth together. "I save lives, Haley."

"I *know* that. I know how important your job is, and you are *so* good at it. But it's not the point. I won't sit on the sidelines being the supportive little woman while you spend all your time here." She waved a hand at the Academy buildings. The range. "My job is important to me too. I'm willing to ease back on my schedule to build a relationship, but I can't see you doing the same."

Anger stirred, heating his blood. "You're deciding all this without giving me a chance?"

"I can't afford to give you time to prove me wrong," she whispered. "As hard as it will be to walk away from this now…"

"There's no 'this,' Haley. Let's be clear. You're walking away from *me*."

She stared at the grass, her lips forming an unhappy downward curve. "You can't deny your job is everything to you."

Quentin waited for the outrage to build that she was making him do this here and now, but all he felt was a growing sense of emptiness that was both horribly familiar and achingly new. His throat worked as he searched for the right words.

"You're right. It *was* everything to me. After I lost my family, putting my all into the job was the only way I could make it through the day. But now..." He moved closer, and she braced as if for a blow. He stroked a finger along her jaw. This brave woman, fighting for the kind of life she deserved, that they both deserved. "Now I've found someone I want to come home to. I love my job, Haley. It is demanding as hell, and it is important, but there is room for you here with me if you want it. I promise you that."

A shout tried to draw his attention toward a group of trainees, but he did not look away from her brilliant blue eyes.

Haley opened her mouth and closed it again. Finally, "Do you mean it?"

He nodded.

"Really?"

He smiled slowly. He had her.

She threw herself at him, and he swayed under the impact, but he didn't falter. He held her tight. Tight enough to convince her he didn't intend to let go. They deserved the chance to figure this thing out.

Darby wolf-whistled at them, and Haley laughed, embarrassed. The blush on her cheeks was cute.

"We still need to talk more," she told him softly. "How about I surprise you with dinner at your place?"

He nodded, hoping he was reading the warmth in her gaze

correctly and that she wasn't gonna dump his ass over a chicken casserole. "Although you kind of spoiled the surprise part," he joked.

"I'm sure I can think of something to shock you." Her tone was flirtatious, her smile back to being the sexy, self-confident woman he'd first met. But he knew she went way deeper than that. People who underestimated and disrespected her were fools.

"I don't doubt it for a minute." He dug in his pocket and removed a key from his fob. "I might be a little late as it's my first full day back." He handed her the key and then texted her his street address with his new cell phone. "But I'll be there by seven or die trying."

CHAPTER THIRTY-FIVE

QUENTIN AND EBAN were on a clandestine video call to Steve McKenzie at SIOC in HQ. The head of the task force didn't want the negotiators involved, but McKenzie knew they might have valuable insight from the work they'd conducted in the region on and off over the years.

Quentin still hadn't caught up on reading all the autopsy and ballistic reports and the mountain of background information that had been collected. He wasn't looking forward to it.

"Someone forces Wenck's wife into a car accident which draws the billionaire away before the attack takes place at the hotel. Any ideas who?" McKenzie asked.

"Wenck greases palms all over Southeast Asia. His mines support entire communities. A lot of people depend on him for their livelihoods, without which they might starve." Eban leaned back in his chair and stretched his legs out under the table.

"Any links between Hurek and Wenck?" McKenzie asked.

"Nothing our guys or Alex could determine," Quentin told him, pissed. "I still don't understand why Hurek attacked the hotel in the first place?"

"Usual motivation for terrorists." McKenzie shrugged. "To create terror, raise their reputation in the terrorist community, raise awareness of their cause."

"Hurek's cause always seemed to be Hurek," Eban put in.

"Pity we can't ask any of his followers questions about their motivation." Quentin clasped his hands together in front of him and rested his chin on his knuckles. "The legat in Jakarta believes Hurek was in league with some of the hardliners in government. Working to undermine the moderates in power on several different fronts."

"Any proof?" McKenzie asked.

"Not yet." He shrugged apologetically.

"Why take hostages?" McKenzie asked.

"For money," Quentin said thoughtfully. "Also to give them a certain amount of terrorist legitimacy that pointed away from their real motivation or backers."

"Might explain why they were so awful at negotiating." Eban yawned. They were all exhausted.

"The big question we're not asking is why target Quentin?" McKenzie looked over his shoulder. He was in the breakout room the negotiators used at SIOC. It was dark, but all it took was the boss to walk past, and they'd have to shut this call down. "Pretty ballsy to attack that conference and kill all those people, but almost suicidal to set their sights on a federal agent."

"Maybe the terrorists wanted to antagonize the relationship between the US and Indonesian governments. Killing civilians and kidnapping a federal agent would do that. Frankly, I'm just glad to be alive. Lucky too." A wave of tiredness hit him, and he looked at his watch, wondering how long before he could go home to Haley.

"Lucky?" Eban rubbed his reddened eyes. "You killed nine men, some with your bare hands, and helped rescue three women."

"Two," Quentin said sharply. He hadn't done a damn thing to help Alice Alexander.

"I still think you're a badass." Eban offered a tired smile.

Quentin wasn't comfortable with the praise. "Haley and Darby are the real heroes. And you guys for finding us." Quentin's team had gone above and beyond. Every single man and woman had pulled together to run the unit and help bring him home. He'd do the same for them. They were damn good agents.

He *was* a lucky man.

He stood, grabbed his jacket. "I need to go. Thank you for all the help and assistance. Now I'm going home and sleeping until Monday."

Hopefully, he wouldn't be sleeping alone.

HALEY KICKED OFF her red-soled heels as she let herself into Quentin's condo with a feeling of excitement and trepidation. The four-inch stilettos made the arches of her feet ache, and she had the horrible feeling there were more jackboots in her future.

She looked around, thrilled Quentin had trusted her with the key to his place. They both knew it would reveal things about him she wanted to know.

After his promise earlier, she felt easier. Things weren't necessarily all resolved, but he'd told her he wanted to make room for her in his life.

That was a hell of a start.

She put the food she'd bought, steaks and makings for a

salad, in the big, empty refrigerator.

She checked the time on her phone, missing her wristwatch and the constant reminder of her grandmother's love wrapped around her wrist. Six PM. Plenty of time to put the grill on and toss the salad.

Did Quentin still want kids? She pushed the question away. It wasn't exactly taking things slow when you were worried about what a family might look like with a guy you'd just started dating. And, so what if they'd met under extreme circumstances and skipped straight to sex. They still needed time to get to know one another properly.

She walked through from the kitchen to the living room. Paused when she caught sight of two framed photographs on a shelf unit. She stepped closer. One was a picture of Quentin and his wife on their wedding day. Their smiles reflected one another's joy. They were obviously so happy Haley had to blink to fight back the emotion. The next photograph was Abbie, hugely pregnant with her hands clasped over her distended belly. Quentin stood beside her, looking goofy and proud.

Haley's throat started to ache with the effort of suppressing tears. Tucked just behind the photograph was a small silver frame with the image of a swaddled newborn.

"Thomas. He was stillborn."

Quentin's voice made her jolt.

Haley looked up. "I'm sorry. I didn't mean to pry."

Quentin tossed a bag and his new wallet on the entryway table. Locked his handgun in a drawer.

"It's fine. I don't mind you looking. I always feel guilty that I don't talk about him more." Quentin walked over and stood beside her, picking the small silver frame up with one hand

and stroking a thumb over the image. "I didn't know him, but I felt him wriggle in his mother's womb and saw his heartbeat on the ultrasound. Held him, afterwards… Loved him." He paused, and Haley felt anguish at the pain he must have endured. "I try to imagine him at each different age, but it's a meaningless fantasy I seem to construct for no other reason than to torment myself."

The suffering in his voice destroyed her. "What happened?"

"Abbie wasn't feeling so great, but she decided to wait for me to get home from work before going to the hospital. She didn't want to bother me. Her placenta ruptured and the cord got tangled and by the time I found them it was already…bad."

Quentin's Adam's apple slid up and down his throat. "It wasn't her fault. She always hated to bother me when I was at work, but I never minded." He sucked in his lips. "I meant what I said today. I love my job, but I'd like a life too." The catch in his voice pushed Haley over the edge, and she caught his hand and pressed it to her cheek.

"I'm so sorry they died, Quentin."

He nodded quietly and put the photograph down. "So am I. But it's been five years now, and it's time for me to move on." He ran his hand through his hair. "I won't ever forget them, but I'm learning to let go." He tipped the wedding photo facedown, then the others.

"Does the fact I can't have children bother you?"

His eyes glittered fiercely when they met hers. "I honestly don't think I could go through that again." He sounded like someone was ripping out his heart.

"If you wanted kids you could always adopt," she said carefully.

"As of a week ago, I never thought I'd need to think about

it again." Then he laughed and squeezed her hand. The sensation was as familiar as her own reflection. "So much for me keeping things light. I made you cry."

Haley wiped her tears. "I can't imagine how you got through it. And I bet you never let anyone help you deal with it, did you?"

"I buried myself in work." He went to turn away, to deflect.

She stopped him. "I want to be with you, Quentin, but you don't have to forget about Abbie or the baby you lost." She gently put the photographs upright again.

The way his lips pressed hard together she could tell he was still trying not to give in to emotion. Instead he swept her up into his arms. "I'm taking you to bed. It's a first for me, having anyone here."

She touched his face. He was so dang beautiful. She thought about her own past and the ghosts she carried. They both needed to adjust to the weight of each other's baggage.

She wiped at her eyes, makeup running. "I look a mess."

"Are you kidding me?"

"I had great plans to feed you and then seduce the shit out of you. Now I need to fix my face."

He lowered her feet onto his bedroom floor. The drapes were drawn. Bed unmade which surprised her. She'd imagined he'd be Mr. Regimented, neat and tidy.

He cupped her face, tipped her chin up with an authority that thrilled her. "You don't need to fix your face. Your face is unbelievably beautiful." He skimmed one hand down her side and rested it on her hip. "You are ridiculously attractive. I thought that in the bar last Saturday night."

Jesus, not even a week ago, and so much had happened.

"I thought it when you were dressed in dirt and a blanket

on the side of a volcano." His hand slipped lower and then stroked up her thigh until his fingers found the silk of her underwear. "And I'm thinking it now."

She shivered as he slowly lowered his mouth to her neck. Making her toes curl as his lips brushed the sensitive skin there.

His fingers found the zipper at the back of her dress, drew it down, and helped the dress fall off her shoulders and onto the floor.

She stepped out of the material and watched his eyes turn black. Her bra and panties were a delicate lavender lace that cupped her breasts and left absolutely nothing to the imagination.

She removed his tie, enjoying the rasp of sound as it came loose. Undid the buttons of his crisp white shirt. Found his belt buckle and unhitched the notch, flicking open the button and easing down the zipper.

He said nothing as she smoothed her hands over his tanned shoulders, outlining the jut of his clavicle, the bulge of his biceps. Dark hair sprinkled his chest, and she traced the downward path until she found him hot and heavy, burning her fingers as she clasped them around him.

"I find you very attractive too," she said, smiling.

The first time they'd had sex had been about two strangers hooking up—superb, but still just animal lust. The second and third times they'd had sex had been desperate bids to relieve stress and prove they were still alive, still fighting. They'd been frantic, glorious bursts of pleasure in a grim survival situation.

"I want to make love to you in my bed." His voice vibrated slow and urgent. He made a move to go down on her, but she shook her head.

"I want you inside me. As fast as possible. I can't wait any longer." The throb between her legs felt like it might consume her if she didn't assuage it soon.

His eyes turned to obsidian. She lay on the bed and drew him down with her. He peeled her bra down her shoulder and latched his mouth onto her nipple, suckling her hard enough to have her crying out, but not in pain. He undid the clasp and tossed the garment onto the floor. While his mouth feasted on her breasts, his hand swept lower, easing into her panties and then sliding deep into her slick folds. Every time his fingers dove inside her, the palm of his hand rubbed against her clit. Her feet pressed hard into the mattress as her hips rose. "Please. Quentin."

"Please what?" He laughed as she stiffened and contorted and spasmed in his arms.

When she collapsed back in a heap, he nuzzled her neck again. "Just taking the edge off."

She tried to shift positions, to repay him by pleasuring his body. He wouldn't let her move.

"Not so fast, Cramer."

"But—"

"I plan on giving you everything you want, but if you touch me right now I'm toast." He rose up and looked down at her, nudging her knees apart and sliding against her vulva, never dropping her gaze. He rubbed her over-sensitized clit with his cock, and she closed her eyes and groaned at the sensation. "Whereas you," he kissed her, slowly, deeply before sliding all the way home, "can hopefully get right back on the orgasm wagon for another go around."

Her fingers gripped his ass tight and hung on as he took her for a long, slow ride. She was completely dazzled. She never wanted this to end.

CHAPTER THIRTY-SIX

THEY'D MADE LOVE, eaten, made love again. Now they lay in bed in each other's arms staring at the ceiling, both of them sated and exhausted and unable to sleep because of body clocks that were set to the other side of the world.

Haley smoothed her hand over his chest, playing with his flat nipples. They fascinated her but not a fraction of the amount hers fascinated him.

"It's funny how the people to come off best out of this are you and me. And Chris Baylor, I suppose."

"What about Tricia Rooks and Grant Gunn?" Quentin queried.

"Neither of them gained a lover or a multimillion-dollar contract out of it. And poor Tricia is still intubated in the hospital."

He frowned. "Chris got a big contract?" He hadn't mentioned it. He liked to brag, although Quentin had taken his friend off guard with his reappearance, and they generally didn't talk business.

"Yeah, although rather him than me." She shuddered. "Wenck decided to renew the security contract he had with Bay-Kar for another couple years. I heard they jacked the price and stiffed the bastard. Couldn't happen to a nicer fellow." Her hand paused over his heart. "I'm going to try and bury the hatchet with Chris. I know he's important to you. I want to be mature enough to at least be able to coexist cordially with him."

"I appreciate the thought, but you don't need to put up with bullshit from anyone on my account." Quentin hugged Haley close and kissed her forehead.

Thoughts kept whirling around and around in his brain, and he couldn't sleep. He waited an hour for Haley to drift off. Something was bugging him. He got out of bed and opened his new laptop, began to slowly trawl through some of the autopsy and ballistics files from the night of the attack.

HALEY BLINKED AWAKE even as fatigue dragged on the edges of her consciousness and tried to pull her right back under. Light slanted through the closed blinds, suggesting it was later than she usually woke. The bed was empty. She looked for a clock and found one on the chest of drawers.

Nine AM. Crap.

She stood and stretched, wondering where Quentin was. Then she spotted a note on the pillow and picked it up.

"I love taking it slow with you. Have to go into work this morning. Sorry. Meet me for dinner?"

Part of her was irritated that he'd gone to work on the weekend, but last night had been so amazing, and neither of them were exactly nine-to-five people. She barely resisted hugging the paper to her chest. She was pretty sure she loved him. Nothing else could account for the giant-sized waves of giddy emotion she was riding.

Her cell buzzed.

Dermot wanted her to come up to D.C. to spend the day with him.

She really didn't want to go, because she wanted to stay here, which scared the hell out of her. She stood naked in Quentin's bedroom and thought for a few moments.

She texted Dermot telling him to book a lunch table at her favorite restaurant in D.C. She didn't need to choose between her friends and Quentin. She was lucky enough and flexible enough to be able to have both.

She wanted Quentin to have both too. As much as it irked her, she would make it a point to reach out to Chris Baylor even if the only place she really wanted to bury the hatchet was in the man's thick skull. But Chris was important to Quentin, and she wouldn't make him choose.

She texted Quentin telling him she was going to D.C. but would be back this evening if he still fancied dinner—unless he wanted to meet her in the city. Then she decided to crawl into the shower before heading to D.C. Maybe Alex and Mal would want to come too?

She texted them both with the invitation. Hell, she felt like throwing a party.

She wanted to tell him.

She wanted to tell Quentin she thought she was falling in love with him. Even though it was so damn scary. But if she was scared of being hurt, she could only imagine how he must feel…to put himself out there after already losing everything once before.

He was incredibly brave.

She wrote a note for him before she could change her mind. Added an "I love you" with a little heart over the top and placed it on the pillow. Her own heart banged painfully against her ribs. He'd never know it was the first time she'd written those words. Or maybe he would.

If anyone seemed to understand her, it was Quentin Savage. She was just grateful the bad things were behind them now, and they could look forward to the future.

CHAPTER THIRTY-SEVEN

QUENTIN DROVE THROUGH the security gates of the Bay-Kar compound at ten AM and parked in front of one of the square block buildings that housed their offices.

"Look who it is!" Nick Karlovac came out to meet him, wearing jeans and a dark t-shirt and combat boots. "Twice in a couple of days! To what do we owe the pleasure?"

Quentin smiled, wishing he was anywhere but here. "Do I need an excuse?"

"Hell, no, but we've been here for four years, and I think this is only the second time you've stopped by." Nick's thick arms were crossed over his chest. "What's up?"

"I was driving up to D.C. and figured I'd drop in. Apologize to the asshole for punching him."

"He deserved it."

"Where is he?"

Nick canted his head to one side. "Driving down from D.C. We're prepping for a job, and he had to pick up some supplies." He checked his watch. "Should be here in the next thirty minutes unless he stops for breakfast on the way. What is it? You want me to be best man again?"

That shot a zinger across Quentin's heart. "Ha. A little early for that."

He didn't want to talk about Haley. He scanned the compound. There were several secure outbuildings, cameras and motion detectors set up around the perimeter. Made sense considering the line of work these guys were in.

Quentin eyed his friend. "I'm worried about Chris. He looks like shit. I take it he's been under a lot of strain lately?"

"I've told him to get his heart checked and cut down on the cigars, but he doesn't listen." Nick shrugged. "We've both been stressed." His expression fell. "Turns out we're better at kicking ass than running a business."

"Running a business?"

"Yeah," Nick huffed out a laugh and glanced around. They could hear the traffic on the nearby road but couldn't see it due to all the trees surrounding the compound. "We almost went bust but now…" Nick planted his hands on his waist and seemed to come to a decision. "Look, I know it's awful, the way things happened, but with all the other firms being in turmoil and our firm already up and running over in Indonesia…"

"You're saying that without the hotel massacre, your firm would have folded? It's understandable you feel this is good news."

"That's right." Nick nodded. "Now we have a chance to get back on course and set things straight."

"That must have been an unsettling time for you and Michelle."

"Michelle didn't know." Nick swallowed tightly. "The idea of losing the house and going bankrupt was pretty goddamn humiliating to be honest. It's all good now. Sorted."

"That must be a big relief."

Nick smiled. "You being alive is an even bigger relief. If you want to come onboard and run the business side of things here, you'd be welcome with open arms any time."

"I'll keep that in mind. You still carry a SIG?"

Nick frowned as he glanced down at his shoulder holster. "Yeah. Why?"

"And Chris. He uses a SIG not a Glock, right?"

"You know as well as I do, Glocks are pieces of shit. We both prefer SIGs." Nick stared pointedly at Quentin's service weapon, a Glock 22.

Quentin hadn't come here to argue the finer points of weaponry. "The thing is—"

"Let's grab a coffee," Nick interrupted. "I'm barely awake."

Quentin followed. He hoped to hell he was wrong about his suspicions. The room was sizeable and open with a big worktable in the middle and a couple of desks pressed up against the wall. Large windows provided pretty views of the surrounding forest and plenty of natural light.

"Truth is, I'm facing a dilemma." Quentin rubbed his sternum as if that would ease the burn beneath his ribs.

"About what?" Nick looked concerned.

Quentin had to be wrong. There had to be some reasonable explanation. "I was going through ballistic reports from the terrorist attack." Hundreds, if not thousands, of rounds had been fired, and the work was still ongoing. "It appears one of the tangos went around putting a bullet in each of the victims to guarantee they were dead."

"That's cold." Nick walked over to the coffee pot, grabbed two coffee-stained mugs and put them down on the counter. One mug had "Best Dad" written on the side. He pulled out his cell, checking a message. "Michelle is asking me what time I'm gonna be home. Fancy coming over for a BBQ later?"

"I'd love to catch up with Michelle and the kids. See what

everyone has been up to. What time?"

"I'll ask her." Nick texted and tossed the cell on the countertop. "You and Chris were lucky to get out of that hellhole alive." He folded his arms and leaned against the sink.

"We were, but also maybe not."

Nick frowned. "What's that mean?"

What Quentin was about to say felt like a betrayal. What he was doing here made him sick to his stomach, but this was his job. More than that, it was the essence of who he was as a person. "The execution-style shots all came from a Glock."

"And?"

"Chris was carrying a Glock when I found him."

Nick's smile dissolved, then his upper lip curled. "Then he took it off one of the tangos before you got there," he snarled.

Quentin watched Nick, looking for signs of deception. "Chris told the agent who interviewed him after the attack that he brought the weapon with him from East Timor."

Nick slammed the mugs down so hard coffee spilled all over the counter. "He had a concussion or your guy misunderstood him. One of the terrorists could have used the Glock, and then Chris picked it up. You know how confusing things get in a firefight."

Nick's words evoked memories of them in battle together. Having each other's backs. Saving each other's lives. And things *did* get confusing in combat—the adrenaline, the fear, the bullets flying and deafening noise, but these men knew weapons better than they knew their own skin.

"Most of the bodies were too charred to identify the caliber of the gunshot wounds, let alone find the bullets intact." Quentin watched Nick's expression as he recounted facts about the murders of people he'd known. "But a couple of victims were recovered where the flames didn't quite reach. And ballistics matched the Glock I dropped on the beach—the one I took from Chris at the hotel—to bullets found in those victims during autopsy."

Nick glared at him. "It wasn't Chris."

"We have an eyewitness. Tricia Rooks—the Raptor operative. She was unhooked from her respirator this morning." Quentin ran a hand around the inside of his collar, which suddenly felt too tight. Because his suspicions were crazy. He had to be wrong, but nothing else fit. "She started to remember things. She says she woke up after being knocked unconscious and saw Chris going around and shooting people in the head. She was hidden by the body of another man. He missed her."

Nick's eyes bounced everywhere in the room except on Quentin. "No. No. This isn't possible."

"Remember at his apartment? He asked me how I 'escaped.' How did he know I escaped?"

Nick snarled. "It's a turn of phrase."

"Why not ask how was I *rescued*?" Quentin shook his head. "It wasn't a turn of phrase. I know it wasn't. Why were you fighting?" Nick looked startled. "The day I went to Chris's apartment, I heard raised voices. What were you fighting about?"

"Fuck you." Nick paced. "So, the FBI has what? Ballistics from a gun anyone could have handled? The eyewitness account of a woman who suffered a brain injury and you overreacting to an innocent comment?" Nick turned and faced him. "That's enough to destroy everything we've meant to each other? A lifetime of friendship? A brotherhood?"

This was the worst thing Quentin had ever had to do—except bury his wife and child, and rescue Haley and Darby from rapists, and kill more men in the past week than he had in three years of war. He would not let a shared past corrupt his soul.

"I need him to come in for an interview," Quentin urged.

"He's your goddamn best friend. How can you accuse him of this bullshit?"

"Nothing else makes sense!" Quentin roared, furious. It had taken him forever to figure it out.

He hadn't been targeted for death; he'd been targeted to *survive*. Because one of his best friends had orchestrated the whole thing. "Chris helped organize the attack and made sure I was taken alive. Why else didn't they shoot me when they shot everyone else?"

Nick raked two trembling hands over his short hair. "No. No. No. Who else have you told this bullshit to?"

"Just you. I want you to help me bring him in."

HALEY HAD BORROWED Alex's Audi again and, although he was a little reluctant with the keys, she knew he didn't really mind. The amount of power under the hood made it tempting to step on the gas, but she was also cognizant that a speeding ticket might reflect badly on Quentin, and she didn't want that. She wanted to make Quentin proud of her.

She rolled her eyes. God, she had it bad.

She passed the sign to Dale City and kicked herself. She could have taken the turn to Hoadly and dropped in on the Bay-Kar compound. She planned to be the bigger person and offer a truce to Baylor and Karlovac. One of them was bound to be there with this renewed contract to honor. Two miles up the road, another turn off appeared, and she was faced with the dilemma again. She knew if she didn't do it now, she'd never do it at all.

She took the turn and got onto Prince William Parkway, turning off into a wooded area a few miles north. She was following a black jeep and, as it pulled into the gateway of the Bay-Kar compound up ahead, she realized it was Chris Baylor's vehicle.

Before she could change her mind, she whipped the sports car through the gap just as the gates were closing and pulled up beside him. He had his phone to his ear. She forced a smile as she climbed out of Alex's low-slung car.

"Chris, I hope you don't mind me dropping in on you unannounced, but I really want to clear the air, for Quentin's sake. I know how much you mean to him and I—"

She stopped talking when her former lover put the barrel of a large black weapon to her temple. Her heart jackknifed in her chest. Her mouth parched. Acid swirled in her stomach.

"If this is a joke," she said raggedly. "It isn't very funny."

Chris grabbed her arm and pushed her in front of him. It was then she noticed Quentin's black SUV parked beyond a big white truck. And she knew, somehow, she'd made a terrible miscalculation.

CHAPTER THIRTY-EIGHT

HALEY'S WORLD NARROWED to the dangerous end of a 9mm as Chris reached past her to open the door and hustle them both through the entrance. Inside the large open space, Nick Karlovac and Quentin stood talking in a small kitchen area.

Quentin took a step forward, clearly startled. "Haley? What the hell?"

"Any closer, and I'll blow her brains out," Chris stated with a coldness that sent an icy rush of fear over her skin. The hard metal dug painfully against her scalp. If the gun went off, she was dead. She forced herself to breathe slowly, in and out. Counting to five each time.

What had happened?

What was going on?

"That's not funny, Chris. Put the damn gun down," Quentin ordered.

Chris ignored his friend, a senior FBI agent. "Sorry, buddy. No can do."

She stayed as still as possible, as compliant as possible, and she was back to being that powerless captive again. Someone without agency, at the mercy of other people's violence. Quentin's dark eyes held hers and seemed to will her to be strong. Then he looked away, back to Chris, whose grip on her arm pinched so painfully she knew it was going to leave bruises, assuming she lived that long.

She tilted her face sideways so she could see Chris's expression. His eyes were regretful, but his mouth was firm. She couldn't believe she'd once been involved with this man. He seemed like a stranger.

"Let her go. She has nothing to do with this." Quentin clenched and unclenched his fists.

"She has everything to do with this. Anyway, she's a witness now."

"She doesn't know anything. Let her go." Quentin shook his head.

Haley didn't have a clue what was happening, but she knew it was bad. Nick stood behind Quentin, looking anxious.

Quentin spoke quietly, urgently. "I know you're worried, Chris. Come in with me. I'll make sure you're treated fairly. Tell us what happened. I'm sure there are mitigating circumstances. A good lawyer will have you out by dinnertime, and we can laugh about this over beers."

Mitigating circumstances for what? Holding an ex-girlfriend at gunpoint?

"We only want to interview you about the Glock I took from you at the hotel," Quentin said evenly.

"It had your fingerprints on it," Chris pointed out.

Quentin frowned. "Are you planning to say I shot those people in the bar—and then tried to rescue them?"

Haley stiffened. Why would Chris shoot anyone in the bar?

Chris shrugged. "Why not? You and Haley hatched a plot to get her company a big contract. You faked the abduction and escape. Rescued a few damsels in distress along the way, came out a goddamn hero."

Her mouth dropped open, but she kept quiet.

"What's Haley's motive?"

Chris shrugged like he didn't care. "Conspiring with her new lover? Getting back at her ex? Wanting Wenck's business and doing anything to get it from lifting her skirts to murder?"

"Bullshit," Haley muttered.

Chris leaned closer to her ear. "No one else is gonna know that, now are they?"

Her eyes widened as she met Quentin's dark gaze across the room. Her pulse hammered. This wasn't some bad joke or some pissed off macho posturing. Chris Baylor was seriously thinking about killing her, and presumably Quentin, to cover up the fact he'd committed cold-blooded murder at the hotel.

Quentin looked calm and composed. She used that. Used what she knew about the man to gather her breath and remember to count, using his poise to bolster her self-control and gain a hold of her body's reaction to the fear that wanted to slay her.

Chris's eyes flicked to Nick. "Is that what he told you?"

Nick nodded.

"I can't believe you went for this one." Chris jostled her in his grip, seeming to change the subject. "I didn't think you went for the slutty type. I thought you were all about cupcake princesses."

Chris's tone was derisive. Haley watched Quentin's expression harden. The fact he had the gall to insult them all and act superior while doing it finally seemed to break through Quentin's control.

He reached for his weapon.

"Watch out!" Haley cried.

Nick pressed the barrel of a gun to the back of Quentin's head.

"Don't hurt him," Haley begged.

Quentin let out a long, steady breath. "You were both in on it."

Nick eased closer and bent to remove Quentin's sidearm. Quentin didn't try to fight him, and Haley's throat closed at what that meant. They were both going to die unless Quentin could talk their way out of this.

"We didn't have any choice," said Nick.

"You have a choice now." Quentin looked grim.

Chris shook his head. Haley could feel the pulse in his thumb throbbing against her bicep. "I don't. Not anymore."

"You set up the hotel attack, didn't you? That's why I was taken alive. And then you ordered the hit on Hurek's people on the island. You couldn't afford any witnesses, could you?"

Haley gasped.

Chris shook his head. "It wasn't my idea. The interior minister ordered it when he discovered the foreign minister had organized a security symposium on Indonesian soil. The guy was furious. I was just the go-between for him and Hurek."

"Chris, shut the fuck up," Nick said angrily.

"Why, for god's sake?" Quentin's voice vibrated with suppressed rage. "At least tell me the truth. I deserve that much if you're going to kill me."

"No one said anything about killing you." Nick looked anxiously at his partner, and his expression sagged at whatever he saw on Chris's face.

Haley froze.

The reality seemed to filter through the room. If these two

men wanted to get away with their crimes, they were going to have to murder their best friend. Killing her would be easy in comparison.

The irony made her want to shake her head, but she was trying not to move. She'd finally found someone to love and they were both about to die.

"I told you we were struggling financially," Nick bit out.

"So rather than file for bankruptcy you opt for mass murder?"

"It wasn't like that," Nick denied. "We were doing good and then a couple of our operatives shot up the wrong house and accidentally killed some Arab kids. We had to pay the families and local officials off. After that, we started to struggle and could never quite get our heads above water. Then that asshole Wenck decided not to renew the only decent contract we had left but instead to put it out for tender…" Nick sucked in a huge breath. "We were going to fold without ARK Mining, but when the interior minister contacted Chris, we realized we still had a chance."

By murdering the competition? Haley's business was important to her, but that was a line she'd never cross.

"How did the minister know Chris?"

"We paid him off a few years ago to get the permits we needed to protect Wenck's mines. Part of the deal was that Chris act as a middleman between him and Hurek. If anyone found out they were communicating directly, the minister would be toast. Hurek was a wanted criminal at that point. We needed the minister to work in the country. He needed us to help direct Hurek's actions when he wanted to stir up a little local strife. It all worked perfectly until a month ago when he decided to attack the conference." Sweat coated Nick's brow.

The guy looked like he was going to throw up. "We tried to get him to change his mind."

Haley tried not to look at Quentin, but her eyes were drawn back to that handsome face. Those intelligent black eyes. She hated that they were once again in a life or death situation. That she might lose him before she really had him. She hadn't even told him how she felt…

"When we found out you were going to be there, we tried again to get him to call it off, but the guy wasn't budging. Chris said he'd get you out of there, but that didn't go to plan either. Now we know why." Nick's eyes raked Haley.

Sure, blame *her* for everything.

"Things went further to shit when Hurek attacked early, and Chris was still in the building."

"You made sure Wenck was out of there before the attack happened," Quentin pointed out. Yeah, they'd warned that asshole. "You didn't want to kill the fatted calf."

Chris laughed. "I'm not a complete idiot."

"Who caused the accident with Wenck's wife?" Quentin glanced over his shoulder at Nick. "You?"

"I hired a guy. She made it easy." Nick's bullish features were set into hard lines now. "She wasn't hurt. Just a little shaken up."

"Why did they attack early?" Quentin asked.

He sounded so like the federal agent she knew he was, collecting information. Haley didn't care. He could ask questions all day as long as it kept them alive for a little bit longer.

Chris wiped his brow with the hand still holding the weapon, but his aim was steady. "They weren't the smartest recruits in the world. That's why I hid at the beginning. Most of the guys knew me but were trigger happy." He gave an ironic little laugh. "I couldn't contact Hurek because he was using the signal blocker I supplied him with. I visited him before I went to the conference and gave him your picture in case my initial plan to get you out of there failed. I told him I wanted you alive."

"You trained them," Quentin said with a note of finality ringing in his tone.

Chris shrugged. She could smell the pungent scent of sweat every time he moved. "What difference does it make?"

"You murdered survivors at the hotel." Quentin sounded sickened and disgusted by this man who'd been his friend.

Haley was sickened by him too. And despondent for Quentin, and terrified for them both.

"I made sure there were no witnesses—almost died in the process. One guy hid behind the reception desk. I'd just taken him out when I was hit on the head by the ceiling collapsing. You saved my life, buddy."

"Did he shoot you or did you do that to yourself as cover?"

Chris's silence spoke volumes.

"You told Hurek to kidnap me." Fury raced over Quentin's features.

"I fucking *saved* you!" Spittle flew out of Chris's mouth. Haley flinched. He was going to pull the trigger any moment, and she didn't want to die.

"And after that, you killed them all, too, didn't you?" Quentin wasn't finished with the guy. Haley stiffened. What Chris and Nick had organized was chilling in its brutality. "All the men you'd worked with in Hurek's camp. You had them killed."

"When Hurek called to say you'd escaped, I knew it was

only a matter of time before the government found you and then him. I sent my guys to get rid of any witnesses." Chris pulled a face. "Hurek escaped though. I have people looking for him."

"You murdered women and children." Quentin sounded strangely calm.

"If you'd stayed put like you were supposed to, I wouldn't have had to kill them!" Chris yelled. "It was all set up. A ransom would have been paid. You'd have had a hood over your head and been driven around for a few hours and then dumped on some island close to a town. You'd have been set free."

Haley couldn't believe Chris was blaming Quentin for the way things had turned out.

"What about Haley?" Quentin met her gaze, his eyes softening.

She wanted to tell him she loved him.

Chris sneered. "When Hurek called to say you'd escaped he mentioned your 'wife' was with you. I told him you didn't have a wife." Haley's heart was racing. "If Hurek had known she wasn't important, he would have treated her the same way he treated the O'Roarke girl until there was nothing left of her worth having. Then he'd have shot her."

She flinched. The imagery was graphic and shocking, designed to hurt.

Nick's skin blanched but he didn't lower the gun he held to Quentin's head.

"You knew where the Alexanders were, all those months. You knew I was negotiating their release. And you knew exactly who took Darby O'Roarke, and you never said a word." The condemnation in Quentin's voice echoed with finality.

"Who do you think told them O'Roarke was there in the first place?" Chris spat on the floor, and Haley edged slightly away from him. He turned her stomach. "They wanted someone to tell them whether or not their volcano was going to blow up, so I pointed them to the nearest expert. I heard some of the boys got to play with her before you rescued her like some damned hero."

Death was too good for him. Haley wanted him to suffer the way Darby had suffered.

"What happened to you?" Quentin's voice shook with anger.

"What happened to *me*? War happened to me. The government treating me like a worn-out piece of shit happened to me. Bitches like this happened to me." Chris shook Haley again.

She set her jaw. She was sick of being pushed around.

Quentin narrowed his eyes. "You can't get away with this. Put the gun down. I'll take you in. Make sure you're treated fairly."

"I did everything I could to save your life, and this is the thanks I get?" Bitterness poured off Chris, and he lashed out. "You want me to give myself up? Confess all? Die in a fucking cell?"

In her peripheral vision, Haley watched Chris's finger tighten on the trigger.

"Wait," Nick said sharply. "There's no point killing them. Let's tie them up and get the hell out of here. The Feds know everything already. Quentin said Tricia Rooks was talking about what you did."

"He's lying." Chris's grin was mirthless. "I dropped in to check on Rooksy before I drove down here. She was still deep-throating a tube of plastic."

Nick let out a deep breath and shook his head at Quentin. "You were fishing for information? You bastard."

Nick had the gall to look disappointed in his friend.

Quentin's lip curled. "Nothing in the rule book says I can't lie."

She tried to remember Alex's self-defense classes. If she whacked Chris in the balls…but Quentin wasn't done trying to save her.

"You guys aren't going to get away with any of this. Not without my help," Quentin told them quietly. "Let Haley go, and I'll destroy the evidence, or make sure its inadmissible in a court of law. I'll help you escape the country. The FBI will never find you."

Chris smiled grimly. "You can't talk your way out of this, buddy. I love you like a brother, but I know you won't destroy evidence or keep your mouth shut. Too many fucking morals. I tried to save you once, and look what it cost us? This time it's us or you. I don't intend for it to be us."

Quentin's lips flattened before he asked, "Nick?"

"Don't worry." Nick sounded miserable, but he wasn't backing down. "We'll make it quick."

Oh, god, no.

"Let me talk to Haley alone for a minute."

"Sorry." Chris shook his head. "Unlike Hurek, I know how resourceful you are, both of you."

Haley might have felt flattered if he wasn't about to shoot her.

"I'm really sorry I got you involved in this." Quentin smiled softly at her. "Try to stand still so it doesn't hurt."

What? Stand still? She swallowed the massive lump that

wanted to choke her. "I love you." The words burst out at last.

Quentin's eyes gleamed.

"Aw, so sweet, although I doubt she means it. You aren't rich enough for a bitch like this." Chris raised his weapon. She tilted her chin to the side and held herself very still, not because Quentin had told her to, but however scared she might be, she didn't intend to cower like a beaten dog. She clenched her fist, about to aim for Chris's balls in a last-ditch effort to get away from the bastard.

Windows shattered.

Chris and Nick both crumpled to the ground.

Haley sobbed.

"STAY RIGHT THERE until HRT is done, Haley. Stand still for another minute so no one makes a mistake." It was a high-stakes situation. If anything happened to her, Quentin would die. He would lay down on the ground and die.

He didn't look at the bodies of his friends or the rivulets of blood that stained the gray vinyl floor. They'd betrayed him and everything they'd believed in, everything they'd fought so hard for when in uniform. He'd known Chris was dirty after looking at the ballistics evidence, but he hadn't been sure about Nick. His throat hurt from suppressing the pain that came from that revelation. His fingernails cut into the palms of his hands as he held back on his desire to race to Haley and shield her with his body.

The nightmare was finally over.

Men in black tactical gear spilled through the door. He waited for a nod from Kurt Montana before he hurried to where another agent was making sure Haley was uninjured. Quentin avoided the blood spatter as much as he could.

A knife twisted in his heart. These people had been his friends for so many years, and yet, they'd been prepared to end him and the woman he loved so that they could get away with their Machiavellian schemes.

When he reached Haley, she sank into his arms, and he held on tight. Relief tore through him. He'd never needed anything as much as he'd needed Haley to come through this alive.

"I don't think I've ever been more scared than when Chris walked in the door with that damn gun pointed at your head," he said.

She grasped his shirt. He'd known they were surrounded and that Chris and Nick were hammering the last nails in their coffins with every word they spoke. She'd thought they were about to die.

He pulled a small recording device from his pocket, barely the size of a lighter. Haley's eyes widened in surprise. He handed it off to an evidence tech already on the scene, although he was sure everything had been caught via his cell and with various parabolic mikes set up in the woods. The FBI had allowed no room for error. The team had come together with record speed once he'd presented his theory to the task force commander.

"You were wearing a wire." The skin between her brows crinkled.

"I knew Chris shot those people in the bar, but I didn't know exactly what else he was involved in. I needed to find out. I wasn't sure about Nick. We decided the best way to get a confession was for me to confront them. FBI had this whole place surrounded." He closed his eyes, thinking about Nick's wife and kids. He had no clue how he would ever be able to face them. "We weren't expecting you to show up."

"I was heading to D.C., and I wanted to make peace with Chris." The pulse in her neck was visibly pounding, and her hand pressed against her throat in a protective gesture. "I knew he was important to you. I know how much this must have hurt you."

Quentin pressed his lips together, refusing to weep for the men he had loved, even though he wanted to. They'd betrayed him. They'd betrayed everyone.

He wiped a few drops of blood from her cheek. *Shit.* She'd been so close to death. She started to shake in reaction, and he didn't know if she'd be able to forgive him for getting her involved in this mess. He'd known the snipers were out there. Waiting for the opportunity to strike. "I'm sorry I couldn't tell you the FBI was outside without warning Chris or Nick." The names tasted bitter on his tongue. "If they'd known they were surrounded, they'd have shot us both and then blown their own brains out." Chris would never have let Haley survive, nor Quentin once Chris realized he'd already told the FBI his suspicions.

Haley clung to him, and he savored her warmth and the tight grip of her strong hands. She'd never been more precious to him.

He led her outside, away from the thick, coppery smell of blood. He brushed the hair away from her face and leaned his forehead against hers. "I love you, Haley Cramer. I'm done taking things slow. Let's move in together and see how we fit."

Her mouth dropped open. "Are you serious?"

"We'll make it work."

Relief shone from her eyes. “I love you, Quentin. Can we *please* do normal, boring things from now on? Like paragliding or abseiling?”

“I hate heights.”

She reared back in mock horror. “I don’t know you at all.”

He laughed and squeezed her against his chest. “Haley Cramer, I want us to spend years figuring out each other’s mysteries.”

“Where would we live?” She bit her lip. She looked daunted. Once again, his timing was lousy.

“You work in D.C. I work in Quantico. Let’s find a place in between. It’ll mean a commute for both of us but not a terrible one.” He touched her face, tipped her chin up with his thumb and stared down into her mystical blue eyes. “I’m not asking you to give up anything. I love you just the way you are, but I don’t want to waste time missing you when you could be in my bed every night. Or I could be in yours.”

Quentin remembered where they were and all the things they still had to do before they could go home and sleep for a week. He took a reluctant step back, but Haley grabbed his arm before he could go too far.

“We can stay at yours to start with. I can go up to D.C. a couple times a week. Alex has been talking about having a satellite office in Quantico anyway. We can see how it works out—”

“It’s going to work out,” Quentin assured her, “because while I might not know what TV shows you like, or food you prefer, I know you are brave and adventurous, and I will do my damnedest to make sure I come home to you as often as I can. And,” he couldn’t stop touching her, “I know you’ll do the same for me. I love you, Haley.”

"First time we've had a declaration of love at a takedown," Montana said as he trudged past with an evidence bag. "I kind of like it."

"I do too," Haley said softly.

"So do I." Quentin kissed her long and slow, despite the audience. "So do I."

EPILOGUE

One Month Later.

HALEY STOOD IN the terminal with her arms wrapped so tight around Darby she wasn't sure she was going to be able to let go. Finally, she made herself release the other woman who felt like a daughter or a sister to her.

"Keep safe," Haley said and then kicked herself. "Call me, *any*time."

Quentin stood beside her, hand on her shoulder. He'd already said his goodbyes.

Eban stood off to one side looking uncomfortable. He and Darby were giving each other the side eye. Haley hadn't told Quentin about Darby propositioning the guy. It was pretty much the only secret she'd kept. She had no intention of getting Eban in trouble with his boss when Darby had been the one to initiate the kiss, and he'd been the one to end it.

"You have your appointment with Dr. Bruce for next week," Haley reminded the other woman.

Darby nodded and grinned. "Yes, Mom."

Quentin's fingers tightened on her shoulder. "Let me know if that supervisor of yours causes you any trouble."

Darby tucked in her chin. "Yes, Dad."

His lips twitched. "Go catch your flight, Madam. Enjoy first-class."

Her father had flown to Virginia. With the help of Quentin and the victims advocate, the visit had been cathartic rather than traumatic. They'd all been surprised when Darby hadn't gone home with him, but she said she wasn't ready. Haley worried she wasn't ready now either, but she knew better than to smother.

Darby grinned at them all. Her eyes darted to Eban.

"Take care," he said gruffly, finally breaking his silence.

Her smile faltered, and she nodded. "You too."

Eban's jaw flexed. He looked miserable. Awkwardness and tension bloomed between them. For once Quentin was oblivious, or pretending to be.

Haley glanced around to make sure the press hadn't arrived. They'd uncovered some of Darby's story, although not the details. She'd made a short statement about being grateful for being rescued and requested privacy.

"Okay. I'll stop stalling. Here goes." Darby swung her backpack onto her shoulder and, after a long wistful look at all three of them, headed through security.

"I'll see you back at the office." Eban walked away, head down.

"What's up with him?" Quentin asked quizzically.

"They were close," Haley hedged. "It's hard to let go. To watch her fly away to try to get on with her life again. We're all going to miss her."

"I have agents watching out for her in Alaska if she needs them." Quentin nodded, and they started walking back to his vehicle.

He seemed preoccupied, but this was difficult for all of them. Since they'd found one another on that island, the three of them had bonded in a way few people could understand.

The added guilt Quentin carried, erroneously, because his friends had been involved, that they'd betrayed him, and the fact he'd watched them die… It had taken time to process. Time for him to forgive himself even though he knew better.

He'd tried talking to Nick Karlovac's widow, but she'd refused to see him. She'd taken her kids and moved in with her parents. Their lives had been irrevocably damaged like so many others.

"Any news on Hurek?" she asked.

He shook his head. "Alex is still tracking the bitcoin."

"Talking of Alex. He told me someone sent Glenda Wenck copies of a bunch of police reports and NDAs signed by women her husband had slept with—some of whom claimed the sex was not consensual. She filed for divorce and plans to take him for hundreds of millions."

A small smile played around Quentin's mouth. "I wonder who'd do something like that?"

Haley's eyes widened. "You didn't."

Quentin just shrugged. "She's about to be thrust into a scandal that will rock her world. Least I could do is make sure she knows the truth about her husband before they're both arrested and go to trial. Maybe it'll persuade her to turn state's evidence against Wenck and the others." He opened her car door and trapped her there for a kiss. "I have something for you."

She wiggled her brows suggestively. They'd spent a lot of time in bed together, healing. They'd also spent a lot of time figuring out who they each were when they weren't running for their lives. Turned out they both liked long hikes and swimming in the ocean. He even had a sweet tooth the same way she did.

He pulled out a jeweler's box, too big for a ring, although her heart gave a little flutter.

When she opened it, everything stopped. She closed her eyes and drew in the sweetest, deepest breath. Her grandmother's antique silver watch. Haley slipped it over her wrist and examined it for any damage. It looked perfect.

She looked up into his intense dark brown eyes. "How did you find it?"

He kissed her. "Alex found it on the net, and I contacted a police officer I know in Australia. They did a sweep of the premises and found a whole bunch of stolen goods. They cut a deal that involves the fence staying out of prison if he gives up all his suppliers. We might catch Hurek this way."

Haley nodded, grateful beyond words. "Quentin?"

"Yes?"

"Thank you."

"You're welcome." He lowered his lids, looking sexy and powerful. "Haley?"

"Yes?"

"I'm done taking things slow. I love you, Haley Cramer. Marry me."

Her mouth dropped open in surprise. "Are you serious?"

"I know what I want. Who I want." He squeezed her shoulders.

She blinked and shook her head. "I love you, Quentin, you know I do. But are you sure?"

He grinned. "I have never been more sure of anything in my life."

Her heart was pounding. She hadn't expected this. Maybe she'd imagined or hoped, but she hadn't been sure being this happy could last. This was all new to her, and old insecurities reared up. She bit her lip. "I'm not going to be the perfect little wife, Quentin."

"Where's the fun in perfect?" He seemed to know exactly what she was thinking, and he cupped her face. "My love for Abbie was like a river, strong and steady and constant. My love for you is like an ocean with calm days in between crashing storms and rogue waves that come out of nowhere to obliterate everything in their path. I will always love Abbie, but she is my past, and I want you to be my future. Marry me?"

She stared at this beautiful man and couldn't utter a single word.

He swallowed, appearing suddenly nervous. "Haley?"

"You're insane, but I love you." She laughed, and it sounded close to a sob.

"Is that a yes?" he asked cautiously.

She flung her arms around him, squeezing hard and holding him close, fitting them together like a lock and a key. "Yes, yes, yes, yes."

"So that's a yes," Quentin teased in obvious relief.

"Shut up." She kissed him, and neither of them spoke for a considerable amount of time.

Finally, she came up for air and pulled back to see his face.

"What?" He hiked a brow.

"I have all these jewels I never wear." His brow rose farther still. "How would you feel if we had the stones from my grandmother's emerald engagement ring put into a simple setting of *your* choice for me to wear as our engagement ring?"

One side of his mouth twitched, and he chuckled. "And save myself tens of thousands of dollars. Why would I do something crazy like that?"

She touched his face. "Plenty of men would resent the

suggestion."

"Yeah." He took her hand. "Well, you're not marrying me because I'm *plenty of men.* I know how much your grandmother meant to you." Love shone brightly in his eyes. "I can't keep up with you in the money stakes, Haley, but I can match you pound for pound in all the things that matter."

"I can't believe how lucky I am."

He pulled her close, and she wrapped her arms around him, her rock, her anchor. "We already sent our kid off to college. Think she'll come back for the wedding?"

"She better." He grinned. "I am so ready to request a transfer to Anchorage."

"She's in Fairbanks," Haley pointed out.

"That's the problem."

She slipped her hand up the warm fabric of his shirt until it rested against his heart. "You might be the best person I have ever known."

He kissed her fingertips. "Did it ever cross your mind that I might feel the same way about you?"

"What?" She blinked up at him.

"You heard." He kissed her, and every little piece of her heart slotted perfectly into place, even as part of it flew far across the country.

USEFUL ACRONYM DEFINITIONS FOR TONI'S BOOKS

AG: Attorney General

ASAC: Assistant Special-Agent-in-Charge

ATF: Alcohol, Tobacco, and Firearms

BAU: Behavioral Analysis Unit

BOLO: Be on the Lookout

BUCAR: Bureau Car.

CBT: Cognitive Behavioral Therapy

CIRG: Critical Incident Response Group

CMU: Crisis Management Unit

CN: Crisis Negotiator

CNU: Crisis Negotiation Unit

CO: Commanding Officer

CODIS: Combined DNA Index System

CP: Command Post

DA: District Attorney

DEA: Drug Enforcement Administration

DOB: Date of Birth

DOD: Department of Defense

DOJ: Department of Justice

DS: Diplomatic Security

DSS: US Diplomatic Security Service

EMDR: Eye Movement Desensitization & Reprocessing

EMT: Emergency Medical Technician

ERT: Evidence Response Team

FOA: First-Office Assignment

FBI: Federal Bureau of Investigation

FO: Field Office

FWO: Federal Wildlife Officer

IC: Incident Commander

HRT: Hostage Rescue Team

HT: Hostage-Taker

JEH: J. Edgar Hoover Building (FBI Headquarters)

K&R: Kidnap and Ransom

LAPD: Los Angeles Police Department

LEO: Law Enforcement Officer

ME: Medical Examiner

MO: Modus Operandi

NAT: New Agent Trainee

NCAVC: National Center for Analysis of Violent Crime

NCIC: National Crime Information Center

NYFO: New York Field Office

OC: Organized Crime

OCU: Organized Crime Unit

OPR: Office of Professional Responsibility

POTUS: President of the United States

PTSD: Post-Traumatic Stress Disorder

RA: Resident Agency

RCMP: Royal Canadian Mounted Police

RSO: Senior Regional Security Officer from the US Diplomatic Service

SA: Special Agent

SAC: Special Agent-in-Charge

SANE: Sexual Assault Nurse Examiners

SAS: Special Air Squadron (British Special Forces unit)

SD: Secure Digital

SIOC: Strategic Information & Operations

SSA: Supervisory Special Agent

SWAT: Special Weapons and Tactics

TC: Tactical Commander

TDY: Temporary Duty Yonder

TOD: Time of Death

UAF: University of Alaska, Fairbanks

UNSUB: Unknown Subject

ViCAP: Violent Criminal Apprehension Program

WFO: Washington Field Office

COLD JUSTICE SERIES OVERVIEW

COLD JUSTICE SERIES
A Cold Dark Place (Book #1)
Cold Pursuit (Book #2)
Cold Light of Day (Book #3)
Cold Fear (Book #4)
Cold in The Shadows (Book #5)
Cold Hearted (Book #6)
Cold Secrets (Book #7)
Cold Malice (Book #8)
A Cold Dark Promise (Book #9~A Wedding Novella)
Cold Blooded (Book #10)

COLD JUSTICE – THE NEGOTIATORS
Cold & Deadly (Book #1)
Colder Than Sin (Book #2)
Cold Wicked Lies (Book #3)
Cold Cruel Kiss (Book #4)
Cold as Ice (Book #5)

COLD JUSTICE – MOST WANTED
Cold Silence (Book #1)

The *Cold Justice Series* books are also available as **audiobooks** narrated by Eric Dove, and in various box set compilations.

Check out all Toni's books on her website (www.toniandersonauthor.com/books-2)

ACKNOWLEDGMENTS

Thanks to all the usual suspects for this one, especially Kathy Altman for the first look, Rachel Grant for her unflinching *beta* read, and Adriana Anders for her awesome quote.

Thanks to my amazing cover designer, Regina Wamba, for her gorgeous artwork, and to my formatter, Paul Salvette, for his hard work. Also, to Tara at Inkslingers PR for her supportive efforts in getting the word out. Credit to my editors, Deb Nemeth, Joan Turner at JRT Editing, and proofreader, Alicia Dean. I obviously need all the help I can get.

As always, I want to thank my husband and kids for their love and understanding. Wouldn't be worth it without you!

ABOUT THE AUTHOR

Toni Anderson writes gritty, sexy, FBI Romantic Thrillers, and is a *New York Times* and a *USA Today* bestselling author. Her books have won the Daphne du Maurier Award for Excellence in Mystery and Suspense, Readers' Choice, Aspen Gold, Book Buyers' Best, Golden Quill, National Excellence in Story Telling (NEST) Contest, and National Excellence in Romance Fiction awards. She's been a finalist in both the Vivian Contest and the RITA Award from the Romance Writers of America. More than two million copies of her books have been downloaded.

Best known for her "COLD" books perhaps it's not surprising to discover Toni lives in one of the most extreme climates on earth—Manitoba, Canada. Formerly a Marine Biologist, Toni still misses the ocean, but is lucky enough to travel for research purposes. In January 2016, she visited FBI Headquarters in Washington DC, including a tour of the Strategic Information and Operations Center. She hopes not to get arrested for her Google searches.

Sign up for Toni Anderson's newsletter:
www.toniandersonauthor.com/newsletter-signup

Like Toni Anderson on Facebook:
facebook.com/toniannanderson

See Toni Anderson's current book list:
www.toniandersonauthor.com/books-2

Follow Toni Anderson on Instagram:
instagram.com/toni_anderson_author